Titles by Dianne Duvall

Immortal Guardians

DARKNESS DAWNS

NIGHT REIGNS

PHANTOM SHADOWS

IN STILL DARKNESS

DARKNESS RISES

SHADOWS STRIKE

The Gifted Ones

A SORCERESS OF HIS OWN

Anthologies

PREDATORY

(includes *In Still Darkness*)

ON THE HUNT

(includes *Phantom Embrace*)

Copyright

A SORCERESS OF HIS OWN
Copyright © 2000 by Leslie Duvall
All Rights Reserved.

Published by Dianne Duvall, 2015
Editor: Jena O'Conner
Cover Art by: Patricia Schmitt
Formatted by: Jessica Lewis

ISBN: 978-0-9864171-1-5

A SORCERESS OF HIS OWN

The Gifted Ones Book 1

By

New York Times Bestselling Author

Dianne Duvall

AUTHOR'S NOTE

Dear Reader,

One of the questions I am asked most often is what inspired my Immortal Guardians series—paranormal romance novels and novellas that feature dark and dangerous heroes, kick-ass heroines, action, passion, and romance. The easy answer is: This book, *A Sorceress of His Own*. There were, of course, other sources of inspiration: a documentary on the water bear, research into possible explanations for the emergence of vampire folklore, and a biography of King George, to name a few. But, long before Sarah Bingham rescued Roland Warbrook with her trusty shovel in *Darkness Dawns*, I wrote *A Sorceress of His Own*... and the *gifted ones* were born.

If you're unfamiliar with my *Immortal Guardians* series, both the vampires and immortals that people it are infected with a very rare, symbiotic virus that conquers, then replaces the immune system, granting those it transforms dramatically enhanced senses, greater speed and strength, and incredible regenerative capabilities, along with an unfortunate photosensitivity and a need for blood. Vampires are humans who have been infected with the virus. Immortals are *gifted ones*—men and women born with advanced DNA that bestows upon them special gifts or abilities ordinary humans lack—who have been infected with it.

Alyssa, the heroine of *A Sorceress of His Own*, was the first *gifted one* I created. And she, along with Seth and Marcus—both of whom are prominent figures in my *Immortal Guardians* series—fired my imagination and inspired many of the *what ifs* that drove me to create my Immortal Guardians. I hope you will enjoy her story.

—DIANNE DUVALL

ACKNOWLEDGMENTS

I'd like to thank all of the readers who have contacted me, asking me when *A Sorceress of His Own* would become available. Many more thanks go to Crystal and my fabulous Street Team, to my friends on Facebook, to bloggers and reviewers, and to all of the wonderful readers who have helped spread the word about my books.

I would also like to thank Patricia for the wonderful cover, and the editor, copyeditors, proofreaders, formatter, and other behind-the-scenes ladies who helped me bring you *A Sorceress of His Own*, guiding me through my first steps into the indie world.

PROLOGUE

England, 1191

"Where is Father?" Alyssa asked, unable to bear the leaden silence a moment longer.

"Outside." Kneeling in the rushes that covered the earthen floor of the modest hut in which Alyssa had been raised, her mother completed one last stitch, then bit off the end of the dangling thread.

Alyssa glanced through the window, but did not spy him.

A brisk, cool breeze wafted in, accompanied by morning sunshine. Leaves the color of a golden sunset had just begun to fall in preparation for winter and painted the forest around the isolated dwelling with bright color.

"Is he angry?" she asked hesitantly.

"He is worried," her mother corrected, "as we all are."

Alyssa's second cousin, Meghan, slumped in a chair by the hearth, brow furrowed, teeth nibbling her lower lip. The two were of a similar age and had been the best of friends in their youth until Meg's parents had been slain when Alyssa was ten. Meghan had gone to live with her grandsire then, far enough away to limit the time the two could see each other.

Rising, her mother crossed to the table in the corner and tucked her needle away.

Matthew, Alyssa's father, may be blind, but he had lost none of his carpentry skills. He had lovingly created every table, chair, stool, and chest in their small home.

Alyssa gave the folds of the long black robe she wore a little shake and checked the length. Perfect. Her grandmother was a couple of inches taller than Alyssa, so all of the robes had needed to be shortened. "Thank you."

The fear and sadness that shadowed her mother's features when she returned tightened Alyssa's chest.

"Please reconsider this, daughter."

Swallowing hard, she shook her head. "This is what I want. I have made my decision."

Male voices erupted outside, one soft and low, the other angry.

Alyssa's brother, Geoffrey, yanked open the door and stomped inside. His lips tightened when they fell upon her, garbed in her grandmother's black robe. "I did not wish to believe Mother when I received her missive. What have you done?"

Alyssa raised her chin. "What I have long wished to do. I have taken steps to replace Grandmother as Westcott's wisewoman."

He swore foully.

"Geoffrey!" her mother reprimanded.

"Well, 'tis madness!" he raged.

Alyssa held on to her own temper, knowing his was fired by concern for her. "'Tis *not* madness. Grandmother grows weaker and more frail every year. She cannot continue to serve as Westcott's wisewoman."

"Then Westcott can do without one."

"I see no reason why they should when, shielded by these robes, I can take her place with none being the wiser."

"They *should*," her brother hissed, "because the path you have chosen will invariably lead to either heartbreak or death."

Her mother's and Meg's expressions betrayed their agreement.

"I know not why it should," Alyssa countered.

He took a step forward. "Think you I know naught of your feelings for him, for the valiant Earl of Westcott? Or the *monstrous* Earl of Westcott, if the rumors are true."

She bristled. "A victim of rumor yourself, you know people are always eager to believe the worst of others. The false rumors told of mother's supposed witchcraft nigh resulted in her death. Yet you would place your faith in the lies told of Lord Dillon?"

"Violence follows him wherever he goes. Can you deny that?"

"You would condemn him for defending his king? *Our* king?"

He clamped his lips shut.

Meg ventured to speak. "Do you not fear him, Alyssa? The rest of England does."

"With good reason," Geoffrey muttered.

"Nay, I do not. You are all well aware the rumors hold no truth. I have seen with mine own eyes the kindness of which Lord Dillon is capable. And Grandmother has said naught but good things of him."

"Too *many* good things. She has filled your head with foolish fancy." Geoffrey paced away a few steps.

Alyssa caught her mother's eye. "Know you where Grandmother is?"

"I think she is fetching her paints. I shall see why she tarries."

Alyssa waited for her mother to leave, then turned to her brother. "Ask me again why I do this."

"Why must you do this?" he asked helplessly as he returned to her side.

"Because I am tired of hiding."

He motioned to the midnight material that covered her. "*This* is not hiding?"

"Do not play the half-wit," she snapped.

"You—"

"I love Mother," she interrupted, keeping her voice low so it would not carry. "But I do not want the life she has chosen. I do not wish to live in total isolation, in constant fear for my life. You know I have always wished to use my gifts the way they were meant to be used. I wish to help others. *Heal* others. Guide them whenever I can. And serving as Lord Dillon's wisewoman will allow me to do that without risking my life."

Her brother snorted. "You will risk your life the very night you begin to serve him. You intend to help Lord Dillon take Brimshire, do you not?"

She nodded. "Are you certain you can gain us entry?"

"Aye. Mother sent me there ere the siege began, saying only that I would be needed. They think me one of them."

"She must have had a vision."

"Aye. And, had she seen the *reason* I would be needed, I would have refused."

"Geoffrey—"

"You will die in his service," Geoffrey predicted, his face full of torment. "Violence *does* follow him wherever he goes. And your love will drive you to heal every wound he incurs, fatal or nay." He shook his head. "I do not wish to lose you and, again, ask you to reconsider this."

She swallowed hard. "I have made my decision."

He stared at her a long moment. "And 'tis yours to make. I shall await you outside." He left without another word.

Alyssa looked to Meg.

Ever her friend and supporter, Meg made no attempt to sway her from the path she had chosen.

Alyssa's mother and grandmother entered.

Her grandmother crossed to Alyssa and offered her a cloth

bag. "The paints for your hands. Show me again you know how to use them."

Alyssa obediently took them and, seating herself at the table, applied them the way her grandmother had instructed. When she finished, her youthful hands bore the appearance of an old woman's, the skin appearing thin and spotted with age.

Her grandmother nodded her approval.

"You taught me well," Alyssa said. "Thank you, Grandmother."

Tucking the paints back in the bag, Alyssa rose.

Her grandmother clasped her hands and stared at her a long moment. "I understand why you do this," she said softly.

And Alyssa could see in her world-weary eyes that she did. She understood *all* of the reasons that had driven Alyssa to take her place as Westcott's wisewoman.

Alyssa's mother took a step toward them. "Mother, do not—"

"Beatrice," her grandmother countered sharply.

Her mother quieted.

"Perhaps I *did* speak too fondly of Lord Dillon," her grandmother mused.

Alyssa shook her head. "You only spoke the truth."

Sadness softened her grandmother's voice. "He will never love you, Alyssa."

She knew her grandmother did not say it to hurt her, but it did, nonetheless. "I am well aware of that. He will think me the same aged wisewoman who served his sire and his grandsire. He will think me *you*. And will continue to believe such as long as I wear these robes."

Alarm lit her mother's face. "You do not intend to remove them, do you?"

"Nay," Alysaa assured her. "Grandmother made me vow I would not, for my own safety."

Her grandmother squeezed her hands. "You are so innocent, Alyssa. You know not what 'tis like to love one who cannot love you in return. What 'tis like to love one who will never be *free* to love you in return. The pain that accompanies the pleasure of being in his presence every day. You know not the misery that awaits you when you inevitably watch the one you covet turn to another."

"I know it well," she insisted, and thought it worth the price she would pay.

Her grandmother sighed. "Nay, you do not. But I fear you soon will." She released Alyssa's hands and crossed to the hearth.

Alyssa's mother stepped forward, tears glistening in her eyes. "We have sheltered you all your life from the hate directed at those who bear gifts such as ours. I fear we sheltered you so much that you do not understand the true danger you will face once you leave here."

"How can I *not* understand it, knowing your past and Grandmother's?" Alyssa asked her. The hate and fear of aught different had nipped at her grandmother's heels all her life. The same hate had led a man of the cloth to set Alyssa's mother afire in an attempt to *purify her of the devil's taint* when her mother was but a girl. And a similar hate had driven men to hunt and slay Meg's parents, who also had been *gifted ones*. "But I will be safe at Westcott, Mother. *No one* will chance earning the fierce Earl of Westcott's wrath by attempting to burn his wisewoman at the stake. All fear him too much."

When her grandmother returned, she bore several wineskins. "Are you certain you wish to begin your service to Lord Dillon with such a grand endeavor?"

"Aye. If I succeed in taking Brimshire for him, he will be too distracted to notice any peculiarities that will arise during my transition."

For the first time, her grandmother's lips twitched with a faint smile. "'Tis bold. And clever. You shall serve Lord Dillon well."

Smiling with just a hint of nerves, Alyssa lifted her robe

and secured the skins to her waist with a rope.

"You must be diligent, Alyssa," her grandmother advised. "And maintain your guise at all times. Never leave your chamber without the robes and cowl. Never allow anyone more than the briefest glimpse of your hands. And never slip and speak in your own voice."

Alyssa adopted the elderly rasp she had been practicing for months. "I shall be most diligent indeed, Grandmother."

Meg's face lit with awe. "She sounds just like you!"

Alyssa grinned.

Her grandmother grimaced. "Surely I do not sound as old as that."

"Of course not," Alyssa lied, returning to her own voice.

Her grandmother's wrinkled features reflected her disbelief as she helped Alyssa straighten her robe. "Should anyone at Westcott seek to harm you, all you need do is duck out of sight and doff these robes. None will know a young woman resides beneath them. When they find the robe, they will search for a doddering old woman, not one who blooms with youth."

Alyssa nodded.

Her grandmother forced a smile and embraced Alyssa with frail arms. "'Tis time."

"Thank you, Grandmother," Alyssa whispered past the lump that rose in her throat.

"Prove them wrong," her grandmother whispered. "Do not let your love for Lord Dillon cost you your life."

When her grandmother stepped back, Meg rose and embraced Alyssa.

Then Beatrice stepped forward and hugged her close. "Be safe, daughter."

Alyssa nodded, unable to speak as tears burned the backs of her eyes and thickened her throat.

As her mother, grandmother, and cousin watched, Alyssa straightened her shoulders and raised the black cowl that would conceal her features from that day forth.

* * *

Alyssa shivered beneath her dark robe as she and Geoffrey stole through the Stygian forest. The light of a full moon dappled the foliage around them, enabling the two to negotiate the forest's maze without the benefit of a torch.

Though brittle leaves carpeted the forest floor, a light rain had softened them, permitting silent footsteps that enabled the two to elude the army encamped outside Brimshire's walls.

Geoffrey touched her arm, bringing her to a halt. Leaning down, he pointed and whispered in her ear, "The postern gate lies through there."

"You are certain you can gain us entry?" she asked again.

He nodded. "They think me one of them. And, should any seek to prevent our entry, I shall use my gifts to attain it."

"I must speak with Lord Dillon first."

Geoffrey's hand tightened on her arm. "There is still time to change your mind, Alyssa. You do not have to do this."

She patted his hand, then gently removed it. "I shall return anon."

Leaving Geoffrey, she once more crept through the forest until she reached the main camp. Simple structures had been erected over the long months to protect the men from arrows should any be let loose by the guards atop the castle walls. They also provided the men with shelter to stave off the illness that could be spawned by poor conditions arising from long sieges.

The light of the fires grew brighter as she approached the break in the trees.

Her heart began to pound when she located the Earl of Westcott.

He sat before a fire with a number of his men. Armor encased his broad shoulders. A sword, nigh as long as Alyssa was tall, lay at the ready beside him. Flickering flames sent golden light dancing across his handsome features, providing a pleasing contrast to the dark stubble that coated his strong jaw and chin. The scowl that creased his brow and made others tremble sparked no fear in Alyssa. She was far too nervous and excited.

Tonight she would begin her service as Lord Dillon's wisewoman.

* * *

Frustration beat at Dillon. Months had passed and the lord of Brimshire seemed no closer to surrender than he had been when the siege began.

"Do you think they are as well-fortified with provisions as Lord Edward would have us believe?" Sir Simon asked.

Several dead cows had been launched over the walls today. At first, Dillon and his men had feared they were diseased. 'Twas a common tactic in sieges.

But the cows had instead been meant to convey a simple message: Those besieging the castle would starve long before the inhabitants of the keep would. They had food aplenty inside the stout walls.

Dillon shook his head. "I know not... and have reached the end of my patience. Tomorrow we will begin constructing siege towers." He had hoped to take the castle—one King Richard had granted him when Dillon had saved his life—without violence. Without death. Without destroying walls and structures he would then have to rebuild once Brimshire became his.

"Do you wish to send for the trebuchet?"

Ready to be done with it, Dillon nodded and started to speak.

A twig snapped in the forest.

Every man present leapt to his feet and drew his sword.

A small, black-robed figure stepped into the firelight, seeming to manifest directly from the darkness itself.

Several knights hastened to cross themselves.

Dillon motioned for all to stand down and waited for them to relax before the fire once more. Sheathing his own weapon, he crossed to the wisewoman's side.

"My lord," she greeted him in her raspy voice.

Dillon guided her away from his men. "What do you here, Wise One? 'Tis not safe." How had she traveled such a distance? He saw none of his men with her. Had she come alone?

"My gifts told me you have need of my services," she whispered.

He could remember a time in his youth when her voice had been stronger. But age had gradually weakened it, first cracking it then reducing it to this faint relic of its former self.

None knew the wisewoman's true age. The more superstitious of his people, those who crossed themselves whenever she passed them, believed she possessed the powers of immortality and could claim centuries to her past. Others placed her age nigh that of the elders, who all swore she had served the Westcott lords for as long as the oldest amongst them had walked the earth. All Dillon knew with any certainty was that she had seen at least two-score and ten years, for she had advised his father throughout Dillon's youth.

He recalled his intense curiosity as a boy. She had stood straighter then, had seemed taller, almost grandiose to a precocious child who would not see his final height of a few inches above six feet for many years. A floor-length black robe with long sleeves that fell beneath her fingertips and a cowl that shielded every feature and defied even the strongest gust of wind had been and still was her constant companion. As Dillon understood it, none had ever looked upon her unmasked. Not even his grandfather, beside whom the elders insisted she had first stood.

Since acquiring the title, Dillon had had little chance to speak with this mysterious woman who had served his family for so many years. He had spent most of his time quashing a cousin's rebellion, then attempting to claim Brimshire. And, though he had known her peripherally all of his life, he had not yet decided how he felt about her coming to him as his advisor.

"All goes well here, Seer," he told her. 'Twas not a lie. There had been no losses on his side. No sickness. As far as sieges went, this had been an uneventful one. "Tomorrow we will begin constructing siege towers—"

"Such will not be necessary."

He stared at her, shocked that she had interrupted him. Everyone else feared him too much to risk the fury they all believed would erupt if they did so. "I know not—"

"Rest easy, my lord," she whispered, interrupting him *again*. "Brimshire will be yours by sunrise."

So saying, she backed away and let the forest swallow her.

Nonplussed, Dillon heard no sound of movement but knew without grabbing a torch and thrusting it forward that she was gone.

He turned to face his men.

Judging by their uneasy expressions, most had overheard.

"What do you suppose she meant by that?" Simon asked.

Dillon knew not and, retaking his place before the fire, decided to forgo sleep until she returned.

Hours later, as the sun rose and painted the land around them with a rosy dawn, a loud clanking sound disrupted the silence.

Dillon stood and faced the castle.

The drawbridge began to lower.

Waking his men with a single command, he mounted his destrier and drew his sword.

Squires fetched mounts. Knights climbed into saddles and drew weapons that glimmered in the strengthening sunlight.

The heavy outer portcullis slowly rose as Dillon and his men took up a position some distance from the end of the drawbridge.

A charged silence followed.

The inner portcullis rose.

All waited in tense anticipation for men to pour forth with

a battle cry.

Minutes passed as bird song serenaded them.

Then a small black-robed figure emerged, face hidden by her cowl. Striding boldly across the drawbridge, she halted when she reached Dillon's side. "As I said, my lord, siege towers will not be necessary. Brimshire is yours."

Dillon stared down at her in astonishment as his men all crossed themselves in a flurry of motion.

She had accomplished in one night what a six-month siege had not.

Just how far did her gifts extend?

CHAPTER ONE

England, 1198

As still as though he were an extension of the ramparts themselves, Dillon stared out over the slumbering keep. The same fog that partially veiled it stroked his skin with ghostly fingers and lent an eerie echo to the sounds of the guards who walked the walls.

She was there. Behind him. He had not heard her approach, but he could feel her presence as surely as he could the damp, chilly breeze.

"What brings you to these battlements on this dreary night, Seer?" he asked without turning around.

"Your troubled spirit called to me," she responded, her voice still but a whisper of its former self. "How may I serve you, my lord?"

He did not speak for many moments. His spirit was indeed troubled. He felt so very weary. And old. As old as some believed the crone hidden in darkness behind him was. "Our king has granted me another keep," he said finally.

"A fitting reward for one of his most loyal subjects."

"Think you he has forgotten I fought in opposition to him at *Le Mans?*"

"He would not hold that against you. You were defending your king. I believe he regrets now being a… less-than-dutiful son to Henry."

"Spoken most diplomatically, Wise One," he murmured, amused by her reference to Richard's hostile rebellions.

"And you have since proven your loyalty to King Richard many times over. You took an arrow for him at Acre. You helped put an end to Prince John's insurrection. 'Tis proper for him to offer his most fearsome knight a prize or two."

The laughter that rumbled forth from him carried a hint of the despair that had weighed him down of late.

"What amuses you, my lord?" she inquired.

He glanced at her over his shoulder. As usual, she stood in shadows, her robe hiding what little may have been revealed by a rogue ray of moonlight. "Take my hand, Wise One," he commanded, extending it toward her, "and tell me what you see."

She reached out and clasped his hand with one of hers. For one brief instant, he caught a glimpse of age-spotted, yellow-tinged skin stretched across blue veins and slender fingers before the sleeve of her robe glided forward to hide both their hands from his view. It was the most he had seen of her in the seven years she had advised him.

The warmth of that hand, so old and frail, surprised him, distracting him for a moment.

"Well?" he prodded. "How fearsome is the man who stands before you? Look closely. What do you see? What do I feel?"

"A great… lassitude, my lord."

"Aye."

"You are dissatisfied with your existence. You have grown weary of battle, of killing."

He looked down at the obscured inner bailey with a sigh. "Sometimes I wonder if I shall ever be able to erase the cursed stench of blood and death from my nostrils, the images of it from my memory." The wind picked up, swirling the night mist into mystical shapes and patterns from dreams. "What else do you see?"

"You know I cannot read your thoughts, my lord."

"Nay, but emotions and desires are clear to you, Seer. Interpret mine as you will."

"Very well."

Focusing intently on that which he wished her to see, he felt his hand heat where she touched it as she delved deeper with her peculiar gift.

"Your greatest wish is for peace."

"Aye."

"And…" She seemed to stall, mayhap mistrusting the information her gift relayed.

"Continue."

"A wife, my lord."

He wondered at the surprise manifested in that statement. With her powers, she saw him more clearly than anyone he knew. Even his younger brother, Robert, with whom he shared almost all of his secrets, did not know him as this one did.

Granted, on those rare instances when she touched him, 'twas usually with the intent to heal. But this desire for a wife had lingered in his heart and mind for some time now, growing stronger alongside his discontent. Surely his soothsayer had become aware of it ere now.

"You sound surprised."

"'Tis true I did not know you wished to wed," she admitted slowly. "But that in itself does not surprise me. 'Tis your reasons for doing so."

He chuckled, a sound rife with self-mockery, and tightened his grip on her fingers. "So, tell me, Seer, why the land's most formidable warrior, save our illustrious lionhearted ruler, desires a bride."

* * *

Shielded by her dark robe, Alyssa hesitated, uncertain of his mood. She had never seen Dillon quite like this before. "'Tis not for the customary reasons, my lord."

His large, rough, battle-scarred hand gripped hers with an almost desperate need for contact. Or mayhap reassurance. One would think that, after seven years of serving him, such a simple touch would no longer speed her pulse or make her breath catch. Yet, as always, she had to struggle to keep her hand from trembling within his grasp, to restrict her voice to the steady whisper she had worked so hard to perfect.

Dillon turned his face away from her, as if to hide his despondency from her view, though he must know she felt it as strongly as he did when they touched. High forehead. Straight nose, despite the numerous battles he had fought. Strong jaw now clenched in an effort to control his emotions.

It was a handsome face, marred only by two small scars. One divided his left eyebrow. A second adorned the right side of his chin. He had acquired both before she had come into his service just after Dillon had turned a score and three. She had let naught mar him since.

Though still a young man, the hair at his temples was almost entirely silver. The rest of his thick locks were only sparsely peppered with gray. Those that teased his collar remained as dark a brown as the day he had come into this world. So dark they were nigh black.

How often had she wished she could reach up and touch those locks, discover if they were as soft as they appeared?

"You do not seek a woman to bear you heirs or increase your lands and fortune as most do," she said.

"Do I not?"

"Nay, my lord."

"What then?"

Energy strummed through her as she sifted through his emotions. She had come to know him well over the years. Better than most. Mayhap that explained why her gift always seemed to stretch a bit further with him, allowed her to *see* more.

"You seek a tender smile and a warm embrace, awaiting you on the steps of the donjon each time you return from venturing forth on the king's business or on your own."

His eyes squinted slightly, deepening the faint lines the sun had placed at their corners. "What else?"

"You want a loving presence to sit with you by the fire of an evening. To converse with you. Teach you how to laugh again, to find joy in life. Someone in whom you can confide." She frowned. "Someone who will be as gentle with you as you wish to be with her."

The hand in her grasp gradually relaxed, as though he were being lulled by her revelation of his deepest fantasy.

Regret that *she* could not fulfill that fantasy left a bitter taste in her mouth.

Alyssa's grandmother had warned her that she would one day come to loathe these robes and the silence they required. Her mother had, too. But she had been young when she had donned them and accepted the many responsibilities of Westcott's wisewoman—a mere ten and six—and had not seen beyond the opportunity to be close to the compassionate, courageous (and, aye, comely) Lord Dillon.

"You wish your bride to come to you innocent," she forced herself to continue. "Pure, but without fear. You dream of spending many long nights… making love with her." Her face heated. "And many more falling asleep with her cradling you close to her, chasing off the grisly nightmares that plague your sleep."

Silence engulfed them when she finished. He withdrew his hand, seeming almost reluctant to sever the contact.

"I ask again," he said softly, his lips turning down at their corners. "How fearsome is the warrior who stands before you?"

"No less fearsome than he was ere I *saw* him."

He shook his head. "How they all would laugh if they knew the truth."

"And what truth might that be, my lord?"

"That one of England's most ruthless killers—a man who inspires terror in all, leaves blood and destruction in his wake wherever he travels, and is rumored to devour small children for supper—desires only peace and a wife who will be little more than a nursemaid to him."

"A nursemaid to your children mayhap. A companion to you. There is no shame in loving, my lord."

He turned to her, his features alight with curiosity. "Know you of love, then?"

Aye, ever since she was a child and had witnessed—from a distance—his kindness toward her grandmother, his defense of her when others repudiated her. "I have not attained this age *without* knowing it, my lord."

"I confess I know not precisely what age you have attained, Seer."

"You are not alone in your ignorance."

He grinned at her evasion, as she had known he would. "Fear not. I will not press you."

"How very wise of you," she drawled, eliciting a sharp laugh.

"Why should I," he continued in teasing tones, "when your age does not rouse nigh as much curiosity as your appearance?"

"I have long considered curiosity a bothersome, unhealthy emotion, my lord."

"Then why do you take such pleasure in generating it amongst my people?" he countered.

She allowed her laughter to emerge as a raspy chuckle. "Mayhap *you* are the true seer here, my lord, for you know me too well."

* * *

Dillon stared at her, wishing that were true. The top of her head barely came to his shoulder. 'Twould be so easy to reach out, drag back the cowl that covered it, and finally discover what he had spent far too much time pondering. But he would not do so. He would never violate her trust in such a way. Not when she treated his own with such care.

"Why is it that you think you will never find the wife you long for?"

His stomach clenched. "Because she does not exist."

"You do not believe there is a woman in all of England capable of the tenderness and devotion you desire?"

"I believe there are many such women. But each and every one of them cringes at my approach. When I come to bed at night, I want my wife to tremble with passion, not fear."

"All women do not fear you," she stated plainly. When he raised a brow, her cowl tilted to one side. "Think you I do not know all that transpires in your domain?"

A warm flush crept up his neck when he realized she referred to the women who occasionally satisfied his needs. "Do not think that because they sought me out and shared my bed those women were not just as frightened as the others."

"If they were frightened, they would not have approached you."

Frowning, he crossed his arms over his chest. "You cannot have lived so many years and remained that naive." When she remained damningly silent, his tone mellowed. "Or have you?" 'Twas something he had never considered before, her innocence or lack thereof. As many years as she had lived and as much of the world as she had seen, he had assumed that at some point…

Well, he had once even found himself wondering if she and his father had not been lovers for a time.

"Very well," he said when no rejoinder was forthcoming. "The women who have offered themselves to me did so because fear excites them. They did not come to me for lovemaking. They came seeking domination."

"And who better to dominate than one with your

reputation," she finished for him.

"Aye." Dillon tamped down the anger and embarrassment that threatened. He had never divulged that particular secret before, not even to Robert, who often bedeviled him about his long, self-imposed bouts of celibacy. A woman had not sought Dillon out with affection since he had left on his first campaign. Even women who desired the power and wealth Dillon possessed kept their distance, dissuaded by the rumors of violence that cloaked him.

The wisewoman stepped up beside him, close, but not touching.

He did not look at her. He could not.

"'Tis true, I know little of such things," she murmured.

And he knew how much that admission cost her. In their years of dealing with each other, she had revealed very little of herself to him, yet did so now as an act of contrition for pushing him to discuss what he obviously did not wish to.

"In this instance, I fear we share the same complaint, my lord," she added sadly.

"What complaint is that?" Dillon found himself holding his breath, unsure how to proceed, since she had never before offered up such personal information to him.

"Very few bother to look beyond our reputations to the individuals they conceal. If you recall, I inspire as much, if not more, fear in those who encounter me."

He realized the truth of her words as soon as she spoke them.

"I see the people cross themselves whenever I walk past, see mothers tug their children closer to them for protection, hear men hurl accusations of witchcraft and link my name with Lucifer's. I have even had a stone or two thrown my way."

His head snapped around in furious disbelief. "Who dared to—?"

"Do not exert yourself on my behalf. 'Twas long ago and the culprits have since been repaid for their actions tenfold."

He found his anger slow to ebb. "Did you…?"

She sighed. "Alas, nay, though the blame *was* placed with me."

"There have been other crimes perpetrated against you, have there not? Crimes you never mentioned to me?"

Her hood swung from side to side. "Only declarations of intent, my lord. The very reputation you despise has been my staunch defender these last seven years. Knowing the trust you place in me, none would dare incur your wrath by following through on their threats."

At least it had done *someone* some good, he thought morosely, wondering at the same time if he should not call his people together and make his displeasure known over their harsh treatment of the woman at his side. The same woman who had healed many of them with her hands, sometimes bringing them or their children back from the brink of death.

"Why does King Richard's gift not please you?" she asked, guiding the subject back to their conversation's origins.

"Because I must lay siege to the keep in order to claim it. 'Twould seem its previous owner is not ready to relinquish his hold on it."

"Yet another battle for you to fight."

"Aye."

"There is more."

He could hide naught from her. "'Tis Pinehurst I've been given."

"Lord Camden's holding?" Camden was son to Dillon's nearest neighbor Lord Everard, Earl of Westmoreland, whom Dillon had admired and respected ever since he was in swaddling clothes. "He has finally done it, then."

"What?"

"Beggared his estate through his own greed. His father worried that he would do as much and should not be surprised by this turn of events."

"I suppose not."

"No doubt Camden compounded the problem by insulting the king. He has always acted rashly and with little thought."

"'Tis the way of it. His support of John during Richard's imprisonment was only the beginning, 'twould seem."

"When do you depart?"

"On the morrow."

"Perchance you could employ the same tactics you used to take Brimshire, thus eliminating the necessity of fighting."

He smiled. "Plan to steal in and lace their food and drink with another of your tasty sleeping potions, do you?" he asked, delighted by her inference that it had been his plan all along. In truth, he had not learned until the keep had fallen how exactly she had aided him that night.

"You need only ask and I shall do as you command."

He shook his head. "I dislike your taking such risks. Were anyone to discover you…"

"They expect treachery to come in the form of brawny soldiers, not"—and he could actually hear her smile—"from a frail, old woman."

Dillon paced away from her. It had worked well the last time. She had succeeded in drugging nigh every soldier within the gates. Those who had retained their faculties had surrendered as soon as they had seen him riding inside, his men directly behind him. No violence. No destruction. No unnecessary deaths. Yet, unease trickled down his spine.

"Nay." He returned to her side. "I like it not. Mix your potion, if you will, Wise One, but I shall find another to smuggle it inside."

She straightened. "A premonition, my lord?"

"You know I do not share your gifts." He dragged an impatient hand through his hair. "I merely sense… danger."

"To me? Or to yourself?"

"Naught so clear as that." He shook his head. "We both know what a knave Camden is. He will not fight honorably. I ask that you remain here, where I may be assured of your safety."

"And what assurances will I have of *your* safety, my lord? I should be by your side should you have need of my services."

He could not help but be pleased by her concern. Whilst others thought him invincible, she worried over his safety as his mother might have had she lived. "I shall send for you, Healer, should I need you."

She nodded with notable reluctance. "And I shall fly to you on the wings of your swiftest stallion, my lord, the moment your messenger arrives."

His lips stretched in a grin others scarcely saw. "So long as you do not truly give the steed wings or my men may flee."

She responded with another raspy chuckle.

* * *

Dillon pondered their conversation later as he lay sleepless in his bed. It might very well have been the most personal they had shared.

It had certainly been the most revealing.

She had always been a solitary figure, the wisewoman, rarely speaking to anyone other than himself unless she was healing a wound. For some reason, he had assumed she wanted it thus. That her powers set her apart. That she preferred her own company to that of others, particularly since others were less than kind to her and seldom thanked her for her efforts when she helped them.

But now…

What a lonely existence she had led. Year after year of enforced solitude, surrounded by people who feared and mistrusted her because of the gifts bestowed upon her at birth. Gifts that were a blessing, but more often were viewed as a curse. Gifts that should have exalted her, but instead had transformed her into a mere vessel to be used by his grandfather, then his father, and now Dillon.

How had they rewarded her? What had they done to make her life easier, to ease her burden when she had eased theirs in so many ways?

The thought unsettled him. His wisewoman had been sorely misused, yet had never in her years of service uttered a single complaint. Even tonight, when she had spoken of those who had thrown stones at her, she had done so matter-of-factly, as if she had never considered that he might be willing to seek justice on her behalf.

It pained him to know she thought as much, that she believed he did not value her more, considering the many days and nights she had staved off the worst of his loneliness. For, when she was not healing an illness, rendering aid to any who incurred an injury, or ensuring that his steward kept his castle running smoothly, the wisewoman frequently remained at his side.

The women he had met at court could barely manage to stutter a greeting when he joined them. The same held true for the men. Rumors of Dillon's supposed cruelty preceded him into every room, stilling a majority of the tongues present and widening all eyes before he entered. 'Twas why he never stayed any longer than he had to and left feeling like a fire-breathing dragon the villagers prayed would not demand a sacrifice.

His companions, his knights, even his brother all knew how to praise and flatter and turn a pretty head. Dillon had no inkling where to begin. His resulting reticence and unsmiling countenance, coupled with the ruthless reputation he had earned on the battlefield, had therefore proven far too intimidating for the noblewomen he had met, inspiring the fear he had eventually, resignedly, come to expect.

But such was not the case with the wisewoman. She alone seemed invariably at ease in his presence. He felt no need to mince words with her. No need to examine every thought before he spoke it for fear of frightening or offending. No need to modulate his tone when vexed nor monitor his bark when angered.

Mayhap 'twas her age and her own power that made her

such a comfortable companion for him. A kindred spirit, as she had implied on the battlements, garnering the same fear in others, unable to function normally in society because of it.

Or mayhap 'twas because she alone was comfortable enough around him to always speak her mind. He knew only that he could relax with her, be more himself, though he always maintained a respectful distance.

A scarcely audible scraping sound met his ears, disrupting his musings. Bolting upright, Dillon grabbed the sword he always kept within reach and prepared to defend himself. He listened, motionless, unable to locate the intruder in the dim light of the dying fire.

"Rest easy, my lord."

"Wise One." His muscles relaxing, he returned his sword to its resting place. "Did my troubled spirit call you to me again?" he queried, wondering what had drawn her to his chamber.

Had she known he was thinking of her?

"Nay." She drew closer, a small silhouette separating itself from a host of others. "This time 'twas my own troubled spirit."

Remembering his desire to repay the debt his family owed her, he waited until she reached his bedside, then asked deferentially, "How may I serve you, Wise One?"

The question seemed to take her aback. "'Tis I who serve you, my lord," she responded with some confusion.

"You said your spirit is troubled. Is there naught I can do to aid you?"

She shifted. "You misunderstand."

"Then, please, explain."

"I was pondering the words we shared earlier," she began haltingly. And he felt his *bothersome*, *unhealthy* curiosity mount. "Though I cannot locate your bride for you, my lord, I *can* ward off your nightmares, if only for one night." Her midnight robe wavered and shimmered as she thrust a mug of rather vile-smelling liquid toward him.

"You would drug me?" he demanded, shocked.

"'Twill not harm you."

He eyed the mug dubiously. "'Tis not the same potion you plied the men of Brimshire with, is it?" It had taken some of the men two or three days to regain consciousness after consuming it.

"Of course not," she retorted, her voice almost, but not quite rising above a whisper for the first time in years. "'Tis very mild. You will merely rest a little deeper, free of the threat of nightmares, and awaken refreshed on the morrow."

He looked from the mug to her hooded figure. 'Twas tempting. He could not remember the last time he had slept the whole night through without waking at least once to the sound of screams reverberating through his head. Unfortunately…

"I cannot leave myself so vulnerable, Healer." Every good soldier knew that sleeping too soundly could endanger a man's life.

"No harm shall come to you whilst you sleep."

"But—"

"I will not allow it, my lord," she added with a conviction that made him wonder once more at the true extent of her gifts.

"What of your troubled spirit?"

"Your sleep will ease it."

Once again he wished he could espy her features. "Very well, Wisewoman." He took the mug from her and, trusting her implicitly, drained its contents with a shudder and a grimace ere he handed it back to her. "I thank you."

"Lie back and close your eyes," she instructed in a gentle voice. "'Twill soon take effect."

He did so, willing his mind to stop racing, silencing the questions that wanted to tumble from his lips.

Her potion came swiftly to his aid. In only minutes, he could feel himself tumbling off the precipice of consciousness.

She was wrong, though. He did dream.

Just once.

He dreamed that, as he succumbed to sleep, his bride's fingers tunneled tenderly through his hair, smoothing it back from his forehead before gentle lips pressed a kiss there.

"Rest well, Dillon," she said in a lilting, melodious voice as delicate fingertips trailed down his temple, past his ear, and followed the line of his jaw to the scar on his chin. "I shall not leave your side."

Then, drawing the blankets up over his broad chest, she lay down atop them and lovingly cradled him against her when he turned into her reverent embrace.

So soft.

So soothing.

So full of long-awaited love for him.

CHAPTER TWO

He had never slept so well.

'Twas the first thought that struck Dillon when his eyelids fluttered open as dawn broke. Nor had he ever dreamed such sweet, tranquil dreams.

"No nightmares beleaguered you, my lord?"

Startled, he looked toward the speaker and found the healer sitting beside his bed. Had she been there all night, watching over him to keep him from harm as she had promised?

"None," he answered, his voice still rough from sleep. "I have never felt so rested."

"I hoped 'twould be so." She sounded pleased. She must be exhausted.

Yet another debt he owed her.

"I did dream, though," he murmured, a face drifting through his memory.

Her hood tilted slightly. "I thought no nightmares visited you."

"'Twas no nightmare who held me close within her warm embrace, but one who must surely be the fairest maid in all the land."

"Who…?"

"My bride, Seer." A languorous smile stretched his lips as he rose onto his elbows. "You were right. She *does* exist. And she is more beauteous than any woman I have ever beheld, with skin as pale as snow and hair the color of midnight."

"But… but… 'tis not possible," she stuttered.

Dillon frowned. Did she think him unworthy of such a maid? Had his disclosures the previous night made her think less of him or convinced her that he was right, that he would never find a woman like the one in his dream, who could love him and would be willing to wed him?

Ere he could press her for an explanation, pounding erupted on the door.

"Enter," he called irritably.

Sir Simon, his second-in-command, threw open the door and strode into the solar with a grin. His gaze flitted from Dillon to the wisewoman. Stopping short, the big man sketched her a clumsy bow. "Good morrow to you, Wise One."

"Good morrow, Sir Simon."

He turned back to Dillon and smiled again. "The Cub approaches the gate."

Thrilled by his unexpected visitor, Dillon eagerly abandoned his concerns and turned bright eyes on the seer. "Robert."

Completely forgetting the revelation of her innocence the previous night, he threw back the covers, leapt naked from the bed, and hurriedly began to dress.

* * *

Lingering in an umbral corner nigh the entrance of the great hall, Alyssa watched their reunion. A vigorous embrace accompanied by the pounding of backs and hearty kisses on stubbled cheeks. At five and twenty, Robert was an inch or so shorter than Dillon, with shoulders equally broad and hair as black as a raven's wing. Both men were incredibly handsome, their blue eyes sparkling with pleasure. But only Dillon made her breath catch and her heart pound within her breast.

Memories surfaced of the way he had turned to her in his sleep last night and wrapped his arms around her, his large muscled thigh slipping between hers, his lips resting upon the sensitive skin at the base of her neck. She had remained awake through the dawn, savoring his nearness, the way his arms would tighten every once in a while and he would unconsciously urge her closer. Never had she felt more alive.

Even now her body tingled in new ways and places, a condition that was not helped by visions of him leaping naked from the bed earlier. She had seen parts of him unclothed many times over the years. An arm. A leg. His chest.

Never had she seen *everything*.

Shaking her head, she forced her attention back to the present.

All that remained of their family, the two Westcott warriors remained as close as siblings could be. Their sister had died in childbirth. One of their elder brothers had met a violent end in the Holy Land. The other had perished whilst defending his king during the revolt of 1174. Their mother had died birthing Robert, almost taking Alyssa's grandmother with her as she had fought for the lives of mother and babe. And their father, the last earl of Westcott, had breathed his last breath without warning one afternoon when his heart had failed him.

So Dillon tended to be very protective of Robert.

"Where are your men?" Dillon guided his younger brother into the great hall with an affectionate arm across his shoulders. "Have they not accompanied you here to eat their way through my stores? I have never seen such appetites as theirs."

"I rode ahead. They shall be here shortly."

"You are limping!"

"Faugh," Robert blustered. "I am stiff from too damned many hours in the saddle."

Dillon called for ale as he and Robert sank into two chairs positioned before the largest of the four hearths the great hall boasted. "You were the one who chose to leave and seek adventure. I have told you often that you are more than welcome to live out your days here with me."

"Aye, and your constant coddling would transform me into a maiden in no time."

Alyssa stifled a laugh.

Dillon grimaced. "Nevertheless. You need not hire out your sword. You take too many risks."

His brother gave a negligent shrug. "At least I am never bored."

Silently, Alyssa moved closer, skirting the hall until she stood in a darkened corner, facing the younger man's back. Robert's unexpected visit pleased her. If anyone could supply a welcome distraction and lift Dillon's spirits, 'twas he.

That limp of his concerned her, though. Robert had ever expressed uneasiness in her presence and would rather have a barber pull a tooth than admit he required her healing skills. Did he not seek her out before nightfall, she would have to find some way to corner him.

"If boredom is your complaint," Dillon broached, "why do you not help me take Pinehurst?"

"Acquired another one, have you?"

"Aye. And Camden's at that. The damned tenants will not open the gates to me unless ordered to do so by their former master."

"Not willing to give it up yet?"

"Camden will never surrender it willingly."

"Sounds like 'twill be a fight. Aye, I will join you."

"You do not sound overly enthusiastic."

Nay, he did not. And she assumed it the result of whatever injury had befallen him.

Robert rubbed his eyes. "I am but weary."

"Then remain here at Westcott, where you belong. Forgo the tournament circuit and fighting other men's wars."

The younger man stubbornly shook his head. "I need land

of my own, brother, and people of my own who will offer me the same loyalty and respect yours do you."

"As my heir, all you see around you will one day be yours."

"I am only your heir until you wed and your wife bears you a son."

Dillon shrugged, his strong features taking on a somewhat bleak cast. "Since I shall likely never wed, you shall remain my heir."

Alyssa bit her lip, regretting her earlier reaction to his dream. Or rather to what he thankfully *believed* had been a dream. She had been so sure he had fallen asleep.

The potion must not have been strong enough. He should not have been conscious, should not have remembered.

It had seemed as though hours had passed ere she had finally given in to temptation, doffed her robe, and—heart slamming against her ribs—lain down beside him. After seven years of loving him, longing for him, she had craved his touch like a man in the desert craved water and had thought him unaware. Had thought herself safe from discovery. Had thought it harmless to steal a moment with him, undisguised.

She closed her eyes for a moment, remembering again how wondrous it had felt when he had drawn her into his warm embrace. She had been so surprised. Her heart had pounded so loudly she had feared he might hear it. And such scandalous desire had claimed her.

Returning her attention to the brothers, she feared her distress this morning at discovering Dillon had *not* succumbed to the herbs—at least not completely—might have sounded more to his ears like mockery.

Robert frowned. "Never wed? What nonsense has the sorceress been filling your ears with now?" He winced and shifted, seeking a more comfortable position.

Watching from the darkness of her hood, Alyssa saw a scowl flit across Dillon's features. He made a slight motion with his hand, one that would go unnoticed by all save herself.

Nodding, she soundlessly moved forward until she stood behind Robert's chair.

"You have not said what brings you to Westcott," Dillon said, changing the subject.

"Can a man not visit his family when the mood strikes him?" Robert griped.

At Dillon's silent instruction, Alyssa rested her fingertips on Robert's shoulder. "He is injured, my lord."

Robert lurched clumsily to his feet and spun around, a slew of epithets spewing from his lips. "Unhand me, Witch!" he shouted last and shoved her arm away.

At least, that is all he had intended to do. Alyssa saw the spark of fever and flash of pain that lit his eyes as his leg buckled and he lost his balance. He swiftly righted himself. But that shove had been forceful enough to send her crashing to the floor, where she landed so hard on her side that it knocked the breath from her.

Fear lanced through her until she realized her cowl had not fallen away from her face to reveal her youth. The relief that followed was so great it almost dulled the throbbing that began just above her temple where her head had struck the floor.

For a moment, all was still as every occupant of the hall stared wide-eyed at her crumpled form lying amidst the rushes, then regarded the earl with fascinated alarm, awaiting his response.

Fury swept across Dillon's features. *"You will treat her with respect!"* he bellowed at Robert, his face mottling, the veins in his neck standing out, ere he faced the knights, men-at-arms, and servants who gaped at them. *"Every one of you* will treat her with respect!"

"My lord, please," Alyssa objected, not wanting him to say or do aught that might foster greater feelings of resentment amongst his people.

Shoving his brother aside, Dillon closed the distance

between them, grasped her elbow in one strong hand, and carefully helped her to her feet.

"He did not do it apurpose," she insisted, stepping away from him and breaking contact as she shook out her robes. "'Tis not necessary."

Speechless, Robert stared at them both with dazed eyes filled with remorse.

Alyssa had never seen Dillon strike his brother in anger, but feared for a moment he might do so now, so furious did he appear.

She jumped when Dillon instead rested a hand upon her shoulder.

He so rarely touched her.

More of his people, upon hearing the commotion, crowded inside, generating a substantial gathering as he commanded their attention.

"This woman," he said, his voice ringing clearly enough to reach every ear, "is responsible for much of our good health and continued prosperity. Yet you all fear her and treat her with contempt."

Alyssa tried to ease back into the shadows, uncomfortable with the attention he drew to her.

Dillon would have none of it and tightened his grip, keeping her at his side. "Know you now that any offense made against her is an offense made against me and will be duly punished. Any kindness she bestows upon you will be repaid with one of your own. The wisewoman has been blessed with gifts we have too often taken for granted. We will do so no longer."

Alyssa stared at him from beneath her cowl as onlookers glanced at one another uneasily. When it became apparent that he intended to say no more, all quietly dispersed.

Dillon sighed and withdrew his touch, allowing her freedom.

Her thoughts churned as she watched him wrap a supportive arm around his brother's waist.

Docile now, Robert looped an arm around Dillon's shoulders and limped along at his side.

Alyssa followed, keeping pace as they made their cautious way to the stairs, climbed them slowly, and headed into the chamber Robert called his own. "I would you had not done that, my lord," she put forth.

"Why?" Dillon grunted, practically carrying Robert the last few steps to his bed.

"Those who are unwilling to treat me kindly will no longer seek my aid." Now that the first shock had worn off, she found his defense of her touching. Gallant. His desire to see her treated with respect heartwarming. But she could not perform her duties if the people of Westcott had even greater reason to avoid her.

He snorted as he settled his brother none too gently against the pillows. "If they cannot treat you kindly, then they deserve not your help. Where is he wounded?"

"I am fine," Robert grumbled.

"His left leg, just above the knee."

Dillon peeled off his brother's chausses and let them fall to the floor. Retrieving the dagger from his belt, he began to cut away the hose beneath that covered the area she had indicated.

"A gift withheld is no gift at all," Alyssa murmured as she leaned forward to get a closer look at the ugly gash he exposed. "It has begun to fester. 'Tis why he is feverish. Had he waited much longer, he would have inevitably lost either his life or his leg."

Robert paled, hearing that.

Dillon, on the other hand, merely looked more furious.

"It must be cleansed first," she announced and straightened.

Dillon stared at her over Robert's inert body, his brow furrowed. "After his actions below, I should not ask this of you."

"You have not," she pointed out, then departed without another word to fetch her herbs and fresh water.

* * *

Dillon watched the wisewoman leave.

"I am sorry," Robert said, breaking the quiet that fell in her absence.

"I am not the one you have abused."

"I know. I shall make amends."

"See that you do," Dillon ordered, disappointed in him. "What made you behave so shamefully? She has come to your aid a number of times in the past. Healing your injuries. Banishing your ailments. Lending you her strength during those early months after Father died whilst I quashed rebellions and settled things at Brimshire. She did not deserve that."

Robert grimaced. "Her presence and her powers have always made me uneasy. I fear my fever made me overreact."

"Do not call her Witch again."

"What?"

"You heard me. Now, tell me how this came about."

It seemed to take Robert a moment to follow the change in subject. Another product of the fever, Dillon assumed. "Thieves."

"Nigh Westcott?"

"Several days march to the south." He shook his dark, tousled head. "I have never seen such a large band. But we managed to cut them all down."

Dillon motioned to the swollen, pus-filled wound. "Not quickly enough apparently."

"A lucky thrust, the bastard. Though they dressed as beggars, I would swear they had been formally trained."

The wisewoman returned, carrying herbs, bandages, a basin filled with water, and a clean cloth. She set the basin down on the table beside the bed, dipped the cloth in the water and squeezed the excess liquid from it.

Dillon glared at his brother pointedly.

Robert turned to the healer. "Forgive me, Wise One. I meant you no harm."

Dillon felt her gaze as she bent over the inflamed injury and began to clean it, miraculously managing to do so without exposing her hands. The glimpse he had caught of them last night had been a rarity.

"Mayhap a bit of sorcery courses through *your* blood, my lord," she murmured.

He smiled at her teasing response to Robert's about-face. When the man in question flinched at her ministrations, Dillon laid a comforting hand on his shoulder. "I made things worse, did I not?" he asked after awhile.

"How so, my lord?"

"Below. With the people."

Her shoulders lifted in a slight shrug. "If you did, I shall hardly notice a difference."

He nodded, consumed with regret. "I only wished to make things easier for you."

"I know." She examined the wound one last time to make certain 'twas clean. "And I appreciate your efforts. But you cannot erase generations of superstition with a few sternly spoken commands, my lord."

Dillon wanted to say more, but was painfully aware of his brother's curious gaze sweeping back and forth between them.

Straightening, the wisewoman set the bowl aside, then placed her hands on the wound. Black material slithered forward to conceal the wonder she performed.

It did not take long. No more than a minute. When she withdrew her hands, her sleeves trailing after her, the wound had closed. Though not completely healed, the angry red of its jagged edges had drawn together in a smooth, pink line that posed no danger.

Minor injuries, Dillon had noted, she healed entirely, leaving behind no trace of their existence. Deeper wounds, however, or those that had festered too long before being brought to her attention, she treated as she had Robert's, first cleaning them, then healing them to the point that they no longer posed a threat or generated too much discomfort. What remained she treated with herbs and poultices.

Mayhap healing the more serious injuries simply took more energy than her fragile form possessed.

He frowned. Although, regardless of their severity, she had always healed *his* wounds entirely.

"Are you unwell, Healer?"

His brother's tentative query made Dillon realize he had been staring fixedly at the pristine white bandage she had wrapped around Robert's thigh after sprinkling it with herbs. His eyes swerved to the wisewoman, who swayed slightly.

The long sleepless night had taken its toll.

As stubborn as she was wise, she shook her head in denial and moved toward the open door, a slight hitch in her step.

Concerned, Dillon started toward her.

"Your brother needs you, my lord," she said without looking at him. "See that he remains abed and does not reopen his wound."

Realizing she did not welcome his assistance, he nodded. "Thank you, Wise One. I shall repay this debt."

"Any debt owed is mine, my lord." With those words, she left.

"What do you suppose she meant by that?" Robert asked, puzzled.

Dillon stared at the empty doorway. "I know not."

* * *

The next morning, Dillon stepped out into the inner bailey and nodded to Sir Simon. Three years his junior, Simon had joined Dillon's service just before the siege of Brimshire had begun. Dillon knew not whence he had come, or whose command he had left, but Simon had proven to be one of the strongest warriors with whom Dillon had ever sparred.

"How is The Cub doing?" Simon asked.

In his early days at Westcott, Simon had remarked upon how fiercely Robert defended his older brother whenever rumors of his supposed cruelty arose. Simon had likened him to a wolf cub and, much to Robert's chagrin, the dubious title had stuck.

Dillon grunted. "Whining to be let out."

"I do not whine," Robert snapped, limping slightly as he joined them. "Nor have I ever. And, considering the number of enemies I have slain and the fact that my ruthless reputation nigh rivals my brother's, do you not think it time you cease calling me Cub?"

Simon nodded solemnly, sunlight glinting off of his dark blond hair. "Mayhap 'tis time I call you *Pup* instead."

Robert swore and cuffed Simon on the side of his head. Laughing, Simon shoved him back. The next thing Dillon knew, the two were down in the dirt, wrestling.

Sighing, he bent down, grasped the backs of their tunics and yanked them up and apart. "Children, please." He gave Robert a little push toward the donjon. "Go seek yourself a place by the fire. Should you reopen your wound, you will answer to the wisewoman."

Muttering beneath his breath, Robert left.

Simon grinned and shook his head. "What news of Camden?"

"'Tis as we expected."

"The weasely bastard. He knows he cannot hold out against your forces. From all we have heard, his stores are already so depleted any siege would be over in little more than a fortnight."

"Yet, a siege 'twill be."

"Camden still being a pain in the arse?" a gravelly voice interjected. His odor preceding him, the burly Gavin joined them. Tall and dark, he was a spirited fighter with a jovial disposition, but possessed such a strong aversion to baths that Dillon always attempted to remain upwind of him.

Simon sighed. "Aye."

"Asking for a siege, he is. When do we depart?"

Dillon considered Simon. "You and I are of a size, would you not say?"

Simon looked at Dillon, then down at himself. "Aye. Close enough."

Dillon glanced at Gavin. "Think you he could pass for me did he don my armor?"

Gavin rubbed the black stubble on his chin, tilting his head first one way, then the other. "As long as he kept the helm on to hide that golden boy hair of his, methinks 'twould work. Why? Not willing to leave The Cub?"

"Nay. Not yet." Dillon looked at Simon and raised his eyebrows. "What say you, Simon? Would you be willing to emulate me for the sake of our Cub?"

"Though your armor will no doubt drag me down with its weight and chafe me endlessly, I would," he quipped with a smile.

"Excellent. Gideon will bring you my armor whilst you and the men make ready to leave. Gavin, you may wait and accompany me and a handful of others by week's end. With any luck, we will join them ere they reach Pinehurst."

Simon nodded. "No doubt you will. Without the supply wagons to slow you down, you will travel much more swiftly."

Gavin grunted his agreement.

"Do not engage Camden in battle if you reach Pinehurst first," Dillon cautioned. "Merely show yourselves and begin assembling the trebuchets." He had no reason to believe Camden would surrender Pinehurst until violence and force drove him to do it.

"We will begin work as soon as we make camp."

Gavin chuckled as Simon walked away.

"What?"

"Just thinking of that fool, Camden. No doubt he will stand atop the walls, cackling and casting insults down upon poor Simon's head, never guessing that he is not you."

Dillon smiled. "Aye. The jest will be on him, will it not?"

* * *

Dillon did not take his leave for three more days, during which he drove Robert mad with mothering. At least, he mothered him when no others save Alyssa were present. The rest of the time he gruffly complained about the inconvenience of having to postpone his departure.

Alyssa found both brothers' behavior amusing and envied them the bond they shared.

Because she disliked straying too far from Dillon's side or shirking her many duties at Westcott, she rarely had the opportunity to visit her own family. She could not safely send them missives for they wished none to know where they resided. Nor would she ask them to seek her here. Westcott and its people had caused both her mother and grandmother great grief over the years. She would not compel them to return.

She could not see Meg simply because 'twas not safe for Meg to travel alone.

And her brother Geoffrey was busy attempting to discover his place in this world.

"He treats me like a child," Robert muttered as he watched Dillon and his men canter across the drawbridge.

"You are all he has," she whispered, walking up behind him.

Jumping, he spun around and squinted against the sunlight as she drew nigh.

Unlike Dillon, who always seemed to sense her approach, Robert rarely seemed to be aware of Alyssa's presence until she spoke.

Another reason, she supposed, for his uneasiness around her.

"After all of the losses the two of you have suffered," she continued, "is it not natural that he might wish to protect you?"

"I suppose," he conceded. "But that does not make his

insistence that I remain at Westcott easier to bear. My leg no longer pains me. *Rarely* pains me," he corrected, no doubt fearing she would *see* the truth. "I have proven my skill in battle many times over. There is no reason I should not accompany him beyond his own stubbornness."

Alyssa studied him a moment. "Is it merely boredom that agitates you?"

He paced away, then back. If she were to doff her cowl, she knew he would avoid her gaze. Such was how troubled he appeared. "Aye. I am sure 'tis all."

She did not speak again for several minutes. She had always felt turmoil in Robert when she had touched him. He had housed it since the first time she had healed him after coming into Dillon's service. Alyssa had assumed, in the beginning, that it resulted from his unease around her, but had gradually come to discern that it stemmed from something else. She knew not the cause, nor how deep it went. Unless his guard was lowered, as it had been when she had healed this latest wound, he sought to hide it from her. Yet, Alyssa was a keen observer of those around her. Being shunned and having little opportunity to converse with others tended to leave one plenty of time in which to study them. And she had noticed that Robert's turmoil always increased during moments of inactivity.

As if inactivity left him too much time to think or remember.

But remember what?

Whilst Robert continued to pace, limping a bit, Alyssa wondered if his desire to accompany Dillon stemmed from his need to stay busy or if he worried that Camden might harm Dillon though treachery.

"Ere your arrival," she ventured at last, "your brother expressed an uneasiness about besieging Pinehurst."

Halting, Robert frowned. "Did he?"

"Aye. 'Twas why he would not hear of my accompanying

him, though I have done so often in the past. I begin to wonder if that is not the true reason *you* have been left behind as well."

"Camden can be a crafty little bastard when he is sober," Robert muttered and returned to tower over her. "Have you seen the future, Wise One? Know you the outcome of this campaign?"

"That is beyond my capabilities," she replied, conveying apology with her aged whisper. "My knowledge of future events is limited to occasional premonitory dreams, which I am afraid my sleep of late has lacked." Nay, her most recent dreams had been consumed with wicked images of Dillon taking her in his arms and tumbling her to his bed. Of him lowering his lips to hers, his hands caressing her.

Robert raked his fingers through his hair, a gesture of frustration he had acquired from his brother. "I will not let Dillon's misguided attempts to protect me keep me from guarding his back as he approaches Pinehurst." He turned sharp eyes on her, as if daring her to disagree with him. "I shall follow him and stay to the trees."

Alyssa nodded, relieved. "I pray such precaution will prove unnecessary."

He seemed surprised. "You will not prevent me from leaving?"

Her eyebrows flew up. "I possess neither the power nor the authority to do so."

He grunted. "My brother places such faith in your counsel that I sometimes forget…"

That she was a servant? A peasant?

Would that Alyssa could forget as well. "I shall gather the herbs you will need, should your leg trouble you further or should anyone incur an injury," she told him as she turned and walked away, wishing she could be there to heal Dillon if he were wounded.

"But I know not how to administer them," Robert protested, following her.

"I shall give you instructions for their uses."

"Why do you not simply accompany me?"

Robert's concern for his brother must be immense if he were willing to endure her company—just the two of them and his squire—for such a trip.

"I cannot go against your brother's wishes, Robert."

"*I* am," he reminded her.

"You are his brother. You are family. I am but a healer. Lord Dillon wishes me to remain here at Westcott, so I shall remain here at Westcott."

"Aye, Wise One," he murmured with a hint of contrition. "Forgive me for pressing you."

She smiled. "You become more like your brother every day."

* * *

Bird song flirted with Dillon and his party, bouncing from one side of the road to the other and back. Faint rustling sounds filled the gaps in between as small creatures foraged in the detritus that littered the forest floor.

A cool breeze wound its way through the men, preventing the bright sun above from roasting them in their mail and thickly padded gambesons. Riffling the manes of the horses, it continued on to pluck golden leaves from the trees.

Dillon listened with only half an ear to the conversations of his men. His thoughts kept returning to recent events. Particularly to those that had involved the wisewoman.

Did she truly believe he would never wed? When he had told her of his dream—a dream he had been so sure was a sign, though he shared not her gifts—she had deemed it impossible.

Had she *seen* the future? Dreamed of it even as he had?

Or, knowing the truth now of his sexual conquests (if one could call them that), did she believe no gentlewoman would have him? That none could love him?

He scowled at the rutted and pitted dirt road that stretched before them.

He supposed she would be the best judge. She knew him better than anyone did.

How many nights had the two of them spent hunched over a game of chess or Nine Men's Morris, exchanging quips or sharing a comfortable silence or even engaging in heated debate?

Why could he not find a bride who would be willing to do such? he wondered, frustration mounting. A bride like the lovely woman in his dream who had, at last, given him a taste of true tenderness?

Another kind of heated debate arose behind him.

Sir Guy and Sir Aubrey had both taken a liking to the cobbler's daughter. Dillon should have left the pair at Westcott and instead brought more seasoned warriors with him. Older, uglier, more seasoned warriors who could not attract a maid's notice if they tried. Then Dillon would not have to hear about it.

Gavin began to sing a bawdy tavern song to drown out the young knights' bickering.

Lucifer's arse! They had been traveling for less than a day and Dillon already tired of their company.

His mood darkening, he opened his mouth to bark out a command to silence them.

Something slammed into his right shoulder.

Grunting, Dillon clamped his teeth shut as fiery pain erupted in his shoulder and traveled down his arm, burning him as though someone had touched a torch to his flesh.

Looking down, he glared at the quarrel that had pierced his armor.

"To arms!" Sir Laurence cried.

Swords left sheaths.

Dillon forced the fingers of his right hand to curl around the hilt of his own sword. Growling in agony, he drew it from its sheath and laid it across his lap as he searched for the archer who wielded the crossbow.

Another bolt embedded itself in his right thigh.

Guy and Aubrey, the men he had only moments earlier regretted bringing, closed in on both sides of him, trying to place themselves between Dillon and the one intent on killing him.

But Dillon had already located the archer.

Bellowing in fury, he urged his mount forward.

The powerful destrier charged off the road and into the forest.

Halting just inside the trees, Dillon dropped the reins, drew a dagger with his left hand, and launched it at the fellow trying to duck behind the trunk of the tree whose branches supported him.

Dillon watched with satisfaction as his blade buried itself deep in the man's chest.

Guy pointed his sword. "There! And there!"

As the archer tumbled to the ground, Dillon followed Guy's aim and saw mayhap a score of men slipping from shadow to shadow.

Low tree limbs made it too difficult to follow on horseback.

Guy leapt to the ground and raced forward. Aubrey followed on his heels, their squabble forgotten.

Dillon slid from the saddle, cursing when it jostled the wound in his thigh, and nigh dropped his sword. His right arm useless, he transferred the sword to his left.

Laurence, Edric, and John headed after the other villains, shouting battle cries.

Squires scrambled forward to grab horses' reins.

"My lord!" Gideon cried, skidding to a halt in front of him.

Dillon motioned for his squire to take control of the destrier beside him, then started forward.

Sir Gavin grabbed him by his uninjured arm and halted him. "Let the others rout them out whilst I tend to your wounds."

Dillon shook his head. "They outnumber us. My wounds can wait. Just break the shafts."

The burly warrior hesitated a moment, then grabbed the shaft of the bolt protruding from his shoulder and snapped off the bulk of it.

Dillon growled as his pain doubled.

Gavin did the same with the quarrel in Dillon's thigh, allowing him to move more freely without the shafts catching on branches.

Sucking air in through his clenched teeth, Dillon tightened his grip on his sword. "Go with Guy and Aubrey."

Nodding, Gavin headed after the duo, who had already caught up with the bandits and engaged them in battle.

Dillon turned to see how Laurence and the others fared.

A third crossbow bolt struck him in the chest with such force he stumbled back a step.

More fiery agony.

Stunned, he looked to the archer he had felled.

The man lay in a motionless, broken heap on the forest floor, no weapon in his hand.

Two archers.

There were two archers.

He opened his mouth to warn his men, but found he could not draw enough breath to do so. His chest, where it did not hurt from the arrow, felt tight. His heart began to race. His legs weakened.

Someone shouted his name. Gideon mayhap?

A roar, like that of an enraged bear, filled the forest.

Staggering backward, Dillon bumped into his destrier, then leaned against it. His eyes searched the trees above and around them until he found the second archer.

"There!" he cried as loudly as he could and pointed his sword at the man.

A dagger embedded itself in the man's throat.

Dillon sank to his knees. His breath grew short and choppy,

crackling in his lungs like dried leaves. His head began to swim. Blood wet his gambeson, tunic, and hose.

Unable to remain upright, he collapsed onto his back.

A large form barreled forward and grabbed the archer before he could hit the ground.

Dillon blinked as the newcomer impaled the dying archer with his sword then found another victim. And another. Tearing through them like a hungry wolf.

Robert?

Satan's blood. What was Robert doing there?

Fighting like a Berserker, 'twould seem, killing anyone within reach with ruthless precision.

Gideon knelt beside Dillon and put pressure on the wound in his chest, attempting to staunch the flow of blood.

Dillon groaned, darkness beginning to cloud his vision.

He knew not how long the battle raged as he lay there, struggling for breath and cursing his inability to fight alongside his men.

Robert dropped to his knees and leaned over him, his blue eyes wild, his face and tunic glistening with the blood of those he had slain. "Dillon!"

Releasing his sword hilt, Dillon raised his left hand.

Robert clasped it. "All but one are dead. And he will only live long enough for us to question him." He looked at someone beyond Dillon. "Guy! My sack! Quickly!"

His brother's blue eyes held such fear when they returned to Dillon's.

"W-Wise One," Dillon uttered.

Robert nodded. "I shall get you to her. *Aubrey!*"

Aubrey joined them down on the ground as the others crowded around. "Aye?"

"Put pressure on his wounds." Robert gave Dillon's hand a squeeze. "I shall be but a moment, brother." Rising, he grabbed Gideon and guided him over to the young squire's horse.

Through the legs of his men, Dillon saw the two engage in heated discourse before Robert bellowed, "*Marcus!*"

Did they argue over how to get him back to Westcott?

If so, it did not matter. Dillon had seen wounds such as this in past battles.

As Gideon and Marcus conferred, Robert returned to Dillon's side and began removing Dillon's mail.

Every jerk, every jostle, sent new waves of pain careening through him.

Robert took a blade to Dillon's gambeson around the base of each arrow shaft. From his sack, he drew packets of herbs he sprinkled on the wounds with hands that shook.

Dillon's thoughts went to the woman who had no doubt supplied those herbs.

When he had told the healer about the bride in his dream, she had as much as said he would never wed.

"Sorceress," he whispered.

"I will get you to her brother," Robert vowed again.

Dillon paid him no heed.

The seer had been right. He would never wed the woman in his dream.

He would not live long enough to find her.

CHAPTER THREE

Whenever Dillon was away, the wisewoman could more often than not be found in her chamber beneath the kitchen's massive storerooms. Speculation ran rampant regarding what secrets might be found within its walls. Other than the lords of the castle, none had ever crossed its threshold and beheld the interior. A few, desperate for her healing skills, had garnered enough courage to knock upon her door. But they always kept their eyes averted, fearing a curse would befall them if they saw whatever sorcery she performed within.

Alyssa knew not if seeing her chamber would ease their fears or enhance them. 'Twas on the sparse side, with very little adornment of any kind. A single enormous tapestry woven by her mother garnished the wall that bordered the dungeon, which frequently lacked occupants. Dillon was neither unduly harsh nor exceptionally lenient when dealing with his people. If punishment was called for, he did not hesitate to exact it. The harsher the crime, the more severe the penalty that must be paid. And sometimes that necessitated imprisonment.

No sunlight touched her chamber. Only candlelight and the flickering flames of the hearth dispelled the gloom. Two wide floor-to-ceiling bookshelves packed with ancient tomes and scrolls divided the room in half. The farther half served as her sleeping chamber, boasting a modest wood-framed bed, a small table, and a trunk containing her clothing and a few keepsakes.

The closer served as a workroom that tended to terrify any who accidentally caught a glimpse of it. A small stool rested beside a long table, strangely organized in all of its bizarre clutter. Stoppered jars, containers, and packets of herbs vied for space on its surface. Bladders filled with strange liquid concoctions hung from the ceiling. Ropes and sticks and staffs of all widths and sizes clustered together in groups. Cauldrons fit for brewing any witch's potion abounded. And, in one dark hidden corner, three cages housed her *pets*.

Standing at her worktable now, Alyssa measured out several herbs that, when mixed together and added to goat's milk, would aid new mothers who were having difficulty nourishing their babes by stimulating healthier milk production. She had performed the task so often in the past that she could do so in her sleep. Which was fortunate, because she seemed to be having difficulty concentrating.

Her mind kept wandering, abandoning the actions of her hands.

Dillon wanted a wife.

A familiar tightness settled in her chest at the thought.

That he would marry eventually she had always known. He was the Earl of Westcott, a man of great power and wealth, friend to the king, with numerous properties and his title to bestow upon an heir. Though Dillon had professed many times that he would happily bequeath it all to his brother, he deserved more than to live out his life alone.

He was a good man. An extraordinary man.

Dillon may be reserved—if not gruff—with others, but he had let *her* see enough of his soul to know that he would make an excellent father, showering his daughters with love and affection, lavishing attention upon his sons and guiding them into becoming fine, honorable men.

But to get those sons and daughters, he must first take a wife. And Alyssa did not know if she could bear to watch him do so from the shadows.

"Healer!"

Starting violently at the sound of that frantic voice shouting through her door, she scattered powder across the table and knocked the remnants of the dried ginger root to the floor.

"Healer, please! 'Tis urgent!"

It must be, she thought, shaking off her morose thoughts. Naught else would prompt the superstitious people of the keep to seek her out whilst she reputedly practiced her *dark arts*.

Pulling the cowl up to shield her face and hair, she strode to the thick wooden door and yanked it open.

A boy, barely old enough to grow a beard, staggered back a step, breathing heavily.

Her heart stopped. Prickles of dread tickled her nape. 'Twas Marcus, Robert's new squire, covered in sweat, grime, and dried blood.

"Speak quickly," she hissed. If aught had happened to Robert…

"Lord Dillon has been wounded," he blurted.

Shock rippled through her. "How badly?"

"Mortally, Wise One."

Ice filled her lungs, choking off her breath.

Mortally.

Spinning around, she grabbed a cloth bag and started to rake bandages and assorted containers into it. "You will take me to him immediately. See that the fastest mount in my lord's stables is readied for me at once—"

"Nay, Wise One. 'Tis too late for that."

The bag slipped from her fingers. "What?" she asked faintly.

His voice softened with regret. "'Tis too late."

Her knees buckled. Collapsing onto the stool beside her worktable, she stared blindly at the floor. Never had she known such despair.

Dillon dead? It could not be. Dillon could *not* be dead. She would have known it. She would have felt something. Why had she not felt something?

"They were ambushed," Marcus said, daring to venture a step or two inside. "Sir Robert and I raced forward as soon as the first shout arose, but Lord Dillon had already been felled."

Felled.

"Sir Robert said 'twas too well timed. They knew everything. They knew 'twas not Lord Dillon who left with the bulk of the troops. They knew how few of his guard accompanied him. When he left. What route he took. They knew *everything*. And he was their only target, Wise One. Had we not routed them out so swiftly, they would have melted back into the trees without engaging the rest of us."

An awful numbness swept through her as she listened, paralyzing her, freezing her insides. She thought that if she were to attempt to move in that instant, her body would shatter into as many pieces as the broken jars in the cloth bag at her feet had when she had dropped it.

"Sir Robert was not injured?" she forced through stiff, unmoving lips.

"Nay, Wise One."

"Had he any instructions for me?"

It cannot be true! It cannot be true! Please, *do not let it be true!*

"He said Lord Dillon was betrayed, Seer. By someone amongst his own, someone with access to my lord's movements and strategies. Only one of the men who attacked him still lives and he will soon be locked in the dungeon."

Hope stirring, she leapt to her feet. "Lord Dillon and Sir Robert are here?"

"Nay. Sir Robert sent several of us onward whilst he

obtained a cart in which to transport Lord Dillon's b—" He broke off, swallowed. "In which to bring Lord Dillon home. He wanted me to deliver his message with all due haste, so I rode ahead with the others. He asks you to ferret out the man who betrayed him."

Robert was bringing Dillon's body home in a cart.

It was true then. Dillon was beyond her reach. He was gone.

Dillon was dead. Dillon was dead. Dillon was dead.

The litany in her mind blocked out all else. She could hear naught. She could see naught. She could *feel* naught. Except the yawning chasm his loss spawned inside her.

It could not be true. How could it be true?

For seven years now, every day of her life had been greeted with a dual purpose—to use all of the powers at her disposal to keep Dillon safe and to serve him in any way he desired. She had begun as his advisor and gradually progressed to his friend and confidant. Though he had been somewhat hesitant to trust her in the beginning, he had rapidly come to rely upon her. He had needed her.

As she had needed him, had he but realized it.

"Come closer," she ordered, her voice hoarse from struggling past the lump in her throat.

Eyes widening, Marcus inched a few steps nearer. He jumped when her hand shot out and grasped his arm.

Unease. Sadness. Concern for Robert.

No hint at all of deception.

Shaken, Alyssa released him and watched mutely as he placed some distance between them.

Dillon truly was dead. He was lost to her.

A future without him stretched before her, empty and frightening. What would she do? What reason would she find for rising from her bed each morning? What would drive her to brave the superstitious mutterings, the surreptitious self-crossings, the fear-filled glances that tormented her so?

The answer came in the form of a single word, slinking insidiously through her mournful thoughts.

Revenge.

Ah, yes. Revenge.

Renewed purpose spread through her limbs, solidifying within her and silencing the screams of denial that clamored for release.

She would do it for Dillon. Avenge his death. Every man, no matter how obscure his involvement, who had been part of Dillon's downfall would pay for it with his life. She would see to it personally. However long it took. She would not let this crime go unpunished.

Fury greater than any she had heretofore experienced flooded her veins, its fiery heat replacing the terrifying cold as she rose.

"Go," she ordered the youth still huddled inside her door.

Marcus did not hesitate to obey her.

Retrieving two cloth bags, Alyssa headed for the cages hidden in the farthest corner of her workroom. Next, she retrieved a wicked-looking dagger that was older than the building that housed her.

She would have her answers.

She would have her revenge.

* * *

The taunts and threats of three guards greeted her as Alyssa entered the dungeon via a secret passage, seeming to magically appear within their midst. Both the guards and the prisoner gasped and fell into silence, their hard faces filling with unease.

The small dungeon boasted two cells. One bore four damp stone walls and a thick, wooden door. The second had three walls of stone and one constructed of bars spaced a hand's breadth apart. 'Twas in this one the transgressor had been placed.

"Tie his wrists to the bars."

Without delay, one of the guards shoved a burly arm through the iron and grasped the man's tunic before he could back away. The other two bound his wrists tightly several feet apart so that his body nigh touched the metal.

Their task finished, they stepped back in tandem and awaited further instructions.

"Leave us." Alyssa's gaze remained on the prisoner, who regarded her with some alarm.

The guards appeared even more eager than Robert's squire had been to leave her presence, their speculative murmurs cut off by the rumbling of the heavy oak door closing behind them.

"So," she said, coldly conversational, "you attacked the Earl of Westcott and survived whilst the rest of your accomplices were cut down."

He curled his fingers nervously around the bars that separated them.

"You shall soon wish you had not."

"I do not fear you," he blustered in a pitiful attempt at bravery.

She could see that rumors of her gifts had reached him and took satisfaction in the fear they inspired. "Fear not. We have time to remedy that."

He remained silent.

"Who is your spy within this keep?"

He laughed, regaining a portion of his flagging courage. Apparently he believed his misbegotten knowledge gave him the upper hand. "I will die ere I tell you aught. What think you of that, Witch?"

She tilted her head to one side. "Methinks you shall pray for death ere I have finished with you. But I shall not give in to your wishes until the betrayer's name has crossed your blood-frothed lips."

Knowing there was more than one way to gain the information she sought, she upended one of the bags she hid beneath her robe and fought the urge to recoil as furry bodies tumbled down her legs.

The front of her robe shivered as though disturbed by a breeze, drawing the prisoner's yellow gaze. He gasped when the hem twitched and shifted as a dozen plump rats skittered out from underneath it, racing toward him, joining him in his cage. Though he hopped from foot to foot and danced away from them as much as the ropes binding his wrists would allow, several found purchase in his hose and began making their way up his legs.

Alyssa had doubted her grandmother's assurances that training rats to do such could be used either to frighten away anyone brazen enough to enter her chamber without her permission or to elicit information from miscreants without applying a blade and using torture.

She should not have. The prisoner grew more frantic the closer the rats came to his groin.

"Give me the name," she prodded between his ghastly screeches.

"Get them off! Get them off me!"

"You will not tell me?"

Not answering, he flung his body against the bars several times in an effort to jostle the creatures and shake them off before they reached their destination.

"Very well." She upended the other bag she concealed. Weight plopped down on her feet. Her robe shimmered again.

Then two hungry snakes large enough to give any man pause slipped from beneath its hem and slithered up after the rats.

The prisoner knew not that the snakes' only interest lay in dining upon the rats. He saw the rodents and serpents heading toward his groin, coupled them with the rumors of Alyssa's sorcery, and drew his own conclusions.

Very dark conclusions, she thought with some satisfaction, were she to judge by his screams.

* * *

The howls and agonized cries of the prisoner echoed up to the great hall for a quarter of an hour or more, growing steadily more frantic and hoarse until they abruptly halted. The knights and men-at-arms taking their evening meal—most of the women having exited upon hearing the first screams—heaved a collective sigh of relief as blessed silence embraced them.

"She must have finally killed the cursed whoreson," one man speculated.

"Put him out of his misery," a second agreed.

"Never heard cries so filled with terror as those were," another commented. "And I have fought in many a bloody battle."

Several men nodded.

"How do you suppose she tortured him?"

An older man shook his head solemnly. "With those unholy powers of hers… I only pray she will never have reason to turn them against me."

The talk continued, each and every man oblivious to her presence. Alyssa stood in the dimness of the stairwell, listening as they competed to see who could guess the most gruesome tactics she may have employed on her deceased lord's behalf.

Making no sound to alert them, she cautiously entered and circumvented the great hall so she could approach the table from the opposite side.

All of her attention remained centered upon one man.

He spoke in a gravelly voice and possessed few of the manners the other knights exhibited. Oily brown hair and a day or two's growth of beard marred a handsome face that still managed to attract women willing to brave his stench. A great hulk of a soldier, he was one of Dillon's personal guard and had ridden out by his side early this morn, laughing and talking with him as though they were the best of friends.

And all the while deceit had driven him.

Her eyes narrowed as she made her move.

By the time the men around the table glimpsed her, 'twas too late. The point of Alyssa's dagger already rested against her target's throat just beneath his left ear.

When her intended victim would have drawn his sword, she applied just enough pressure to elicit a single drop of blood.

All movement in the hall ceased. The knights, the men-at-arms, the servants… everyone froze. Even the hounds that foraged for scraps beneath the table went still, emitting periodic whines.

"What means this, Wise One?" Baldwin, the eldest of the soldiers across from her, questioned hesitantly.

Her focus did not stray from the man glaring up at her, though her cowl showed him only darkness. "On whose orders did you act?" she hissed, placing her empty hand on his shoulder to *see* the truth of his response.

"All here know I follow Lord Dillon's orders," he gritted, his face full of malevolence.

Very slowly, Alyssa dragged the blade across his neck to his right ear, leaving a raw red mark in its wake. "On whose orders did you betray my lord?" she repeated evenly.

Baldwin stood as her meaning sank in. "'Twas you, Gavin? *You* are the one who—?"

"Nay!" he exclaimed. "The witch lies!"

Her blade retraced its path to his left ear, dipping a little deeper, drawing blood this time.

He stiffened, beads of sweat popping up on his forehead.

"I ask you again. Whose orders did you follow?"

His eyes darted to the men around them. "Will you do naught but stand and stare? She is mad, I tell you! Take her!"

They moved restlessly, glancing at each other, then at the seer. All were wary of her sorcery. All were loyal to Lord Dillon. Most of the eyes that returned to him filled with contempt.

A sneer twisted Gavin's lips… until the blade followed the

shallow trench back to his right ear.

"You are running out of time."

Swallowing jerkily, eyes rolling nervously, he finally bit out a name. "Sir Robert." Someone gasped. "'Twas Sir Robert. He covets his brother's land and wealth."

"You lie."

He whimpered when the blade moved yet again across his throat. Warm blood now trailed down to soak his collar.

"Answer me truly this time or your life will be forfeit," she lied. She would leave this man's fate up to Robert, confident that he would avenge his brother's murder in a manner that would satisfy them both.

Whatever bravado Gavin had managed to maintain left him in a rush. "'Twas Lord Camden of Pinehurst!"

"Why?"

"He will not relinquish his land and title and thought to buy himself time enough to get back in the king's good graces."

"The king is not a fool. He would know him for the knave he is."

"Camden plans to blame the thieves who attacked Sir Robert. The same thieves, he will say, absconded with the money he owes in delinquent taxes and killed Lord Dillon."

"Thieves do not assassinate, then withdraw without collecting the booty."

"They did not expect Sir Robert to be there and panicked when they heard his battle cry."

"You speak the truth?" she persisted, although her gift had already confirmed it. She wanted to be certain those seated and standing around the table were left with no doubts.

"Aye! I swear it! 'Tis the truth!"

"Very well."

His shoulders wilted with relief.

"Surely you do not think your admission absolves you of your guilt," she stated coldly. "Lord Robert no doubt will kill you upon his return. You have merely earned yourself a brief stay of execution."

Withdrawing her blade, she turned to leave, trusting Dillon's men to see to the beast's incarceration.

A slender knight moved out of her path, then looked over her shoulder. His eyes widened.

Alyssa spun around.

Gavin loomed over her, one arm raised high, a dagger clenched in his fist.

Fear pummeling her, Alyssa reacted without thought.

Her blade sank deep into Gavin's slick throat before he could drive his own down into her flesh.

His eyes bulged and flew to her hood.

Alyssa's heart pounded in her chest as the moment stretched.

The men at the table jumped when she abruptly jerked her blade back, liberating Gavin's blood. His fist slackened, dropping the dagger with which he had meant to impale her as he fell back onto the table.

"Do with him what you will," she instructed, struggling to keep her elderly wisewoman voice steady so none would guess how shaken she was.

Turning, she exited the hall, her carriage painstakingly correct. The violent trembling of her legs went unseen beneath the many folds of her robe, the rapid thumping of her heart unheard in the hush that followed her down to her chamber. Closing the door silently behind her, she took two steps and halted. The ancient, blood-soaked dagger fell from now nerveless fingers, hitting the floor with a clatter and splattering small, crimson droplets in its wake.

She had slain Sir Gavin.

A hairline fracture formed in the ice that filled her, lengthening in both directions, branching, growing, allowing pain to seep in through the cracks.

"A life for a life," she murmured hoarsely and sank to her knees. At last her grief found its release in tears that erupted from her in harsh, rending sobs. "Forgive me, Dillon."

* * *

Robert burst through the door he had never before even dared knock upon and tripped over a figure kneeling on the floor. "Umph!" Sprawled facedown, he rolled to his back and propped himself up on his hands to view the damage.

The wisewoman crouched amongst the rushes, her arms wrapped around knees drawn up to her chest, her unseen forehead resting upon them.

"Healer! Forgive me. I did not see you there."

She made a slight gesture with one hidden hand. "Please leave me, Robert."

Hearing the odd catch in her speech, he rose to his knees and scooted closer to her. "Are you hurt? Did I injure you?"

"Nay," she said, her voice a bit stronger. "Please, go."

"Go!" He scowled and pushed himself to his feet. "I have no time for this. We must—"

"I have already located and dispatched the spy, as well as identified the man who filled his pockets. What more could you ask of me?"

Fury flooded him. "How can you ask that? My brother lies in his bed. Why are you not by his side?"

"To what purpose?" she demanded, her voice full of resentment as her body unfolded and rose. "Your brother is dead. My powers do not extend to resurrection."

"Unless he expires as we speak, my brother still fights for his life!"

"Dillon lives?" she breathed, falling back a step. "Marcus said…"

Understanding struck. "'Twas Gideon! Damned useless whelp!"

"Dillon's squire?"

"Aye. 'Twas chaos. And the boy refused to leave Dillon's side to carry my message to you, so I had him send Marcus in his stead. I *told* Gideon 'twas not too late, but all he saw was the blood. He was inconsolable. He must have told Marcus… Wise One, Dillon is *not* dead. But he soon will be do you not—"

He broke off when she spun around and fled the room. "Your herbs!" he shouted after her to no avail. He had not realized a woman her age could move so swiftly.

Not knowing what she would need, he grabbed a nearby basket, swept a number of containers into it, and took off after her.

* * *

More than one servant shrieked as the wisewoman raced past, her black robes fluttering above and behind her like demon wings. Up the stairs and into the solar she flew, desperate to confirm Robert's words.

As long as he draws breath, there is hope. As long as he draws breath, there is hope, she chanted silently. She had healed harsh wounds on Dillon's large, muscled body before and would eagerly do so again.

She tore through the doorway, his name upon her lips, and felt her stomach sink. Robert had warned her that there was a great deal of blood. Nevertheless, her first glimpse of Dillon devastated.

Skidding to a halt beside the bed, she stared down at him in horror. She had expected a sword thrust, a puncture, a gaping slash mayhap deep enough to expose bone beneath the muscle. Instead, not one, but three quarrels protruded from his body.

The shafts had been broken, allowing his surcoat, hauberk, gambeson, and chausses to be carefully removed, leaving him in his hose, braies, and linen undershirt—all a sticky ruby red. Cloths had been stuffed into the ragged holes the quarrels had carved. There was some evidence of the herbs she had given Robert before he had left to join Dillon, but the outpouring of blood had washed away most of them.

The quarrel in Dillon's right shoulder did not concern her

greatly. She extended a hand over the one in his right side just above his waist and confirmed that it, too, had damaged naught vital. But she did not need her gift to tell her that the remaining one had.

It had struck Dillon in the chest. He could only take tiny, gasping breaths. And she could hear fluid rattling around inside him with each. Crimson liquid pooled on his lips and forged paths down both stubbled cheeks. With shaking fingers, she reached out and turned his head to the side so he would not choke on it, then felt for the pulse in his throat. Almost indiscernible, it weakened rapidly as the internal devastation took its toll.

Alyssa bit her lip, suppressing a sob as sorrow pressed down upon her, crushing the hope that had so fleetingly flared to life.

Naught had changed. Dillon was no less lost to her now than he had been only minutes earlier when she had believed him dead. With wounds such as these, he would perish did she not heal him with her hands. And once she did, she would never look upon his cherished face again. She could not heal so severe an injury as the one in his chest without surrendering her own life. But she would not hesitate to do so. For him.

Tears once more overflowed her lashes as she let her fingers trace the scar on his eyebrow, then follow a path down his temple, along his rugged jaw to the one on his chin. If only he would open his eyes and speak to her. Let her hear the deep rumble of his voice one last time. Let her pour out the words that had been bottled up inside her for so long ere they were forever separated.

Leaning forward, Alyssa pressed trembling lips to his in a brief kiss that expressed but a fraction of what she felt for him, then rested her warm, damp cheek against his.

"Good-bye, Dillon," she uttered brokenly, knowing what she must do. "I love you."

* * *

Robert sprinted into the room. "Does he still live?"

The healer seemed to be listening for Dillon's breath. "Aye."

Stepping up to the opposite side of the bed, he thrust the basket toward her. "Your herbs."

"There is not time. Set them aside."

Scowling, he did as she directed, then watched as she climbed onto the bed and knelt beside his brother's motionless form. Dillon had been conscious for a few precious moments after they had cautiously loaded him into the cart, and the black-robed figure bending over him was the one he had repeatedly asked for. He had called out every name he had ever given her—Wise One, Seer, Healer, Soothsayer, Sorceress (a title he only used when she vexed him), Wisewoman—as if by doing so he could make her miraculously appear at his side.

Well, she was there now, swiftly cutting away his clothing and tossing it to the floor. Robert prayed she was not too late, for the faint gray hue his brother's skin had acquired terrified him.

"As quickly as you can, I want you to pull the quarrel from his chest and stand clear," she ordered.

"Would it not be better to push it through to—?"

"Your brother will die in the time 'twill take me to explain! Just do as I ask! *Now!*" she shouted in a voice so loud and clear that it shocked him into obeying. Wrapping fingers that trembled around what remained of the shaft at the quarrel's base, he yanked it out.

The healer slammed both hands down over the ragged hole. Robert caught a glimpse of blood inundating age-spotted skin before the sleeves of her robe slipped down to hide her from his view.

Still holding the warm, slick quarrel, he moved back a step, then another, to give her whatever room she needed and hoped that every rumor he had heard about the depth of her sorcery was true.

She kept her arms as stiff and straight as a sword's blade, applying pressure as she infused Dillon with that strange tingling heat Robert had felt when she had healed his thigh. The cowl of her robe masked her features. Though she had always remained silent in the past when healing, a faint murmuring met his ears. Words indecipherable.

Soon, an opalescent glow unlike aught he had ever seen began to seep from beneath those sleeves. Swallowing hard, Robert retreated another step and continued to watch with wide, disbelieving eyes.

Minutes passed, lengthening until hours seemed to pass instead. The glow grew brighter. He imagined he could feel the heat himself from where he stood.

At last, the murmuring ceased. The light faded to nothingness. Those thin, straight arms bent. The healer swayed, slowly sliding her hands off the wound. Only a pale pink, puckered scar remained beneath rapidly drying blood.

Sweet relief rushed through Robert. Dillon's breathing was now slow and easy.

"Come forward…, Robert," the healer summoned.

His head jerked toward her. Dillon's breath may have eased, but the wisewoman's had grown ragged.

Dropping the quarrel he had forgotten he held, he approached the bed. "Wise One, are you—?"

"Remove… the last two quarrels."

As much as he loved his brother and wanted Dillon's suffering to end, he hesitated. "Should you not rest ere you—?"

"There is no time," she gritted. A guttural cough racked her body. "He has lost… too much blood. Blood I cannot… replace. I must heal the remaining wounds now… ere he loses more."

Uneasy, Robert leaned forward, grasped the quarrels, and pulled them out—gently this time, since panic no longer rode him so rigorously.

The healer's hands slipped forward to cover the wounds. "Place your hands... over mine," she instructed haltingly.

He dropped the quarrels and stared down at her hands in confusion. Surprisingly small, they were sticky with congealing blood where the robe did not conceal them. "I do not understand."

"Cover... my hands with your own. Hold them fast... against the wounds. Do not allow me... to release him."

His gaze swinging to the hood, Robert wiped his moist, bloody hands on his tunic. She was too weak. 'Twas why she asked for his help. She could not even trust herself to maintain her hold.

His hands clenched into fists, everything within him telling him he should refuse her. Dillon would want him to, fearing the healing would tax her too greatly. But she was a sorceress, was she not? Healings had never harmed her in the past. He had witnessed too many to believe otherwise.

"Robert."

If this one taxed her overly or harmed her in some way, Robert vowed he would be her servant until she fully recovered. His brother's life was worth the risk.

"Now, Robert."

Tentatively, he placed his much larger hands atop hers.

"Harder."

Sweat began to bead on his brow as he increased the pressure. Her hands felt so fragile—almost childlike—beneath his that he feared crushing them.

Seconds passed.

A slow heat began to build beneath his rough palms. At first, 'twas like the welcome warmth of the sun. It proceeded to intensify, however, and soon grew uncomfortable, as though he held his hand above a candle flame. A dim glow seeped up between his fingers, much as blood had through the healer's when she had first covered the wounds. He stared, awed, as the light grew in strength.

Chanting accompanied the marvelous illumination, barely audible, as though lips moved, but breath did not pass them.

So intent was Robert on his hands and the action taking place beneath them that he almost cried out when his brother sighed.

"Dillon?" Robert said.

The light flickered, then vanished. The chanting concluded. The hands beneath his grew cold.

"Is it... Are you finished?" he asked her uncertainly.

The healer nodded, shoulders slumped, head drooping.

"I should release you then?"

"Aye," she wheezed.

He did so. Straightening, he rolled his shoulders to ease the stiffness in them.

A sinking feeling hit his stomach when he heard her increasingly burdened breath.

She did not even try to straighten. Withdrawing her hands, the wisewoman sagged sideways.

Robert lunged forward across Dillon in an attempt to catch her. But she fell so swiftly his fingers barely grazed the hem of her robe.

"Umph! What the hell?" Dillon's drowsy voice uttered. "Robert? Get off me. What are you doing?"

Wincing with dismay, Robert rapidly reversed directions and removed himself from his brother's newly healed chest. "Dillon?"

"Are you surprised 'tis me?" he countered dryly. "'Tis *my* chamber, is it not?"

"I am not surprised 'tis *you*," he denied, so grateful to hear his brother's voice that tears burned the backs of his eyes as he hastened around the foot of the bed. "I am surprised you are talking and breathing as if you have not just escaped death by a hair's breadth."

* * *

Dillon frowned. What was Robert talking about? And why did he look as if he were struggling not to weep?

Dillon glanced around the room.

What was he doing at Westcott? In bed? Had he not ridden for Pinehurst?

"What happened? Why am I so sluggish? Did you talk me out of leaving and drink me under the table again?"

A watery chuckle burst forth from Robert's lips as he halted on the other side of the bed and knelt. "Do you not remember?" he managed to ask.

"Remember what?" Dillon demanded. Every muscle in his body felt weighted down, as if he were wearing a full suit of armor. Taking a deep breath, he shoved himself up onto his elbows.

His head swam. The chamber dipped and swayed. And it took a moment for him to focus clearly again.

When he could, he glanced down. His heart stopped, then resumed beating much more urgently, pounding in his ears.

His body was bare, his torso sticky with congealing blood. A hasty exploration with one hand sent shivers dancing through his limbs. Three wounds. One in the side. One in the shoulder. One practically covering his heart.

By all rights, he should be dead.

"You were ambushed," Robert explained as he leaned over something on the floor, "and took three quarrels."

Dillon only half listened. The wounds were healed. All three of them. Something he had not believed the healer capable of accomplishing. "Where is she?"

"She collapsed."

Dillon bolted into a sitting position as Robert lifted a small figure swathed in black into his arms. *"What?"*

"Only seconds ere you woke." He rose, then hesitated, brow furrowing with uncertainty.

Throwing back the covers, Dillon scooted over to make room. "Place her here beside me."

Gingerly, Robert complied.

"Careful!" Dillon snapped, wishing he had sufficient strength to perform the task himself. Instead, he busied himself with placing a pillow beneath her hooded head, wondering if she would view his imminent removal of that hood as a betrayal of her trust.

"Dillon…"

Dragging his attention away, he looked up at his brother and froze. Terror filled him.

The front of Robert's tunic, his sleeves, and his hands glistened with fresh blood. Their eyes met, then flew to the wisewoman.

"Nay." Tremors coursed through Dillon's hands as he reached for the front of the healer's robe. He knew deep within his heart what it concealed. "Please," he whispered.

Bunching the material up in both hands, he rent her shroud from neck to hem.

CHAPTER FOUR

Dillon squeezed his eyes shut against the sight that met them. The simple gown she wore beneath had torn away with the darker robe. Three gaping, gushing wounds marred the healer's porcelain skin. One in her side. One in her shoulder. One puncturing her left breast. All located precisely where his had been, where the tiny pink scars remained.

This was why she had avoided healing such wounds in the past.

"But... how?" Robert questioned.

"She took my wounds into herself. 'Twas the only way she could save me."

"What?"

Opening his eyes, he saw that Robert had scarcely even noticed her wounds. He stared instead at her face, or at least the part that was now visible.

Leaning over her, Dillon smoothed the cowl back until all was finally revealed.

"'Tis not possible," Robert exclaimed and crossed himself.

Dillon shared his astonishment, but for a different reason. He recognized her.

The figure lying beside him suddenly gave new meaning to the dream he had experienced a few nights past of his future bride.

The wisewoman was no aged crone. She was young, little more than a score in age, he guessed. And beautiful, with flawless alabaster skin and raven tresses that would reach her waist when she stood. Delicately winged brows. A small, pert nose. Full, shapely lips that parted to expose straight white teeth stained with the blood that trailed from the corners of her mouth as she drew in short, jagged breaths.

"How can this be?" Robert asked.

His eyes never leaving her, Dillon shook his head. "Not now. We must find a way to help her."

"How?"

Dillon shoved her garments aside. Tearing the sheet into strips, he wadded them up and pressed them to her wounds. He could only reach two at a time—the one in her chest and the one in her side—so he handed the rest to his brother.

Robert wrapped her slender shoulder and tied the cloth tight to keep pressure there.

"There must be *someone* here who can heal her."

"Dillon, you are not thinking clearly. No one else here shares her gifts."

He swore. "I know that. But she cannot be the only one amongst my people with a knowledge of herbs and poultices and such. There must be a midwife. A leech. *Someone*. Find them and bring them to me. Now!"

Robert promptly vacated the room.

Dillon replaced the already crimson cloths with fresh ones, applying as much pressure as he dared without doing further damage.

His eyes returned to her face, taking in every detail of her features, struggling to come to terms with the fact that this lovely young woman was the same treasured friend and companion who had been by his side for the past seven years.

The same one who had seen through his formidable facade to the quiet man beneath. Who had advised him so wisely, never once thinking him weak for seeking her counsel. Who had argued with him, challenged him, comforted him, brought laughter into his life, and been there for him in so many ways.

The wisewoman had possessed every quality he desired in a bride save youth.

Now she possessed that, too.

His heart pounded a frantic rhythm. "Please," he entreated, "do not leave me, Seer. Not now, when the woman we spoke of, the woman I dreamed of, is finally within my grasp." How gentle she had been that night, cradling his head to her breast, pressing her lips to his brow. Closing his eyes, he leaned down and rested his forehead against hers. "Wise One, answer me. Please."

"How… mm… may I… s-serve you…, my lord?"

His eyes flew open and met hazy cinnamon. Rearing back, he abandoned the puncture in her side long enough to cup her face in one unsteady hand. "You may serve me by healing yourself."

Her lips tilted up ever-so-slightly as she turned her face into his palm. "Y-You have asked… the one thing… I cannot grant you…, Dillon."

She had such difficulty speaking.

An emotion so strong he almost did not recognize it as fear engulfed him, leaving him shaking like the greatest of cowards.

"Say it again," he implored, not bothering to explain.

"Dillon," she sighed, seeming to enjoy voicing it as much as he took pleasure in hearing it. She had always addressed him formally in the past.

With regret, he removed his hand and bore down on the wound in her side.

She sucked in a breath through gritted teeth and was instantly repaid with violent coughs that sent more blood pouring from between her lips.

"Forgive me," he murmured.

A slight movement of her head told him there was naught to forgive. "W-What think you… of your… healer… n-now that… she is… visible?"

Bending, he placed a tender kiss upon her brow. "'Twas you that night, was it not, holding me in your arms?"

Her thick lashes lowered to blanket her cheeks, as though her actions shamed her.

"I thought it all a dream," he admitted.

"I sh-should not have…" Stiffening, she grimaced in pain.

"You should not have hidden the truth from me."

"W-What truth?"

"That the woman I have waited and searched so long for has been by my side for years."

Tears welled in her eyes as they met his, then spilled down her temples. Another series of coughs racked her body, the agony they spawned eliciting a moan and almost driving her back into unconsciousness.

Dillon watched her anxiously. "Tell me what to do," he beseeched. "Tell me what I must do to heal you."

She closed her eyes, struggling for breath. "There is… naught."

"I cannot accept that," he said fiercely. "I *will* not accept that."

"F-Forgive me." She seemed to weaken more every second.

Dillon swallowed past the lump that rose in his throat. For the first time in his adult life, he felt completely helpless. "Why? *Why* did you heal me if you knew 'twould mean your life?"

She roused just enough to answer him. "Your life… is… p-precious to me…, Dillon. W-What I did… I did… willingly."

He swore.

Fumbling blindly, she rested a hand on his thigh and opened her eyes once more.

She was trying to comfort him, he realized.

The backs of his own eyes began to burn.

"M-My choice… was clear." The fingers on his thigh clenched as another spasm tightened her features. "I chose n-not to live… in a… w-world with… out you in it."

"Then do not condemn me to a similar fate," he pleaded. "Do not leave me. I need you. You were right that night, when we talked of the woman I longed to have by my side, to grow old with. She *does* exist. But if you die, you will take her with you and deny me the happiness I have sought. Stay with me, please, and I shall spend the rest of my days thanking you."

"It could… n-never be." The hand on his thigh released him. Her body went slack. Her lids fluttered shut as her head rolled to one side.

"Nay," he denied, his heartbeat thundering in his ears. "Nay! *Nay!*" he repeated, his voice rising to a shout. "Do not leave me, Seer! You cannot! I will not let you! Do not *leave* me!"

"Dillon!"

The highly agitated voice jarred him.

Blinking hard, he turned to the figure standing beside the bed.

Robert, his face ashen, gazed back with wide eyes. "Dillon, I-I think she still breathes."

Holding his own breath, Dillon finally heard the rattling of blood in her lungs that his shouting had drowned out. "Where is the healer you sought?"

Robert shook his head. "There is none."

"None?" Dillon parroted, failing to comprehend.

"None. No midwife. No leech. No one. I asked Harry and he would know."

"Ask him again."

Robert hesitated. "As you wish, brother." Reaching out, he clasped Dillon's shoulder in a strong, consoling grip, then left.

Dillon sighed. The cloths he held against the healer's wounds were wet with blood again. Tearing a few more strips from the linen sheet, he placed them atop the others and resumed applying pressure. Her short, ugly breaths, though terrible to hear, were music to his ears. As long as air found its way to her lungs and blood to her heart, she lived.

* * *

"My lord?" a timid female voice said in the doorway.

Scowling, Dillon looked up. A plain, fairly familiar young woman stood there, clutching a basket tightly to her waist and looking as if she were poised to bolt.

"What is it?"

She took a tentative step forward and bobbed a curtsy. "Harry told me that Sir Robert sought a healer."

Hope stirred. "Know you of herbs and medicines?"

"Aye, my lord. A little. I hoped I might one day offer my services to the wisewoman and help her care for the people of Westcott."

"Come closer. And close the door behind you."

Obediently, she shut the heavy oaken door and approached the bed. Her wide eyes fastened on the dried blood that coated his chest. "You have been sorely wounded, my lord."

"Aye, but the wisewoman has already healed my injuries. 'Tis *she* who requires your aid."

Her forehead crinkling, she transferred her attention to the healer, then gaped. "*This* is the wisewoman?" Her astounded gaze took in the pale skin free of wrinkles, the midnight hair tumbling across the pillow and bedclothes, the youthful beauty present despite the pain that twisted the seer's features.

"Aye. Where I was wounded, she now bleeds. Can you help her?"

"I shall do all I can, my lord." Sitting on the edge of the bed, she placed her basket at the healer's feet. "You will have to release her so that I may attend her," she instructed gently.

Nodding, he withdrew his hands. The wisewoman's blood stained them red, coating them so completely that he could only stare.

The woman pressed a moist cloth into them. "Use this, my

lord," she stated, her voice kind.

Dismayed that she should read his vulnerability so keenly, he avoided her gaze and scrubbed at his hands. "You have not given me your name."

"Ann Marie, my lord."

He soon transferred all of the blood from his skin to the cloth, but would swear he could still feel it cleaving to him.

Ann Marie began to peel back the cloths, disturbing the wounds as little as possible. "I do not know nigh as much as the healer does, but I have—" She broke off as she removed the last of the material covering the wisewoman's chest.

A sick, bilious feeling engulfed Dillon when he saw the wound above her heart. The bleeding had slowed, but massive bruises now painted her skin. "Did I do that?" he choked out, his gut churning at the thought that he had applied too much pressure.

"Nay, my lord." Ann Marie's face lost all color. "She bleeds inside. I believe 'tis what causes it."

"Can you stop it?" The last of his hope faltered when she shook her head.

"All I can do is clean the wound, pack it, and bind it tightly. I am only just learning."

'Twas not enough. He knew 'twould not be, as did Ann Marie, who went about performing the tasks she had named. She proceeded as gently as possible, but her ministrations nevertheless caused her patient pain. When the wisewoman moaned, Dillon took the hand nearest him in one of his and brought it to his lips whilst he stroked her hair back from her forehead with the other.

It felt so natural to touch her thusly. He could have spent the last seven years doing so had she not hidden herself from him.

Why had she hidden herself from him?

"You did not hesitate to help her," he mentioned at length, needing to break the oppressive silence. "Why?"

"When my husband and I made Westcott our home, I feared her greatly. Though it shames me to admit, I heard dark tales told of her and believed every one of them. For years, I managed to avoid her until she caught me alone one day down by the well. She told me she knew I lamented the fact that I had given my husband no children and said she wished to help me. I feared her sorcery too much to deny her."

With Dillon's aid, Ann Marie wrapped tight bandages around the wisewoman, from wounded shoulder to waist. "She advised me and plied me with herbs. My husband as well. Six months ago, I took to my bed, laboring to bring our first child into the world, but the babe was turned in the wrong position. Neither my son nor I would have survived had the wisewoman not used her gift to save us. 'Tis why I began studying herbs and their uses. 'Twas foolish mayhap, but I had hoped I might be of some service to her to repay her for all she has done for us."

Dillon gazed down at the healer as he stroked her hair. "Your babe is well then?"

"Aye, my lord. Simon is quite proud of him."

"Sir Simon, my second-in-command, is your husband?"

"Aye, my lord."

So that is where he had seen her. "You did not react to her youth as I would have expected." She had not crossed herself or shrieked in fear or babbled nonsense about the devil's work.

She nodded. "I should have guessed she was not the aged woman all believe her to be."

He looked at her with some surprise. "How *could* you have?" *He* certainly had not.

"After she delivered my son and cleaned herself up a bit, I noticed this." Her hands went to the arm Dillon did not hold.

He had himself discarded the wisewoman's clothing earlier, leaving her arm bare to their view from fingertips to bandaged shoulder. The hand Ann Marie now clasped loosely and lifted for his inspection was coated with blood. His, Dillon assumed.

The skin on her wrist, however, was not. And he could see that it bore traces of yellow and gray that—at a glance—gave the illusion of age and wrinkles. The paint or stain or whatever it was only reached a few inches above her wrist. The rest of her arm matched the pale skin of her face and chest.

When he examined the hand he held, Dillon discovered the same strange disguise.

Ann Marie dipped a cloth in fresh water and bathed away the blood and paint. "There were traces of this left on the cloth she used. I was never quite certain whence it came until now."

She passed the cloth to Dillon, who cleansed the other hand and arm.

"You should rest, my lord," Ann Marie advised timorously when he handed it back to her.

Nodding, he lay back beside the healer, turned onto his side so he could keep an eye on her, and tucked her hand against his chest.

Ann Marie flushed. "I did not mean… Mayhap you would rest easier—"

"I shall not leave her," he whispered, the words lacking volume, not force.

"Aye, my lord." She stood awkwardly beside the bed.

"You have done all you can for her," Dillon told her patiently. "Go now. But stay within the donjon. I shall send for you when her bandages need changing or should she worsen."

"Aye, my lord." She bobbed a curtsy. "Thank you, my lord. With your permission, I shall have Cook prepare you some hearty stew. 'Twill help you regain your strength and rebuild the blood you have lost. I shall bring it up myself and see that no one else disturbs you."

"Very well. And tell no one what you have seen this night."

"As you wish, my lord." She curtsied again and started for the door.

"Ann Marie."

"Aye?"

"I shall not forget what you have done here. You and your family will want for naught as long as you remain at Westcott."

"Thank you, my lord," she breathed, her face flushing with pleasure, and left him alone with the wisewoman.

At last Dillon was free to examine the healer without curious eyes perusing him. Taking a deep breath, he sat up—a simple task that nigh sapped the remainder of his strength—and turned toward her.

His cobalt gaze fastened on the top of her head and began a slow foray down a high forehead just beginning to bead with moisture. Slipped over thin, sloping eyebrows that drew together in pain. Past eyelids garnished with thick lashes. Along a thin, straight nose that turned up the tiniest bit at the tip. Pallid cheeks smudged with blood. Full lips similarly painted. A chin that he imagined had been thrust forward in stubbornness often during their many *discussions*.

She was stunning.

He could understand, somewhat, Robert's assumption that her appearance stemmed from sorcery. They had believed her an old woman. The shoulders they had thought stooped with age were in fact smooth and gently rounded, one left bare by the bandages.

His gaze dipped lower. He had used so much of the bed linens for bandages that what remained barely covered her to her waist. She was of slender build. Her injuries, combined with her diminutive height, lent her a fragile air. He knew from experience, however, that she possessed great strength.

Who *was* this wise young woman who had been so loyal to him? This woman who, for years, had been his closest friend?

* * *

Ann Marie returned sometime later with his meal, fresh water, and clean linens. Though he was reluctant to move the wisewoman, Dillon agreed she would rest more comfortably were the blood-encrusted sheets beneath them replaced.

The many years of combat he had endured enabled Dillon to conquer the weakness that plagued him enough to rise and lift the wisewoman into his arms. Ann Marie suggested he enlist Robert's aid, but Dillon simply could not stomach the notion of someone else cradling her in his arms. Even his own brother, who had done so briefly earlier.

Her face flushing a florid red, Ann Marie suggested they garb the seer in one of his tunics, but Dillon refused, not wanting anything to restrict access to her wounds or interfere in her care.

Naked save the bandages, the wisewoman felt right, curled up against him, her head resting on his bare shoulder. Her skin was so soft. Softer than down. Her long hair fell over his arm and brushed his hip, distracting him from her narrow waist, full hips, long supple legs, and the dark thatch of curls between them.

"'Tis done, my lord."

He breathed a sigh of relief and carefully settled the wisewoman against the pillows.

Propping himself against a bedpost, he watched Ann Marie cover the healer and finish arranging the linens to her satisfaction.

She stepped back. "Do you wish aught else, my lord?"

"Only that you do not stray far, Ann Marie, and may be easily located should she worsen."

"Aye, my lord. Gideon is just outside your door. I shall keep him apprised of my whereabouts."

As soon as she left, Dillon availed himself of some of the water Ann Marie had fetched and washed the dried blood from his body. The tiny portion of strength he had managed to muster soon abandoned him. Unable to remain standing any longer, he climbed into bed and reached for the steaming bowl of venison stew Cook had prepared for him.

Robert returned, having found no other healer, and paced

whilst Dillon ate. His attention vacillated between the healer and the three new scars that adorned Dillon's torso. When he finally ceased his restless prowling, Robert seated himself and stared at Dillon for so long it made him downright self-conscious.

"The scars are not *that* bad, are they?" Dillon posed gruffly.

"Nay. We have both seen worse."

"Then why do you stare at me in such a way?"

A long moment passed.

"I thought you were lost to me." Emotion roughened Robert's voice. "I thought the healer would be able to serve you better here, but…" He shook his head. "The ride home never seemed so long."

Dillon set his empty bowl aside.

"In my imagination, your breath stopped at least a dozen times," his brother continued raggedly. "Each time, I panicked and frantically searched for your pulse, cursing myself for not having had Marcus tell the healer to meet us halfway. Even when the gates were in sight, I was sure you would expire ere the cart rolled to a halt in the bailey."

"You did the right thing, Robert. You kept a clear head and did what you thought necessary."

Robert's lips turned up in a weak smile. "My head was not clear when I saw you collapse to the ground with so many quarrels sticking out of you. I thought you dead and went into a berserker's rage, killing every man within reach of me. I damn nigh skewered Sir Aubrey ere my mind cleared. The men had to restrain me to keep me from slaughtering the last attacker." He paused. "Mayhap 'twould have been better for him if I had."

"Why? To spare him my wrath?"

"Nay. They are saying the wisewoman tortured him to obtain your betrayer's name."

Dillon thought he must not have heard correctly. "What? Who is saying it?"

"All of Westcott. I was not here, so I know not what methods she employed. But whatever they were, I suspect it has driven him mad. At least, 'tis how it appeared when I went down to the dungeon to see if he lived. Everyone else was afraid to, having witnessed the seer slit Gavin's throat."

"Gavin!"

"Aye. Gavin betrayed you. He was in league with Camden, who engineered the attack. She forced his confession in the great hall, then slew him when he would have buried a blade in her back."

Fury and shock inundated Dillon, leaving him speechless.

The brothers stared down at the healer, listening to her continued fight for breath.

"She is very loyal to you," Robert said softly. "I knew not asking her to save your life would cost her her own."

"She will not die," Dillon informed him.

"Dillon."

"She will not die," he repeated, refusing to consider the alternative. He had just found her. He could not lose her.

Robert studied him for several long moments, then turned his gaze back to the healer. "Did you know?"

"That she is so young?"

"Is she?" he queried uneasily. "Or does her sorcery merely make her appear so?"

"Do not be a fool," Dillon snapped. "You are letting the people's fear sway you. And nay, I did not know. I should have guessed the truth long ago, but believed my eyes and ears over my heart. I thought her the same aged wisewoman who served our father."

Robert frowned. "'Tis a mystery, is it not?"

Dillon nodded, knowing his brother believed 'twould remain one.

Robert's jaw cracked open in a wide yawn.

"Go seek your bed," Dillon enjoined. "You need not stay with me."

Loosing a weary sigh, his brother stood and drew his thickly muscled arms above his head in a mighty stretch. "Gideon guards your door. Send him to me should you need aught during the night."

Or should the healer perish. The words went unspoken.

"I will." Dillon reached out and grabbed his arm in a rough-tender grip. "Thank you, brother, for following me and saving my life."

Robert smiled and, leaning down, gave him as hardy a hug as he could without disturbing the young woman by his side. "Thank *you*, brother, for living. I know not what I would have done if I had lost you." Pulling back, he grinned mischievously. "After all, I've yet to best you in combat."

Dillon cuffed him playfully and bid him good night.

Exhaustion pulled at him, leaving him light-headed. A great sigh escaped him as he lay back and let his eyes roam the healer.

The blankets had slipped to her waist. Dillon started to draw them back up, but stopped when something caught his eye. Frowning, he leaned in closer and confirmed it. She had a nasty scar the length of his middle finger on her left upper arm, halfway between her shoulder and her elbow. He had failed to notice it earlier because of his preoccupation with her injuries.

Slowly, he traced it with one finger.

It was an old scar. Seven years old if he guessed correctly. He had been wounded in the same place shortly after they had taken Brimshire. *He* did not carry the scar from it, however. *She* did.

Had *all* of his wounds left their mark on her?

Dreading the answer, he drew the covers back.

There—on her left side, partially obscured by her bandage—was a scar from the wound he had received when the former lord of Northaven had sought to regain by force what King Richard had given Dillon four years past. The battle had been brief, violent, and bloody. Despite Dillon's protests, the wisewoman had never been far from his side and had healed the wound for him only minutes after he had run through the one who had given it to him.

A smaller scar marred the pale flesh just beneath her right collarbone. She had acquired that one healing him after Robert had inadvertently dealt him an injury whilst they were training together one day. One pale thigh bore a scar where he had been wounded at Shepford. The knee beneath it bore another. And there were more. On her forearm. Her wrist.

He had no such scars on his own body. It sickened him to think that all of those wounds had opened on her flesh as they had closed on his. He would never have asked her to heal them had he known doing so would cause her pain, that 'twould scar her. The fact that the lesser wounds he had suffered had left no marks upon her did not ease his conscience in the least.

She shivered.

Swearing, Dillon pulled the blankets up to her chin, not wanting her to catch a chill on top of everything else, and lay back beside her.

Searching beneath the sheet, he found her hand and brought it to his lips. "How did you know me so well?" Without the paints she used to disguise it, her hand was a smooth, milky white with graceful fingers capped by glossy, rounded nails. He gently uncurled it and sized it against his own.

The whole of her hand fit within his palm.

"So small." He traced the light blue veins on the back of it.

And cold. She was as cold as winter snow. Dillon inched closer to her until only an inch or two separated them from chest to toes, offering her his warmth. Whilst he would love to roll her to her side, spoon his body around hers, and hold her close, he could not risk reopening her wounds.

Instead, he tucked her hand to his chest and, leaning forward, nuzzled his face between her chin and shoulder. "Do not leave me. Please. Give me the chance to know you."

"Dillon."

Heart skipping, he retreated just enough to glimpse her face.

Glazed brown eyes stared back at him.

"Wise One?" He retrieved one of the cloths Ann Marie had left beside the bed and gently wiped the blood from her lips.

"Dillon." Her voice was weak, thready, bracketed by gasping breaths.

"I am here."

"I… I did not think… 'twould take so long."

"What, Seer?"

She closed her eyes. "Dying."

His throat thickened. "You will not die. You *can*not die."

She stiffened suddenly and moaned in pain.

"Tell me how to help you," he begged.

Her eyes opened, met his. "Please," she whispered. The hand he held tightened around his. "Do not leave me. I am… s-so afraid."

As he watched, a tear spilled over her lashes and trailed down one temple.

His own eyes burned as he brushed her hair back with his free hand and cupped her soft cheek in his palm. "I shall not leave you," he vowed thickly.

"Y-You will stay with me?"

He nodded. "I shall stay with you, Seer. I shall stay with you forever if it be your will."

The corners of her lips tilted up in a faint smile. Her grip on his hand loosened. "You will stay," she repeated softly, eyes closing, her body relaxing as unconsciousness claimed her once more.

Dillon lay beside her in silent despair and pressed a fervent kiss to her unbound shoulder.

He was losing her.

He clenched his eyes shut and, bringing her hand to his

cheek, held it there.

She withered before his eyes as an autumn flower did when touched by winter's first frosty fingers and there was naught he could do to stop it.

She began to tremble.

Moving closer, he draped one leg across both of hers, wishing he could wrap an arm around her waist without disturbing her injuries.

He buried his face in the fragrant hair that blanketed the pillow they shared, inhaling deeply as he confronted the truth at last.

His breath hitched as he damned himself for living when she would not.

Hope fading, Dillon gave the tears that had been building within him free rein.

CHAPTER FIVE

"Someone comes."

Meghan looked up from the bowl she had just filled with stew.

Her grandsire stared into the fire, a familiar faraway look in his faded brown eyes.

"Who comes, Grandfather?" She set the bowl on the board before him.

He shook his head. "Someone with great power."

Unease trickled through her. Her grandfather, like Alyssa's mother, had been born with the sight. If he said someone approached, then someone approached. But who? He had said someone of great power, surely he did not mean their liege lord. Did he?

A knock shook their door.

Meg jumped.

Lord Osmond did not intend to call her grandsire forth to serve in battle, did he? Her grandfather had barely survived the last battle he had fought on their lord's behalf.

Heart pounding, she crossed to the door and opened it.

The man standing outside, nigh swallowed by the darkness,

was so tall she had to tilt her head way back to find his face.

Her mouth fell open.

He was strikingly handsome, with a strong angular jaw and piercing brown eyes so dark she at first thought them black. His shoulders were nigh as broad as the doorway. And his garb was indeed that of a nobleman.

But this was not Lord Osmond. She had never met this man before.

He offered her a slight bow. "Greetings, Mistress Meghan."

Or had she? Her heart pounded in her chest as she bobbed a curtsy. "My lord. Forgive me, I cannot recall—"

"We two have never met," he interrupted with a smile. "I know your name because I am like you."

Her grandfather moved to stand behind her. "Let him enter, Meg," he instructed, then addressed the stranger. "You are most welcome, my lord."

"My thanks," he said as he ducked his head and entered.

"You are a *gifted one*," her grandfather said.

Meghan studied the giant curiously.

His tall form was clad in black chain mail, the likes of which she had never seen. A black tunic, plain but woven of fine cloth, covered it. And the sword he bore in a scabbard looked as though it was longer than she was tall.

"Aye, I am a *gifted one*," he confirmed in a warm, deep voice.

Meghan had not realized others born with peculiar gifts existed outside of her and Alyssa's bloodline.

Her grandfather offered his arm. "I am Albert."

The stranger clasped her grandfather's arm. "I am called Seth." As he did, Meghan noticed his hair. Pulled back and secured with a leather tie, it fell to his waist in raven waves that glinted in the firelight.

"I sense great power in you," her grandfather said, gazing up at the man.

A faint smile curled Seth's lips. "I am quite powerful, aye."

"And you bring us news, eh?"

"Aye."

"My vision told me as much."

Seth turned to Meghan, surprising her. "Alyssa needs you, Meghan. I have come to take you to her."

"I do not understand. If she wishes to see me…"

He shook his head. "She has done what you all feared she would do when she donned her grandmother's robes. She has healed mortal wounds Lord Dillon suffered in an ambush and now lies dying in his stead."

Icy fear lodged in her chest, then clawed its way down her spine. "How know you this?"

"I have seen it in a vision not unlike your grandsire's. If you believe me not…" Reaching out, he touched the fingertips of one large hand to her shoulder.

Images flooded her mind of the Earl of Westcott being felled by three bolts from a crossbow. Of Alyssa healing him, then collapsing.

Meg's breath left her in a rush. "No."

"I can take you to her tonight."

She shook her head, tears welling in her eyes and spilling over her lashes. "She lives several days march to the north."

"We will not walk or ride there," he informed her. "If you will place your trust in me, I can and will take you there tonight."

Meghan looked to her grandfather.

"Go with him."

But go with him where? The man couldn't sprout wings and fly her there.

She eyed the stranger uneasily. Could he?

His lips twitched. "There are faster means than even that to convey you."

Again her mouth fell open. Had he read her thoughts?

"Aye." He turned to her grandfather. "I shall return her anon, and thank you for trusting me to ensure her safety."

So saying, he again reached out and touched Meghan's

shoulder.

Darkness engulfed her, shutting out all light. Her head swam with dizziness. Then she found herself standing in a moonlit forest.

Seth chuckled. "'Tis a bit unsettling the first time, but 'twill pass."

"Where are we?" she managed to gasp, her heart beating so fast she feared it might burst from her breast.

"Two days march from Broughston castle."

She frowned. Alyssa's brother, Geoffrey, lived on Lord Humphrey's lands.

"Roland," Seth said.

Foliage rustled as a dark figure emerged from the shadows. "Aye?"

Though not as tall as Seth, this man towered over Meghan, as well. Short black hair. A handsome face that made her wonder if he and Seth were brothers. Broad shoulders encased in chain mail and the garb of a nobleman.

"Protect Meghan whilst I seek out Geoffrey."

Roland nodded.

Seth closed his eyes, then vanished.

Meg gasped.

Roland's stony face lit with a faint smile. "I reacted the same in the beginning."

She gripped her skirts in clenched fists. "You are not like him?"

He shook his head. "I am like Alyssa. I can heal with my hands."

Another *gifted one*. How had she and her family never heard of them?

"How do you know of Alyssa?"

"Seth told me." His brow furrowed. "He seems to know of us all."

"I knew not there were others like us."

"Nor did I until…" His expression darkened.

"Until?"

He shook his head. "Until Seth found me and helped me understand otherwise."

An uncomfortable silence descended upon them.

"If Seth is so powerful, why does he not simply heal Alyssa himself?"

"I know not. But, if he wishes you and your family to learn how to do it yourselves, I have no doubt that he believes such knowledge will benefit you in the future."

An unsettling notion. Did he think Alyssa would sacrifice herself again for Lord Dillon? Or had he foreseen Meg or one of the others suffering a fatal wound? "Who is he?" she asked, unable to stifle her curiosity. "Whence came he?"

"I know not his origins. I know only that he is the eldest and most powerful amongst us."

That sparked another frown.

If Seth was the oldest amongst the *gifted ones*, how did he appear so young?

The trees around them swayed and whispered as a brisk breeze buffeted them. Lightning flashed in the distance, the rumble of thunder chasing it. 'Twould rain soon.

Seth reappeared, Geoffrey at his side.

Geoffrey's face lost all color as he stumbled backward and looked around with wide eyes.

"Geoffrey!" Meg rushed forward and embraced him.

Closing his arms around her, he held her tight. "Meg? Who are these men? How did… how came I to be here? I was—"

"They're *gifted ones*, like us." Drawing back, she clung to his hand. "Only more powerful. I was home with my grandfather only moments ago."

Eyes wide, Geoffrey looked up at Seth. "Who are you?"

"I am called Seth. And, as your cousin has told you, I am a *gifted one*. As is Roland." He motioned to the other man.

Roland dipped his head in a slight nod.

Meg squeezed Geoffrey's hand. "Alyssa needs us. Lord

Dillon suffered mortal wounds, and she healed them. She now lies, dying, at Westcott."

"Nay." Alarm and fury returned the color to his features. Geoffrey had warned Alyssa that the black robes would mean her death. He had warned her that she would one day sacrifice her life to save Dillon's. "Nay!"

"Seth said he can take us to her and show us how to heal her."

Geoffrey eyed Seth with rising resentment and no little suspicion. "I am not a healer. Neither is Meg. We do not bear that gift. And, even if we did, my sister will not live long enough for us to reach her."

"You can be with her tonight," Seth said. "We've still your mother and grandmother to collect. Let us tarry no longer." He touched Geoffrey's shoulder. The second man touched Seth's.

Darkness blanketed them.

Then the four found themselves standing outside the home in which Alyssa and Geoffrey had been raised. Far from Lord Humphrey's lands.

The door opened. Light from the fire within spilled into the night as Geoffrey's mother and grandmother stepped into view. Matthew, his father, opened the door wider and joined them, his head turned slightly aside as he sought to hear with his ears what his sightless eyes could not tell him.

Beatrice's face creased with despair as she looked at the four of them. "My vision was true then? Alyssa has sacrificed herself to save Lord Dillon?"

Seth answered her. "I fear 'tis so. You do not seem surprised by my presence. Did you foresee my coming as well?"

"Aye." Tears welled in her eyes. "In my vision, my daughter suffered such pain."

"And still does, but you can remedy that. All of you together. Matthew, I know you fear for their safety, so you may accompany us."

Matthew frowned. "If you are as powerful as my wife suspects, why do you not heal Alyssa yourself?"

"I could. But should Alyssa again suffer grievous wounds in the future, at a time when I cannot be present, you will need to know how to work together to heal her yourselves. I will show you how tonight."

Meg saw Geoffrey look to his mother, asking her with his eyes if her vision had told her they should trust this man.

She nodded.

Seth removed a pack from his shoulder and opened it. "You should all don these."

Geoffrey took the black robe Seth held out to him. It looked much like the one Alyssa always wore, but larger. "Why? Would we not draw less notice without them?"

Shaking his head, Seth handed similar robes to Meg and the others. "No one else will see you. And these will keep Lord Dillon from skewering you when he awakens to find you all in his chamber." Dropping the sack, he donned a black robe of his own. "Alyssa is the only one he has seen wear these robes. He associates them with healers and will accept both your presence and your purpose more readily if he thinks you are like her."

Confusion and concern for Alyssa muddling her thoughts, Meg donned the midnight robe and moved to stand with the family. Matthew, she noticed, clutched one of his carving knives, the tip peeking out from beneath the sleeve of his robe. Apparently, he too did not trust easily.

"Are you all ready?" Seth asked.

Geoffrey's father stepped outside and closed the door. "Aye."

"Then come closer and link your arms."

Meg linked one arm through Alyssa's grandmother's and one through Geoffrey's.

"Roland," Seth said.

The stranger with Seth moved forward to touch Geoffrey's

shoulder.

Then Seth touched Matthew's shoulder and darkness enfolded them all.

* * *

A voice woke Dillon in the still moments that preceded dawn. Deep and soft, yet filled with barely suppressed violence, it brought Dillon to instant alertness. "I should kill him whilst he sleeps."

"Nay, Geoffrey," a feminine voice countered. "He has done her no harm."

"She lies moments from death, in agony, and you would defend him?"

As soon as the deep voice predicted her death, Dillon's eyes flew open and focused on the form he held.

The wisewoman's face bore a faint bluish cast. Dark hollows had formed beneath her eyes. Dried blood flecked her cheeks. The tiny breaths she took were few, the lengths between them growing with each erratic heartbeat.

"He does not understand her gifts," the female voice continued.

"That does not excuse—"

"She was forewarned," a third voice, aged and wise, interrupted. 'Twas familiar, almost identical to the voice he was accustomed to hearing emerge from the wisewoman's lips. "She chose to follow this path, knowing full well where it would lead her. You warned her yourself, when she donned my robes, and must not condemn him for a decision that was hers alone."

Dillon swept the room with his gaze, seeking the source of the voices. Several black-robed figures formed a horseshoe around the foot of the bed. Startled, he yanked a dagger from beneath his pillow and sat up, leaning over the healer in a gesture of protection. "Who are you?"

"See how he defends her?" the old woman asked. He could not tell which one she was. There were six of them, and all wore cowls that hid their faces as efficiently as the seer's did.

"Who are you?" he demanded again. "Why are you here?"

Had she said the wisewoman had donned her robes? Was one of these figures the wisewoman who had served his father? Was that why their voices sounded so similar?

"We have come to undo the damage you have wrought," the deep voice answered, teeming with rage over the wisewoman's condition. Dillon guessed it was that of the tall figure closest to him, for the one next to him placed a restraining hand on his arm and stepped forward.

"We were told you sought a healer," the younger woman who had spoken earlier announced evenly. "We are like the wisewoman." She reached up and doffed her cowl, revealing black hair streaked with gray pulled back from a face so similar to his wisewoman's that the two were most certainly mother and daughter. As her brown eyes slid to the still figure on the bed beside him, tears welled in them, and her pale throat moved in a swallow. "We wish to aid her."

Dillon lowered the dagger, hope rising. "Do you share her gifts? Can you help her? Will you heal her?"

"We will do what we can for her," she replied.

Dressed as his Wise One did and appearing as silently as they had without disturbing Gideon, they *must* share her extraordinary gifts, he thought.

Dillon glanced down at the wisewoman. "There is little time. Please, do not let her perish. I shall give you aught you ask do you heal her."

"Think you material goods mean aught to us?" the tall one growled.

"Then tell me what *does* matter to you and I will—"

The wisewoman made a sound—half gasp, half cough—and fell silent. His wide-eyed gaze locked on her as his heart thudded in his chest and his stomach clenched painfully. "Wise One?" he cried. His dagger fell from lax fingers, slipped over the edge of the bed, and clattered to the floor, obscenely loud in the pregnant silence.

She gasped again, her chest barely rising.

Shards of excruciating relief at the reprieve cut through Dillon's veins as he turned back to the robed figures. "Any boon you ask of me is yours, just *heal her ere 'tis too late!*"

"Will you give your life for her?" the tall one challenged.

"Aye," he answered instantly.

"Enough," a deeper, resonant voice boomed.

The six robed figures all started, then swiveled as one to peer into the dark corner behind them.

Dillon eased up a bit so he could see over their heads.

The shadows beyond deepened as a seventh dark-robed figure stepped forward. A figure who must surely be the tallest man Dillon had ever beheld. Dillon stood a couple of inches above six feet himself. Yet this man, whose face remained hidden beneath his cowl, was at least half a foot taller.

"I brought you here to heal her," the man said, his voice carrying an accent Dillon could not place, "not to taunt Lord Dillon. And I would see her suffer no longer. Remove her bandages, my lord."

Fingers fumbling, he hastily did so.

Gasps sounded when the last of them were removed.

He swallowed hard. "I know naught of healing, of herbs and medicines. There is one here who is just learning. She did all she could for her, but 'tis not enough."

"We shall reward her for her efforts," the female who looked like Alyssa promised thickly.

"I have already vowed that she will want for naught as long as she resides at Westcott," he informed her, stroking the seer's hair as he turned to the giant. "Please, will you heal her now? I, too, would have her suffer no longer."

"You must withdraw first, my lord."

"I will not leave her."

The other six swung their attention back and forth between them, waiting to see what would happen.

"Very well," the giant conceded. "But you must remove yourself from the bed and retreat some distance to give us room."

"As you wish."

As soon as Dillon slipped naked from the bed, five of the black robes flowed forward to surround the wisewoman on three sides. The giant remained where he stood, another at his side.

Dillon retrieved a tunic, braies, and hose from his trunk and pulled them on as the dark figures glanced at the tallest one, then clasped each other's hands and extended them above her. The eldest woman began to chant softly, the words indecipherable to him. Soon the others joined her.

Spent from the simple exercise of clothing himself, Dillon remained still, awe striking him when their exposed hands—male, female, old, young—began to glow with an eerie iridescence. The elderly woman touched a hand to the wisewoman's shoulder. Light flowed over the seer and settled upon her like a blanket, molding itself to her limbs and torso. Shifting from white to gold, it suffused the seer with a healing warmth so great the temperature of the room rose.

Sweat trickled down Dillon's temple. The ugly, seeping wounds on the wisewoman's body sealed themselves, healed themselves, vanished as he watched with wide, fascinated eyes. The bruising and old scars followed suit, disappearing without a trace. Color returned to her pallid features, cloaking her form with a healthy flush. Her chest rose and fell in deep, even breaths.

"Enough," the giant said.

The chanting ended. The light vanished as quickly as candlelight snuffed out by damp fingers.

Silence reigned as nigh darkness cloaked them. Dillon blinked furiously, attempting to banish the ghostly shapes the peculiar light had planted in his vision. He brought his hands to his eyes and rubbed them impatiently. When he lowered them, all but the tallest of the robed figures had vanished.

Dillon glanced at the door that had not opened, then back to the giant in the corner.

"They await me outside," was his only explanation.

Slowly, Dillon approached the bed. Every inch of the wisewoman's flesh now appeared flawless. No quarrel wounds, no cuts, no bruises, no scars. No blood rattled in her lungs. No haggard coughs racked her torso.

Yet something was awry.

Her body glowed not with health, but with a more moderate form of that unearthly iridescence, much as the horizon often glows with the residual warmth of the setting sun. Instead of the calm serenity he had expected to encompass her once the pain receded, she lay as stiffly as his shield, her muscles tense and trembling. A frown creased her brow. And she gritted her teeth as if she waged some fierce internal war.

"What have you done?" he asked hoarsely.

"Shown them how to combine their powers to heal her, so they may do so again should she require aid in the future."

"She will not." Dillon would not let her sacrifice herself for him again. He would not have let her do so this time had he been conscious and aware of the price she would pay. Sitting on the edge of the bed, he reached out to stroke the hair back from her damp forehead. Heat seared his skin. "She burns with fever!"

"'Tis not with fever she burns," the dark one denied as Dillon searched for something to dip in water.

"Are you mad? Do you not see how she trembles?" The cool, damp cloth Dillon pressed against her burning skin warmed within seconds.

"She burns and she trembles, but 'tis from the healing."

"I do not understand. She has healed me many times and it did not affect me thusly." Dipping the cloth into the cool water, he rung it out, then tried again.

"You do not share her gifts, Lord Dillon."

He frowned. "You are saying 'tis because she is a healer herself?"

"Aye. It affects her differently than it does you."

"Her injuries are healed, are they not?"

"Aye."

"Is she in pain?"

The robed figure seemed to choose his words carefully. "She is experiencing some discomfort, aye, and will continue to do so until her body has adjusted. But 'tis mild compared to that which came before it."

Dillon knew not what the man meant, why the healing had done this to her, what kind of *adjustments* her body must undergo. He knew only that he did not like seeing his wisewoman so uncomfortable.

"How long will she be like this? What can I do to bring her ease?"

"You are already doing it, my lord. It may take some time for her to awaken. Until then, see that she consumes water frequently. The heat will leave her with a great thirst." He turned to leave.

"Wait!"

"Aye, my lord?"

"Who are you?"

A pause ensued. "I am known only as Seth."

"Where can I find you? If she should worsen, I will need to know where to send for you."

"You will have no further need of my assistance."

He glanced down at the wisewoman dubiously. When he looked up, the last robed figure was gone.

Once more, there had been no sound of the large oak door opening or closing, leaving Dillon to wonder at his means of escape. The idea that all of the black-robed figures had simply vanished through some magical means made gooseflesh pepper his skin. He quickly shook it off, admonishing himself for letting the keep's superstitions infect him, and dipped the cloth in cool water once more.

CHAPTER SIX

Her body woke her. Or rather, the energy raging through it did. Reminiscent of the power that engulfed her whenever she healed a wound, this was a hundredfold stronger.

Alyssa burned inside, as though roasting above a spit. Her mouth and throat felt as dry as the desert, her tongue swollen and raw. Miniature bolts of lightning pricked her skin. Her ears buzzed with the sounds of insects that were not there. Tension stiffened her limbs, made it difficult to move.

As alarm and confusion swelled, battling for dominance, wave after wave of shudders inundated her. Unclenching her teeth, Alyssa tried to relax and will the pain away as she often had in the past. But, as soon as she began to concentrate her gift, the cacophony magnified. Sound exploded in her head. Fire consumed her insides. Stinging nettles whipped her flesh.

Barely aware of her actions, she gripped her hair and tugged at it, unable to bear it.

Large, gentle hands covered hers, untangling her fingers and pulling them away. A voice intruded upon the chaos, soft yet insistent, shocking her into realizing she was not alone.

The buzz faded, yielding to warm masculine tones. Alyssa

opened her eyes and focused blearily on the face that swam above her.

It was a familiar one. A trusted one.

A beloved one.

"Dillon?" Her voice sounded muffled to her own ears. With fear and pain scattering her thoughts, formality did not occur to her.

Nor did whispering.

He smiled, though concern creased his features. "Aye, Wise One."

"W-What is amiss?" Her gaze made a jerky exploration of the chamber, then returned to his handsome, haggard face. Shadows underscored his eyes. Several rogue hairs stood up on one side of his head where he had speared his fingers through the thick dark locks as he was wont to do whenever he was angry or agitated. "What happened? Why am I here?"

Naught could have surprised her more than what occurred next.

Supreme relief blanketing his features, he drew one of her hands to his lips and kissed her palm. Stubble abraded her fingers.

"Why did you do that?" Had she not been gritting her teeth, her mouth would have fallen open.

"I began to think you would never awaken," he admitted.

It occurred to her then that he looked her in the eye. Gasping, she jerked her other hand up and fought the prickling stiffness to make it do her bidding. Under Dillon's watchful gaze, she drew quaking fingers across her face, up, and over her hair.

Her cowl. Her robe. Where was it? And why was she here, in Dillon's chamber, in Dillon's bed, utterly naked if she could trust her jumbled senses?

Some sound of distress must have escaped her, for he began to stroke her hair with languid movements.

"Be at ease, Wise One. You are safe."

"I do not… I cannot remember how I came to be here."

He leaned away from her to reach for something. "Will it harm you if I lift you enough to drink?"

Since she had no idea what afflicted her, she was unsure. "I know not. But I feel a great thirst."

He nodded. "Tell me if this causes you pain."

Leaning forward, he slipped an arm beneath her head and shoulders and eased her up so she could drink. Voices immediately filled her head, all talking at once. All his. Overlapping.

Careful. Ease her up slowly.

Her eyes are clear. I could easily lose myself in them.

Easy. Good. Good.

Will it last this time? Or will she again fall victim to that unnatural slumber?

Those eyes… so warm and dark. What thoughts do they conceal?

Almost finished now.

Why does she look at me in such a way? How many times has she done so in the past unbeknownst to me?

Her flesh is cold. Shivers shake her. Does she not find warmth soon, I shall peel off my clothes, crawl beneath the blankets, and warm her with mine own body.

Her eyes widened at the fragments that filled her mind then. Heat crept up her neck to her cheeks, her ears. Her heart began to pound.

"What is amiss?" he asked, noticing the change in her. "Has the fever returned?"

She shook her head, mute.

"Are you certain? You are flushed of a sudden."

"'Tis naught," she lied, unwilling to admit that 'twas his own sensual fantasies that had shaken her.

Never had she read him so well, so easily, so clearly.

Another violent shudder shook her, setting her teeth on edge.

Dillon sat on the edge of the bed, still supporting her.

"You are cold."

She *was* a bit chilled, she realized. When had frost replaced the fire that had seared her when first she had awoken? "Aye."

Alyssa could not fathom Dillon's intentions at first when he dragged back the blankets.

Why would he uncover her when he knew she needed warmth?

Then she remembered his thoughts and…

Stretching out beside her, he reclined against the pillows and settled her so that her right hip and the length of her thigh were melded to his left. Her back rested against his chest. Thick, tunic-clad muscles pillowed her head.

Reaching around her, he tugged the covers up to her chin and slipped his hands beneath them. Her heart nigh stopped beating when his arms crept under hers and wrapped themselves around her waist.

"Are you warmer now?" The deep rumble of his voice tickled her ear and encouraged the chaos within her.

"Aye," she responded softly. Dillon was treating her like a… like a woman. Why? What had happened?

Memory gradually began to resurface.

He had been injured. So severely he had barely survived the trip home. Three wounds. One fatal.

"You were injured!" When she would have sat up and spun around to inspect him, the arm around her waist tightened, preventing her from resurrecting the worst of the pain. She had to settle instead for tilting her head back to look up at him.

His budding beard swam into focus first, as dark as the hair on the nape of his neck with a few sprinkles of silver.

"Aye. And you healed me."

"All three wounds?"

He nodded.

Confused, she looked away. 'Twas not possible. "I should not have survived."

"You *would* not have survived had others with your gifts

not come forward and offered aid." He went on to describe the bizarre circumstances surrounding her healing. "Who were they, Wise One?"

Her family. Geoffrey he named. Even had he not, the temper her brother had demonstrated would have betrayed his identity. How she had missed him this past year.

The woman who had doffed her cowl sounded like her mother. Her grandmother had surely been present as well. She was uncertain who the others had been. Meg's grandfather was surely too old to render aid. And Alyssa had not known there were others out there who possessed similar gifts.

Nor had she known that any save for a healer could help her… and do so without perishing.

"Had you told me how to reach them, I would have sent for them as soon as I became aware of your condition."

"I did not think 'twas possible."

"That there were others like you?"

She shook her head. "That they could heal me."

His fingers moved to her forehead, smoothing away the creases there and making her flesh tingle. "You did not think they could save you?" Though his words remained neutral, she could feel tension building within him. It distressed him to know that she had healed him, believing there would be no hope for herself. "Have you never been healed before?"

"Only with herbs and tonics and poultices. Not with hands."

"You know not these healers?"

"Some. Mayhap four of them."

"Why then have they never healed you? Surely there must have been times—"

"I heal more swiftly than others do. Only rarely did I suffer injuries that lingered. And I was told as a child that 'twas too dangerous for them to be healed with aught but herbs. That I would not react the same way you do."

"Yet you are better than you were."

"Am I?" How nigh death had she traveled?

"Why did you never explain to me the true nature of your gifts?"

"You always knew I could heal with my hands."

"But I was not aware that doing so harmed you." A hint of steel entered his voice, reflecting the anger she could feel rising inside him. At himself for hurting her. At her for not telling him she suffered.

She read him easily. "The pain was fleeting, negligible. I saw no reason—"

"Do not lie to me," he growled. "I saw the scars."

Emotion flowed into her like lava, scalding her from the inside out. Not hers. Dillon's. Images flashed before her eyes, scenes spawned by *his* vision, so quickly she could not grasp them all. His wounds. Her scars. His body. Her hands. His hands. Her blood.

Pulling away, he threw his legs over the side of the bed and stood. Before he could rail at her, however, a knock sounded at the door.

"My lord?" Gideon, called.

Dillon cursed. "Hold!"

As she watched, he reined in his temper, then leaned down and fluffed the pillows beneath her befuddled head. Dragging the covers up, he added a few more blankets until all was arranged to his satisfaction.

He raised his eyebrows in silent question.

She smiled gratefully, touched by his fussing over her, and murmured a shy, "Thank you, Dillon."

He stilled. His eyes dropped to her lips.

Her smile faltered under his regard. For some reason her pulse skipped, picking up and thrumming through her veins. Her mouth went dry as she was struck with the sudden need to lick those lips that held his attention. A need to which she surrendered.

His eyes narrowed, darkening with an emotion she did not

recognize.

* * *

"My lord?" Gideon repeated.

Dillon hesitated an instant more.

His heart pounded like the hooves of a galloping warhorse. A single timid smile was all it had taken to make time stop. A small pink tongue gliding sensually across soft lips in what he knew was an innocent gesture. Yet his body reacted as if she had just thrown back the blankets and invited him to take her.

Yanking the curtains surrounding the bed closed, he called, "Enter."

His squire slipped into the room and closed the door behind him. "Harry is outside asking to see you, my lord. I told him only Robert and the sorceress are allowed to visit you, but he is insisting."

"Is it a matter of defense?"

The boy shrugged, face creasing with irritation. "He will not say. His mouth is sealed tighter than William's purse."

"Where is Robert?"

"Training with the men in the tiltyard."

"Send Harry to him."

"I tried to. Harry refuses to budge from yon hallway until he sees you."

Scowling, Dillon sighed and settled himself in a chair by the hearth. "Send him in."

Harry strode in on slightly bowed legs, balding pate uncovered, helmet held in his beefy hands. When Gideon slammed the door on his way out, Harry jumped. Eyes darting around the room, lingering momentarily on the bed, he cleared his throat.

Dillon watched him shift from foot to foot and waited, arms folded across his chest. He had known this man all of his life and could not remember ever having seen him look so anxious.

"You seem to be on the mend, milord," Harry blurted,

wincing when the words emerged unnaturally loud and hearty.

"Aye."

A pained look crossed the older man's face when Dillon offered no more. "Uh… 'tis pleased I am to hear it. The men will be glad to see you return to your duties. Not that they have any complaints about Sir Robert, mind you," he added hastily. "A fine leader he is."

"Harry."

"Aye?"

"Did you come here to commend my brother's leadership skills or was there aught else you wished to discuss?"

The gatekeeper's shoulders slumped. "I *do* have a concern, milord." He glanced over his shoulder, then leaned forward as if he feared Gideon might have his ear pressed to the door.

Intrigued, Dillon leaned toward him. "Go on. You may speak freely here."

"Well, I come to ask about the wisewoman."

Instantly alert, Dillon kept his expression neutral. He had asked Ann Marie to don the wisewoman's robes and venture out a few times so his people would not know the healer was ill. "As far as I know, the wisewoman is down below, either with Robert or in her chamber. If you wish to speak with her, you will have to seek her there."

Harry shook his head. "Not *that* wisewoman. *Our* wisewoman. I come to see how she fares."

Whilst Harry had been privy to Robert's search for another healer two nights earlier, he had *not* known the reason for it. Ann Marie's impersonation of the sorceress had been questioned by no others. Why would Harry doubt it? "I do not—"

"He knows, my lord."

Both men spun to face the bed as a portion of the curtains retreated and the seer's face appeared. She sat up, her face pale as she clutched the blankets to her chest.

Harry's face broke into a wide smile, several creases

forming alongside his mouth and at the corners of his eyes as he hurried toward the bed. "Lass, I was worried about you, I was."

Scowling, Dillon rose and followed him.

"You have not been to your garden in days. Not since Sir Robert came searching for another healer."

Her startled gaze met Dillon's. Mayhap she did not realize she had been lost to unconsciousness for three days.

"I thought at first 'twas for Lord Dillon," Harry went on, "but when I did not see you, I feared the worst."

The wisewoman smiled sweetly and reached out to pat one of Harry's oversized hands. "I am well, Harry. Please do not fret over me."

Something ugly and seething coiled within Dillon's gut— loathsome, blisteringly hot jealousy.

Harry knew.

Harry knew *her*. Not the facade she had shown Dillon and the others over the years, but that which had always been hidden beneath her robes and her whisper.

Harry alone was unsurprised by her youth.

He *knew*.

"You are so pale," he declared now in the closest thing to a fatherly tone Dillon had heard him use. "What ails you, child?"

Dillon gritted his teeth. *He* did not even know the healer's name and *this* man spoke to her as if they were old friends!

"I have been ill," she admitted, "but am better now, Harry. Truly." When he opened his mouth to object, she hurried to change the subject. "Have my plants begun to wither?"

"Nay."

Whilst Harry clamored on about watering her garden for her, Dillon stalked over to his trunk and yanked a linen shirt out of it.

Why had she confided in Harry instead of him? Did she not consider Dillon her friend? Was he not worthy of her trust? In the past seven years, they had scarcely left each other's sight. Yet she had kept *him* in the dark and shared her secret with *Harry*.

Returning to the bed, Dillon shoved Harry aside and tugged the soft material down over the wisewoman's head. He did not like the other man seeing the little bit of shoulder visible above the furs that covered her.

Startled, she blinked several times and blew the hair out of her eyes. Dillon took a moment to brush it back for her, gentle in spite of the irate thoughts that rode him. His hand tingled when he smoothed it around to the back of her neck and carefully released the rest of her long, dark tresses from their prison.

As soon as his callused skin met hers, her eyes widened and flew to his face. He refused to meet them, however, knowing she could feel the turmoil raging within him. Instead, he held the shirt down, modestly covering her whilst her arms found the sleeves.

Harry yammered on as if naught were amiss whilst Dillon swiftly laced up the tunic, piled pillows behind her back, and covered her with the blankets once more.

Though the wisewoman offered comments and answers whenever prompted, her gaze remained fixed on Dillon.

Oddly unsettled, he retreated to stand by the fire and gave them his back.

At last, Harry wished her well and turned to leave.

"You will speak of this to no one," Dillon informed him curtly.

Harry spun about and puffed up like a rooster. "Of course I will not! I would not betray our wisewoman for aught!"

Dillon strode forward, not stopping until Harry had to crane his neck to look up at him. "Not *our* wisewoman," he gritted, "*my* wisewoman. And anyone who betrays her will find a quick end at the point of my sword."

Harry's disgruntled look swiftly altered to one of astonishment. A knowing grin spread across his worn features.

Dillon did not know what he wanted to do more, wipe that smile off with his fist or take back those hasty, dreadfully possessive words.

He settled for grimacing and waving toward the door. "Get you gone, old man."

He could have sworn he heard the blasted soldier chuckle as the door closed behind him. Beset with restless anger, Dillon prowled the room and wished he were outside, training with his men. He would challenge Robert if he were. Or Simon. Only they could offer him a good fight.

Shoving aside his trunks and the small table and two chairs that rested nigh the hearth, he drew his sword and began to drill himself and measure his returning strength. He had done so each day whilst the wisewoman slept her dreamless sleep, cursing when he quickly tired.

Today differed, though. Consumed with a fury that powered his muscles and infused him with energy, he pushed himself further than he had all week.

"Harry can be trusted, my lord," the wisewoman assured him.

Dillon's sword made the air hum as it severed the arm of an invisible opponent. "You do not hesitate to call him Harry, yet until now refused to call me Dillon." He heaped silent epithets upon his own head. Why had he said that? He had sounded as petulant as a boy denied a sweetmeat.

Another slash of his sword, another invisible limb severed. Several more imaginary foes fell before she spoke.

"I have a garden."

Dillon missed a stroke, so surprised was he. He stopped and glanced at her, breathing hard from his exertions.

Crimson color rushed to her cheeks as she looked down at her lap. She had almost never spoken of herself to him. Mayhap doing so now left her uneasy.

Returning to his swordplay, he offered a casual, "Do you? I have not seen it." He thought he heard her sigh with relief.

"I keep it in that section of the forest where the villagers fear to tread."

"The glen to the south they all swear is cursed?"

She smiled. "Precisely the one. I grow many of the herbs I use there. But 'tis as much a source of peace for me as 'tis a source of medicines."

As Dillon's muscles grew fatigued, his swings and parries and lunges slowed.

"There I can escape the fear and hatred that are constantly directed at me here," she confessed. "In my garden, no one crosses himself as I pass or mutters curses in my wake. The birds and animals that visit do not shy away at my approach. They welcome me with warmth and song and playful mischief. I can remove my cowl there and feel the sun kiss my face, push my sleeves back and bury my fingers in the soil without worrying that someone will see them and know that I am not all that I seem."

Dillon stopped, more interested in hearing the healer speak than in listening to the air complain as his weapon sliced through it. He returned his sword to its scabbard and wearily sank into the chair by the hearth. Closing his eyes, he leaned his head back and let her low, husky voice wash over him.

"I seek refuge there nigh every day," she continued. "And each time I encounter Harry as I pass through the gate. He was wary of me for a long time, having heard the nightmarish tales that circulate about me. But, unlike the others, he seemed to grow accustomed to my comings and goings, offering a greeting, asking how I fared, even giving me word of those who might have need of my aid but were too fearful to approach me."

When she paused, he opened his eyes to find her staring at him.

"I know a greeting here or there may seem trivial to you," she said, "but, other than you, Robert, and Ann Marie, he is the only person in your domain who has ever spoken kindly to me when not in need or under orders to do so."

Without the cowl to conceal it, the loneliness she had suffered these last seven years lay bare before him.

Was it true? Had no one save himself and Harry and, in rare moments, Robert addressed her kindly? Even Ann Marie had avoided her until the healer had saved her life and that of her babe.

Dillon had been so preoccupied with defending his lands and his king that he had been unaware of the extent of the wisewoman's ill treatment. Was that why she had confided in Harry rather than in him?

"Harry learned of my true age and appearance quite by accident," she said as if he had spoken his thoughts aloud. "Though strong and of good health, his limbs are beginning to ache and stiffen with age. He hoped that, as a healer, I might be able to help him with a tisane or a compress that would bring him ease on the worst days. He did not want the other soldiers to know, so he sought me out in the one place he knew no one would chance to overhear us speak."

"Your garden."

She nodded, lips twitching. "I cannot tell you what a fright we gave each other. One minute I was alone, and the next a man stood across the clearing."

Apprehension suffused Dillon. What if it had not been Harry? If one of the village men had decided to brave the curse and follow her to her sanctuary, no one would have been there to protect her.

"Harry had come searching for an elderly sorceress, not a young woman who grubbed about in the dirt and feigned an ability to sing. I fear it came as a bit of a shock to him."

Dillon made some sound of agreement, still fretting over her safety.

"He is a good man." Smiling fondly, she peeled back a couple of furs. "Verily, once he recovered himself, I believe he pitied me. Or mayhap he felt we were allied in some way, each not quite what we appear. Whatever his reasons, he has been kind to me and has kept my secret well. He will not betray us."

Us.

Not *me* or *you*, but *us*.

Dillon noticed with some concern that she had removed all but one of the blankets he had draped across her. "Your chill," he murmured. ""Tis gone?"

"Aye." She hid a yawn behind one dainty hand. "In truth, I find it quite warm. Do you not?"

He frowned as she sank back against the pillows, eyelids drooping. Rising, he approached the bed. "Mayhap your fever returns." He rested a palm, callused from years of wielding weapons, upon her forehead.

She started slightly, then drew away, forcing a smile.

Dillon's stomach clenched. Did his touch displease her?

"You worry over neglecting your men," she commented.

Though such concerns had flitted through his mind at least a dozen times since waking, he denied it. "Nay. Robert oversees them."

"You would rather do so yourself."

He shook his head. "I wanted no one else to tend you."

Her brow furrowed. "Do they all know…?"

"Nay. I could not forget that someone had cast stones at you in the past. If they knew you could be hurt, you would lose the protection your robes and the rumors of immortality lend you. And I feared that someone might try to harm you in my absence. So Ann Marie has donned your robe and worn it these three days past."

She stared at him. "Three days? I have slept that long?"

He nodded.

"And Ann Marie is pretending to be me?"

"Aye. 'Twas she who treated and bandaged your wounds, enabling you to live long enough for the other healers to reach you."

"Then all of Westcott believes…"

"That I lay abed, recovering from my injuries whilst you tend me."

She seemed to need a moment to digest it.

Dillon strolled over to the narrow window and peered down through the precious glass he had added at great expense a few years ago. "The men do not suffer from my absence. Robert is more than capable of leading them."

"Robert has inherited your sire's fierce pride and stubborn temperament," she said after a moment. "He will not be satisfied until he has acquired lands and wealth of his own."

"Aye. He has told me as much. It seems he is bent on following in my footsteps." Dillon wished he could spare his brother that. Hiring out his sword, constantly having to prove himself in tournaments and one bloody battle after another, fighting other men's wars, hardening his heart against the taunts and cries of those he killed in combat, those who sought to kill him. As a third son, Dillon had done it all himself and, after gaining Henry II's notice at a very early age, had acquired his own wealth and property long before he had inherited the title.

"Gavin attempted to lay the blame for your betrayal at Robert's feet," she told him.

Shocked, he glanced at her over his shoulder. "Did you believe him?"

"I never doubted he spoke falsely." She tilted her head. "The same may not be true of your men, however. The seed of doubt Gavin planted has taken root and spawned suspicion. I can feel it." Closing her eyes, she seemed to listen to voices he could not hear. "Your men may not be content for much longer. They question Robert's word that you are recovering. His refusal to allow anyone but your squire to see you only encourages more speculation." She paused and opened her eyes. "'Tis time to make an appearance, my lord."

'Twas the truth. Yet he was reluctant to leave her. She had only just begun to improve. She was alert, if a little drowsy.

She spoke to him, confiding in him and looking at him with less shyness and self-consciousness, as she grew accustomed to being with him unconcealed.

There were so many things he wanted to ask her. So many things he wished to know. Could Westcott not wait one more day?

"Surely they do not think you would allow my brother to usurp my position," he murmured.

She shook her head, her lips forming a sad smile. "Your people trust me less than they do your enemies, my lord. Have you not guessed that yet?"

Lucifer's toes. "All right," he snapped, irritated by his people's persistent blindness, resenting it for luring him from her side. "You are to rest until I return. You are still weak."

"Aye, my lord."

"Dillon," he corrected in a growl.

"Aye, Dillon," she corrected dutifully. Her lips twitched.

His eyes narrowed suspiciously.

A laugh escaped her, hastily cut off as she clamped her lips more firmly together, eyes widening. It was such a youthful, joyous sound—so unlike his somber sorceress—that his irritation fled.

Smiling sheepishly, he crossed to the bed. "I am a poor substitute for a healer, am I not? Churlish and overbearing."

The tender smile she gave him muddled his insides. "You have done very well, Dillon. I would not have healed so quickly had someone else tended me. I thank you for your kindness."

Needing to touch her, even fleetingly, he again pretended to check for the return of her fever. Her forehead was cool beneath his hand, her hair like silk where he smoothed it back.

Her eyes softened.

"Rest," he repeated quietly.

She nodded.

He had to force himself to walk away, unwilling to leave her presence.

"Dillon." Her voice stopped him as he reached the door.

He looked back. "Aye?"

Deep brown eyes rose to meet sapphire. "'Tis Alyssa."

He tilted his head. "What is?"

"My name."

CHAPTER SEVEN

Lord Camden drew back his leg and slammed his boot into the side of the boy curled into a ball on the floor of the kitchen. Then kicked him again. And again. And again. In the ribs. The stomach. The back. Whatever body part happened to roll in front of his foot. His fury rising with every blow.

The little bastard had been caught filching food for his family.

Every crumb in Pinehurst's measly stores would be needed until Westcott's men were called away to mourn the death of their lord and cease this cursed siege. Camden would be damned if even one of those crumbs went into the mouth of a thieving whelp like the one moaning and weeping on the floor.

One of the women present whimpered.

"Silence," Camden roared, spittle flying from his lower lip. "Or you will be next." By the time he finished with this piece of filth, no other would even *think* of stealing from his larder.

"My lord," a gruff voice said just as Camden prepared to kick the boy in the head.

"What?" he barked mid-kick and looked over his shoulder.

Osbert, one of the men who guarded the walls stood just inside the doorway. "Sir Simon is demanding to speak to you."

Sir Simon, the burly knight from Westcott who had believed he could pass for Lord Dillon. Foolish knave. Even had Camden's spy not revealed the ruse in a missive, Camden was certain he would have swiftly guessed the truth. *None* were more clever than he.

"Have an archer fell him."

"He says he has received word from Westcott. He says you will wish to hear it."

Camden stilled. Tilting his head to one side, he ignored the groans of the boy at his feet and considered the soldier thoughtfully.

Had the ambush already taken place? Had Lord Dillon been slain?

Grim satisfaction suffused him, twisting his lips in a smile that made the other occupants of the kitchen take fearful steps backward. At last, the cursed whoreson was dead. How Camden wished he had been the one who had wielded the crossbow.

No more would Camden have to hear the praise heaped upon Lord Dillon's head. No more would he have to endure seeing the admiration that filled his father's eyes each time he spoke of Dillon turn to disappointment when he regarded his own son.

Delivering a final kick to the moaning boy, Camden spun around and preceded the soldier out of the kitchens. Across the bailey they strode. And, with every step, anticipation thrummed through Camden and swelled his chest.

The siege that had barely begun would end now. Sir Simon and the rest of Westcott's men would withdraw to mourn the loss of their lord. Lord Robert would be too buried by grief to begin the siege anew.

Camden would send missives to the king, alerting him to the tragic loss of his friend. The kind missive would, of course, include a fabricated account of Camden valiantly having hunted down and slain the thieves who were responsible. The same thieves, he would add, who had attacked Lord Robert *and* stolen the coin Lord Camden had sent to pay the delinquent taxes he owed. Alas, the coin had not been recovered.

The king, in his benevolent gratitude, Camden thought with an inward sneer, would reverse his decision to take Pinehurst from him. Mayhap King Richard would even grant him some of Lord Dillon's lands. He seemed to reward Lord Dillon for every minuscule act he performed. If Dillon so much as visited the garderobe, he was granted another keep, the bastard. So why would King Richard *not* give Camden a boon for avenging the death of his beloved friend?

Lord Dillon of Westcott would, at last, no longer be the most feared and revered warrior in England.

Nay. Camden would assume that position.

Upon reaching the gatehouse, he scaled the steps to the wall walk two at a time.

The men who manned it all bore grim expressions.

Ignoring them, Camden leaned into one of the crenellated openings in the wall, Osbert at his side.

Sir Simon stood in the meadow below, what appeared to be every man he had brought with him lined up behind him.

Had they not had their shields at the ready, Camden would have ordered his archers to fell them all.

"I am told you wish to speak with me," Camden called.

Even work on the trebuchets had halted, he noted with triumph.

Sir Simon removed his helm. "Aye. I've news to share with you."

"Speak it," Camden commanded.

A malicious smile lit Simon's face. "Your plot has failed," he shouted.

Unease trickled through Camden.

The men behind Simon did not mimic his smile. Nay, they

all bore murderous expressions.

"Plot?" Camden called back. "I know not—"

"The ambush you arranged did not gain you what you hoped it would," Simon interrupted. "Lord Dillon survived. Gavin has revealed your perfidy. And a missive has already been sent to the king, granting him the details of your attempt to murder his most trusted warrior."

Camden's blood went cold. Gavin had betrayed him? Dillon had survived the ambush?

"You should have at least had the bollocks to try to kill him yourself, you bloody coward," Simon mocked him.

A rumble of agreement swelled behind Simon.

Humiliation heated Camden's face. "Kill him," he whispered hoarsely, his hands beginning to tremble.

"What?" Osbert asked.

"Surrender the keep now," Simon ordered in a voice all of Pinehurst could hear, "and mayhap, when Lord Dillon arrives, he will let you live."

"Kill him!" Camden hissed furiously.

Osbert murmured something.

One of the archers behind Camden stepped into the next crenellated opening and raised his bow.

An arrow struck the archer in the chest with a *thwup*.

Camden watched him stagger backward and collapse. Heart racing, he returned his attention to Sir Simon.

"Did you fail to notice we have our own archers?" he drawled. "Sleep well tonight, cur, whilst you ponder the fate that awaits you."

Simon turned and strode away as though he had not a care. The other warriors closed ranks around him.

Lord Dillon had survived.

Camden's heart slammed against his ribs. And he cursed the fear that drove it.

Dillon had survived. The king knew of the murder plot. And Simon had named Camden a coward loud enough for everyone at Pinehurst to hear.

The corner of one eye began to twitch as fury battled fear.

They thought themselves so much better than he?

They were not fit to eat the shit that clung to the bottom of his boot.

All was not lost, he silently vowed.

Nay, all was not lost.

They could not defeat him. They could not outwit him.

Camden would punish Dillon, that bastard Simon, and every man they led who thought him a coward. Then he would claw his way up out of the mire.

There would be a reckoning.

Ah yes. He would see to it.

There would be a reckoning indeed.

* * *

Alyssa awoke, a slow, gradual return to consciousness. She did not think she had slept long after Dillon's exit. An hour, mayhap. The deep sleep, bereft of dreams, had gone far toward easing her body's weakness. That odd humming was almost a memory. Her limbs no longer prickled with pain. Neither heat nor cold bombarded her. She was quite comfortable actually.

And yet, something seemed amiss.

Frowning, Alyssa cautiously opened her eyes. The shutters had been closed whilst she had slept, leaving the chamber thick with shadows.

One such shadow detached itself from the rest and loomed over her.

Gasping, she lashed out with her fist, striking her assailant squarely in the nose. A slew of curses filled her ears as he stumbled backward, tripped over something, and went down. Alyssa scrambled out of bed and raced for the door.

"Wait!"

Skidding to a halt, she spun around.

The intruder abruptly shoved open the shudders, allowing

the golden light of a setting sun to flood the room and illuminate its occupants. "'Tis only me."

"Robert?"

"Aye." Straightening, he wiped the blood from beneath his nose and dropped his hand. "Forgive me. I did not mean to frighten you." He took a halting step toward her. "Dillon will run me through if he learns I woke you. Please, do not tell him."

She would have been amused if Robert were not staring at her with an awkward combination of hesitance, apology, and fascination.

Heat crept up her neck when his gaze assessed her in a disturbingly masculine way.

Where was her robe? She felt *naked* standing before him without it. Dillon's tunic hung off one shoulder and covered her to just below her knees, leaving her calves, feet, and— worse yet—her face bare.

Dismay swamping her, Alyssa ducked behind one of the bed curtains.

"Robert!" a voice bellowed behind her.

Alyssa jumped and spun around in time to see Dillon slam the door shut.

"I specifically ordered you not to disturb her!"

"Dillon." She did not realize she said his name. Nor did she hear the relief and pleasure her voice carried to his ears.

His attention shifted to her. Both his expression and tone sweetened. "You should be abed. You are not yet recovered."

Surely that explained why her knees suddenly went weak.

"I made a vow, Dillon," Robert began.

"I come here and find her cowering behind the bed curtains whilst you leer at her and slaver over her soft white skin and you prattle on about a *vow?*"

Alyssa started to protest his description of her—she was *not* cowering—but the *soft white skin* part distracted her.

All thoughts fled entirely then as Dillon closed the distance between them and lifted her into his arms. Cradling her to him, he tenderly pressed his cheek to her forehead. Her heartbeat stuttered. Her flesh tingled where his whiskers abraded it.

"No fever," he murmured, raising his head and giving her a proud smile as though she had some control over her body's temperature.

"I was not leering at her," Robert gritted. "If you would but listen—"

"I grow tired of listening."

"Then allow me to do my duty! I am a man of honor, Dillon. I have never been forsworn and will not be so now. I made a vow and 'tis time I…"

The brothers continued to bicker as Dillon lowered her to the bed and tucked her beneath the covers. Alyssa knew not what kind of vow Robert had made, but she could feel the irritation it inspired in Dillon.

As soon as a lull arose, she cleared her throat and asked Robert, "Of what vow do you speak?"

Lips tightening, Dillon crossed his arms over his massive chest and glared at his brother.

Broad shoulders back, one hand resting casually on the hilt of his sword, Robert said, "I vowed that if healing Dillon weakened you, I would be your servant until you recovered. Whatever you ask that is within my powers to grant, I shall grant you." Gallantly dropping to one knee beside the bed, he finished earnestly, "I am yours to command, Wise One."

Her mouth fell open. She looked to Dillon for his reaction.

Dillon's arms fell to his sides as he snapped, "Oh, get up, you horse's arse!"

She looked back at Robert, who did not budge. "Aye. Please rise, Robert." Her eyes widened. "My lord. Please rise, my lord," she corrected, shocked that she had forgotten his proper address.

Robert shook his head as he rose to stand beside the bed. "We are alone here. There is no need for formality, particularly when I owe you so much."

"You owe me naught. I release you from your vow."

"Nay. The vow was made to myself, Seer. I have sorely wronged you in the past and regret the unkindnesses I have dealt you. I allowed myself to be swayed by the words of others instead of judging you on your own merit."

Alyssa stared. "But—"

"I will not be swayed, Healer. I am your servant. Command me as you will." He sniffed and swiped at his nose again.

She blinked. "Very well. Come closer."

Dillon scowled and eyed them suspiciously as Robert drew nigh.

"Kneel down as you did before."

He did so, curiosity replacing the unease she usually saw in his eyes.

"Now, lean forward." She reached a hand toward him. "Your nose still bleeds. I would heal it for you."

"Nay!" The brothers spoke simultaneously.

Robert reared back as Dillon dove forward and grabbed her wrist, stopping her.

Confused, Alyssa studied them. "Why?"

Robert looked to his brother.

Avoiding her eyes, Dillon lowered her hand to her lap and gave it a pat as he withdrew his own.

Her eyes narrowed. "You think I am too weak?"

"Aye," Dillon said.

"Aye," Robert parroted.

"I am not so weak as that," she protested indignantly.

"'Twas only today that you awakened fully," Dillon informed her. "I shall not risk your falling into another decline."

An indecipherable look passed between the brothers, leading her to suspect that something more was at work here.

Robert cleared his throat. "Mayhap some broth might appeal to you, Wise One. I would be happy to fetch you some from the kitchen."

Alyssa's gaze went from one to the other.

"Make it something a little more substantial, Robert," Dillon instructed. "'Twill help her recover more swiftly."

Nodding, Robert bowed to Alyssa, then left. She stared at the closed door, wondering silently if she had not transferred her fever to Robert.

Dillon laughed, drawing her gaze.

"What amuses you?"

Seating himself on the bed, he leaned to one side and rested an elbow beside her thigh. "If you could but see your expression."

She sent him a wry smile. "'Tis the truth I feel as if I have awakened into an odd dream."

He winked. "More like a nightmare? Robert is quite determined to serve you and make amends. He will not be dissuaded."

"But he is not at fault," she repeated. "He did not force me to heal you."

"I have told him so a number of times. I suspect more of his guilt lies elsewhere. He is thankful and amazed that you went to such lengths to save my sorry hide. It has made him regret being less than kind to you in the past."

She shook her head. "'Tis bewildering."

His eyebrows rose. "Is the change in him so difficult to accept?"

She let her gaze rove his muscled body, lounging so casually and comfortably nigh her own. "'Tis not only the change in Sir Robert that confuses me."

Dillon's expression sobered. His cerulean eyes turned watchful. "Am *I* different with you, Alyssa?"

The sound of her name falling so smoothly from his lips after so many years should not inspire this depth of pleasure. Swallowing nervously, she wished now that she had held her tongue. "You know that you are."

"In what way?" His gaze swept her hidden form. His voice

deepened, turned husky. "Tell me."

Alyssa's heart hammered beneath her breast. What was he doing to her? With just a look… such a look… he peeled away her exterior and threatened to expose all of her hidden desires.

"In this way," she managed to say, heart pounding. "The way you look at me." *As though you are a starving wolfhound and I a choice bit of venison that has fallen at your feet.*

"I thought you gray-haired and wrinkled beneath your robes. Yet, here you are, younger than myself by several summers unless I miss my guess. To discover such exquisite beauty… 'Tis not surprising that I look at you differently." Still reclining on one elbow, he leaned forward and, with his free hand, brushed his fingers across her forehead, traced the arch of one brow and trailed down her temple to her cheek.

Images stirred in her mind. Erotic images that stole her breath and began a flash fire in her body.

Dillon drawing back the blankets, baring her body to his heated gaze.
Dillon's hands and mouth touching her in the most shocking places.
His clothing miraculously vanishing as he lowered his body to hers.

Sucking in a breath, she drew away.

Hurt dimmed the sparkle in his eyes as he dropped his hand.

"That does not explain why you…" She bit her lip, afraid he would laugh if she finished her thought. What if it was all her imagination? Could it not be that the earthly desires that frequently flooded her at his touch were her own, rather than his?

"Continue," he urged her.

"You do not treat me as formally as you used to." She danced around the issue, of course. Without her robes to hide her expression, she found herself battling a new shyness and uncertainty when nigh him.

Flattening his hand on the bed, he splayed his fingers and frowned down at it. "You would prefer formality? Distance?"

She opened her mouth, ready to say *aye*, that aught would

be better than this confusion he inspired.

Unfortunately, to do so would be to lie outright and—with the exception of neglecting to correct his assumptions regarding her age—she had always dealt honestly with him.

"Nay," she admitted softly.

"Then what troubles you about my recent behavior toward you, Alyssa?"

She closed her eyes and repressed a shudder of pleasure. What troubled her about it? That she craved more and more and more of it and feared she would soon become a glutton.

Lifting her lashes, she stared at his bent head. "I simply do not understand why you are treating me with such… tenderness."

His eyes rose and captured hers. "Because you are letting me."

You seek a woman who will be as gentle with you as you wish to be with her.

Was this what he had meant, what he had longed for? Someone with whom he could share his warmth? Someone who would welcome his caresses, his fingers combing through her hair, as she had several times since waking?

Alyssa thought of the women who had occasionally satisfied his physical needs during their long acquaintance.

How hard it had been for her, watching him disappear with this wench or that.

She had known the name of every one of them. Brazen women all. Enticing him to their beds. Touching him boldly for all to see. Pushing him until he dragged them wide-eyed from the great hall to the nearest place of privacy. Never to his chamber.

What fools. They had gone to him seeking domination when what he had wanted most was tenderness. Both to give and to receive it.

She had envied them the intimacy they had shared with him, yet now understood that beyond the act itself, there had been no such intimacy.

Was she the first woman to whom he had shown this side of himself? The first woman who had *allowed* him to?

If so, what did it mean?

To him? To her? For the future?

She was his advisor. His sorceress. His servant.

He was her lord.

That could never change.

"I know not how to react, Dillon. I know not how I *should* react."

He smiled. "Do not tax yourself so. How oft have you lectured me on the necessity of change, of accepting it and learning what one can from it?"

She grimaced. "Aye, but that change has never affected *me* before."

He chuckled. "Mayhap 'tis time that fate *did* bring a few changes into your dull, dreary life. Nay, do not wrinkle your lovely brow. I but jest."

Those wrinkles he mentioned deepened as heat crept into her cheeks. She simply did not know how to deal with him when he acted this way. Less the fierce, commanding warrior she was accustomed to and more the buoyant young swain who was completely unfamiliar and far too appealing.

He leaned closer, eyes glittering. "Ahh. She blushes at compliments. And so very prettily."

The heat in her face increased.

"I shall have to compliment you often in order to make up for all the times your cowl hid your rosy cheeks from me in the past," he murmured playfully.

Alyssa grabbed a pillow, the only weapon available to her, and hit him squarely in his smile.

Dillon laughed in delight.

Alyssa pursed her lips, fighting a smile of her own. "I begin to think that when you were struck by those quarrels you must have fallen and hit your astoundingly hard head. You are behaving most strangely, Dillon."

Tucking the pillow beneath his arm, he ran a hand through his mussed hair. "Well, you had better accustom yourself to it," he warned with a wicked grin. "Now that I know we are of a similar age—"

Robert entered, cutting off whatever Dillon intended to say. Kicking the door shut, he circled the bed and placed a large cloth-covered tray in Alyssa's lap. "Your dinner, Wise One."

She smiled up at him. "Thank you, Robert." When he removed the cloth with a flourish, her eyes widened. A virtual feast lay before her, with numerous mouthwatering selections and… a small bouquet of wildflowers tied with a pink ribbon.

Thunder rolled across Dillon's features even as Alyssa glanced up to gauge his response. "You are not courting her, Cub! You are only supposed to *serve* her."

Robert's face tightened. "Of course I am not courting her. I merely thought to please her after all she has done for us."

"And what do you suppose Cook thought when he saw you add posies to the platter you no doubt claimed you were preparing for your brother?"

"Cook never saw them," Robert retorted. "I hid them under my tunic until I was sure no one was about." His smile was charmingly rueful as he looked at her. "I fear they are a bit bedraggled."

"It matters not, Robert," she assured him. "'Twas very thoughtful of you."

He tossed Dillon a triumphant smile.

Alyssa spoke up quickly to head off the impending explosion. "I assume by the bounty before me that the two of you will be sharing my meal."

"Robert will dine below with the men," Dillon stated when Robert opened his mouth to reply.

For a moment, she thought Robert would protest just to provoke him. But, in the end, he merely shrugged. "Is there aught more I may do for you, Wise One?"

She shook her head, moved by his desire to please her. "I thank you, Robert, but nay."

"As you wish." He offered her a chivalrous bow, then strolled from the room.

* * *

Scowling, Dillon watched his brother leave. *Curse his hide.* Robert *always* knew the right thing to do when it came to women. The right thing to say. Exactly how to brighten a pretty face.

Flowers.

As much as his people distrusted her, Alyssa had probably never been gifted with flowers in her life. And Dillon could have been the first to do so had he thought of it.

He could have been the one to receive her sweet smile of thanks.

Instead, Robert had.

Sitting up, he swiveled on the bed to face her and crossed his legs.

"Pay him no mind, Dillon," she advised with a sweet smile. "'Tis only as you say. He wishes to make amends. As soon as I return to my duties, his vow will have been fulfilled and he will move on to more interesting endeavors, leaving us to enjoy our ordinary world."

Relief suffused him. "You are right, of course." He reached for a piece of bread, relaxing as his jealousy subsided. Though jealousy was new to him, he began to understand why it repeatedly drove men to make idiots of themselves. "I should not complain. His wariness around you has always troubled me."

She nodded. "As it has me. I have hoped over the years that—as close as the two of you are—your trust and acceptance of me would in time find its way past his superstitions." She took the tasty bit of venison he offered with a smile, then chewed thoughtfully.

Dillon's food went untouched for long moments as he watched her lips, entranced. She reached for the wine. His gaze fell to the graceful lines of her throat as she sipped, noting the gentle motions as she swallowed. A hint of liquid sparkled upon her lips when she finished, and he waited impatiently for her to sweep it away with her tongue.

Ah, yes. He had had no idea a man could derive such pleasure simply from watching a woman eat, watching her drink. The movements of her hands. Her lips. Her tongue.

A new hunger rose within him, superseding the other.

"You should eat, Dillon. 'Twill help you regain the remainder of your strength. Though you appear fit, I am sure you tire more quickly than does please you."

She truly is *an innocent*, he thought when she tendered him a piece of roasted venison with her fingers.

Dillon leaned forward and opened his mouth, allowing her to carefully place her offering inside. Before she could withdraw completely, he closed his lips, trapping one of her fingers within. He heard her breath catch and drew his tongue leisurely across her skin in a brief caress, circling and stroking. Her eyes focused on his lips as the pulse at the base of her neck began to pound erratically.

So. She was as affected as he.

Pleased with his discovery, he gave her fingertip a little nip and released it.

Her dazed eyes met his, blinked, then flickered away as she ducked her head and nervously stuffed a piece of bread in her mouth. The finger he had teased, she curled into a loose fist and tucked against her chest.

"Am I mistaken in believing that you did not serve my father?" he asked as though naught unusual had passed between them.

She cleared her throat and avoided his gaze, color still ripe in her cheeks. "Nay, my lord. I have served no other but you."

He paused. Had she reverted to formality apurpose to

remind him of their mutual positions or inadvertently because he had unsettled her? "And you have been with me since my father's passing?"

"Almost," she answered, her voice barely audible. "I began serving you the night I helped you take Brimshire."

"You alone?" He wondered how she could have advised him so wisely at such an early age.

"Aye."

"What age had you attained when you came into my service?"

"I was ten and six, my lord." She glanced at him from the corner of her eye and, finding him watching her, occupied herself with taking a sip of wine.

Dillon began to regret making her so uncomfortable. It had not been his intention. Instinct had driven him. Instinct and a desire to learn whether the attraction he felt sparking between them was mutual or one-sided.

Unfortunately, having never pursued an innocent, he lacked Robert's smoother skills.

"You should eat, Alyssa," he murmured, mimicking her earlier words to him. "'Twill help you regain the remainder of your strength."

Her lips lifted in a wry smile. "You have acquired the most irritating habit of late of tossing my words back at me like a discarded bone."

He grinned as she took another bite. "Should good advice not be shared?"

She opened her mouth to offer what he suspected would be a traditionally dry reply, then rolled her eyes and went back to eating.

He fought a laugh. "I have one more question for you, then I shall leave the rest for the morrow and let you concentrate on your meal." She seemed to relax and even managed to keep from blushing when she sent him an inquiring look.

Sobering, he asked the question that had been poised on

the tip of his tongue ever since he had removed her cowl. "Why have you hidden yourself from me these many years?"

Swallowing, she dabbed her lips with her napkin. "The previous wisewoman would not relinquish her position until I vowed to conceal my true age and appearance beneath the robes, allowing others to believe she and I were one and the same."

He nodded his acceptance of her explanation, but battled disappointment. The fact that she did not distinguish *him* from the others discouraged him. He had thought they had grown closer than that over the years.

"She left no room for exceptions, Dillon," she continued. "And I did ask. My adherence to the robes is not a reflection of any lack of trust in you. You were the one person I would have willingly shared my secret with had I been given a choice in the matter."

His spirit lightened. Curiosity rose.

He had been too quick to promise to pose no further questions.

She smiled. "I can see the wheels turning in that inquisitive mind of yours. But I intend to hold you to your promise and will answer no more questions this night."

He grinned. "Ah, Seer, you know me well."

A crash resounded from below, drawing a sigh from him. "My men appear to be celebrating my return to health and the resumption of my duties more exuberantly than 'tis wise, particularly when one considers that there was an enemy within our midst only a few days past. I'd best go down and see to them ere they destroy the trestle tables and drink themselves into oblivion."

Pushing himself to his feet, he strode over to the door, where he donned his most stern expression and pointed an authoritative finger at her. "You are to consume every crumb on that tray, Alyssa, ere I return. You have gone too long without sustenance and have desperate need of it."

She eyed the wealth of food before her doubtfully. "I shall try, Dillon."

He grinned at the sight of her sitting there, so small in his oversized bed, seeming almost a child. When she glanced back up, he winked, earning himself another treasured smile, then ducked out into the hallway.

He would not return until he was sure she slept. After resting beside her, always touching some part of her and drinking in her sweet presence, he was loath to give it up. 'Twas the first time in his life he had ever spent an entire night (three actually) in bed with a woman.

He found it addictive and could not imagine sleeping without her by his side. Yet he felt certain she would object should he return early, doff his clothing, and climb into bed with her.

Nay. He would wait until sleep claimed her, slip beneath the covers, hold her close through the darkest hours, then leave before dawn broke. That way he would be content.

And she would remain none the wiser.

CHAPTER EIGHT

*A*lyssa squinted up at the sun above her. Reigning over the sky, it glared back, so bright that no clouds dared challenge it. Heat pressed down upon her like heavy hands on her shoulders. The ground beneath her feet would burn them as swiftly as hot coals were she to remove her boots and walk upon it in her bare feet. Her clothing clung to her with suffocating determination, saturated with perspiration.

Dragging in a strained breath, she coughed when the wind peppered her with granules of sand. Fatigue pulled at her. Injuries she could not see pained her.

Where was she?

Chaos surrounded her, courted her. Everywhere Alyssa looked, harsh sunlight gleamed on weapons, shields, and armor stained crimson. Bodies moved in a grisly dance as hundreds of men sought to slay each other.

Sound abruptly filled the silence, as though she had been covering her ears and had lowered her hands. The clang of swords striking swords made her wince. Voices called out as men were cut down. Limbs severed. Bodies cleaved in twain. Her heart slammed against her ribs as warriors bumped into her, buffeted her. Her ears rang with screams of agony and fear. Cries for mercy.

A dark figure suddenly rose up before her, robes rippling in the arid *breeze, and eclipsed the sun. At the same moment, arms imprisoned her from behind, tightening like a vice and cutting off her air. As she watched in horror, the man in front of her—unidentifiable with the light behind him blinding her—released a great war cry, raised his mighty curved scimitar, and swung it in an arc that would end with her head being separated from her body.*

Alyssa screamed and struggled to free herself. Bucking and rearing, kicking and clawing at the arms wrapped around her, she whimpered and fought for air as panic engulfed her.

"Wha… Alyssa?"

She stilled, heart pounding, breath coming in harsh gasps. Her eyes flew open. The thick, sinewy arms that had been clutching her jerked with surprise, then abruptly released her.

The vision vanished. The cries ceased. The fear receded.

Yet, the metallic scent of blood seemed to linger in the air. *Dillon.*

She lay in bed with Dillon. Or rather he lay in bed with her. He must have come to bed after she had fallen asleep and…

Well, she had not devoted any thought as to where he had been sleeping during her illness. Or where he would do so tonight. But this *was* his chamber, his bed. He must have turned to her in his sleep, unaware of his actions, and curled his body around hers. Then his dream had become her own.

"Alyssa? Are you all right?" His voice wavered slightly. Mayhap he still fought the grip of his nightmare.

"Aye," she responded shakily, rolling onto her back so she could look at him.

"You cried out."

"'Twas a nightmare." She could barely isolate him from the night. "Only a nightmare."

His eyes glinted in the moonlight that weakly wrestled its way through the window and into the room. He lay on his side, his face nigh hers on the pillow. As she watched, he crossed his arms over his broad chest and tucked his hands beneath them as though he could not trust them to do his bidding. "I was likewise troubled by sinister dreams."

Alyssa's heart began to slow its frantic pace. Her muscles relaxed, one by one. Brushing the hair from her eyes, she turned onto her side to face him. The move brought him even closer. So close his warmth reached toward her beneath the blankets and banished the chill fright had produced.

"I did not harm you, did I?" he asked tentatively. Mayhap he feared he had squeezed her too tightly in his sleep.

"Nay. You woke me at a most opportune moment, my lord. I should thank you."

He looked at her strangely, but 'twas too dark to read whatever might have been visible in his eyes.

"Was yours the same specter that visits you nightly?" she queried, remembering with a shudder the carnage that had surrounded her.

He sighed and reached up to rub his eyes. "'Tis not always the same dream, but… aye, 'twas of a similar nature."

Unbidden, tears threatened. No wonder he slept so poorly. If she knew such dreams awaited her each time she rested, Alyssa would *never* want to sleep. And, unlike all of the other wounds she had healed for him, she knew not how to remedy this.

"Of what did you dream?" he asked softly.

She could not bring herself to tell him. 'Twould distress him to learn that his dream had invaded hers and terrified her so.

Throat tight, she shook her head. "I do not wish to speak of it."

His large hand swam out of the shadows and cupped her cheek, testing it for tears. He frowned when he found them. "Shh. 'Tis all right," he murmured, pulling her toward him. "You need not. 'Twas but a dream, Alyssa. Let it trouble you no more."

She let him draw her head to his chest, press her body to his. He stroked her back with one hand, her hair with the other.

Long, leisurely brushes.

Slow, soothing circles.

Tranquility suffused her as she slipped her arms around his waist and mirrored his actions. He was so large and muscular, his back wide and strong. When he pressed a kiss to the top of her head and rested his cheek against her hair, she smiled and nuzzled his chest, the coarse hair there tickling her nose.

Alyssa knew not what spell had befallen her. Never had she felt this sense of peace, this sense of freedom. Not a breath of air separated them. Her full breasts pressed against his chest and rippling abdomen. Her hips rested against his. Their legs were loosely entwined.

'Twas, for all intents and purposes, a lovers' embrace. Yet, she felt no shame, no embarrassment. Only a rising tide of heat as her pulse quickened once more, this time with something other than fear. The muscles beneath her hands gradually went taut, his tension finding its way into her. She felt the one part of him she had always modestly avoided viewing (but had glimpsed the morn he had leapt out of bed naked) lengthen against her stomach in the most shocking way. Breathing became difficult. The large hand at her back now *incited* instead of soothed. But incited what? Such feelings were foreign to her, alternately exciting and frightening.

He shifted, one muscular thigh slipping between hers. His thoughts fought their way past whatever haze afflicted her.

Absently acting on them, she moved her right leg up a little higher. He moaned, a low rumble just short of a growl, and she was surprised by the pleasure she felt course through him. Sliding his hand across her hip, over her bottom, and down her thigh—leaving tingling fire in his wake—he hooked his fingers beneath her knee and drew it up until it rested over his hip.

She had not realized until then that he was bare.

Her calf met naught but heated flesh that flexed as he leaned into her, practically rolling her onto her back and generating an even greater heat within her. The only thing separating that most intimate part of her from the most intimate part of him was the thin linen shirt she wore, which had ridden up almost to her bottom.

He must have heard her gasp, for he stilled of a sudden, his hand motionless on her thigh. His fingers paused in the process of slipping beneath her shirt to caress smooth, bare skin. "Alyssa?"

Insecurity, desire, astonishment, guilt, need. She could not differentiate her emotions from his. Not whilst her body hummed and begged her to ignore her obligations, to be selfish and give in to the wondrous feelings Dillon nurtured within her.

Oh, how she wanted to lean into him, rub her body against his, and fan the flames higher.

"Alyssa…"

He intended to apologize. She could feel it, rising within him alongside embarrassment over what he considered his clumsiness with women. She frowned over that because she had never once seen evidence of such and had herself just experienced the opposite. Yet Dillon feared she would turn from him and think him crude for giving in to his base desires and touching her. Even now his body ached with need and she could feel how he fought the urge to move against her, carefully holding himself in check.

When he drew in a breath and opened his mouth, she slipped a hand up to cover it.

He hesitated, then pressed a kiss to her fingertips.

She closed her eyes, the knowledge that she could never have him for her own weighing her down. "Good night, Dillon," she whispered, disappointing him… and herself.

"Good night."

She felt him tense when she slid her leg down his. Her body protesting every move, she rolled away from him onto her other side. Cool air rushed in between them, contrasting sadly with the heady flush he had left on her skin.

Alyssa listened carefully, expecting him to turn away from her.

He did not. He remained exactly as she had left him, utterly still.

Was he as full of regrets as she?

Minutes passed.

Neither found solace in sleep.

"Dillon?" Silently, she cursed herself for her weakness.

"Aye?"

"I am cold."

A moment's hesitation followed. Then she heard the bedding rustle and felt his big warm body mold itself to her back. The tops of his thighs met the backs of hers. One of his thick arms came around her waist, holding her close, his hand just beneath her breast. The other slipped under her head to form a pillow.

Emitting a sigh of contentment, he burrowed his face into her hair and awaited her response.

Surely she could allow herself this much. "Thank you, Dillon."

Was that a kiss pressed lightly to her shoulder?

"Good night, Alyssa."

* * *

Dillon dragged his fingers through sweat-dampened hair and detained a passing servant long enough to request a drink.

"You seem to be in fine form again, brother," Robert said beside him. "I thought 'twould take you longer to regain your strength."

"Why?" Dillon surveyed the hall around them to ensure no one else listened. "My wounds were healed days ago. Had I not been otherwise occupied, I would have long since joined Simon in the battle for Pinehurst."

Giving him a wry smile, Robert shook his head. "You did not see the frightening amount of blood that spilled from your body. I did not know a man could lose so much and yet live."

Dillon recalled his and Ann Marie's fruitless attempts to stop the unceasing crimson rivulets that had escaped Alyssa's wounds. Wounds *he* had put there.

His lips tightened. His teeth ground together.

"No good will come of such thoughts."

He glanced at Robert with surprised censure. "Presume you to know my thoughts?"

Both men took the tankards a serving woman offered them, then waited until she was out of earshot.

"You blame yourself for the pain she suffered healing your injuries."

Dillon tossed his head back and drank deeply. The scars his wounds had left on her body may no longer be visible, but they had been indelibly carved into his memory. As had the more recent wounds that had nigh stolen her from him. "I blame myself with good reason. 'Twas my fault."

"You did not knowingly step into the path of those quarrels. Nor did you encourage her to heal you, knowing it might harm her in some way. If with anyone, the fault lies with me."

"Nay. We have already dismissed that." Dillon took a step or two away and stood watching the servants put the hall in order. Alyssa had always ensured that his home was clean and freshly scented, that colorful tapestries adorned the stone walls. 'Twas another of her tasks he had taken for granted. "In all of the years I have known her, I have never questioned her method of healing, never asked her the consequences."

"One often does not question what one has seen and been told since birth. Our father never asked after the health of his healer. She never exhibited any weakness. Since you thought them one and the same, 'twas natural for you to assume your own came to no harm when she exercised her gift."

"Ignorance is no excuse. It does not erase the pain she felt each time my wounds ripped open her flesh."

"Dillon…" Robert stopped, then nodded to the entrance, where a man stood, searching the room's few occupants. "Look you there. 'Tis no doubt a message from Simon."

Spotting his lord, the man hurried to Dillon's side and held out a missive. "My lord. A missive from Sir Simon."

Taking the roll of parchment, Dillon waved the man toward the kitchen. "Seek yourself refreshment."

"Aye, my lord."

Dillon heard fading footsteps as he scanned Simon's careless scrawl.

"What news?" Robert asked.

"They are tunneling under the walls and await my orders ere they break through and take the castle. Camden suspects naught because he expects them to use the trebuchets instead."

"A clever ploy, assembling the trebuchets within his sight to fool him into thinking he will know how and when the attack will come. I sent word to Simon of your injuries and of the failed ambush the day after you fell so he would not wonder at your delay."

"And he has apprised Camden of my good health." Dillon's lips twitched. "And called him a cowardly cur for not trying to kill me himself whilst he did so."

His brother laughed. "Would that I could have seen Camden's face. No doubt he soiled his armor when he heard you survived and will soon seek justice."

Dillon grunted, staring down at the parchment. Unexpected resentment bubbled up inside him. Yet another battle that would tear him from his home. Only this time the parting would be far more difficult.

He did not wish to leave Alyssa. He wanted to remain by her side, coaxing more fetching smiles from her lips, building upon the feelings that had caught them both unawares the previous night.

"I will go in your stead, should you desire me to do so," Robert offered softly.

Looking up, Dillon read understanding in the blue eyes that so closely resembled his own. "Nay. Inconvenient though it may be, 'tis my responsibility as the new liege lord of Pinehurst to take it myself. I must ensure the people will be loyal to me and demand their oaths of homage."

Robert nodded. "Then I shall remain here and watch over the wisewoman for you. No harm shall come to her in your absence, brother. I shall guard her with my life."

Dillon eyed him uneasily. For a man who shunned boredom and often clamored for battle, he was awfully eager to sit this one out. "You are not becoming overly fond of her, are you?"

"Of course not," Robert snapped. "Have you forgotten my vow to be her servant until she is recovered?"

"Nay, but—"

"She saved your life, Dillon. Think you I would repay her in such a way? By making her my next conquest?"

Dillon scowled, feeling like a fool. 'Twas time he conquered this jealousy once and for all before its talons became too deeply embedded to be extracted.

Grimacing, Robert admitted, "Besides, it may not seem so, but I have not lost all of my uneasiness around her yet. Her comely face can sometimes make me forget whilst in her presence. But her powers… what I witnessed and experienced when she healed you…" He shook his head. "I try not to think about it."

"My lord?"

He turned to see his steward approaching.

William had seen three-score years and had served the family honestly and competently for decades. Of average height, thin as a whip, with long white tufts of hair that formed a horseshoe around his bald crown, he was a sober man who had always seemed more at ease around Dillon and the sorceress than most.

"Aye, William?"

"Your bath will grow cold do you not take advantage of it soon."

"My bath?"

"Aye, my lord. The wisewoman saw to its preparation some time ago."

"Thank you, William. I had forgotten."

When the steward left, Dillon turned and found Robert regarding him with one raised eyebrow. "What?"

"You have not allowed her to resume her duties, have you?"

"Nay. I am sure 'twas Ann Marie's doing. The wisewoman is resting. She did not sleep well last night." He fell silent as a new worry pricked him.

He had not seen Alyssa since he had awoken with her in his arms nigh dawn. The fragrant tangles of her hair had been his blanket, as had the warm curves of her body. He had lain there, sprawled on his back, he knew not how long, savoring the wondrous feel of her arm resting upon his chest. Her hand curled around his neck in a loose embrace. Her breasts pressed against his side. Her peaceful face pillowed by his shoulder. Her thigh draped across his groin. Her tiny foot tucked between his calves.

He had not wanted to move, had wanted to linger, awaken her with kisses and teasing caresses. Yet, fearing her reaction, he had instead carefully extricated himself from her enticing clasp and slipped silently from the bed, then from the chamber.

Were he honest with himself, he would admit that he was a little anxious about speaking with her. For the first time in years, he was reluctant to approach her. Guilt gnawed at him, enhanced by ever-present desire.

Last night Alyssa had been vulnerable, plagued by the remnants of whatever illness the healing had spawned within her. She had been struggling to adjust to the fact that he and Robert now knew her secret. And what had he done to aid her? He had flirted shamelessly with her, acted like a jealous lover whenever Robert paid her a visit, frightened her into waking from what appeared to have been a ghastly nightmare, then attempted to make love to her ere she could regain her equilibrium, fully cognizant of her innocence.

And he had longed to do so again this morn.

"What is amiss?" Robert asked, interrupting Dillon's self-recriminations. "You look as though you just quaffed two goblets of that wine that went sour last spring."

How could he answer? *I am disgusted with myself for sinking so low as to attempt to seduce the woman I respect and admire above all others when she was at her most vulnerable?*

Robert had appointed himself her protector. He was the *last* person Dillon could confide in, or confess to, whichever the case may be.

"'Tis naught. I was merely considering the arrangements that must be made ere I depart."

"When do you leave?"

"On the morrow."

Robert nodded and clapped him on the back. "I shall see to it for you. Go and have your bath. You will no doubt be sore after the paces I put you through this morn."

Dillon cuffed his brother playfully. "'Tis too soon to gloat, Cub. You've yet to best me, even as *weak* and *frail* as I am after my injuries."

Robert had a few choice words to say about that. Dillon imagined Alyssa's cheeks would have turned quite pink if she had heard them. The fact that he could now view and treasure those lovely blushes brought a smile to his face as he climbed the stairs and approached the solar.

Very quietly, he opened the door, slipped inside, then closed it, hoping his bath would not disturb Alyssa if she rested. Or offend her modesty if she did not. Swiveling to face the room, he froze. His smile slowly slipped away as everything within him went still. Then his heart began to pound a hard, heavy beat. His stomach did a funny little turn. And all of the self-castigating thoughts that had beleaguered him below threw up their hands in defeat and fled.

Alyssa was indeed asleep… in the bath he had mistakenly believed was meant for him. Her head rested against the back rim of the tub, tilted the slightest bit toward the hearth in which a fire had been built to ensure she did not catch a chill. The flickering flames cast golden highlights across her dewy skin.

Desire carried Dillon's feet forward.

Sitting behind her on the floor, brushing Alyssa's hair and fanning it out to speed its drying, Ann Marie gasped when she noticed him. "My lord! I did not hear you enter. When I came in to see if I could aid the healer in some way, she requested a bath and I—"

"Leave us," he instructed, never taking his gaze from Alyssa.

He knew not what Ann Marie saw in his face, but it sent her fleeing across the room to retrieve a bundle from the bed, then out the door without donning Alyssa's dark robe.

Dillon stood beside the tub for many long moments, simply drinking in the sight of her.

Alyssa's hair had begun to dry and spilled down to the floor in rivulets of midnight satin that would soon draw up into waves and curls. The hollows that had formed under her eyes lay hidden beneath the thick lashes that brushed them. The full lips he had neglected to kiss whilst his hands had made their sojourn over her body the previous night parted just enough for him to glimpse the edges of her teeth. Soft lips. Pink and pouty. His mouth went dry as he pondered how they would taste, how easily they would mold to his own.

The slender arms she had wrapped around him last night now balanced on the rim of the tub. The graceful hands that had stroked his back dangled limply over the side. Her tempting breasts drew his gaze next, their hard pinks tips hovering just above the water's edge. The waist beneath was so small he was sure he could span it with his hands. Full hips bracketed the thatch of dark curls he had pressed his arousal against in his moment of weakness, then yielded to shapely legs he thought surprisingly long considering her diminutive height. Legs he wanted her to wrap around him in passion.

Staring at her, Dillon thought her more beautiful than any other woman he had ever laid eyes upon. The longer he stood there, the harder his body became, the shorter his breath grew, and the fewer scruples remained to battle his erotic impulses.

Leaning down, he drew fingers that shook across her shining temple and back to circle her ear. His palm cradled her cheek as her eyelids fluttered, then lifted.

"Dillon," she murmured, a sleepy welcome that touched him deeply. Smiling, she raised one hand to stroke his cheek. He heard the rasp of his beard stubble as she stroked him again, further heating his blood.

Her smile faltered. A tiny crease formed between her eyebrows as she tilted her head the other way. Again she stroked him. Her eyes widened. "Dillon!"

Jerking her hand back, she bolted upright, splashing water over the edge of the tub and saturating his feet, his legs, and the floor around him. He just managed to keep their heads from colliding.

As Alyssa glanced down at herself then around the room in unmistakable dismay, Dillon realized he had made another colossal blunder. The woman had spent seven years completely hidden beneath black robes. Naturally she would not be pleased to wake up and find a gawking male salivating over her naked body.

What should he do? How could he repair the situation?

Dillon started to straighten, already searching in vain both for a suitable apology and for a towel or robe to hand her.

Alyssa made a sound of protest, grabbed his tunic with both fists, and yanked him to her.

Caught off guard, he felt his balance waver and grabbed

156 | DIANNE DUVALL

for the tub's rim.

He missed.

His arms plunged into water. One foot went up. The other skidded in the puddle she had just produced. And the next thing he knew he was in the tub under water with his face smashed between her breasts.

A great deal of squirming and splashing took place next on both their parts. In the end, Dillon wound up in a position that made his head spin. His hands were braced on the bottom of the tub behind and to either side of her. His lower body was settled oh-so-wonderfully between her thighs, balanced on his knees with his feet in the air and his shins wedged against the foot of the tub.

Heat surged to his groin, which was flush against her center. What lust he had felt before trebled as he met her astonished gaze.

The chamber door abruptly opened.

"Dillon, how large a contingent did you—?" The words ended in a gasp.

Alyssa shrieked and threw her arms around Dillon's neck to keep him from rearing back and exposing her. He bit back a groan when her legs encircled him as well to lock him into position as her shield.

Gritting his teeth, he glared over his shoulder at his brother, impaling him with visual daggers.

Robert stared at them with wide eyes and gaping mouth.

"Well?" Dillon growled.

Face reddening, Robert snapped out of his shock and straightened. "I, uh… uh…" Blinking, he looked around the room with exaggerated surprise and blurted, "Why, this is not my chamber!" Spinning around, he exited and slammed the door behind him.

Nonplussed, Dillon looked down at Alyssa.

Now that their unwelcome audience had left them, she relaxed her hold and leaned back so she could meet his gaze.

His lips twitched.

Hers followed suit.

Both burst into merry laughter.

"Not his chamber?" Dillon choked.

"Mayhap Robert has had one too many shocks of late."

"I believe you are right."

Their laughter quieted. Awareness returned.

Silence descended upon them as they stared into each other's eyes.

"Why did you do that?" Dillon whispered finally, wondering how long it would take her to realize that her legs were still wound around him.

"Do what?" she responded, her voice equally hushed.

Supporting himself on one hand, Dillon raised the other and waggled his fingers to draw her attention to the water that dripped from them. "Invite me into your bath." He gave her a teasing grin to stave off the nervousness he could see creeping in.

"I did not wish you to look upon me," she admitted.

His eyes crinkled with suppressed laughter. "And you thought pulling me down atop you would prevent that?"

Tears unexpectedly filled her eyes, contradicting the smile she forced and erasing his own. "You were the only covering available to me."

Dillon stroked her cheek, sensing that more than simple modesty troubled her. "Why did you not want me to look upon you?"

She shook her head mutely.

"Is it your promise to the other wisewoman? Your vow not to voluntarily show yourself to others?"

"Nay." A sparkling teardrop overflowed her lashes and bathed his thumb.

"What then?"

"I did not wish to disgust you."

'Twas not at all what he had expected. "Disgust me?" he

repeated, disbelieving.

"I am scarred." Her brow furrowed. "Or I *was*. When I woke to find you standing over me, I forgot the scars had healed and…" She swallowed hard. "I did not want you to see them."

"Alyssa, those scars were mine. You acquired them healing me." When she parted her lips to speak, he touched a finger to them. "If those scars had remained where they belonged—on *my* body—would they have disgusted *you?*"

"Nay, but you are a warrior."

"As are you. You have ridden into battle by my side more than once. And…" He shook his head. "Do you not know how beautiful you are to me? So lovely your image lingers always in my mind when we are apart, distracting me from whatever task I am attempting to perform and leaving me utterly useless to those around me. 'Twould be no different were you still scarred."

Another tear fell. "You must not say such things when they are not true."

"But they *are* true," he insisted. "You are touching me." He brought one of her hands to his cheek and held it there. "Can you not *see* the truth in my words? Can you not feel it?"

She stared at him, unspeaking.

"Alyssa?"

"I cannot think clearly when you touch me," she whispered.

His heart skipped a beat. He could feel hers pounding wildly against his chest. "You must forgive me."

"For what?"

His head dipped. "For this."

* * *

Dillon's lips brushed hers in a first tentative kiss that was wild in its restraint. Devastating in its tenderness.

Alyssa suddenly found it hard to breathe. Her pulse raced. Her skin tingled. Every muscle tightened. And the things she heard… the things she saw…

Dillon's jumbled, passion-driven thoughts. The erotic images they spawned.

Her whole body heated and began to ache with the same need that consumed him.

He drew back slightly, his blue eyes dark, breath short. He bore such a look on his face, one that reflected all of the hungry chaos that devoured him inside. Awe coupled with need softened by affection she would not allow herself to believe might be love. A look that told her no other woman could stir him this way. No one else could make him forget himself so completely.

She whispered his name. "Dillon."

His eyes closed as something like rapture blanketed his features. "I love it when you say my name."

He was so beautiful. Her gaze fell to the lips that had only seconds earlier claimed her own. Warm and full and inviting. She knew she had to taste them again.

"Dillon."

His eyes opened, met hers, read the desire there, and blazed with heat. Through her gifts, Alyssa felt his control fray, then snap. Scalding hunger that obliterated all reason flooded her, as though a dam had burst. Groaning, he leaned into her and lowered his lips to devour hers. When she parted them on a gasp, his tongue delved within to engage hers in a seductive dance.

One muscular arm clamped around her waist and pulled her to him. Driven by need—both her own and his—she slipped her arms up around his neck once more, hugging him close, flattening her aching breasts against his chest. She tightened the legs she had wrapped about his waist, locking them at the ankles, forcing him ever closer in an attempt to assuage the heat building at her core.

Dillon growled his approval and left the haven of her lips to trail a scorching path down her neck. Abandoning the support of the base of the tub, he grasped the back of her head with his other hand and surged upward. Moving their entwined bodies forward, he lowered his legs into the water, sat back on his heels, and settled Alyssa astride his thighs with her womanhood flush against his arousal.

Never had she experienced such intense need, such desperate longing. Virginal fear crumpled before it as Dillon's mind and heart guided her hands. Clumsy, shaking, she divested him of his sodden tunic and threw it aside. The linen shirt he wore beneath met a similar fate. Heated flesh met hers as he pressed her against his naked chest, hard and yielding at the same time.

"Alyssa," he groaned, one hand going to her hips and urging her to rock against him. "Can you see it now?" he asked between heated kisses that followed the line of her neck to her shoulder. He glanced it with his teeth, then continued on to her collarbone and lower still. "Can you *feel* it now? How beautiful you are to me? How desirable? How all-consuming and impossible for me to resist? Your skin." He laved the skin between her breasts with his tongue. *Like that of a pearl. Glowing. Opalescent. How did you hide it from me? I should have seen it shining forth from beneath your black robes like the moon defying the cover of clouds.*

"Your breasts." He claimed one pebbled peak with his lips, his tongue, his teeth. The other he fitted to his rough palm, setting off a roaring fire she knew only he could extinguish. *They were made for my hands. Only mine. So soft and round and perfect.*

"Your waist." *I can more than span it with my hands. Such delicacy compared to my strength and bulk makes my head spin.*

"Your hips." The hand at her breast slipped around to splay across her back, always roaming, as if he could not get enough of touching her. The other remained at her hip, sliding around to her bottom as he ground himself against her. *I tremble with the need to be inside you. To feel you all around me, warm and welcoming, as frantic for me as I am for you.*

"Your legs." *In a thousand years I would never have dreamed they would be where they are now, locked around me, urging me against you.*

"And your face." Bestowing one last kiss upon each breast, he leaned back a few inches and stared, almost mesmerized, into her eyes. "Your lovely face." He removed his hand from her back and drew fingers that quaked over her forehead to brush back her thick locks, wet once more from their splashing. *I lack the words necessary to describe its beauty and know only that in hiding it from me, you were robbing me of my greatest treasure.*

Moisture blurred Alyssa's vision. Tunneling her hands through his hair, she pulled him to her and kissed him with all of the love and desire and yearning he inspired. If only he knew how deeply his words, his thoughts, his touch affected her, he would have no reason to envy Robert his way with women.

The kiss broke. Dillon's heart thundered in his chest where it pressed to hers. His eyes sparkled with need, with hope. "Alyssa."

She heard what he dared not speak aloud: *Let me make love to you. Let me make you mine.* "Aye," she whispered, shocking them both.

He seemed to stop breathing. "I have not asked…"

She stroked his cheek. "You need not, Dillon."

Air left his lungs in a rush. Burying his face in her neck, he squeezed her against him. *I do not deserve this.*

Clenching her eyes shut, she pressed a kiss above his ear. "You deserve better."

He froze for a moment, then relaxed and kissed her throat. "There *are* none better." Anchoring one arm around her back and one under her hips, he whispered, "Hold tightly to me."

Nodding, she curled her arms around his neck and held on as he rose to his feet, graceful despite being encumbered by her weight. The delicious friction of their bodies rubbing against each other kept her warm as he stepped out of the tub with care and onto the driest section of floor available. A few strides later, he lowered her to the bed.

She smiled when he retrieved a towel and took the time to squeeze the excess water from her hair before he drew the cloth gently down over her body. First the front. Then the back.

"I do not wish you to catch a chill," he explained.

"With you as my blanket, I shall not," she murmured, wondering at her own brazenness. She grinned when his hands flew into action, shucking his boots and his soggy hose and braies in seconds.

Once naked, he stood beside the bed for a moment to let her drink her fill of him. Blushing furiously, she let her gaze dip below his waist… and swallowed. She had seen the uncovered loins of a few men in her years as a healer. But those had all been aged, infirm men who were far from being aroused.

"You are very large, Dillon."

He smiled and lay down beside her, cradling her close as he had after their shared nightmare. "Are you frightened?" He pressed his lips to the top of her head.

Again, any maidenly fear she might have felt was eclipsed by their combined hunger. "Only a little."

Dillon cupped her face in one palm and forced her to look up at him. "Should you wish me to stop at any time, you need only speak the words and I shall do so without complaint. I wish to do naught that does not bring you pleasure, Alyssa," he told her, face and voice earnest.

As love for him swelled within her, she turned her head slightly and kissed his palm. "Judging by the minutes we just passed together in yon tub, you know very well what brings me pleasure."

A faint smile lit his features as he surrendered at last. Claiming her lips with his own, he rolled her to her back and began a fervent exploration of her body with his hands and mouth. Her lips, her breasts, her navel, and lower.

She writhed helplessly, tangled in the web of desire he wove as Dillon made several of the scandalous fantasies she had seen in his thoughts become reality. Though he touched her and kissed her in ways and places that shocked her, Alyssa uttered not a word of complaint, moaning his name instead and arching into him. And, when he settled himself between her thighs and she felt his body begging entrance, she felt no fear.

"I do not wish to hurt you," he groaned, his muscles trembling with restraint.

She kissed his earlobe. "Then do not stop."

There *was* pain despite the care he took in breaching her maidenhead, but 'twas soon forgotten, buried beneath the wonder she felt at their bodies being joined so intimately.

After giving her a moment to adjust to his intrusion, Dillon began to move, thrusting and withdrawing, his muscles bunching. Sparks of desire struck her with increasing intensity. She arched up against him, needing more, needing to be closer and closer still. He slid a hand to her hip, guiding her, teaching her the motions, feeding the fire that consumed her and urging her toward something she did not recognize.

He recognized it. He *wanted* it. Craved it. She could feel it. But he would deny himself until she found it.

His movements quickened, as did her breath.

"Dillon," she moaned, holding him tighter, reaching for it, straining for it…

His hand left her hip, and she felt his fingers slide over to the dark curls that shielded her core. Lightning danced through her as he stroked and teased with the same rhythm of his body moving inside her.

Ecstasy swept through her in wave after wave, tightening her muscles and drawing his name from her lips a final time.

Groaning, he stiffened above her, his head flung back, and the pleasure began anew as his ecstasy became hers.

He collapsed upon her, the bulk of his weight balanced on his forearms.

Panting, replete, they held each other as their breathing

slowed. Their pulses grew more even. Their muscles relaxed. Still joined, Dillon rolled them to their sides and—hooking a hand behind her knee—drew her leg up to rest atop his hip as he had the previous night.

Content, Alyssa snuggled her head to his chest and let her lashes drift shut.

Tranquility embraced them.

Far more attuned to his thoughts and emotions, she could feel that—for the first time in years—Dillon was at peace. He was happy.

But she knew 'twould not last.

"You leave for Pinehurst on the morrow," she whispered.

He sighed. "Aye."

"You will not allow me to accompany you."

"I cannot." He stroked her hair, kissed her forehead. "Please do not argue with me, Alyssa."

She *would* have argued had she not been privy to his thoughts. Her own safety was not all that would be at risk if she followed him. Dillon, too, would be in danger, his mind on her instead of his enemy. Such was the power of their attraction, their newfound passion.

"I fear for you," she admitted. The last time he had left her behind she had nigh lost him.

"Do not. All will be well."

But the fear would not leave her. Seeking comfort, she wrapped an arm around him and pulled herself closer to him. He stiffened, and she felt him move inside her.

All fear fled, replaced by the first tinglings of returning desire.

Curious, she flexed the muscles in the leg draped over him, pressing her hips flush against his, pulling him in deeper. Her pulse leapt as hunger streaked through her. She heard Dillon hiss in a short breath, felt his fingers clench in her hair.

"Alyssa," he uttered gruffly. Though clearly ready to make love again, he was determined to restrain himself. For *her* sake, she discerned.

"Aye?" she asked, all innocence, and drew back a bit. He sighed with relief… until she pulled him to her again.

Groaning, he dropped a hand to her hip to still her enticing movements. "You must not. 'Tis too soon."

"Is it?"

"Aye."

"Oh." Ignoring him, she continued to move her hips, remembering the rhythm he had taught her. Forward and backward. Together, apart. Appetite rising. "Are you quite certain?" she persisted, quelling the urge to let her hands explore him.

"Aye," he groaned. He did not even realize that his hand at her hip had slid around to cup her bottom and now urged her on. "Mmm. Aye."

She bit back a grin. "Well, you do know more about this sort of thing than I do."

"More," he muttered. "Much more."

Breath quickening, she managed to say, "Then I bow to your greater knowledge. If you need more time to recover, I shall simply have to restrain myself."

"Aye." He stilled. Leaning back, he stared down at her through glazed, suspicious eyes. "What?"

She tried, but could not keep her lips from twitching.

He barked out a laugh and hugged her. "Precious imp. See what you have done to me? My lips say one thing whilst my body shouts another."

"'Tis not me," she insisted with a grin.

"Not you, eh? Just your luscious, utterly distracting form!" His hands found her ribs and tickled giggles from her as he rolled her about the bed.

When at last she was able to catch her breath again, he lay atop her.

His face lit with a warm smile as he combed her damp, tangled hair back from her face with gentle fingers. "How you tempt me."

The truth of his statement was very evident in the body pressed to hers.

"The reverse is also true."

"I fear 'twill hurt you." *Surely she is sore.*

"Listen to your healer," she advised him with a wink. "There is no reason for you to halt your amorous pursuits."

"Well then." He grinned and waggled his eyebrows. "I would never presume to ignore the advice of such a wise wisewoman."

Alyssa welcomed his kiss as his hands slipped down to her breasts. In all of the times she had allowed herself to consider the act of lovemaking, she had never dreamed that it could be accompanied by the laughter and teasing in which they continued to engage. Softer, slower, their second joining may have lacked the desperate urgency of the first, but 'twas no less intimate or moving.

Afterward, both exhausted, they slept.

Curled together.

Complete.

CHAPTER NINE

Dillon came awake slowly. Eyes still closed, he smiled, more at peace than he had been in years. If only he could remain thus, spooned around Alyssa's sleeping form, and never again need to emerge into the real world.

She stirred in his arms, sighing as she released her hold on sleep.

They lay amongst the tangled bed linens, facing the window. Dillon pried first one, then the other eyelid open and located the sun. Judging by its position in the sky, they had not slept long. Dusk would not blanket the earth for a few hours yet.

"Robert would think you have fallen ill if he knew you were lazing the day away," she murmured drowsily.

Smiling, he nuzzled her hair away from her ear and graced it with a kiss. "More like he would suspect you of casting a spell on me. I have not slept in the afternoon since I was in swaddling clothes."

"You deserve a restful afternoon." Sadness crept into her voice. "The days ahead will be difficult."

Dillon tightened his arms around her. "Were it not so dangerous, you know I would not leave here on the morrow without you."

"I know, Dillon. You need not explain."

Their tranquility shattered as visions of his imminent departure engulfed them.

"Would you do something for me ere I leave?" he asked after a moment.

"Of course," came her immediate response. "How may I serve y—?"

"Nay," he snapped, pushing himself up onto his elbow and urging her to her back. "Nay," he repeated more gently. "I do not ask you as your lord. I ask you as your…" Dillon hesitated. What exactly was he to her now?

"My friend?" she supplied tentatively.

He smiled down at her. Friend. Lover. She was so much more than that. "Aye."

Pink touched her cheeks as she returned his smile. "Then I shall answer as your friend. What boon do you ask?"

"I would like you to show me your garden. I wish to know more of you."

Reaching up, she combed her fingers through the hair above his forehead, smoothing it back in a gesture so casual and endearing that he felt his heart contract.

"Will you show me?" 'Twas the first time he had asked her to share something so personal with him… other than her body, of course, he thought with a twinge of guilt.

"Aye, Dillon."

Relieved, excited, he planted an exuberant kiss on her lips, then leapt from the bed. "Come. Let us rise."

They used the now-cool bathwater to wash before donning their clothes. Alyssa seemed embarrassed by her nudity despite Dillon's attempts to put her at ease. And he reminded himself once more that she had kept every aspect of her face and form hidden for seven years. 'Twould be folly to think that shifting from showing none of herself to showing all of herself would be easy. He knew not how he had conquered her shyness last night. How he had coaxed her into letting him explore every lovely curve.

Pushing away the amorous thoughts that began to form, he frowned at the kirtle she pulled on over her shift. Although not the same garments he had torn off of her when she had lain bleeding to death, both were in very poor condition.

She deserves better, he thought, as he buckled on his sword belt. *Silks and satins and velvets, adorned with jewels that mimic the sparkle in her eyes.* She should be garbed as the lady of the castle. She should *be* the lady of the castle. *His* lady. His *Countess.*

Yet something told him she would balk if he dared suggest as much.

"You are staring, Dillon."

Blinking, he realized he had indeed been staring.

A flush of uncertainty painted her features.

He smiled and closed the distance between them. "Forgive me. I was merely committing your beauty to memory ere you hide it beneath this." Reaching up, he helped her tug the black robe down over her head.

Her color deepened. "You flatter me."

"I speak the truth." Dillon clasped the lowered cowl loosely in both hands, one on either side of her face. Her pale skin provided stark contrast to the midnight material. Her glossy raven hair had been tamed into a single braid, accompanied by so much muttering and grumbling that he had chuckled as he stopped to watch her wrestle with it. Her full lips were still rosy and slightly swollen from his kisses.

So much warmth and understanding filled her gaze as she stood staring up at him that he wanted to crush her to him and never let her go.

"Dillon?" She waited for him to raise the hood into place.

"I cannot," he murmured, unmoving. He should feel some guilt, he supposed, for the main motivation of his refusal appeared to be greed.

He was greedy for the sight of her. Every smile, every

twitch or purse of her lips. Every blink of her entrancing brown eyes. Every flicker of her long lashes. Every rising, falling, and drawing together of her sculpted eyebrows. Every crinkling of her forehead. Every wrinkling of her nose.

How could he bear to have it hidden from him again now that he knew all that he would be missing?

Even more unthinkable… once she raised the cowl, would Alyssa slip back into her role of advisor and forget all that they had shared?

Her hands came up to clasp his wrists. "You know this is how it must be."

"For now," he conceded with reluctance.

She shook her head, eyes full of regret. "For always."

Nay. That he would not, *could* not accept. Leaning down, he pressed a quick, hard kiss to her lips, then drew the hood up to shield her face.

"We shall speak more of this later," he intoned and led her from the solar.

* * *

Alyssa did not realize just how much she had changed since her healing until she followed Dillon out of the solar and down to the great hall. His easy acceptance of her appearance had made her complacent. The kindness he, Robert, and Ann Marie had heaped upon her had been a healing balm for her soul. Yet it could not safeguard her from the pain inflicted by others.

Throughout the keep, the mood toward her had shifted, deteriorated. Those who had feared and mistrusted her before now seemed utterly repulsed, alarmingly hostile. Their narrowed gazes impaled her. Their mouths moved in mutters. Even the precious few who had been civil in their dealings with her in the past now crossed themselves and scurried away as she neared them.

"I have been negligent," Dillon confessed through tight lips as he noted her reception. "I assure you the problem will be dealt with ere I depart."

"What has altered?" she whispered.

Starting, he glanced down at her, then frowned and gave his head a slight shake as if her elderly woman's voice had caught him off guard.

Had he forgotten so swiftly that her guise went beyond the robes?

"Is it…?" She swallowed. "Is it because I killed Gavin?" Her hands still shook and her stomach still knotted whenever she thought of it. Though she had ridden into battle at Dillon's side in the past, Gavin's life was the first she had ever taken.

"In part. Those who were not present in the great hall fail to understand why you killed him. They do not know that, had you *not* done so, he would have impaled you with his dagger. Every man who was in that great hall can attest to it—and would have done the same as you in your position—but none have spoken in your defense."

Nor would they. Such should not surprise her.

"I shudder to think what might have transpired had Sir Rolfe's reaction not warned you in time," he continued. "Those who were there are wrong to condemn you for defending yourself. *And* unwise. Had you done naught to stop him, Gavin—and Camden—would have emerged the victors. You would have died. And, without your healing skills, I would have perished as well."

'Twas a relief that Dillon did not condemn her for it. "What else angers them?" she asked as they stepped out into the crisp autumn air.

He sighed. "A rumor that you took the life of the spy in the dungeon."

"Did you not tell me he hanged himself?" He had been alive and unharmed when she had left him.

"Aye." He lowered his voice as they as they descended the steps of the keep and began crossing the inner bailey. "Around the time you were being healed by the other soothsayers, which makes me wonder if one of them might not have snuck down there before leaving and… aided him in finding the rope. But some of the people whisper that you bespelled him."

"They believe I tortured him, too," she murmured.

"Aye." A moment passed. "Did you?" 'Twas the first time he had broached the subject.

She shook her head. "I merely frightened him into telling the truth."

"How?"

"Rats and snakes, if you can believe it."

He huffed a laugh. "Rats and snakes frightened him?"

"Aye. But they did not bite him," she hastened to clarify. "I simply sent the rats up his hose then released two snakes who thought the rats would make a fine meal."

"And that worked?" he asked, brow puckering with disbelief.

She smiled. Dillon was fearless. It should not surprise her that he expected others to be as well. "In truth, I did not expect it to succeed either, but 'twould seem the man had a most grave fear of snakes."

He grunted. "Not at all the gruesome torture of which you have been accused."

Alyssa sighed, weary of it all. "They are all so eager to believe the worst of me." Until that night, she had injured not one resident of Westcott. Had never used her gifts for aught but healing and helping those who now spread the vicious rumors about her.

"'Tis infuriating," he growled. "They offer *me* their loyalty when I give them so little whilst *you*, who have aided almost every individual at Westcott at one time or another, are rebuffed."

She stopped him with a hand on his arm, the black material of her robe hiding it from others' view. "Do not underestimate your worth, my lord. Your father was a good man and kept his people fed, but they have *flourished* under your care."

"And *your* guidance," he added. Poised on the steps of the keep, he surveyed his holding with a troubled frown.

It was beginning to dawn on him, she realized. One of the many insurmountable obstacles that would prevent them from seeking a future together. If she could not find favor with his people as their healer, they certainly would not accept her as his leman. And she could *never* be his wife, despite the strong attachment for her she could feel growing within him.

"Your people may be wary of your temper and overly preoccupied with the fearsome reputation you have earned," she continued, "but you won their hearts long ago. Each time you defended them from marauders and villains and thieves. Each time you helped them bury loved ones and ordered their dwellings repaired. You built a wall around the village to further ensure their safety. You—"

"—do not know their names," he interrupted.

"What?"

"There is not a man, woman, or child at Westcott whom you do not know by name. You have healed someone in every family. You have that link with them, and I do not. Yet they persist in…" He sighed and ran a hand down over his face. "I did not express my displeasure so that you would sing my praises…, Wisewoman."

Even his inability to call her by name frustrated him.

Releasing his arm, she followed him down the steps and matched his strides—slowed so as not to tire her—as he began traversing the inner bailey. "I appreciate your concern, my lord, but naught can be done to alter things as they are. A life's worth of superstition and distrust cannot be erased in a day. Or a fortnight. Or even a year for that matter."

"Aye, it *can* change in a day," he declared gruffly. "It *will* change in a day. I must simply apply myself to discovering the means I shall use to induce the metamorphosis."

"And a great metamorphosis 'twould be. Even more so now." Alyssa's lips twitched. Glancing around to ensure their privacy, she murmured teasingly from the safety of her cowl, "A few hours in my arms and you believe yourself capable of sorcery. Mayhap wizardry *does* course through my veins."

A burst of laughter escaped him, turning heads as far as the stables. His eyes twinkled merrily. "A few more such hours and I could work miracles. What say you, Healer?"

When she made no response, her boldness now lurking behind timidity, he laughed again. "Would that I could see your face," he pronounced, lowering his voice. "'Tis no doubt as flushed as the rest of your beautiful body was when I—"

"Ahem." The sound of a man clearing his throat behind them interrupted him.

Dillon closed his eyes and gripped his forehead in a visible attempt to generate patience.

Alyssa bit her lip to keep from laughing.

"Dillon? A moment, if you will?"

They turned in unison to confront his brother. Robert's gaze flickered from one to the other then away as an unexpected blush crept up his neck.

"What is it, Robert?"

As actively and enthusiastically as Robert entertained the women of Westcott, Alyssa thought it odd that catching Dillon in the act of invading her bath would embarrass him so.

"I wanted to confirm the number of men you wish to accompany you on the morrow. After the difficulties you encountered the last time…" His eyes went to Alyssa, then returned to Dillon as if he were hesitant to mention it in front of her.

Because Dillon had been wounded? Because she had almost perished saving him? Who knew?

Alyssa took a step back, hands clasped in front of her inside the long, black sleeves. "I shall leave you to your discussion."

She started to turn.

"Wait." Dillon's protest stopped her.

Glancing up at him, she realized he feared she would not

show him her garden if she left now.

"I shall speak with Harry until you are finished. We can continue our business then, my lord."

"You will await me at the gates?" he persisted.

Robert studied them, his shrewd eyes missing naught.

"Aye," she affirmed. "I shall be there."

Dillon smiled, relaxing once more. "Very well. I shall not tarry long."

"As you will." She felt their gazes follow her as she continued across the inner bailey.

Westcott was quite large. Impressive. The envy of many, both landed and landless alike. It possessed two separate baileys, each surrounded by a high wall and a moat. The inner curtain wall was broken by four round towers. The outer boasted six. The smaller inner bailey encased the stables, the mews, the garrison. The armory. The smithy. A tiltyard. Two spacious training fields, both of which were currently occupied by sweating, straining soldiers and sparring squires. A third for practicing archery. A large, profuse garden just outside the kitchen. A pond stocked with fish. A well-tended orchard. Carefully cultivated hives.

The ringing of the blacksmith's hammer followed Alyssa as she passed through the first formidable barbican, across the drawbridge and into the outer bailey, which housed the village. She tried to ignore the fearful looks she received as she passed. Hands rapidly made the sign of the cross. Others fisted with forefingers and pinky fingers extended to ward off the evil eye.

The only friendly face in the sea of suspicion that surrounded her was the one that swam into view as she approached the outer barbican.

Harry greeted her with a wide, open smile, oblivious to the odd looks to which his companions treated him. "Wise One! 'Tis a glorious day, is it not?" he offered brightly.

Though he could not see the face her cowl concealed, he

seemed to know 'twas Alyssa.

"Aye. 'Tis beautiful," she agreed, warmed by his happiness to see her.

"The nights grow cold. Mayhap winter will fall across the land early this year."

"Verily, I had not noticed." She had been ensconced in Dillon's solar, snug beneath layer upon layer of furs and blankets with a fire in the hearth to dispel any cold air that attempted to seep in through the cracks.

If winter *did* approach early, she would do well to prepare a large quantity of the medicines Harry and others like him used to soothe the pain that settled in their joints each time the temperature dipped or a storm rolled in.

"Agnes, the weaver's wife, was complaining only yesterday of the ache plaguing her hands and wrists," he continued, confirming her thoughts.

She nodded. "Who else requires my aid, Harry?"

* * *

"Have you lost your senses?"

Dillon smiled inwardly, staring at the place where Alyssa's small, black-robed figure had disappeared through the gate house several minutes ago. *Aye. Twice this afternoon.*

"Well?"

"You would not ask me such a question had you not already formed your own opinion. What troubles you, Cub?"

"You mean other than walking in on you fornicating with the healer?"

He shrugged, surprised Robert had waited until they had concluded their business to mention it. "You should have knocked."

"Have you no shame?" Robert hissed, careful not to raise his voice and draw attention to them. The depth of his brother's agitation surprised Dillon. "She saved your life—nigh forfeiting her own in the process—and you would repay her by seducing her and robbing her of her innocence?"

Dillon's eyes narrowed. "What know *you* of her innocence?" His brother had spent far less time in her presence than *he* had.

The look Robert gave him next said, *Look who you are asking.* "I have been with enough women to recognize one who is pure, brother, and those I always give a wide berth."

"I knew not you possessed such a weighty conscience," Dillon commented dryly. He had to admit he had not realized his brother was so discriminate and—before Alyssa—had, in fact, envied him his many lovers.

Robert shrugged. "I am not so noble as that."

"Then think you a maiden would not offer you as much sport as a widow or a whore?" If so, he was sadly mistaken. Dillon had never tasted such ecstasy as he had found in Alyssa's sweet embrace.

Robert smiled a little. "I do not believe a virgin would be as inventive as the women who seek me out, nay. Nor would she know how to prevent conception. My strict avoidance of innocents is the reason I have not peopled Westcott with bastards."

Despite his efforts to the contrary, Dillon felt himself pale.

"I see you understand now." Robert eyed him somberly. "After all she has done for us, 'twould not be right for you to use her, then leave her with a babe in her belly."

Mayhap he already had. Mayhap his seed had already taken root and Alyssa even now carried his child. Should that thought not alarm him? Should fear or worry or anxiety not assail him now instead of the warm jubilation that sifted through him?

How would she look swollen with his child? As slender and graceful as she was, he found it difficult to imagine her waddling ponderously into the solar with one hand resting protectively on their unborn babe. Even the idea of such made him want to smile.

"Dillon?"

"What? Oh. What makes you think I would discard her?"

Robert's gaze sharpened. "Are you saying you would not?"

"I care a great deal for her," he avowed softly.

A worried frown marred the younger man's forehead. He brought his hands to his hips and sighed. "Do you love her?"

Dillon stared out over the busy bailey. "I believe so, aye."

If aught, his words seemed to increase his brother's concern.

Much to his surprise, Dillon himself felt... liberated. Pleased to have reached the realization.

"Dillon, she is not of noble blood."

"Her bloodlines mean naught to me."

"If you seek to take her as your mistress, nay. Nor will the rest of the nobility care as long as she remains your mistress for but a short time. But should you seek to make the wisewoman your bride, they will *never* accept her. Nor you."

Irritation tightened Dillon's jaw. "They do not accept me now. They merely tolerate my presence because of my title and the power I wield."

"Even that will be lost to you should you pursue this. You know well their cruelty. That which the wisewoman suffers here will be naught compared to the barbarism she will face at the hands of those of our station if she weds you," Robert persisted. "And what of the king? King Richard will want you to wed a noblewoman from—"

"Enough! I will speak no more of this." Stiff with anger, he spun around to leave.

Robert grabbed his arm before he could get away. "Dillon."

Gritting his teeth, he turned back to hear whatever else his doomsaying brother felt impelled to impart. "What?"

"As your brother, I support you in your every endeavor. Should marriage to the sorceress be what you truly desire, then I shall welcome her as my sister with an open heart. I merely wanted you to be aware of the obstacles you will face in trying to make her yours."

His anger melting, Dillon clamped a hand on Robert's shoulder. "Thank you, brother. But, in listing those obstacles, you neglected to include the people's fear and distrust of her."

Robert grimaced. "I did consider that, but thought the people's superstitions would be easier to overcome than the circumstances of her birth or our king's love of making gainful matches."

"Have you any suggestions?" Dillon asked. He suspected these were all the reasons Alyssa had told him she would forever remain his advisor, hidden beneath the robes.

He watched his brother squint, peering thoughtfully at the people around them.

"Nay," Robert admitted. "Not yet. But I shall think of something."

Dillon smiled. "Thank you, Robert. You give me reason to hope."

Crossing his arms over his chest, Robert raised both eyebrows. "You seem to have already made your decision."

"She brings me peace, Robert, and makes me happy in a way I have never been before. I would be a fool did I not cherish her for it." Eager to return to Alyssa's side, he left his brother and made his way through the inner and outer baileys with long swift strides.

Though he could not see it, Dillon could feel Alyssa's smile when he joined her at the outer barbican. Harry stood close to her, his face wreathed in a smile that puzzled onlookers as he listed the names of men, women, and children who suffered from this ailment or that.

Dread coiled within Dillon as he pondered the decision he now faced. No doubt Alyssa would seek out each one mentioned to offer aid, whether they overcame their fear of her and sent for her or not. Some she would heal with herbs. Others she would heal with her hands.

He swallowed. How could he let her do it? Allow her to use her gift to take their pain and illness and injuries into herself? Leave those who reviled her and would give her not a word of thanks or kindness to bask in their restored good health whilst she suffered in their stead?

'Twas unthinkable. And so soon after her brush with death, after her own illness?

On the other hand, how could he say her nay? 'Twas only recently that she had told him that a gift withheld was no gift at all. Would she not resent him if he forbade her the use of her special healing skills? Would she not see such as a rejection of that part of her that had inspired so much distrust in others? As a rejection of *her*?

He would gladly cut off his sword arm before he would hurt her apurpose. So, he found himself in something of a quandary. Now that he knew the true nature of her gifts, to permit her to use them freely would be to invite her to do herself harm. To forbid her to utilize them would be to watch her die a little inside each time another suffered as a result. And she would never forgive him should one of his people perish for lack of her care.

"You seem troubled, my lord," she whispered as they left Harry and the rest of Westcott behind them.

He followed her into the dense, dark forest to the south. The fact that she had not abandoned her guise now that the trees had swallowed them up and hid them from others' view unsettled him. Did she mean for their relationship to return so soon to what it had been before she had healed him? Before he had looked upon her unveiled? Before they had made love so tenderly? So passionately?

He had always enjoyed her company, but could not bear the thought of retreating to the scrupulously respectful distance that had stood between them in the past.

"Aye," he answered, finding comfort in the familiar despite his concern. For seven years now he had taken his troubles to Alyssa, seeking her counsel, respecting and valuing her opinions. 'Twas one of the reasons he had not believed he would ever marry, though 'twas one he had not mentioned to her. He had wanted a wife who would prove to be as good a helpmeet as his wisewoman had. A partner in whom he could confide, not merely another pretty ornament to decorate his household.

Had he not been injured so gravely, would he ever have discovered that Alyssa was the one he had sought?

"Mayhap if you were to share your problem with me, we might endeavor to solve it together," she suggested.

Were her cowl folded back, he would run an affectionate hand over her hair and pull her close for a kiss, telling her without words how much he appreciated her.

Instead, he smiled to soften his refusal. "Nay. This time 'tis something I must struggle with alone. You have my thanks, though."

She nodded, her disappointment palpable as they made their way through dappled sunlight. The trees and bushes conferred with one another as a cool breeze tickled its way through them. Uncertain of the quality of her robe, he began to worry she might catch a chill.

"Are you warm enough, Seer?" he asked, reaching for the clasp that held his cloak together, ready to wrap it around her for increased warmth.

"Aye, Dillon. These robes are very warm."

Just as he noted that she had abandoned formality and once more spoke in youthful, dulcet tones, she parted the brush in front of him and stepped into a pool of bright sunshine.

Swiveling to face him, she drew back her cowl and proffered a proud smile. "Welcome to my sanctuary."

Dillon froze as his breath left him. No air replaced it. He could not seem to squeeze any into his lungs, past the throat that rapidly grew tight.

Dazzling sunlight bathed her features, lending her ivory skin an unearthly glow. Her brown eyes sparkled with golden highlights he had been unable to discern in the dimness of the castle. Radiant rays reflected off of full pink lips, making him hunger for them anew.

She was so lovely his heart ached.

Her smile faltered as the silence lengthened, broken only by the twittering of birds that watched from the tree limbs. "Dillon?"

The hand he raised shook as he folded his fingers in and drew his knuckles down her cheek.

Alarm flared in her eyes, burning brightly as she frowned up at him. "Dillon, what is amiss?"

He had to swallow once to force his voice to cooperate. "'Tis the first time I have beheld you in sunlight." His voice sounded hoarse. "You are so beautiful. I wish I had the words to describe you, Alyssa, so that you might see yourself through my eyes."

She bit her lower lip, but not before he saw it quiver.

Had he said it right? Had he managed to convey what it meant to him to see her like this—so incandescent in the sun's beams?

One of her small hands came up to clasp his own and brought it to her lips. "You need no other words. You said it perfectly."

His gaze went to her hair. "Take it down," he implored. "I would see it loose, watch it dance on the wind."

Smiling, she turned her back to him, tugged her braid from her robes, and waited for him to perform the task himself.

Dillon grinned, feeling like a boy rewarded with a treat. He swiftly went to work, giving her captivating curls their freedom, and combed his fingers through them until they fell loosely down her back to graze her hips.

The scent of lavender rose up to tease him. Welcoming it with a deep inhale, he walked around to stand before her.

"It shimmers like a moonlit lake," he whispered. And indeed it did, the sun's rays uniting with the breeze to make the dark strands come alive.

He wanted so badly to kiss her in that moment.

Alyssa must have been of the same mind, for she rose

onto her toes and touched her soft lips to his. Her arms came around his neck, the black material of her sleeves sliding back as she leaned her slight weight into him.

Settling his hands at her waist, Dillon enjoyed the leisurely kiss.

I love you. The words formed in his mind without any forethought and he knew them at once to be true. *I love you, Alyssa. I shall find a way for us to be together.*

She drew away, umber eyes glinting with moisture, and gave him a smile imbued with melancholy. 'Twas almost as though she had read his thoughts and saw no hope for them.

"Come." Taking one of his hands in her own, she began to walk backward, tugging him after her. "Let me show you my garden."

CHAPTER TEN

Alyssa led Dillon forward, happiness and hopelessness vying within her.

Dillon loved her. He *loved* her.

Never, in all of her imaginings, could she have foreseen that the friendship they had cultivated for years would—overnight—transform into so much more. One simple act, the removal of her cowl, had changed everything.

She should not have allowed herself to lose control, to give herself to him with such wanton abandon. But she had been alone for so many years. Had craved his touch. *His* touch. Only his. Always his. Had imagined it every time she had seen him slip away with one woman or another. Had imagined him turning to *her* instead.

And she had loved him for so long. Since that moment when—she but a child and he newly knighted—she had seen him come to her grandmother's aid and defend her with such valor, castigating her tormentors.

He was Dillon.

Her Dillon.

She had always thought him so.

How could she *not* have succumbed?

But they could never be together, she thought sadly as she stared up at him.

"Amazing," Dillon breathed as he beheld her beloved garden.

Forcing dark thoughts away, she entwined her fingers through his and moved to walk beside him. "'Tis more than you anticipated mayhap?"

"I did not expect it to be so grand."

She nodded. "Although I would like to assume the credit for it, I am not solely responsible. It has taken decades to become thus."

Pausing nigh the center of the clearing, Dillon twisted this way and that. "I can well believe it."

The garden *was* immense, she had to admit, larger even than the vegetable garden outside the kitchens at Westcott. Row after row of square and rectangular raised beds stretched before them. Wattle—a basketlike border constructed of branches woven horizontally in and out of vertical sticks—held the dirt neatly in place. Leaves and other materials gleaned from the surrounding forest provided mulch that nourished the herbs even as it smothered and prevented the growth of weeds.

A heady conglomeration of scents shifted and changed with each breath of wind. Lavender, basil, rosemary, mint, sage, and many more. A kaleidoscope of colors dazzled them. Every shade of green imaginable. Silver. Powdery gray. Purple. Striped. Solid. Spotted. And that was just the leaves.

Some of the herbs still bloomed, preparing to produce the seeds she would use to regenerate them in the spring and work medicinal magic. Ivory, azure, scarlet, saffron, coral, and combinations thereof.

"All the years I have watched you grind dried, shriveled roots to powder, steep brittle brown leaves in water, mix some foul-smelling poultice or other…," he murmured. "I would never have believed you had you told me your concoctions found their origins in such beauty."

Beaming, she gave his hand a squeeze. "I am glad it pleases you."

"Tell me about them," he urged with a happy smile.

Alyssa touched her fingers to a fern as they came abreast it. "The roots of this fern may be used to rid one of worms." She laughed when he grimaced. "And this…" She motioned to a plant with spotted leaves. "This is lungwort. 'Tis used in remedies for coughs and inflammations of the lungs." She pointed to another. "Bloodwort aids in healing wounds."

She pointed out several others she thought he might have heard her mention over the years. Comfrey, mouse-ear, feverfew, yarrow, centaury.

"'Tis truly a sanctuary," he commented at last and seemed to savor the peaceful atmosphere as much as she did.

"Your father thought so. He came here often after your mother died."

"Did he?" Dillon's visits home had been infrequent after he had been fostered out. And once knighted, he had been preoccupied with winning his own fortune and land through tournaments and such, not to mention crusading with King Richard.

It did not surprise her that he had failed to notice his father slipping away for an hour or two here or there during his visits.

"Who tended these beds ere you?" he queried curiously.

"My grandmother."

His eyebrows rose. "Your grandmother lives at Westcott?"

"She did for many years, but no longer. She was the wisewoman who preceded me. The one who served your father and his father before him."

He nodded, his handsome face thoughtful. Drawing her hand through his arm, he began to lazily stroll down the rows. "Does she still live?" he asked hesitantly.

"Aye. Two day's ride from here, deep within the forest

where none will disturb her or threaten her safety."

They turned down another row.

His brows drew together. For a moment, he looked almost ill. "Did your grandmother… That is, were she and my grandsire or my father ever…"

"Lovers?" she supplied, understanding dawning.

"Aye."

"Nay. She was never more than advisor, healer, and friend to either of the men she served."

"She was wed then?"

"Nay." She turned a pensive gaze on the trees on the opposite side of the clearing. "My mother was bastard born." Would it trouble Dillon to learn that Alyssa had been bastard born, as well?

"Before or after your grandmother came to Westcott?"

"After." The usual anger rose within her. "Lord Bertram killed the man who sired her."

His head snapping around, Dillon stared at her. "*My* grandsire killed *yours?* Alyssa, I am sorry."

"Do not be. I am not. Were the man standing before me now, I would drag your sword from its scabbard and run him through myself." Such fury filled her whenever she thought of him.

Abandoning her hand, Dillon curled an arm around her stiff shoulders. "Tell me."

A great sigh escaped her as she forced herself to relax. "Grandmother was a midwife at Westmoreland."

The Earl of Westmoreland's property bordered Westcott to the north.

A troubled frown made its way to Dillon's brow. "Think you Lord Everard blames me for Camden's losing Pinehurst?"

"Nay. He is well aware of his heir's many faults."

"I would think he would be furious."

"Disappointed more like. He and your father fostered together and remained the best of friends until your father's death. He loves you and Robert as though you were his own. What grieves him is the knowledge that his son will never be what Lord Everard wishes him to be—more like you."

Dillon muttered a denial, clearly thrown by the unexpected praise.

Alyssa smiled and gave his chest a tender pat. "He said as much to me only last summer." Like Dillon, the Earl of Westmoreland had always treated her kindly and often sought her out during his visits to pass a pleasing word.

Dillon brought her hand to his lips. "Forgive me for interrupting you. Please continue."

"Grandmother and I possess the same gifts," she told him. "She hid hers as well as she could, fearing she would be branded a witch if the truth were known. But her talents as a healer soon became renowned throughout the countryside."

They began to walk again, arms around each other, as comfortable as they had always been together.

Every once in a while, she paused to pluck a leaf and crush it to release its fragrance. "Lord Bertram's newly widowed sister was in residence at Westcott, visiting for a time. She was with child, the babe not due for two months yet, when her pains began. When Lord Bertram sent for Westmoreland's healer, Grandmother used her gift to stop the labor. But the lady was so distraught and afraid she would yet lose her babe that Lord Bertram asked Grandmother to remain at Westcott until the danger had passed."

Alyssa quieted for a moment. She had never spoken of her grandmother's past to anyone outside the family. "She did not wear robes then and… she was very beautiful. Westcott's men were all quite taken with her, arguing and wagering over who would gain her favor first. They were very determined."

She hesitated, unsure how to continue.

Dillon folded his arms around her and pulled her into a comforting embrace. "Did one of them force himself on her, Alyssa?"

She nodded, glad she did not have to say it, and rested her head against his chest. "Your grandsire stumbled upon the crime in time to punish it, but sadly too late to prevent it."

He swore beneath his breath. "Did he slay the villain?"

"Aye. Lord Bertram was horrified that a woman he had brought into his household to care for his sister—a woman solely responsible for saving the babe's life—had been brutalized by one of his own men-at-arms. Thereafter he forbade any man to touch her on penalty of death and, in recompense, invited her to remain and reside in the donjon as his healer. He vowed to protect her and her child, if she bore one, as long as they made Westcott their home."

"So she stayed."

She nodded. "Your grandsire upheld his vow and saw to her protection. Eventually she came to trust him and confessed the true extent of her gifts."

"And the robes?"

"She donned the robes after my mother was born. She could bear no man's touch and sought to hide her beauty in hopes that they would soon forget."

"And that is why she made you vow never to remove your robes?"

"In part. She feared I would meet a similar fate."

"What of your mother? Did she serve my father?"

"Nay. She left Westcott when she was very young. As Grandmother's unusual healing abilities became known, superstition grew and rapidly poisoned the people's minds. The priest sowed the first seeds, naming her *Witch, Satan's Handmaiden,* and other such nonsense."

"There has been no priest at Westcott for as long as I have lived," he commented.

"Your grandfather banished him when the man set my mother afire to *purify* her."

"*What?*" Shock cut through him.

"And Lord Bertram allowed no other to take his place,

fearing similar repercussions. Your father followed his example after a similar episode occurred when he caught another priest, one he believed was different, encouraging the people to stone Grandmother to death."

"'Tis the first I have heard of this," Dillon told her, and she could feel how much the thought sickened him.

"I know. 'Tis the other reason for the robes. As long as others believe my grandmother and I are one and the same, they have difficulty determining just how long we have been *wielding our sorcery*. People are far less inclined to try to burn or drown a witch if they think her immortal and capable of exacting retribution."

"Ah."

"And, since none have ever seen me without the robes, should they ever overcome their hesitation and seek to harm me, I can merely duck out of sight, discard the robes at a moment's notice, and walk away unharmed. None would recognize me, because they all think the wisewoman old."

"'Tis a clever shield and deterrent," he admitted. "Was my father aware of your grandmother's history? That she bore a child?"

"I do not believe so," she answered. "He was but a child himself when Grandmother sent my mother away. I doubt he would remember her. No one else does."

"And your mother? Does she also share your gifts?"

"Nay, her gifts differ from ours. She cannot heal with a touch. But she sees things. The future is frequently very clear when it comes to her. She does not have to wait for dreams as I do. Ofttimes it comes when she beckons."

"So *that* is it," Dillon muttered.

Alyssa looked up at him. "What?"

"I wondered how your grandmother arrived at Westcott in time to heal you if she lives at such a distance. Your mother must have foreseen your injury and alerted her."

"Most likely 'tis as you say." Alyssa had had no opportunity to visit her family and learn all that had happened that night. And she trusted no one at Westcott to carry a missive to them.

"But why did she not simply come to Westcott and prevent you from healing me?"

"Because she knew there was naught she could have said that would have stopped me." Alyssa's grandmother and mother were both well aware of her attraction to Dillon, the love she felt for him.

Dillon frowned. He did not seem to care for her determination to sacrifice herself for him.

She smiled up at him. "She also may not have had time. Though she can view the future at will, she rarely can choose whose future she will see. Sometimes her visions come too late to prevent harm from being done and the only course of action left her is to attempt to repair the damage."

Tightening his arms, Dillon drew her closer and rested his chin atop her head. "I am sorry for what happened to your grandmother, Alyssa. I would she had not suffered so."

"Your grandsire avenged the wrong."

"'Tis not enough. It pains me to think of the solitary life she led."

"She has always spoken of your grandsire with great fondness," Alyssa murmured, nuzzling his chest. He smelled so good. "I suspect she loved him as much as she could love any man. And, from the stories I overheard as a child, I believe your grandsire's motives—his swift and violent justice, his generosity in placing her under his protection and giving her a position of respect—were driven by more than guilt."

Dillon leaned back so he could meet her gaze. "Love?"

"Aye. From the day she arrived to tend his sister, 'twas said Lord Bertram was smitten with her."

He frowned. "But he married another."

Filled with regret, she took a half step back from him, raised her chin, and firmly addressed that which they had danced around since she had awakened in his bed. "Aye," she confirmed softly, yet firmly. "He married another. As *you* will marry another, Dillon."

"Nay!" The word burst from his lips as he dropped his arms and moved away from her. "Nay. Why would you say such?"

"I am your advisor. 'Tis my duty to counsel you wisely and I am doing so."

His face turned to stone. "Did what we shared only hours past mean so little to you?" he demanded.

"That can have no consequence in this decision."

"No consequence?"

"Aye, no consequence," she repeated, her voice rising as she lost the battle she fought with anger and fruitless resentment. "'Tis the way of things, Dillon. You are an earl, one of the wealthiest in the land, a favorite of the king, the Lord of Westcott, Brimshire, Northaven, Shepford, and soon Pinehurst, not to mention half a dozen others. With that power comes obligation. You are expected to take a noblewoman to wife." She paused long enough to cultivate some semblance of calm. "No noble blood courses through my veins, no matter how oft I have wished otherwise. And, if that is not enough, I am bastard born."

He swallowed what she feared would have been a scathing retort. "Your mother... she was not..."

"Nay, she was not taken against her will. But I shall not discuss that now. 'Tis essential that I take this time to make you understand."

He took a forbidding step toward her, features darkening as he towered over her.

And Alyssa could not prevent herself from taking a hasty step backward.

"If what you wish me to understand," he said, his voice deep and angry, "is that my future lies with some heiress who will quake in her slippers each time I approach her, then you shall *never* succeed. What of the words we spoke when you lay so nigh death? Were yours false?"

She frowned, her anger giving way to confusion. "I know not what you mean."

"After you healed me, you collapsed. Whilst Robert sought a healer to minister to you, you opened your eyes and spoke to me for the first time without robes or pretense."

Alyssa shifted her weight from one foot to the other. "I have no memory of such, Dillon. What did I say? Of what did we speak?"

He hesitated, heightening her concern even more.

What had she said that he would not repeat?

"You would watch me wed another woman?" he asked gravely in lieu of answering her questions. "Know that I take her to my bed?"

Pain knifed through her, but Alyssa would not let it defeat her. She lifted her chin. "You have not bedded a woman without my knowledge since I arrived at Westcott."

A muscle in his jaw twitched. "'Tis not the same, Alyssa. A wife deserves more consideration than those women. They wanted only a quick tumble, craved domination at my hands. A wife requires special care. Tenderness. Passion."

His voice dropping, he took another step closer.

Though her heart gave a little stutter, Alyssa held her ground.

"Would you feel naught then," he asked, "knowing that each night I did to her all of the things that I spent much of this afternoon doing to you? That my hands and mouth spent hour upon hour seeking out all of the places on her body where you welcomed my touch on yours? All of the places that made you cry out and clutch me closer, your nails leaving marks upon my back, your heels digging into my hips, pulling me in deeper…"

She swallowed, eyes locked with his. Mute. Miserable.

"You would feel naught when she began to quicken with my babe? When I doted upon her and cosseted her and smoothed my hand across her burgeoning belly with husbandly pride? When you delivered my son into your hands and stared down at him, knowing he could have been ours? That he *should* have been ours?"

Wanting to weep at the image he conjured, she squeezed her eyes shut and touched her fingers to her lips to hide their trembling.

Dillon grasped her upper arms and gave her a little shake. "Look at me, Alyssa."

She did so, tears welling in her eyes and blurring his cherished visage.

Cupping her face in one rough palm, he smoothed his thumb across her cheek. "You see me better than anyone. You *must* know how I feel about you." When she would have spoken, he shook his head. "You are a brilliant strategist and have guided me well these seven years past. Do not abandon this particular quest so easily." He brushed her lips with a gentle kiss. "Please, Alyssa. You have fought by my side before. Do so one last time and I promise you the reward will be far greater than we ever dreamed."

Heartsick, she let her head fall forward against his chest. "Oh, Dillon. The only lesson you have yet to learn is that some battles are lost ere they have even begun."

He wrapped his strong arms around her, rocking her from side to side. "'Tis a lesson I shall *never* learn," he responded.

But she could feel the concern that plagued him, his fear that she may be right.

They held each other for many long moments.

"A storm approaches," she whispered at last, pulling away. "We should make haste back to Westcott."

Eyeing the blue sky doubtfully, Dillon agreed to leave.

They turned as one and made their way back through the fragrant beds to the point where they had exited the forest earlier. Dillon halted and faced her, grasping her hood as he had in his chamber.

She stood silently whilst he studied her.

"Mark my words, Alyssa," he said. "These robes will not be necessary for much longer. I *will* find a way to free you. To free *us*." Bending, he captured her lips in a long, determined kiss.

Then, tucking her hair inside her robes, he covered it with her cowl and slowly led her back into the shadows.

* * *

The great hall was rife with delicious aromas as servants brought forth platter after platter heaped with steaming foods that would make any mouth water.

Any mouth, that is, save Dillon's.

He did *not* want to be there. He would prefer to be up in the solar, dining with Alyssa, whom he had sent back to bed—his bed—upon their return.

Right now he could be laughing with her, teasing her, tempting her as he had the previous night. Offering her the choicest morsels. Stealing kisses in between. Enjoying her company.

But a feast had been prepared to celebrate his return to health, so he had sent Robert up to her with food enough to keep her busy for at least an hour and orders to consume every crumb.

Thunder rumbled overhead, almost drowned out by the laughter and boisterous conversation that flowed around him. Moisture blew in with the wind as the large, heavy doors opened and two knights stumbled inside, their cloaks and hair dripping wet. A storm had indeed rolled in, its wrath reflective of Dillon's mood.

Face frozen in a perpetual scowl, he leaned back in his chair, food untouched, and glared at the people who packed the trestle tables and crowded the hall. Even the wives who usually stayed away, ever leery of him, had joined them for this *joyous* occasion.

One hand absently toyed with his goblet, rotating it this way and that, before he raised it to his lips for a brief, distracted taste. Behind him, he heard Gideon shift his stance. Alerted to his lord's foul disposition, the boy no doubt worried over its cause. Baldwin and the other knights whom he had invited to join him at the high table restricted their comments to murmurs and darted wary sidelong glances at him.

Eventually notice that something was amiss filtered down through the lower tables to the other occupants of the hall.

The noise level decreased.

Conversation switched to whispered speculation.

All kept one eye on the glowering Earl of Westcott whilst they dined.

William appeared at Dillon's elbow and motioned to his full trencher. "You are displeased, my lord?"

"Aye," Dillon growled, "but 'tis my people who displease me, not the fare."

With the exception of Ann Marie's baby, who grunted as he attempted to stuff as much of her kirtle as possible into his little mouth, everyone in the great hall froze. Tankards halted halfway from table to lips. Mouths ceased their chewing. Tongues stopped wagging. All eyes widened with trepidation and focused on Dillon, who altered neither his position—lounging in his chair like a lion awaiting the chance to pounce upon its prey—nor his expression.

Thunder roared through the hall, startlingly loud now that all else was quiet. One of the dogs beneath the trestle tables whined.

Nearby a throat cleared, drawing his attention to Baldwin. Rising, the older man bowed respectfully and said, "If it pleases you, my lord, I ask that you inform us how we have wronged you so that we may make amends." Retaking his seat, he waited with the others for Dillon's response.

Dillon abandoned his study of Baldwin and raked his gaze over several of the faces turned expectantly toward him. "All here know I was ready to receive the last rites when my brother brought me home."

Murmurs of agreement rose up around him, words such as *blood, quarrels,* and *death* standing out above the others.

"'Tis glad we are to see you hale and hearty again, my lord," someone called out nigh the entrance.

A rousing chorus of *aye's* ensued.

If anything, Dillon's mood darkened. "Are you?"

Smiles faltered, replaced by frowns of confusion.

William nodded earnestly. "Of course, my lord. 'Twas worried about you we all were."

Confirmation again sounded from the people.

Dillon merely stared at them frigidly. "Your actions tell me otherwise."

All exchanged uneasy glances.

"Though I doubt not you have all heard the tale several times, I tell you now that I took three quarrels in that ambush. One in the shoulder. One in the side. And one in the chest. My own squire thought me dead ere I was carried through the gates, and he was not the only one."

Some of the men nodded grimly. A few women uttered swift prayers.

"The wisewoman risked much to save my life," he informed them dourly. "Had she not used her gifts to heal me, I would not have seen another dawn. Yet were I to judge you by your reactions to her today, I would have to say that you scorn her for coming to my aid and would have preferred instead that she let me find my grave."

Since the *nay's* that followed were not nigh as adamant as they should have been, Dillon guessed they began to see where he was leading them.

William stepped forward. "My lord—"

Dillon raised a hand to stop him. "Your loyalty is not in question, William. Nor is Robert's. Nor Ann Marie's."

All heads swiveled to look at Ann Marie, who stood nigh the great hearth, offering Dillon a proud smile.

"Nor is Harry's or Gideon's," he continued. "'Tis the rest

of my people whose loyalty is suspect."

No one seemed to know quite what to say to that.

"Sir Richard," he called suddenly.

The young knight who had shouted his good wishes only moments before reluctantly stepped forward. "Aye, my lord?"

"You say you are happy to see me hale and hearty again."

"Aye, my lord. I vow 'tis the truth."

"Have you proffered your thanks to the healer for caring for me so well during my recovery?"

The young man's Adam's apple bobbed up and down as he swallowed. "Nay, my lord."

"Why have you not?"

"It... it did not occur to me, my lord."

"It did not occur to you," Dillon repeated amiably, though any watching him could see the danger that lurked just beneath the surface. "Did it also not occur to you to greet her civilly when she passed you on her way across the inner bailey this afternoon?"

All waited with bated breath for Richard's answer.

Sweat began to bead on the knight's forehead and trail down his temples. "I cannot say as I recall seeing her, my lord."

Dillon nodded. "'Tis fortunate then that my memory does not suffer as yours does." He allowed the fury he felt to enter his voice and expression. "You see, I recall quite clearly that she did indeed draw your notice. You glared at her most fiercely as she passed, then spat dangerously close to the hem of her robe."

Dillon wanted to kill the man as he recalled the incident.

Eyes widened when the metal goblet Dillon clutched began to bend beneath the pressure of his clenching fist, slowly sinking in upon itself.

"Know you the punishment you would have been dealt had your aim been more true?" he questioned menacingly.

The knight shook his head.

"I warned you all, did I not, ere I left for Pinehurst that

any offense made against her is an offense made against me."

Richard blanched.

"What say you now to the earl upon whose feet you spat today in his own bailey?"

The young man trembled beneath Dillon's wrath. "F-Forgive me, my lord. I—"

Lunging to his feet, Dillon slammed the twisted goblet down on the table, causing everyone to jump and those nearest him to skitter away. "*'Tis not* me *you should be begging to forgive you!*" he bellowed. "*She saved my life!* And you all treat her with contempt! If 'tis not because you wish she had let me perish, then I would hear your explanations now!"

Deadly silence filled the hall, the air thick with fear.

One of his men at arms, Kenneth, slowly rose beside his place at a lower table. He looked to be only a tad less frightened than Richard. "Verily, my lord, not one of us here is sorry you live. 'Tis thankful we are that you survived. If some of us possess… unkind feelings toward the healer, 'tis because of Gavin."

"I see." Dillon leaned forward and braced his hands on the table. "So you claim you are loyal to me, yet admit to mourning the death of my betrayer."

"Nay, my lord," he corrected. "'Tis not Gavin's *death* that troubles us, but the *way* he died."

"And how is that?" he inquired, wanting to stamp out once and for all whatever nonsense was being bandied about.

Kenneth glanced at the faces around him, then returned his attention to Dillon. "I was told his head was nigh severed from his body and that she… that the sorceress… mutilated his body in unmentionable ways"—his gaze went pointedly to a few of the women in the hall—"ere she was finished with him."

Appalled, Dillon turned his head and speared Baldwin with a look. "Baldwin." His voice was hushed and laced with barely restrained rage.

The man scrambled to his feet. "Aye, my lord."

"You were there, were you not?"

"Aye, my lord."

"Who else was present? Name as many as you can remember. Those of you whose names are called will rise and make yourselves known," he commanded.

One by one, Baldwin called out names. Most were men. Several of Dillon's knights and men at arms. A few servants, both men and women. Each remained standing as Baldwin's voice droned on until he could recall no more.

"Ann Marie," Dillon said more kindly, turning toward her. "You may be seated. As I said before, your loyalty remains unquestioned."

She smiled and bobbed a curtsy, her son bouncing on her hip. "Thank you, my lord."

The others watched with envy as she took her seat.

Dillon's scowl returned as he faced the assembly. "The rest of you... hear you what Kenneth said?"

"Aye," they chorused.

"Why have you not come forward with the truth and cleared the healer of such obscene false charges?"

Their eyes fell beneath his furious regard.

"Baldwin, inform the others what transpired here that night."

Features tight with guilt, he did so, abandoning any and all exaggeration. Frowns and murmurs filtered through the listeners. Dillon was pleased to hear more than one admit that Gavin had left the wisewoman no choice.

"What about the man in the dungeon?" someone called out, not so eager to absolve her.

Dillon raised one eyebrow. "What of him?"

"She tortured him, did she not?"

Straightening, Dillon folded his arms across his chest. "As long as the betrayer's identity remained unknown, Westcott was vulnerable and all of your lives were in danger. The wisewoman was well aware of this and questioned the man until he confessed his conspirator's name. Would you condemn her for protecting you?"

"But what she done to him… 'Twas terrible."

"You watched, did you?"

The man shifted awkwardly. "Nay. But we all heard his screams. And once he gave her Gavin's name, she hanged him."

His teeth grinding in frustration, Dillon held up a hand to arrest the growing grumbles. "The man still breathed when she left him. He was also unharmed. My brother can confirm this, as can the men he ordered to guard him. Since the wisewoman spent the rest of the night tending my wounds in my solar and had no further contact with him, I assume you are laboring under the foolish belief that she cast some sort of spell upon him?"

Abashed looks.

"Then allow me to ease your minds. If aught drove the man to hang himself, 'twas the knowledge that I lived and he would soon face my wrath. Knowing my reputation, he would have had no reason to expect mercy. If he did, I am sure my brother rid him of the false hope. Like all of you here, I doubt he had any difficulty imagining the fate that would befall him when I resumed my duties. So 'tis lunacy to suggest that sorcery had aught to do with it."

He saw a change in some of their faces as the logic of his words began to penetrate and conquer the lies. No doubt they would still be wary of Alyssa. But mayhap acknowledging the truth of what had happened that night would take them one step closer to acceptance.

At least, he prayed 'twould be so.

Dropping his arms to his sides, he relaxed a bit. "The wisewoman has healed almost every one of you at one time or another. Many of us would not be here today had she not and owe her our very lives. She has treated you all with kindness

202 | DIANNE DUVALL

and compassion and should in return be treated with deference and respect. She has in no way *earned* your fear or distrust."

He paused. "I suggest that from this day forward, if you intend to continue judging the healer, judge her solely by her actions toward *you* and remember the numerous ways you have benefited from her care."

Stepping back from the high table, he headed for the stairs. When he drew even with Richard, he paused long enough to slam a fist into the quaking man's face, knocking him unconscious. Then, nodding to Ann Marie, Dillon left the hall.

The rest of the gathering found their seats once more and resumed supping, suitably subdued as they pondered his words.

Not one of them went to Richard's aid.

CHAPTER ELEVEN

Robert and Alyssa sat at a small table by the hearth, playing Nine Men's Morris, when Dillon entered the solar. Her cowl lay back on her shoulders, discarded and nigh hidden beneath her lovely obsidian tresses. Her pale hands were bare, the sleeves of her robes having been folded back.

Judging by the number of pegs she had captured, his brother was in danger of losing quite badly.

Both looked up with a smile as he closed the door behind him.

"What goes, brother?" Robert asked with good humor.

He shrugged, taking in the empty tray left on the bed. Shifting his focus to Alyssa, he narrowed his eyes. "How much of your supper did my hulking brother consume?"

She cast Robert a guilty glance.

Dillon looked to Robert, who grinned unrepentantly.

"'Twas too large a meal for a maid her size. Chivalry demanded that I lend her my aid." He winked at Alyssa, earning him a smile.

Dillon frowned. "Get you down below, Cub, and see that my people do not get into further trouble."

Rising, Robert stretched. "Since I have in some way managed to lose every match we have played this evening, I must admit I am not sorry to go." He offered Alyssa a gallant bow. "Although your company, as always, has been enchanting, Healer."

"As has yours," she replied.

Just as jealousy began to reawaken from its slumber, Robert leaned toward Dillon and said in a loud, conspiratorial whisper, "She must have bespelled the board for it absolutely refuses to allow any save herself to triumph."

When Dillon glanced at Alyssa, he was pleased to see a spark of amusement light her eyes. He slapped Robert on the back. "She is an excellent tactician, brother. Did you truly expect to win?"

Chagrined, Robert raised a humble hand to his chest and lowered his head in a comical gesture of defeat. "In fact, my manly pride did assure me I would. I shall know better in the future than to listen to it."

Alyssa chuckled, obviously charmed. But this time it did not trouble Dillon.

"Is there aught I can do for you ere I take my leave?" Robert asked her.

"Nay, Robert. I thank you for entertaining me."

"'Twas my pleasure." Swiveling on his heel, he headed for the door. "Next time 'twill be chess, Wise One."

Dillon laughed. "You shall have no better luck winning that game than you did this one."

Grimacing playfully, Robert ducked out into the hallway.

Dillon closed and barred the door.

"He is more at ease in my presence each time I see him," Alyssa commented.

"A little too at ease," he muttered, crossing to sink down on the side of the bed.

"I tried to release him from it again tonight."

"His vow to serve you?"

"Aye. He would have none of it."

"My brother is a good man," Dillon said as he unbuckled his sword belt, "with a soft heart that is oft eclipsed by his monumental stubbornness. He clings to his beliefs like a hound to the only bone in the province. It sometimes takes a force of nature to shake him loose." He sighed, feeling weary of a sudden, and wondered if he were not still suffering a bit from his recent blood loss.

Then again, it could just be a result of the confrontation below and the stress of battling his people's unreasonable fears regarding Alyssa. As well as her own belief that they could have no future together.

"Let me help you, my lord," the woman of his thoughts offered, moving to his side and bending to take hold of his boot to tug it off.

"My thanks," he mumbled, distracted by her scent and the sight of her loose curls cascading down over her shoulders.

"So you believe 'tis Robert's soft heart guiding him now?" she asked, setting the first boot aside and moving to the second.

"Hmm? Oh. Aye. He rarely makes the same mistake twice. And this time his mistake was trusting in rumor and hearsay. Now he is taking his own measure of you and—as with me—you appear to have succeeded in capturing his heart."

She straightened, his other boot dangling from her hand as she cast him a look of dismay.

He grinned. "Only not in the same fashion."

Emitting a sigh of relief, she twisted to place both boots beside his trunk.

Dillon caught a glimpse of dainty bare feet as the hem of her robe shifted. Strength flowed back into his limbs. The blood in his veins began to warm. Grinning, he leaned forward, snagged a handful of the fluid black material, and gave it a tug.

She pivoted, glancing down to see what her robe had caught on, then followed a path from his hand to his face.

Using his hold as leverage, he slowly drew her closer. "What wear you beneath this robe, Healer?" he questioned in a low, suggestive voice. Color immediately flooded her cheeks. "Not much, I would wager." He gave the material another yank. "Why do you not remove it and come to bed?"

Her face an intriguing shade of crimson, she nodded and walked around the foot of the bed to the other side. Dillon stood and turned to face her. When Alyssa's eyes flickered up to shyly meet his, he sent her an encouraging smile.

Taking a deep breath, she whipped the robes over her head, revealing an almost-transparent shift, then dove beneath the covers. By the time he could breathe again, she lay against the pillows with the blankets drawn up to her chin.

Dillon stared down at her, unable to help himself, his heart slamming against his ribs. Would she always affect him thusly? One glimpse of her tantalizing form had left his pulse racing, his hands shaking, and his body hard with desire.

Yet he would not make love to her tonight. 'Twas too soon. She had been so ill. She had been a maiden as well. And he had already taken her twice today.

Giving her his back, he sat on the edge of the bed and attempted to cool his raging ardor.

"You did it again, did you not?" she asked softly.

He glanced at her over his shoulder. "Did what?"

"Spoke to your people about me."

He swore silently. "How did you know?"

Her lips curled up in an indulgent smile. "Dillon, your voice makes thunder seem a whisper when you are angry. I had little difficulty discerning some of your words, despite your brother's not-very-subtle attempts to drown them out."

Berating himself for not restricting his shouts, he faced forward and dragged his tunic over his head.

"You cannot order your people to befriend me," she admonished gently.

"I did not," he protested, his linen shirt landing atop his

discarded tunic. "I merely ensured that they learned the truth of what transpired the night of my wounding, exposed the lies they had been told, and suggested that those were not the only misconceptions they have been harboring. There is no harm in that, is there?"

The bedding rustled behind him. His flesh jumped when her smooth hand touched it, stroking a path of fire down his back.

"I simply do not wish to see your hopes crushed."

"Their attitudes will change in time, Alyssa," he insisted.

"But my parentage will not."

Closing his eyes, he lay back and rested his head in her lap. Some of the tension eased from his neck and shoulders when she began to comb her fingers through his hair.

"You never told me who your father is," he said sometime later, half asleep, lulled by her soothing hands.

"Your skin grows cold," she whispered. "Why do you not finish disrobing and join me beneath the blankets?"

Dillon nodded drowsily and stood. Once he removed his hose and braies, he slipped beneath the furs and slid over until cool flesh met warmth. A sigh of contentment escaped him as he wrapped his arms around her and pulled her close, her face snuggled to his chest, their legs entwined.

* * *

"I know not my father's name, nor whence he came," Alyssa said. "Nor would I recognize him did he stand before me, for I have never seen his face."

Leaning back, Dillon reached down for the hem of her shift, deftly divested her of it, then pulled her close once more, no barriers between them. "Better."

Her heart pounded, as it always did at the feel of his warm muscled body pressed to hers.

"Continue," he murmured.

She smiled against his chest "He sought out my grandmother, a serf dressed in his cleanest rags, his face concealed by the shadow of his cowl, and asked her for her aid. My mother had foreseen his coming and told my grandmother to direct him to her cottage in the forest."

"From what ailment did he suffer?"

"He knew not. 'Twas what he wished to discover. He had been wed for several years, but despaired because his wife had borne him no children."

"Was she barren?"

"Nay. His marriage was not a happy one, you see. He had known his wife for most of their lives and wed her to remove her from her cruel father's clutches."

"Very noble of him," he commended.

"Aye. He felt genuine affection for her at the time, but soon realized he had been played for a fool. She cared naught for him and had only used him to escape her father's household. Once they were wed, her manner toward him changed. And he was wretchedly disappointed. His one hope for happiness, he said, was to sire a son who would lighten his days and bring him laughter as they toiled side by side."

"Did his wife deny him his husbandly rights?" Dillon asked.

"Nay." Yawning, she rubbed her cheek against his chest. "I mentioned earlier that my mother can *see* things."

"Aye. What did she see when he sought her out?"

"His wife was using herbs to prevent conception without his knowledge."

Dillon swore. "Did he confront her?"

She shook her head. "My mother advised him to say naught, but to discern through stealth the location of the hidden cache of herbs, showing him what to search for. He was to return in a fortnight, at which time she would give him alternate herbs that were similar in appearance and taste to those in his wife's possession. These, however, would do naught to prevent his wife's body from ripening with his seed."

"I do not understand why he did not simply acknowledge her deception and take the herbs from her."

"He feared that if he did so, she would refuse him his rights as husband, and he could not stomach the notion of forcing her until she became with child."

He grimaced. "I see his point. Did he return as bidden?"

"He did. 'Twas then my mother named her price for aiding him."

"If he was a serf, I do not expect he had much to offer her."

"He could offer this."

"What did he give her?"

"Me," she said simply.

A startled pause ensued. "The price was to get her with child?"

"One night in my mother's arms was his payment," she corrected. "And 'twas all she told him. But my mother had seen in a vision that he would give her a daughter."

"And she… surrendered herself to him? A man who was a stranger to her?"

"You must understand. She was very lonely, Dillon. Her turbulent childhood had made her fearful of living amongst others. Having spent most of her days in almost total isolation, she was eager for someone with whom she could share her life, a child who would love her and not fear her."

"I see."

She smiled again. "Her visions had not informed her that she would meet, fall in love with, and marry a wonderful man less than a year later."

"Who?"

"A carpenter who had been blinded in an accident and sought her aid, mistaking her for my grandmother. He is the one I have called Father all my life."

Dillon hugged her tighter. "Did he treat you well, Alyssa?" Some men would not accept a child who had not sprung from their own loins.

She nodded. "He has told me often that he could not have

loved me more had he been the man to sire me."

"Good. 'Tis a most unusual story. An extraordinary beginning for an extraordinary woman."

She yawned again. "You do not think less of me?"

"Of course not." Tilting her chin up with one finger, he touched his lips to hers. "Thank you for sharing your tale with me."

Her pulse jumping, she curled her hand around his neck and drew his lips down for another, longer melding. "If I could, I would share everything with you, Dillon."

* * *

The room was unfamiliar to her. Deserted. Lacking any furniture or adornment. Dark and shadowed. 'Twas a great hall that seemed to have been uninhabited for many years.

The rushes beneath her feet were old and soiled, musty-smelling, infested with insects and animal excrement. Dirt and soot had turned the barren walls gray, a sharp contrast to Westcott's clean, whitewashed interior and colorful tapestries. 'Twas smaller, too, its corners—barely definable amongst the gloom—draped in gossamer gowns of translucent webs that rippled from a breeze that did not touch her.

Her feet carried her forward, down a long passageway. No torches lit it, yet the darkness was not complete. Alyssa had no difficulty discerning where she strode.

A doorway lay ahead. To a tower? To the kitchens?

Nay. To a bed chamber.

Cautiously, she entered. Darkness cloaked this chamber, too. Begrimed and thick with shadows, it boasted only a bed and a chest.

A man sat upon the chest with his back to her, his head bent as he stroked a brown cat that sprawled in his lap. Another cat, yellow with brown and black splotches, emerged from beneath the bed and rubbed against his leg, purring loudly. Two more trotted past from the hallway behind her. All were fat. All received a stroke or a pat from the man.

Something about him made her heart pound and her throat tighten with fear. Wanting to see his face, she began to circle the room, keeping a careful distance between them. Slowly. One half step at a time, her back to the wall.

The occasional feline of various hues continued to appear and stroll past her.

'Twas too dark to determine his hair color. Red mayhap? Light brown? She simply could not tell, only noting that it curled over the collar of his dark tunic.

She squinted, his profile gradually taking form.

Suddenly, he raised his head, shoulders straightening, as if he sensed her presence for the first time.

Breathless, she watched as he swiveled on the chest to face her.

* * *

Alyssa jerked awake. Blinking against the blackness, she felt Dillon move beside her. She lay on her back, his arm looped around her waist, one of his muscled thighs draped heavily across hers.

His face burrowed deeper into her hair, breath tickling her ear. His arm tightened. "Another nightmare?" he asked, voice gravelly.

"I dreamed," she whispered, anxiety coursing through her.

His head came up. "What?"

"I dreamed," she repeated, sitting up. "I need parchment. A quill and ink."

When she started to toss back the covers, he stopped her. "I shall fetch them for you. Stay here, where 'tis warm."

Before she could protest, he exited the bed and touched a candle to the coals that still glowed in the hearth.

A light shiver shook her. Watching Dillon, Alyssa drew the covers up over her breasts and tucked them beneath her arms.

Golden light bathed his beautiful bare body and sleep-tousled hair as he retrieved the items she requested. Setting the candle on the bedside table, he handed her the rest, then turned away.

Alyssa opened the ink bottle, dipped her quill into it, then frowned.

"Here, love. Use this." He placed the now-empty supper

tray in her lap and arranged the parchment and ink bottle upon it for her.

Her heart leaping at the endearment and how naturally it had flowed from his lips, she smiled up at him. "Thank you, Dillon."

He returned her smile and bent to place a chaste kiss on her forehead, his love and concern pouring into her like the purest of wines, warming her insides and strengthening his hold on her. It took a heroic effort to drag her attention away from him as he bent to stoke the fire, then retook his place beside her beneath the blankets. But she wanted to record the dream ere any of the details escaped her memory.

It did not take long. Once she finished, Alyssa read back through it, frowning as key words and phrases leapt out at her. At last, she transferred the tray to the table and lay back against the pillows.

Dillon's hand found hers beneath the blankets and brought it to his lips. "Was it another nightmare?"

"Nay. But now I wish more than ever that I were accompanying you to Pinehurst. I fear for you, Dillon."

He frowned. "Did you see me wounded then?"

"Nay."

His thumb smoothed over her palm, circling, stroking, tempting unintentionally as he considered her words. "What did you see, Alyssa?"

She told him, relating every detail that had drawn her attention. All except for the ending, which she had forgotten upon waking.

"You remember naught of the man's features?"

"Only a feeling that he was young and was smiling."

"Hmm." His frown deepened. She could feel his confusion as he began to slide his hand slowly up and down her forearm in an absent caress. "In truth, I fail to comprehend what has upset you. I see naught sinister in a man stroking a cat. It seems a harmless dream."

"Cats," she corrected, stressing the *s*. "There were several. Half a dozen at least."

He shrugged apologetically, telling her without words that it made no difference in terms of his understanding.

"My dreams are rarely meant to be taken literally," she explained. "What is straightforward to you is symbolic to me."

It had always been so. Her mother had taught her how to decipher dreams, to identify symbols and who or what they represented, at a very young age. Sometimes Alyssa did not discern the full meaning of a dream until it came to pass, only translating enough of it to be forewarned. 'Twas frustrating. But her dreams had often aided her in advising Dillon wisely in the past.

He gave her wrist a little squeeze. "Help me to understand."

"You see a man stroking a cat," she began. "I see a villain plotting adversity. Cats frequently represent mischief in dreams. They howl and spit and tear things with their claws. To pet one is to invite trouble. To welcome it. The fatter the cat, the greater the mischief and these were all large cats. Some were yellow, indicating cowardice. Others were brown or black, indicating darkness, death, mystery. The man enjoyed stroking them, took pleasure in his negative emotions. His clothing was dark, possibly brown. That is negative. There were spiders' webs aplenty. Webs ensnare or trap one. The castle was poorly kept and dirty. That, too, is negative. The darkness. 'Twas *all* negative, Dillon."

He said naught for long minutes, digesting the information given him. Though the newly acquired ability disturbed her, she was glad she was privy to his thoughts, for they told her that he took her concern seriously and doubted not her interpretation of the dream's symbols.

"How does the dream relate to me?" he queried, puzzled because he had not appeared in it.

"Hallways indicate transition. You leave on the morrow to wrest Pinehurst from Camden. Both the castle and your life will be in transition until the siege ends and you have succeeded in ousting any and all who refuse to pledge their loyalty to you."

"But 'twas *you* who negotiated the hallway, not I."

Alyssa frowned. "Aye. But your departure weighs heavily on my mind. I am almost certain 'tis a warning for *you*, that more trouble awaits you at Pinehurst than we anticipate."

Dillon was apparently unconvinced, however, for he directed his mind toward identifying possible threats to *her* safety, rather than his own. "I want either Robert or Harry to accompany you if you must tend your garden in my absence," he stated and her heart sank. "Both if 'tis possible, though I would prefer that you remain inside the gates until my return."

"But that could be months," she protested. "'Tis said that Pinehurst was in poor condition, its people starving, long before the siege began. Even if you forego utilizing the destructive siege engines, 'twill take time for you to put it in order. My garden is my only solace, Dillon. Do not take that away from me. I truly do not believe I am in any danger. 'Tis *you* the dream seeks to protect."

"What of the people? Did my lecture not reach them, I fear they may seek to harm you."

She smiled. "In which case my garden is the safest place for me, for all here are terrified of that section of the forest."

His brows knitted in a scowl as she felt frustration bubble up inside him. When his lips parted to demand she take this seriously, she covered them with her own, stealing his voice. She placed her free hand on his lightly furred chest, sliding it up to curve around his neck and toy with his thick, silken hair. His beard stubble abraded her skin as she moved her mouth across his, teasing him, tasting him, taking his lower lip gently between her teeth before surrendering her hold and backing away.

Heart thudding in her chest, she stared up at him in the light provided by the candle and the fire.

His eyes were smoky and unreadable. But his pulse beat faster beneath the hand she had curled around his neck.

He cleared his throat. "Do not ignore the threats to your own safety, Alyssa. My reputation may not be enough to protect you this time." He brought a hand up to tuck a thick lock of hair behind her ear, then slipped it down to fondle her bare shoulder. "I have only just found you, sweetling," he added more softly. "Should aught happen to you…"

Sensing his fear, his despair at just the *thought* of losing her, she tightened her hold on him and drew his head down for another kiss. His thoughts scattered, as did her own, swept away by the rising tide of desire.

He loved her. Without question. Knowing everything he did about her.

The wonder of it overwhelmed her, made her eyes fill with tears, her body burn for his touch. To know that she mattered so much to him, to this man she had wanted for so long… 'Twas not lust or mere infatuation that made him quake at the idea of her being harmed, but the same deep abiding love she had carried in her heart for him for years.

Urging him closer, she slipped her tongue past his lips to boldly tangle with his. He groaned his approval and rolled atop her, sliding his legs between her own. One hand burrowed into her hair. The other eagerly captured her breast, thumb circling its hardened peak and sending shards of pleasure cutting through her.

Alyssa gasped and arched into him.

His lips left hers and scorched a searing path down her throat, over her collarbone, to her other breast.

Their bodies hummed in unison, trembling with need.

"I should not," he whispered, lips hovering above the pink tip.

"You should," she moaned. Combing her fingers through his hair, she pressed him to her. "I need you, Dillon."

When the hand at her breast tightened, she cried out for

more. His teeth found the bud she guided him to, then his tongue, making her squirm with pleasure. She could not get close enough. She needed more and more and more. She would *never* get enough of him.

And he was ravenous for her, unknowingly driving her mad with his erotic thoughts. Thoughts he did not hesitate to act upon as he glided down her body, tucked his arms beneath her bent knees, and took her with his mouth.

"*Dillon.*" Shocked, she fisted his hair to pull him up. (Men were not supposed to kiss women there, were they?) Then he stroked the heart of her with his tongue and pleasure arced through her. She gasped. Again his tongue moved. She moaned. And again and again. The hands she had buried in his hair now held him to her and urged him on until ecstasy exploded within her, wringing a cry from her throat.

"More," she heard him utter, voice hoarse with hunger, as he renewed his sensual assault, his fingers joining his tongue in tormenting her. On and on it went. So good. So devastating.

Moans poured from between her lips as she moved her hips, the pleasure building until ecstasy once more seized her.

Replete, breath coming in gasps, she welcomed Dillon's weight as he rose above her, then whispered in her ear, "You will tell me if I hurt you."

"You will not hurt me," she assured him, knowing no amount of pain would make her stop him now.

He touched his tongue to her earlobe, sending shivers dancing through her. "Do you speak as a woman or as a healer?"

"A woman." Alyssa wrapped her legs around him the way she knew he wanted her to. "Please, Dillon. I need to feel you inside me." She kissed his bristly jaw just below his ear. "Now."

Groaning, he complied, his arousal teasing her entrance, then sliding in deep. She *was* a bit tender, but... oh, the feel of him. Stroking her. Filling her. The way he worshipped her with his mind, heart, and body. So completely. So desperately.

Calling her name in a voice both beautiful and rough with passion as he found his release and flung them both over the edge.

The way he held her close, pressing tender kisses to her lips, her throat, her shoulder, whilst she floated back down to earth, his body curled possessively around hers.

As she drifted off to sleep, a contented smile curling her lips, Alyssa prayed that he was right, that there was some hope of a future together for them. A future as man and wife, free from the condemnation of others. Free from the shackles of superstition.

For Dillon had given her more than wave after wave of unspeakable pleasure that night.

So much more.

* * *

Alyssa found their parting the next morning unbearable. Surrounded by men on horseback and numerous onlookers, she stood placidly in her dark robes and watched as Dillon mounted his loyal destrier.

They had dressed silently at dawn, each trapped in his or her own thoughts. Before calling Gideon in to dress him in Simon's armor, Dillon had repeated what Alyssa now thought of as his ritual. Helping her don her robe, he had gazed down at her for many long minutes before dipping his head to steal a quick, hard kiss. Then, his resentment clear, he had drawn the hood up to hide her features. But he had embraced her, too, clutching her so tightly she had thought she might break, his fear still for *her* rather than for himself.

Were she his wife, she would run to him now and beg a passionate farewell kiss, admonishing him to have a care for his safety and to return to her with all due haste.

Were she his wife, she would tell him she loved him.

But that honor would never be hers. So, tamping down her emotions, she simply nodded and wished him a quick and easy victory from within the confines of her cowl.

After delivering a few last-minute instructions to Robert, Dillon herded his men toward the barbican, the hooves of their warhorses churning up the ground. There he paused to look back at her, where she waited on the steps of the keep.

Alyssa need not touch him to know how much it disturbed him that he could not see her face just then.

His wishes thwarted, he turned and charged through the gate, disappearing from view.

She bit her lip, the tears he could not see forging slick paths down her cheeks. Why could things not be different? Why must people be so suspicious of that which they did not understand? Why could they not accept her for who she was, not what she could do, how she was dissimilar, who her parents were, or whether or not she had been born on the right side of the blanket?

Why could she not leap at this chance for happiness with Dillon and say to hell with what everyone else thought?

Her shoulders slumped. Because, in the end, 'twould bring Dillon more headache than happiness. And she would do naught that might endanger his position as Earl of Westcott.

But his expression…

How she wished she could have doffed her hood, waved wildly, and given him a smile that would have sent him on his quest with a grin and a light heart. Mayhap then she would not be plagued by this feeling that something dreadful hovered just over the horizon.

"Wise One." Robert stood at her side, having joined her as the men crossed the drawbridge. "I would speak with you privately. In the solar, if 'tis satisfactory."

"I have work I must attend to in my chamber," she choked out.

"'Twill take but a moment." His face impassive, he motioned for her to precede him into the castle.

Swallowing past the lump in her throat, Alyssa did so, struggling to regain some sense of control as she trod up the stairs and into the solar. She stopped in the center of the room, facing the oversized bed that held so many new and tender memories.

The door closed behind her with a thud.

Robert's footsteps echoed loudly in the silence as his boots carried him toward her, stopping close to her back. Though she tried to concentrate on donning her role of advisor for whatever difficulty Robert brought to her, Alyssa could think of naught other than her desire to be at Dillon's side, ensuring his safety and healing the wounds he would inevitably incur in the coming battle.

Her breath gave an involuntary hitch that she fervently hoped went unnoticed.

Robert circled her slowly, halting in front of her, legs braced apart in a stance reminiscent of his brother. Before she could guess his intent, he reached out and swiftly drew back her cowl.

She tried to duck her chin to hide her wet cheeks.

Robert would have none of it. Touching a finger to her chin, he applied gentle pressure to raise it. "He will fare well, Seer," he stated, forcing her to meet his gaze. "Dillon would not give up his life in so puny an undertaking as this after you labored so hard to save it."

Alyssa bit her lip. Though she tried to prevent it, another fat tear spilled over her lashes and raced down her cheek.

Brow furrowing, Robert lifted one hand and slowly—as though he feared she might object—cupped her face in his large rough palm. He smoothed his thumb across her cheek, sweeping away her tears. "All will be well," he insisted.

'Twas odd, she thought. There had been several times during her years at Westcott when she had broken down and wept. From loneliness. From pain, both physical and emotional. And she had always believed that if she could just unburden herself… to Dillon… to her family… to anyone who cared… that the need for catharsis through tears would

220 | DIANNE DUVALL

vanish. Yet, now, as Robert smiled reassuringly and offered her his sympathy and understanding, something seemed to shatter deep inside her. Violent sobs erupted. Tears flowed freely. Simply drawing in air became a struggle.

He swore. Shifted his weight from one foot to the other. Then, after another moment's hesitation, he drew her into a loose embrace and pressed her head to his chest. "Shh," he crooned. "All will be well."

Illogical though it may seem, it only made her cry harder. Dragging in great gulping breaths, Alyssa drowned herself in his kindness.

"You will make yourself ill do you not cease," he chided in soothing tones as he patted her back and patiently waited for the storm to subside. "And all for naught. Dillon will be as irascible and full of bluster as always when next you see him."

Touching him as she was, she knew he firmly believed that. "But I had a dream…"

"I know," he admitted with some reluctance. "Dillon took me into his confidence so I would be prepared should trouble arrive at Westcott during his absence. I hope that does not anger you. He meant no disrespect."

"Nay. I trust you, Robert." When, at last, the wellspring of tears dried up, Alyssa stepped back with a sigh and swiped at her cheeks. "Forgive me. I am not accustomed to… I did not intend to…"

He held up a hand. "You are worried and overtired."

She hoped fervently that he did not know *why* she was overtired.

"Why do you not rest for a bit? Here, where Dillon's presence and belongings will surround you and bring you comfort. I shall see to it that no one disturbs you."

Her eyes burned anew. Robert said so much with that request.

That he knew she cared for Dillon. That he did not object.

"Thank you," she whispered.

With a smile and wink, he headed for the door. "Oh." He turned back, his handsome face crinkling with a wince, "You will no doubt be displeased by this, but I must insist that you do not leave the inner bailey without my protection. Dillon expressed some concerns for your safety. And you are still vulnerable from your illness."

She sighed once more in defeat. "As you wish, Robert."

His smile returned. "Rest now."

* * *

Shame settled on Robert's shoulders as he descended the stairs to the great hall. Its talons digging into his chest, it pecked and pecked and pecked at him until a scowl as ferocious as his brother's darkened his features.

He had never seen anyone weep with such intensity. 'Twas as if all the pain the wisewoman had suffered during her years of service at Westcott had come pouring out to bathe his chest. And all she had needed to relieve herself of it was a little kindness. Just a little. Not so very much to ask, was it?

Several foul names came to mind, all of which Robert heaped upon his own head. He cursed himself for every instance he could have shown her a kindness in the past and had not, every grudging thanks he had offered her for healing one wound or another instead of showing her true gratitude for taking away his pain. Knowing she had taken it into herself only worsened his guilt.

"William!" he bellowed, sighting the man across the hall, where he upbraided a servant nigh the entrance to the kitchens.

Tossing one last rebuke over his shoulder, the snowy-haired man hurried to Robert's side. "Aye, my lord?"

"No one is to enter the solar unless ordered to do so by myself or the healer."

"As you wish."

Expression still dark, Robert took himself outside and crossed to the stables. His favorite destrier had been wounded during the ambush that had nigh taken Dillon's life and he worried that it would no longer be strong and agile enough to carry him into battle.

Bright sunlight gave way to darkness as the stables, musty with the scents of hay and animal, enveloped him. A muted male voice broke the hush, drawing him toward Berserker's stall.

The stable master murmured something in the warhorse's twitching ear as he stroked its sleek chestnut coat, hypnotizing it into nigh motionlessness. At least a head shorter than Robert, Thomas boasted a stocky build, a quick smile, and an easy disposition. Mayhap two-score in age, he was well-liked by the people of Westcott.

Hearing his approach, Thomas looked up.

"How fares he?" Robert asked. As soon as Berserker saw him, the horse stretched his neck out and nudged Robert with his velvety nose.

"On the mend, milord. Another sennight and he will be all that he was before, if a little bit uglier. No lasting damage."

Relief brought a broad smile to Robert's face. He watched Thomas check the wound on Berserker's right shoulder without any protest from the huge stallion. The man had a fascinating rapport with animals. Even Dillon's vile-tempered beast calmed when Thomas gave him his attention.

Hmmm… Now, there is an idea.

Mayhap he could do something for the wisewoman after all.

Hiding a smile, Robert leaned casually against the stall door. "You have an amazing way with animals, Thomas."

He grinned. "That I have, milord. That I have. Been that way all my life."

"I suppose I am not the first to notice it."

Chuckling, Thomas straightened. "Nay. There have been many over the years what have commented upon it."

Robert furrowed his brow. "Does that not concern you?"

"Why would it?" he responded.

"Well, there are some who might suggest your gift with animals may have… unnatural origins."

Thomas's smile faded. "I am not sure as I follow you, milord."

Robert offered a negligent shrug. "I have heard it whispered about that one with a gift such as yours must surely have surrendered his soul to the devil in exchange for it."

The man's mouth, normally so eager to boast of his skills, fell open. His face turned a mottled red, then paled when he looked past Robert and saw two stable lads cross themselves.

"'Tis a lie!" he exclaimed belligerently. "I was *born* with this gift, I was. Like my father before me. I did not acquire it through wicked means. 'Tis shameful for any to suggest such a thing!"

Straightening, Robert kept his tone light. "The wisewoman was born with *her* gifts, like her mother before her." He had no idea if her mother shared her gifts or not, but saying so suited his purpose. "Yet you believe *she* gained them through wicked means. Why then should it surprise you that others believe the same of you?"

The only sounds in the stables were those made by the horses.

Giving Berserker one last loving stroke, Robert smiled. "I suppose the miraculous job you have done on Berserker here will only fuel their speculation. I am very pleased with the progress he is making. You have my gratitude."

Poor Thomas looked terribly disturbed as Robert turned and walked away. "Aye, milord."

Robert did not miss the strange sidelong looks the other occupants of the stables gave Thomas.

Whistling a cheerful ditty, he stepped out into the brisk wind and decided to pay the weaver a visit. He could use a couple of new tunics. And the man just happened to have a true *gift* when it came to turning out the finest quality materials.

CHAPTER TWELVE

"*Do you see him?*"

"Nay!"

"*Where the hell is he?*" Dillon roared, deflecting a thrust meant to pierce his heart and nigh severing his opponent's sword arm in return.

The man howled in agony as he fell to his knees. The corpses of his companions littered the ground around him.

Dillon and his men had poured into the castle's only bailey just as the sun had crested the horizon. The fog had not yet burned away and seemed in some way to enhance the noise of weapons clashing, the scents of blood and death, as the battle continued to rage. The sea and the long sheer drop of a cliff's face protected the back of the castle. Having tunneled under two of the three remaining walls, shoring them up as they went to prevent unnecessary damage, Dillon's men had swiftly surrounded Camden's undisciplined crew and squelched any thoughts of retreat.

They were a ragged band, Camden's army, lacking the rigid discipline and rigorous training required at Westcott. Dillon and his men would soon defeat them, likely without suffering any grievous wounds themselves.

The peasants raised not a hand to aid Camden, whom Dillon had yet to glimpse amongst the crowd of inadequately armed men. Judging by the gaunt faces that peered out from the shelter of poorly kept buildings, the fool had been starving them all for months.

"He must have taken refuge in the donjon!" Simon shouted above the shouts of rage and cries of pain.

"Then let us seek the coward there!"

With the help of a battering ram and several of his men, Dillon burst through the large, barred doors, his entrance heralded by the crack of splintering wood. An equal number of mailed soldiers awaited them inside.

He did not see Camden amongst them.

When the fighting at last ground to a halt, Dillon's men performed a thorough search of Pinehurst to no avail.

"He is nowhere to be found," Simon informed him, his blood-splattered face grim, as he collapsed onto a bench in the great hall. "He must have slithered away ere the fighting began, though I know not how. I saw to it that our men watched the castle every hour of the day."

Dillon swore foully. "Run home to his father, no doubt, with his tail betwixt his legs."

"Aye. I pity Westmoreland."

Nodding, Dillon sank wearily into the ornate lord's chair. "Lord Everard is a good man. Too good to be saddled with the likes of Camden for an heir. He will be sorely disappointed by his son's actions this day."

Simon snorted. "Not just *this* day, I wager."

Dillon watched the emaciated servants bustle about the hall, mopping up blood and carrying out soiled rushes. "Have you noticed the condition of the people?"

Simon nodded. "The buildings as well."

"The storerooms must be nigh empty."

"There is a goodly supply of ale, but little else."

"We can send to Westcott for our immediate needs once we have determined what they are. Our larders there are always overflowing. Gideon!" he called over his shoulder.

His squire—dirty, unkempt, and covered in his own fair share of blood—hurried forward. "Aye, my lord?"

"See if you can locate the steward and have him report to me at once. Tell him to bring the books with him."

"Aye, my lord."

"The sooner I get started, the sooner I shall finish," he told Simon dolefully as the boy left the great hall.

"There is much to be done," his second-in-command agreed. "'Twill take days just to assess the damage. Other than the castle, the only structure that looks reasonably sound is the stables. Everything else is either on the verge of collapse or has already done so."

Dillon nodded, unhappy. Alyssa had been right. There was much he must do here ere he could return to Westcott. He would not see her again for at least two months.

Two months was too long. *One night* was too long. Yet, until he discovered to what haven Camden had absconded, he could not safely send for her to join him.

A slew of malcontent epithets exploded from his tight lips as he rose and began to pace, ignoring the servants' nervous glances.

"What troubles you?" Simon queried in a low voice, conscious of their audience.

"I like not Camden's disappearance." Alyssa's dream floated on the periphery of his thoughts. Was this the trouble of which it had warned? Was Camden bent on breeding more mischief? "I want another search made of Pinehurst. Every corner of this castle. Every croft in the village. Every privy, every stall, every chest, every cask."

"I shall see to it immediately."

"And send a party of men out to search the surrounding forest. If Camden escaped—as it appears he has, the cursed whoreson—I want to know how. And I want to know where the bastard has gone."

Simon nodded. "If he is here, we shall find him. If he is not, we shall hunt him down."

The steward entered as Simon exited, swiftly stumbling out of the fierce knight's path. He looked to be roughly Dillon's age, with closely cropped blond hair, a beakish nose, and a body thinner than William's. The top of his head barely reached Dillon's shoulder.

Bowing, radiating fear, the man stuttered a greeting. "You s-summoned me, my lord?"

"Did you bring the books?"

He held up the requested items, which looked as in danger of disintegrating as everything else at Pinehurst.

"Very well. Have you a name?"

"Aye, m-my lord. I am called Edward."

Dillon loosed a gusty sigh. "Very well, Edward, shall we begin?"

* * *

"Sir Robert," Alyssa whispered.

Jumping, he barked out a curse. And she thought, for an instant, that he would stomp his foot in frustration ere he pivoted to face her with a rueful frown. "How do you do that?" he challenged.

The men he had been training paused in their mock battles and gave them their undivided attention.

"Do what?" she asked, biting back a smile.

"Manage to approach me without making even a breath of sound that would alert me to your presence."

She shrugged. "I did make a sound." Nay, she had not. Years of following Dillon into battle and being his eyes and ears at Westcott had taught her how to move silently under almost any conditions. "You were simply distracted, watching these fine soldiers train."

'Twas well-known that Dillon's men were amongst the

most magnificently trained warriors in the land. So she was quite shocked to see several of the men grin and nudge each other, puffing out their chests with pride.

Within the darkness of her hood, she frowned. Why were they not crossing themselves?

Then they did, disappointing her with their predictability… until she realized that they were looking not at *her*, but at someone behind her.

Curious, she turned.

Thomas the stable master hurried past, his face red and creased with a vicious scowl.

"Good day, Thomas," she whispered.

Halting abruptly, he looked up. "Good day to you, Healer," he responded, giving her a preoccupied smile as he offered a respectful bow.

Astonished by this new behavior, she decided to say more. "Sir Robert tells me that your mending of Berserker's wound has been quite extraordinary."

His eyes darted to the men around her, who crossed themselves again. "'Twas naught extraordinary about it," he insisted, a sort of furious vulnerability sweeping his visage. "All I did was stitch up his wound and slap a poultice on it."

"He underestimates his skills," Robert interrupted smoothly. "His way with horses always amazes me. Dillon is fortunate to have him in his stables."

The soldiers began to lean toward each other in two's and three's, speaking in low voices swallowed up by the breeze.

Alyssa pursed her lips and studied them all.

What precisely was amiss here? Thomas looked as if he wanted to either weep or scream. And Robert looked far too innocent.

"Either way you are to be commended, Thomas," she told him.

"Thank you, Wise One," he mumbled somewhat pitifully.

"We have rarely discussed your methods of healing the

horses' wounds and ailments," she ventured, intrigued by the continued lack of fear in his bearing. "But, should you have need of medicinal herbs, I have a goodly supply I would share with you."

He perked up a bit at that. "Thank you, Healer. 'Twould be most helpful." He started to smile. But a group of children chose that moment to scurry past him, their little hands fisting in a manner to ward off the evil eye.

For once, they ignored Alyssa's presence entirely.

As Thomas stomped off in a huff, his face all but purple now, she swung her gaze back to Robert. "Sir Robert."

"Aye, Wise One?" His lips twitched. His blue eyes sparkled with mirth.

"There is a matter I would discuss with you."

"As you wish." Robert issued a few instructions to the men, then accompanied her to the great hall. When he would have ascended the stairs to the solar, she stopped him.

"In my chamber, if you will." 'Twas a test, really, to see if he had truly conquered his fear of her.

Shrugging, he motioned for her to precede him.

"Healer!"

Alyssa stopped as one of the women who worked in the kitchen hurried toward her.

Upon reaching them, the woman thrust a cloth-covered bundle forward. "I baked you this loaf of nut bread. 'Tis a special recipe passed down by my grandmother."

Careful to keep her hands from showing, Alyssa took the proffered bundle. "I do not understand."

"'Tis my way of thanking you for laboring so hard to save Lord Dillon's life and for healing my son's leg when he broke it falling out of that tree last summer. He might have been crippled had it not been for you."

Without waiting for a response, the woman curtsied to them both and hastened away.

Alyssa looked to Robert, whose lips had stretched in a grin

so wide it barely fit his face. Refraining from commenting, she led him down into her chamber and closed the door behind them. The bread she set on her worktable, unsure what to think of either the gift or its giver. Then, eyes narrowing, forehead crunching up in a scowl, she faced a smug Robert and lowered her hood.

"What did you do?" she demanded.

When he caught sight of her less than pleased expression, Robert gave an exaggerated grimace, reached forward, and cautiously tried to raise her hood again to hide her frown from his view.

Alyssa fought back a laugh and swatted his hands away. "What did you do, Robert?" she repeated, less severe this time. "The world outside that door is not the same world it was when Dillon left three days ago."

"I know not of what you speak," he stalled, quickly backing out of arm's reach so she could not touch him and *see* his lie.

She rolled her eyes. "At least half a dozen others have come forward to thank me for saving Dillon's life."

"That was *his* doing," he protested, pointing in the direction of Pinehurst. "Not mine. Whatever he said to them that night must have finally penetrated their thick skulls."

Crossing her arms, Alyssa raised her eyebrows. "And the rest of Westcott?"

He dropped his arm. "They have *all* thanked you?"

"Nay, not that," she said, exasperated. "They are so busy cultivating suspicions of each *other* that they seem to have forgotten to fear *me*."

"Is that not a good thing?"

She groaned. "Not when anyone who possesses even a modicum of talent—the stable master, the weaver, the falconer, the blacksmith, the armorer, the *cook* to name a few—is now suspected of having evil ties!"

He shrugged and began a slow circle of her workroom, his handsome face alight with curiosity regarding the chamber that had spawned so much speculation. "I am merely making a point. They shall comprehend it eventually."

"Before or after they wage internal war here at Westcott?"

"Ann Marie told Dillon she did not realize how badly you were treated until she donned your robe and trod in your path. I thought 'twas time the rest of the people did the same."

"And?"

"And what?" He leaned forward to cautiously sniff a packet of herbs.

"The rumors of the priests. Care to explain how those came about?"

At last, Robert began to look uncomfortable. "Do you mean the priests Dillon told me about?"

She raised one eyebrow, waiting.

"Aye," he mumbled, straightening. "Well, I *might* have put it about that the priests only turned against you because you, ah, refused to fall in with their plans to heal only in exchange for contributions. That 'twas their greed, not any wickedness on your part, that guided their actions so many years ago. Of course, 'twas *not* you. 'Twas the other healer."

"My grandmother."

"Your grandmother was the last healer?"

"Aye." She shook her head, confused. "I have not even told Dillon of the priests' motives. How did you know?"

"*Aha!* So I *was* right!" he crowed.

Her eyes widened. "You *guessed?* You bandied it about amongst the people without even confirming that 'twas true?"

He nodded, unrepentant. "I knew there had to have been *some* less than pious reason for their intense condemnation of you, or rather your grandmother. Besides, it worked. Those whose ears I filled with the tale were displeased to learn that the priests in whom they had placed their trust would have denied them access to your healing skills unless they could spare the proper coin."

"Oh, Robert. I do not think 'twas very wise of you."

"I do." The cages caught his attention then.

"But you may have shaken the people's faith."

"Considering in whom they chose to place their faith, I do not consider that a crime."

Alyssa shook her head, thoroughly vexed. "Even if they come to view *all* priests in such a way?"

He shrugged. "Are these snakes poisonous?"

"Mildly."

"What does that mean?"

Sighing, she seated herself on the stool by her workbench and began to unwrap the bread. "Their bites are painful and will make you ill if they inject enough venom, but are not fatal. You would have to be bitten many times over ere death would find you."

"Hmm."

"Robert, I worry that you are becoming as ill-disposed as Dillon is with regards to religion."

"Dillon believes in God," he offered absently, leaning down to peer at the reptiles. "He just does not believe in priests."

"But all priests are not like the two banished from Westcott," she persisted. Leaning forward, she drank in the delicious aroma that rose from the bread.

"After seeing quite a few corpulent priests, garbed in raiment as luxurious as that of the king, beg alms from the poor and seduce their innocent womenfolk, I am inclined to disagree."

She clutched the loaf in both hands and broke off a generous chunk. "But I have heard that some take vows of poverty and truly do practice the chastity they preach."

"Well, I have yet to meet any of those." Glancing at her over his shoulder, he frowned. "Do not eat that until I have tasted it."

"Why? Have you reason to believe 'tis poisoned?" It hurt to think that the first gift she had received—other than Robert's flowers, that was—might have been given with wicked intent.

Robert abandoned his study of her animals for the moment and turned to approach her. "Dillon bade me watch for trouble from even the most unlikely sources. Therefore I shall do so."

As she watched, he broke another piece off and started to bring it to his mouth. "Wait. Feed it to the rodents. If they sicken or die, I shall not eat it. But I will not risk your poisoning yourself on my behalf."

He smiled down at her with a twist of his lips that seemed somehow sad. "I am sorry. I wish 'twere not necessary."

She took the bread from him and went to drop it in one of the cages. "Well, let us see what your outrageous rumors will accomplish. Mayhap by the time Dillon returns, 'twill not be."

* * *

Exhaustion pulled at him as Dillon climbed the tower stairs to the solar. He had ridden almost nonstop for three and a half days. After only a brief rest, he had then attacked Pinehurst at dawn, eager to confront the man who had ordered the ambush that had nigh claimed his life (and Alyssa's as well when she had healed him afterward), not to mention the one that had brought Robert to his doorstep with a limp.

'Twould seem, however, that Camden was not in residence.

Both searches the men had conducted had come up empty. The party Dillon had sent into the surrounding forest had found a trail far from the walls that seemed to begin in the middle of nowhere and lead toward Westmoreland, but naught more.

It had to have been Camden. But how he had escaped Pinehurst remained a mystery. One that left Dillon uneasy. None of the servants would admit to knowing the answer. And none of Dillon's men would confess to falling asleep whilst on watch.

How did he manage it? Dillon wondered for the hundredth time, closing the door behind him. He needed Alyssa by his side, to help him discern truth from falsehood whilst he conducted his interrogations.

And to dispel the loneliness he could feel closing in on him like winter.

He missed her.

Wearier by the moment, he sank down on the edge of the bed and sighed. He would sleep in his mailed chausses and hauberk, his thickly padded gambeson easing much of the discomfort. Until the knights he had sent to Westmoreland returned to confirm that Camden was indeed there, Dillon would not rest well. Nor would his men, guarding the walls, relax their vigil.

Dillon would have *liked* to leave on the morrow, hunt the bastard down, and finish the matter once and for all. Unfortunately, with winter fast approaching, he could not delay the repairs needed at Pinehurst for even a few days. The people needed shelter before the first snowfall. They needed food—great quantities of it—to replace what nigh-starvation had taken from them and to increase their stores. 'Twould take many hunts to bring down enough meat to satisfy both present and future needs.

They must have clothing as well. The rags they had been reduced to wearing would neither keep them warm nor stave off illness. Trees needed to be felled, to be used both for repairs and to keep the hearth fires going. There seemed an endless list of tasks that must be taken care of as swiftly as possible.

Lying back on the bed in the recently cleaned, nigh-spotless chamber, he let his mind drift away from his responsibilities and toward Alyssa.

Alyssa...

His lips stretched in a slow smile.

Aye. He would deal with Camden later.

* * *

"Robert, would you please stop tormenting my animals," Alyssa reprimanded for the fourth time.

"I am not tormenting them," he protested around a mouthful of the delicious bread she had shared with him.

Hours had passed and the rats that had consumed the bread had shown no signs of illness, easing their fears that the gift had been given with foul intent.

The castle had wound down for the night. Servants had cleared the hall, then wearily found their pallets. Dillon's men either patrolled the walls, slept, or sought a willing wench to warm their beds. Alyssa would have thought Robert would choose the last. But he had instead made his way back down to her chamber.

It surprised her, how comfortable he was in her presence now. He actually appeared to enjoy her company, as she enjoyed his. She missed Dillon terribly, and managing Robert's many questions helped distract her a bit from the emptiness. And her concern.

"One would think you had never seen a snake before," she commented, placing a stopper in the jar of ointment she had just prepared for Harry.

"I have not. Not like these. 'Tis the first time I have had the opportunity to study a snake whilst it still lives."

"You would have more such opportunities were you not so quick to slay them whenever you see them."

He shrugged. "I know not which ones are poisonous." Backing away from the cages, he dusted the crumbs from his fingers and disappeared between her bookshelves. "I must admit that I am in awe of your usage of those creatures. I would not have believed one could use them to extract information from a man."

She had told him the purpose her *pets* had recently served. "Why?"

"A *woman* recoiling from rats and snakes would not surprise me, but a *man?*"

Irritation struck. "Are you telling me that—were two or more of those serpents to slither up your hose and tunnel their way through your braies—you would not be at all concerned?"

Robert's face reappeared, his expression horrified. "You did not tell me you trained them to bite him *there!* That is—"

"I cannot train a snake to bite a person, Robert, nor would I."

"Then he was not bitten?"

"Nay, he was not bitten."

"What did you train them to do?"

"The snakes? Naught."

He frowned. "If you did not train the snakes, how did you get them to slither up his hose?"

She shrugged. "I trained the rats." She had thought her grandmother's orders to do so most peculiar when she had donned these robes, never guessing that such would someday serve a purpose. "'Twas a surprisingly easy task, if you can believe it."

"Actually, I can," he said with a wry smile. "I once knew a boy who trained a field mouse to scurry up ladies' skirts so he could glimpse their legs when they frantically shook their gowns to dislodge it."

Alyssa laughed. "Well, once the rats clambered up the man's hose, all I had to do was release the snakes, which—fortunately—were in need of a meal that night."

"So they followed the rats." He pursed his lips. "I still do not understand why that would frighten the man so badly if none bit him. The prisoner still shook and searched his cell with wide eyes when I looked in on him hours later."

She winced. "'Twould seem his fear of serpents far surpassed that of most men. He was quite terrified of them. I told him I would remove them as soon as the betrayer's name crossed his lips. But… I admit that after hearing of Dillon's death—you do recall I thought him dead—I wanted to see him suffer a little as payment." She bit her lip. "That sounds hideous, does it not?"

"Nay. I would have gutted him myself."

Alyssa shuddered. "You are very like your brother."

He grinned. "I hope so."

Ducking back between the bookshelves, Robert left her to her work. Occasionally she heard a slight scraping sound as he pulled one of her precious tomes down to examine it, then returned it to its home. There were many he would not be able to read. Books from faraway lands—from Asia, Africa, and the Holy Land—that contained irreplaceable healing knowledge.

He came around the corner and set a large, heavy volume on her workbench. Leaning forward, he bracketed the ancient leather-bound book with his elbows. "I envy him, you know," he admitted softly.

"Dillon?"

"Aye. I envy him what he has found in you."

She sent him a skeptical frown. "A quarrelsome sorceress who can heal with her hands?"

He shook his head. "A woman in whom he can confide. One with whom he can share both his triumphs and his troubles. One who makes him happy, makes him laugh." His gaze dropped. "A woman who would not love him less even were he to fail her in some way."

Something told her he spoke from experience. An experience that had not ended happily for him.

"I had that once myself," he confirmed, with so much melancholy that she did not need to touch him to recognize his grief. "For a time."

Alyssa knew not what to say. The way Robert went from woman to woman… She had not realized he had formed an attachment to any one in particular. Not at Westcott. She would have heard.

"Dillon never told me," she murmured, wondering what had happened.

"He knew not. 'Twas whilst he was crusading with King

Richard. Father sent me to train with Lord Edmund ere I earned my spurs and…" He could not have been more than ten and eight at the time. "It only lasted a year. I do not talk about it. But I see how Dillon looks at you and remember how it was with her." His eyes met hers. "I am happy for him."

Regret gripped her. "Robert, even were your bizarre rumors to succeed in softening the people's attitude toward me, 'twould not change the fact that I am the bastard daughter of a peasant. 'Twould be unseemly for a man of his station to pursue a legitimate union with me. Think you the king would approve?"

"We shall see," he countered with a healthy dose of Dillon's stubbornness, then briskly changed the subject. "What is that you are concocting?"

"'Tis for Sir Michael's lung ailment."

Only a year older than Robert and—other than Dillon—his closest friend, Michael often experienced difficulty breathing. He would wheeze audibly, sometimes gasping for breath. On rare occasions, he would suffer dreadful attacks and once had nigh perished before she could reach him. It frustrated Alyssa that, though her gift could ease his breathing and bring a quick end to such attacks, she had been unable to prevent a recurrence of them.

Some illnesses were like that. Simply beyond her ability to mend completely.

Opening the book he had chosen, Robert turned to the first page.

Alyssa let her thoughts wander again to the fierce warrior who owned her heart. Worrying. Wondering.

Had he reached Pinehurst yet?

Would he take the keep on the morrow? Confront Camden? She asked Robert what he thought.

"I doubt not Pinehurst is his by now. As for Camden's fate, we shall have to wait for Dillon's messenger to bring us news."

"How soon might that be?"

"'Twill take three or four days of nigh constant riding to reach us. We can begin looking for him then."

Four days. 'Twas too long, Alyssa fretted. She needed to know Dillon was safe *now*. Needed to know he had heeded the warning they had been given.

"You are thinking of your dream?" Robert asked, contemplating her.

"Aye."

"He will be fine. I am certain of it."

"If only I could read the dream more clearly…" She ran the details over in her mind like a checklist, marking off everything she was certain she had deciphered accurately, focusing on the more ambiguous.

"The man *must* represent Camden," she muttered. "Camden inviting trouble. Taking pleasure in orchestrating it. Laying a trap. In the bed chamber. Bed chambers are private. Secret. Camden doing something secret. Camden some *place* secret?" Her voice lowered further. "Camden somewhere secret… plotting trouble…"

But what? And where?

Pain struck her with the quickness and ferocity of a lightning bolt, nigh splitting her head in two. Crying out, she dropped the herbs she had been measuring and pressed white-knuckled fists to her temples.

"Wise One?"

She squeezed her eyes shut and clenched her teeth. That terrible hum that had plagued her when she had awoken after being healed returned to vengefully assault her senses.

"Wise One?"

'Twas as if a thousand bees swarmed around her, filling her ears with their buzzing, pricking her flesh with their wicked stingers.

"*Wise One!*" Robert called anxiously as he grasped her arms. "What ails you?"

She could not speak, could not move. She could barely

draw a breath as the pain magnified a hundredfold. Groaning, she felt her knees buckle (she had not even realized she had risen) and was dimly aware of Robert catching her as she fell.

* * *

*D*arkness. *The pain abruptly receded. Alyssa no longer stood in her chamber. Was no longer at Westcott. She could see naught of her surroundings, yet was certain nonetheless.*

Raising her chin, she drew in a deep breath. The air was thick, stale. It smelled of many unwashed bodies and—she sniffed again—stagnant sea water.

Where was she?

Thrusting her hands out in front of her, she moved them in wide arcs. Behind her they scraped across a rough wall of stone, which she decided to use as her guide. Swiveling to her right, she took a hesitant step forward, then stopped.

Nay. She must go the other way. Why this was so Alyssa knew not. She simply obeyed the impulse.

Reversing direction, she made her way forward, trailing her left hand along the wall. Occasional scuttling noises alerted her to the presence of rodents or other small creatures. She herself made no sound, moving as silently as the wind with no leaves to rustle.

Soon she heard whispering and saw faint light up ahead.

There. Men. Clothed in ragged armor, with dented shields and weapons in hand or within reach. A ragtag band that would seem pathetic should they stand beside Dillon's disciplined army.

They lounged against the walls of the cave, which she now saw was a long, narrow tunnel of natural origins. 'Twas mayhap wide enough for a dozen men to stand shoulder to shoulder across it, though most of those present either sat or lay propped against the walls with their legs sprawled in front of them. A few meager torches attempted to battle the blackness, their smoke hanging like storm clouds nigh the ceiling.

Reaching up to ensure her cowl was raised, Alyssa stepped into the light and boldly strode into their midst. Straight down the middle of the tunnel she walked, stepping over a foot here, a leg there, virtually unnoticed by all. There were dozens of them. Some rested. Others were wounded.

At the end of the tunnel lay a door before which three men stood, their backs to her, discussing their imminent victory over…

Dillon.

She gasped. A man to her right, sitting at her feet, glanced up sharply, seeming to look directly at her.

"You do not see me," she whispered, heart pounding.

He looked around, confused, then rubbed his eyes wearily and went back to sharpening his sword.

As baffled as he must feel, Alyssa continued forward until only a few paces separated her from those she assumed were the leaders of this motley band. One in particular she recognized.

Camden.

"I want to see his face when he realizes I slaughtered his entire army whilst he slept," he said with relish.

"'Twill kill him," one of the others uttered gleefully.

"Nay. I will kill him," Camden growled. "'Tis what he deserves for attempting to take what is mine."

Panic flooded her.

They intended to murder Dillon? How? Where? Was there time enough to warn him?

"I will be glad when 'tis finished," the third grumbled and nodded toward the door. "I thought all of our planning would be for naught when I heard his men searching just on the other side."

Camden waved off his concerns. "Nay. I knew the ale and the sad state of the stores would distract them. The door is too well hidden, blending easily with the rest of the wall."

The complainer shifted. "How much longer must we wait?"

"Only a few servants will be awake at this hour. Soon they, too, will seek their pallets. Then we shall strike, swiftly and silently, killing them all as they sleep."

Alyssa shook her head violently, backing away.

No.

Dillon.

Dillon!

Blinding white light engulfed her, erasing everything, then faded to darkness broken only by the struggling flames of a dying hearth fire.

CHAPTER THIRTEEN

"Dillon."

A smile lifted the corners of Dillon's lips. He dreamed of Alyssa again. He had done so every night since he had left her standing on the steps of the castle, frustrated by his inability to glimpse her features.

No nightmares had haunted him. Only warm, passionate interludes with his beloved wisewoman.

"Dillon, you must awaken."

He frowned. This dream differed, though. She sounded urgent. Frightened. She had been playful and affectionate in all of his other dreams.

"Alyssa?" he murmured.

Prying open eyelids that weighed almost as much as his horse, Dillon propped himself up on his elbows and searched the room. A familiar shadow, nigh lost amongst the others, stood several paces from his bed. Her hands, the color of moonbeams, emerged from her sleeves and rose to divest herself of her hood.

Anxiety creased the beautiful features she revealed.

This was no dream.

Dillon bolted upright. "Alyssa?" Swinging his legs over the side of the bed, he rose and started toward her. "How came you here? Did you follow me after I ordered you to remain at Westcott? Know you the danger you have placed yourself in?"

"Cease," she commanded, thrusting a hand out in front of her to prevent him from coming any closer.

He halted, astonished. Did she fear him? "Alyssa—"

"You must make haste, Dillon. Camden's men tarry below."

"*What?*" His hand went to his sword.

"In a secret tunnel that opens onto a storeroom that contains several barrels of ale and little else. The door is well-hidden and was overlooked by your men when they searched earlier."

He took a step toward her, but stopped when she stepped backward. "How know you this?"

"I was there. They plan to kill your men whilst they sleep and you with them, taking the keep from the inside out."

'Twas not until then—until she took that step that placed her between him and the hearth—that he perceived that something was awry.

His breath stopped. His eyes widened. His heartbeat increased.

He could see through her to the glowing coals and insignificant flames behind her.

"Alyssa," he whispered, not knowing what else to say, how to ask her what was happening.

"You must leave *now*, Dillon," she urged him. "You have little time. Go quickly and wake your men. Prepare them for Camden's assault and lead them to victory."

Shock nigh rendering him mute, he nodded, ordered her to remain within the solar, and raced for the door. Gideon leapt to his feet as soon as he opened it.

Dillon cautioned him to be quiet.

"Is it Camden, my lord?" the boy whispered, wide-eyed.

"Aye. I want you to stay here and guard…" He glanced

over his shoulder and fell silent when he saw the room was empty.

Alyssa had vanished as suddenly as she had appeared.

"My lord?"

He shook his head. "Come with me and make no sound. We must prepare the others."

* * *

Darkness surrounded Alyssa once more, taking her by the hand and leading her back toward awareness. Whispering Dillon's name, she wished she did not have to leave him and longed for his reassuring presence.

"Nay, 'tis Robert," a familiar voice responded. "Open your eyes for me," he coaxed.

She did so and realized she lay in her bed at Westcott. Robert sat beside her on the edge, his face grave, eyes brimming with concern. A cold, damp compress draped across her forehead, alleviating the warmth burning there.

Dread filled her. Had it all been a dream? A hallucination? Naught more?

It had seemed so real.

"Dillon."

Robert shook his head. "Dillon is at Pinehurst, Wise One."

"Alyssa." She corrected without thinking. Sitting up, she discarded the cloth that fell to her lap.

"What?"

"Alyssa. My name is Alyssa."

"Is it?"

A stab of guilt pricked her. After the kindness he had shown her, she really should have told him earlier, but instead had selfishly cherished hearing only Dillon call her by name.

Dillon.

She did not doubt that her vision of Camden and his men had been accurate because it confirmed her dream. But she knew not what to think of the rest.

Praying that Dillon would remain safe, she started to rise.

Robert held up a hand to halt her. "You should rest. I fear your illness has returned."

She shook her head and scrambled off the bed. "Dillon needs me."

He rose. "I do not understand."

Alyssa retrieved her empty valise and crossed to the shelves that contained her herbs and medicines.

"You have been unconscious for over two hours," Robert continued, "shivering and muttering things beneath your breath. Your skin burned with the same fiery heat that I felt in your hands when you healed Dillon. Your skin is yet flushed with it. What has happened?"

"I cannot explain it."

"You have not tried to."

She frowned. "Treachery stalks Dillon at Pinehurst. Camden and the remainder of his men will attack tonight, pouring into the castle from a secret passageway beneath it. I only pray my... warning... reached your brother in time. If it reached him at all."

"*What* warning? You have not left my sight. And just what is it you are doing?"

"Packing my medicines and a few other necessities. I shall leave for Pinehurst immediately."

"Nay, you will not," he countered firmly. "You shall not step foot outside these walls until Dillon returns."

Satisfied with the herbs she had chosen, Alyssa stuffed a bundle of clothing into the bag next. "I shall leave with or without your permission, Robert."

"Do not make me restrain you, Alyssa."

"You would not." He would never tie or bind her. She was certain of it.

"Then I shall confine you to this chamber."

"Nay, you will not," she stated, distracted. What was she forgetting? Alyssa studied the contents of her valise.

"If 'twill prevent you from placing yourself in danger, I

shall," he assured her, the determination in his voice reaching her at last.

Lowering the bag in one hand, she gave him her full attention. "Do not cross me on this, Robert," she advised him, half pleading, half commanding. "'Tis something I must do."

"I have no choice. Dillon has entrusted me with your care. 'Twould be foolhardy to allow you to leave the protection of Westcott and ride into almost certain danger."

He meant it, she realized. He had no intention of letting her leave. Even if it meant locking her in her chamber and setting men to guard her.

Panic vied with fury as Alyssa stared up at him. She had no time for this. She needed to see Dillon. She needed to be there to heal him if Camden caught him unawares. She needed to see that he was all right, that he still lived.

"I will not let you stop me," she gritted, her resolve unshakable. Dillon needed her. He *needed* her. Could Robert not see that?

"Nevertheless I will," he bit out. Then his voice and expression calmed. "I understand your concern, Alyssa. I shall dispatch men to Westcott posthaste so that we might know the truth. Until then—"

Her patience snapped. Adrenaline and apprehension driving her, Alyssa grabbed the front of his tunic with her free hand and yanked him closer, forcing him through sheer surprise at her actions to bend until their faces were only inches apart.

"You did not see what I saw," she nigh shouted, trembling with fear and frustration. "You do not know what I know. He needs me, Robert. Pinehurst is under attack and Camden *will not* fight honorably. Dillon may even now be bleeding from wounds that treacherous dog has inflicted and I am not there to heal him. Do you understand me? He could be dying and I am not there! *I should be there!*"

Her breath catching on a sob, she shoved him away and

248 | DIANNE DUVALL

raked quaking fingers through her hair. "Y-You do not know what I know," she repeated anxiously, seeing again all the men who had filled that cave. The men who waited to massacre the unsuspecting occupants of the keep, undetected by the guards posted outside until 'twas too late. "I will not rest until mine own eyes have confirmed that Dillon lives," she whispered passionately. "I *must* see him."

The quiet that filled the room in the aftermath of her outburst was deafening. His face unreadable, Robert reached up with slow, deliberate hands and smoothed his tunic where she had grasped it.

"Please, Robert," she implored. "I will come to no harm on the ride to Pinehurst."

"I know you will not," he said finally. "I shall accompany you myself."

She blinked. "What?"

"I shall take you to my brother."

"Nay. You must remain here and protect Westcott in Dillon's absence."

"Then you, too, shall remain."

"A score of men may escort me," she blurted. "Put Sir Michael in command of them. You trust him above all others, save Dillon. With such an impressive guard, I shall surely be safe."

He scowled. "I do not feel right letting you out of my sight."

"'Tis imperative that you tarry here a while longer, Robert."

"Why?"

"I know not. 'Tis more than defending the castle. I…" She shook her head, helpless to explain. "I know only that the feeling that you must abide at Westcott is nigh as strong as my need to see Dillon."

He studied her long and hard, then nodded curtly. "I shall choose carefully the men who will accompany you and shall place Michael over them as you suggested. Be ready to leave in half an hour."

"Thank you."

Striding resolutely for the door, he paused as he passed her. Some of the harshness left his face. "Do not make me regret this, Alyssa. Reach Pinehurst safely and send me good tidings of my brother."

She nodded, appreciating his concern. "I will."

* * *

The men waited nigh the base of the castle steps when she emerged. All were heavily armed and armored. All eyed her warily, uneasy with the task they had been given—to guard a woman labeled *Sorceress* as she fled the keep in the dead of night.

Alyssa could not blame them. The air was thick with menace, heavy with cloying humidity. The moon had chosen not to bathe the earth with its illusory light. In its place, a phantom fog danced around their ankles and wrapped skeletal arms around them.

The horses picked up on the tension and pranced nervously despite the soothing words offered by the warriors who stood beside them.

Her cowl shielding her from the men's scrutiny, Alyssa descended the steps and strode past them. She took note of each man's identity as she did and soon came to the conclusion that they had been chosen on the basis of three qualifications: strength, prowess, and a recent softening in attitude toward her. In fact, many of them had been amongst those who had surprised her earlier by smiling at her praise.

Well, they did not smile now.

She approached Robert, who spoke with Sir Michael.

Noting her presence, Michael nodded, unsmiling. "Wise One."

Her hood dipped with her own nod of acknowledgment. "I regret having to disturb you all at this hour, but time is short," she whispered. "I could not wait for the morrow."

"Robert has explained as much. If you are ready, we can depart forthwith."

"Nay," Robert declared, overriding her agreement as he faced the anxious knights. "Ere you leave, I will hear every one of you vow to protect the wisewoman with your life."

Much to Alyssa's astonishment, they did not hesitate to offer their oaths.

Robert guided her over to a powerful black stallion, one of Dillon's favorites. "Can you handle him?" he asked softly as the others mounted their battle-hardened destriers.

Alyssa stroked one hand down the muscled neck and shoulder of the beast only Dillon and Robert had been able to ride in the past. "Aye," she answered, confident that she could.

"Good. Should you come under attack, he is the best mount to have beneath you. But I worry that he may be too spirited."

"He and I shall do well together."

She handed Robert her bag and stood patiently whilst he fastened it to the back of her saddle. Once finished, he turned and stared down at her, his handsome face dark with misgivings.

"Worry not, Robert," she said, voice low, and placed a hand on his arm.

He covered it with his own. "I shall worry until you send me news of your safe arrival at Pinehurst and of my brother's well-being."

"A messenger should arrive by week's end."

"Does he not, I will assume the worst and lead an army in your wake."

She nodded. When she would have pulled away, he tightened his grip on her hand.

"How Dillon must hate those robes," he murmured, beyond the hearing of others. "'Tis difficult to bid you farewell when I am unable to see your face. It must be a hundred times harder for him."

Tears threatened to choke her as she recalled Dillon's expression just before he had thundered through the gates to conquer Pinehurst. "'Tis difficult for me as well."

He hesitated for a long moment, his fear for her and Dillon inundating her and clutching at her heart. "Fare you well, Alyssa."

"And you, Robert."

Dropping his hands to her waist, he lifted her and set her in the saddle. "Michael," he called.

Michael directed his beige warhorse over to Alyssa's.

"'Tis time."

The two turned their horses and, side by side, rode swiftly through the gates, the others falling in behind and stonily keeping pace.

* * *

Darkness enshrouded the tarnished great hall. Only the diminishing flames of a single hearth allowed Dillon to see the figures creeping forth from the storeroom like rats looking for a bit of cheese.

He and his men remained utterly still, cloaked by the shadows that swallowed the walls.

Alyssa had been right. How had she known?

Making only the slightest sounds, Camden's men slunk toward the pallets in the center of the room. Pallets that supported lumpy forms covered with blankets, which they mistakenly believed were the men who instead watched them with carefully restrained wrath from their positions around the hall.

Dillon strained to see the soldiers' faces as they closed in on their counterfeit prey. He had hoped he would be able to locate the one who had escaped his clutches ere he launched his attack, but 'twas too dark to see individual features.

When a man stood over every pallet, the intruders raised their weapons and looked to the doorway of the storeroom. The auburn hair of the one who stepped through it glinted with red highlights.

Camden.

Camden nodded. The ragged army he commanded instantly buried their weapons in the hapless lumps of clothing.

Dillon roared a battle cry as he and his men leapt forward.

The slayers jumped and looked around wildly.

Gleaming in the light of the dying flames, swords swung toward bodies frozen in shock.

Steel met flesh. Cries of pain shattered the night.

Panicked, Camden's men began to fight with feral desperation.

Dillon saw Camden's auburn head disappear through the doorway of the storeroom and swore foully.

Not this time, he vowed. The bastard would *not* escape him again.

Stepping over his opponent's fallen body, Dillon began to cut a swath toward his absent enemy. "There!" he called, alerting Simon to their quarry's whereabouts.

Nodding, Simon swung his sword and joined Dillon in forging a path.

Camden's men preceded them, backing toward the doorway through which they had crept with such malicious glee earlier. Dillon could not tell if they sought to protect their cowardly leader or merely wished to retreat and thought this their only means of escape.

With swords clashing, curses spewing, and blood spilling, all flowed toward the storeroom. Bodies began to fall beneath the superior might of Dillon's men and formed a dam before the entrance, blocking access.

Frustration mounted. Then Gideon and several other squires plunged forward to pull the bodies away.

Dillon sucked in a breath as a blade barely missed Gideon's neck. But the boy was fast and remained alert enough to evade injury as he cleared the path.

Camden's men, their panic rising, pried open the hidden

door and hurtled themselves through it in a bid to flee with their leader.

Dillon would have none of it. He and Simon followed, his men—those who were not still engaged in battle in the great hall—fast on their heels. They had just enough time to register a long tunnel mayhap wide enough for a dozen men to stand shoulder to shoulder ere Camden's ragged army began to extinguish the torches.

"Gideon!" Dillon bellowed even as he caught up to the first man and cut him down.

"Aye?" he barely heard Gideon call from the storeroom.

"Torches!"

If Gideon responded, Dillon did not hear him. The sounds of battle resumed as Dillon and his men raced forward to end the retreat of Camden's. So little light remained that he would have been unable to tell friend from foe if his men's armor— far better cared for than that of the malefactors they fought— did not reflect the flames of the torch or two that remained. Such also made them clearer targets, however.

Past the straining, swearing warriors in front of him, Dillon caught a glimpse of Camden. 'Twas too dark to see with whom he fought.

Dillon had to look away to cut down his opponent. When he turned back, Camden was gone.

Had he fallen? Escaped?

The battle slowed as bodies crumpled to the ground.

Gideon and several other squires, poured into the tunnel, each bearing a torch in one hand and a sword in the other.

Blessed light bathed Dillon and his warriors as they defeated the last of Camden's army, their shadows engaging in a phantom battle on the walls around them.

Dillon took the torch Gideon offered him and began to search the faces of those fallen.

Simon grabbed a torch of his own and examined the faces of the dead and wounded. "Was he here when we entered the tunnel?" he asked after a moment.

"Aye. I saw him, but lost him in the fray." Dillon's frustration mounted as he continued to scrutinize the carnage, but failed to find the face he sought.

"Here!" Simon called.

Head snapping up, Dillon crossed to Simon and knelt beside the body his second-in-command studied.

The fallen man lay facedown, but bore the auburn hair for which Dillon's enemy had been known.

Simon turned the man onto his back.

Both grimaced.

He appeared to have taken a mace to the face, amongst other things. His chest no longer rose and fell with breath. Though badly mangled, his features still managed to carry the look of Westmoreland, his father.

"'Tis Camden," Simon said.

Dillon nodded. "Aye." Relief relaxed the muscles knotted in his neck and shoulders.

Camden was dead.

'Twas finally over.

* * *

In the distance, she saw him. Dillon stood, silent and stoic, staring at the road leading to the unfamiliar gates below him. He was watching for her. Waiting for her. Was desperate for the sight of her.

He, too, sought reassurance and prayed for her safety, knowing that somewhere out there her robe blended in with the night as she steadfastly made her way toward him.

"I am coming, Dillon," she whispered.

A hand gently grasped her arm, steadying her. Blinking, Alyssa realized Michael had just kept her from sliding out of the saddle. She had fallen asleep again.

And dreamed of Dillon.

Over forty hours had come and gone since they had left the safety of Westcott's walls. She had not slept for more hours than that and craved rest. Yet she would not allow them to halt.

Thrice she had dozed off and caught glimpses of Dillon. Hazy, cryptic impressions of him seeing to his wounded men and disposing of the bodies of Camden's army.

Did he know she was coming?

Her heart leapt with anticipation, but she would not abandon her fears for him just yet. Such brief visions were new to her. She was reluctant to place much faith in them, particularly since they were not as strong as that which had assaulted her in Robert's presence.

"I thank you," she whispered, struggling to sit straighter and stave off her fatigue.

He released her. "There is a clearing up ahead. We shall rest there until dawn breaks."

"Nay. We shall continue on until we reach Pinehurst's gates."

"Pray do not argue with me, Wise One. A woman of your advanced years must not push herself so. 'Twill make you ill."

She sighed. She *was* exhausted. Too exhausted to engage in another battle of wills similar to the one she had fought with Robert.

"Does it trouble you, Sir Michael?" she posed in her whispery voice.

His brow creased. "What?"

"When others do not allow you to perform tasks you are more than capable of carrying out because of the weakness they perceive in you, does it trouble you?"

His lips tightened. "I am no weaker than they."

"Some believe otherwise."

"They are wrong."

"Then it *does* trouble you."

"Aye, Sorceress, it troubles me," he grated.

She nodded. "Now reverse our conversation. Apply your frustration to me and cease grappling with me over this. I give you now the same words I gave Sir Robert. I will not rest until mine own eyes have seen Lord Dillon. If you have to tie me to this saddle to keep me from falling out of it and slowing us down, so be it. But we will none of us seek shelter for the night. I wish to have crossed Pinehurst's drawbridge by the noon hour on the morrow."

Turning her head, Alyssa awaited his response.

Michael studied her dark form for several long moments. "As you wish, Wise One. I meant no insult."

She smiled, though he could not see it. "I know. And I appreciate your patience. You must all be nigh as weary as I."

He shrugged. "We are accustomed to such, Healer. You are not."

The clearing Michael had mentioned came and went on their right. Hopefully the men would not be too angry with her over her insistence that they keep moving.

Michael seemed to understand.

"I hope you did not mistake my words," Alyssa said, worried that she may have injured his feelings. "I merely sought to make a point."

He regarded her curiously.

"I see no weakness in you, Michael. You are one of the strongest, bravest men under Lord Dillon's command. Anyone who fails to comprehend that is too great a fool to look beyond what they consider your *flaw* and see you for what you are." She nodded for emphasis, knowing that there were many men at Westcott who underestimated his abilities. "And I assure you that neither Lord Dillon nor Sir Robert are fools. Nor am I. We know your true value."

For a moment, he did not seem to know what to say. She feared he had received very little validation in his six and twenty years.

"I thank you, Wise One," he said at last. "'Tis good to know there are some at Westcott who believe in me. And to hear those words come from you, who know the extent of my illness, gladdens my heart."

Alyssa smiled, pleased she had spoken.

He continued to stare at her, almost as though he could see through the midnight material that enshrouded her. "It makes me wonder, though, if I have not been as great a fool as those who have misjudged *me*," he murmured, alluding to his own beliefs regarding her.

Surprised, she faced forward. "We are all fools at some point in our lives."

"Aye," he agreed, "but some are greater fools than others."

* * *

Dillon stood on the wall walk nigh the barbican, gazing out over the pitted road that led to Pinehurst. The sun shone high overhead, bleaching the sky to a pale, pale blue. A nigh constant breeze bent the trees in an awkward dance and made the tall grasses in the meadow between forest and wall ripple like ocean waves.

She was close. He could feel Alyssa's presence growing stronger. Thrice he had seen her since her mysterious appearance in the solar the night of Camden's failed invasion. Her face and form had been ghostly, indistinct, not as vivid as they had been that first night. Her voice when she had spoken—*I am coming, Dillon*—had been barely audible. One might even have surmised it a trick of the wind or a figment of his lonely imagination. And he did wonder.

Those around him appeared to have seen and heard naught, though he had been in the company of others each time he had glimpsed her. It puzzled him. Alyssa's warnings were normally delivered in person and stemmed from dreams, not prophetic visions. Those, she had said, were only granted her mother.

As for Dillon, the only dreams that had toyed with him in recent years were nightmares spawned by his time in the holy land and, more recently, erotic dreams of hours spent making love with Alyssa.

So, what did it mean? What had changed? Or had anything?

Simon approached and leaned into one of the crenellated openings in the wall. Dillon had felt the intense scrutiny of his second-in-command often in the hours he had stood there.

"What do you watch for, Dillon?"

His gaze did not stray from the road. "You will see it with your own eyes soon."

"You anticipate trouble?"

"Nay."

"What then?"

"Have the men raise the portcullis," he pronounced in lieu of an answer.

Brows drawing together, Simon opened his mouth to respond, then closed it. He knew better than to question a command issued by the Earl of Westcott, friend or no friend. Turning on his heel, he left to convey his lord's orders.

Soon the clunking and clanking of the heavy metal gate raising assaulted Dillon's ears.

Simon returned and, without saying a word, joined his friend in a silent vigil.

Not five minutes later the first figures rounded the bend in the road and came into view.

"Riders approach," Simon announced unnecessarily, straightening.

Dillon nodded, squinting against the sun's brightness.

"At least a score, riding hard," his companion continued. "Too far away to see what banner they carry."

"They carry my banner," Dillon stated with absolute certainty.

Simon darted him a look, then leaned forward and squinted in an attempt to confirm his words. "'Tis as you say. I was not aware you had sent for reinforcements."

"I did not." A deep scowl creased Dillon's forehead as he searched the figures for the one he awaited with scarcely contained impatience. His gaze roved one armored knight after another until he found her. There. In the center. Riding beside Michael. Protected in front and behind. A small, dark figure that could only be Alyssa.

Relief swept through him. *At last. She is here. She made it safely.* Yet…

His pulse leapt with trepidation. She was slumped forward over her stallion's neck, Michael's careful hold on her arm the only thing keeping her in the saddle.

Ignoring Simon's rapid-fire questions, Dillon turned and raced for the gatehouse, down the stairs, and into the spacious single bailey the castle offered. The rumbling of hooves meeting dry, packed earth accompanied the party's arrival as the horses cantered through the barbican.

"Secure the gate behind them," Dillon ordered Simon, who was fast on his heels.

A look of sublime relief lit Michael's features when he marked Dillon's approach. "My lord, I—"

"I know why you are here." Grabbing the reins of Alyssa's horse, he brushed Michael's hand aside and steadied her with his own. "What happened to her? Is she wounded?"

"Nay, she is unharmed." Dismounting wearily, Michael stared up at the wisewoman and shook his head. "She is simply exhausted. She refused to halt. And she would not ride with me or any of the others in order to find rest, despite my urging." He shrugged helplessly. "Forgive me, my lord, but I did try. I knew not what else to do short of forcing her."

"I understand," he said, wishing he could see her face, to confirm with his own eyes Michael's words. "She can be quite stubborn at times."

"My lord?"

Some of the tension left him at her familiar whisper. "Aye."

Her cowl lifted as she straightened sluggishly and turned to face him. "Have we reached Pinehurst then?"

"Aye, you have." He could not stop the tender smile that crossed his lips, despite their audience. Most of the men who had accompanied her as her guard remained seated atop their destriers, watching them with avid curiosity. "Allow me to help you dismount."

At her slow nod, he placed his hands on her waist and lifted her down. Had he not maintained his hold, she would have crumpled to the ground. Her hands, cloaked in her customary midnight garb, came up to grip his biceps. He could feel her trembling and wanted naught more than to yank her into his arms and hold her.

But he could not. Not until they were inside, away from prying eyes.

At last she raised her head. "You are well?"

"Aye. Your message reached me in time."

"Message?" he heard Simon mumble as he stepped up to Michael's side.

She nodded, her grip tightening as she wavered where she stood. "I was so afraid that it had not. 'Tis why I would not stop until I reached you. I feared you would be wounded."

"Well, you may rest easy. 'Tis over. Camden's plot failed and he and his men are dead. Come now. You are weary from your arduous journey." Ignoring his fascinated men, he draped an arm around her shoulders and turned her toward the castle. He knew not what shocked them more, that he had performed the act with such casual affection or that she had allowed it, leaning into him to let him take some of her weight.

They had only gone a few steps when she stopped short. "Wait." Alyssa faced the men. "I thank you for escorting me with such patience and diligence. You are all strong, loyal, honorable men. I could not have asked for a better guard."

Several mouths dropped open. A few rough-hewn, beard-stubbled faces flushed. Heads dipped and nodded in response.

Michael sketched her a formal bow. "The honor was ours, Wise One."

"You are very kind," she whispered. When she swiveled to face the donjon, she staggered into Dillon.

"Easy," he murmured as he steadied her. Supporting her

with a hand at her elbow, he practically held her upright. "Can you walk?" he whispered.

"I must," she returned, valiantly forcing her shoulders back and her head up, determined to maintain a show of strength.

"Then we shall take it slowly."

The men behind them remained motionless, watching as he and Alyssa painstakingly made their way to the steps that led up to the castle doors. How badly he wanted to scoop her up into his arms and cradle her against him. To let her head rest against his shoulder, feel her face burrow into his neck, as he carried her to their destination instead.

"Do not let them think me weak."

"They dare not after the way you drove them to cover so much ground in so little time." He knew of no other woman who could have pushed his men, all of whom towered above her and were twice her weight—thrice it if you counted their weapons and armor—so hard, forcing them to do her bidding and flattening any protests that arose. Who else but Alyssa could have made it to Pinehurst so quickly? Who else would have even dared try, not knowing what danger might confront her upon reaching her destination?

As usual she had placed his safety above her own. 'Twas an affliction of hers he would soon have to cure.

"'Tis not an affliction," she whispered lethargically as they stepped through the massive double doors.

Dillon's head snapped around. "What?"

"My need to see you safe. 'Tis not an affliction, but love that feeds it. Should that not please you?" Her words began to slur with fatigue.

Dillon wondered, heart pounding, if she was even aware of what she had said.

Did she mean it? Did she truly love him?

"Of course I am aware. And aye, I meant it. I love you, Dillon. I wanted to tell you ere you left Westcott, but did not think I had the right."

Which answered the other question that had arisen. The question he had dared not even ask.

Stopping at the foot of the stairs that led to the sleeping chambers above, she swayed as she peered up them. "Oh, Dillon. I do not think I can climb those stairs. I am so weary. If no one is looking, would you please carry me?"

Carefully guarding his thoughts, he swept her up into his arms, not giving a damn if they had an audience, and carried her up the stairs and into the solar, kicking the door closed behind them.

He crossed to the large, comfortable bed he had spent the last three nights in and lay her down atop it. Only then was he able to push back her cowl and gaze at the face he had so swiftly grown to cherish.

Sleep already claimed her.

Drawing gentle fingers down her pale cheek, Dillon sat beside her on the bed and savored the sight of her. Her long, raven hair was pulled back in a loose braid. Several resilient curls had sprung free about her face, refusing to be bridled. Dark circles pooled beneath her eyes.

So deeply did Alyssa sleep that she did not stir whilst he divested her of her clothing and slipped her naked beneath the covers. Her hands were free of the paints she often used to give the illusion of age, her arms as limp as a rag doll's.

Smiling, Dillon leaned over to stroke her hair and pressed a kiss to her temple. "Sleep, love," he whispered. "We shall talk when you awaken."

And they *would* talk, he vowed as he exited the chamber, went below, and sent Gideon up to stand guard.

Aye, they would talk. For Dillon was suddenly quite certain that she did indeed experience the same visions her mother did, as well as the ability to project them into the minds of others over great distances. And, mayhap more disturbing, that she possessed the ability to read his thoughts as clearly as her own.

Why had she lied? Why had she hidden it from him for so long? And how could she continue to deny it after today?

For, exhausted by days without sleep, she had grown less cautious and answered his thoughts as easily as though he had spoken them aloud.

Thinking back to their tour of her garden at Westcott and their recent forays into lovemaking, he suddenly understood that it had not been the first time she had done so either. There had been quite a few instances in which she had responded to his unspoken ideas and desires. He had marveled at the time over how well she knew him, thinking she simply reacted to his emotions—all that she had claimed she could read. Yet such was clearly untrue.

Dillon could not bring himself to believe that she intended to harm him in some way with the knowledge she gained from perusing his uncensored thoughts. Nay. She had given him too much of herself for that, had nigh sacrificed her life for him. She had ceded her love and placed her heart in his admittedly clumsy and less-than-capable hands, always putting his well-being and happiness before her own.

Why, then, had she lied?

Could it be that, despite her professed love, she did not trust him? Did she fear his response should he learn the true extent of her gifts? Did she think he would spurn her, believing as others did that she was the devil's get?

Surely not. Not when she knew how deeply he loved her, how completely he adored her. As she *must* know.

Several of the men who had escorted Alyssa to Pinehurst entered the great hall and trod dully over to the trestle tables that had been erected for them. Dillon watched from his place nigh the great hearth as timid women, still far too thin, brought food and drink from the kitchen to bolster the tired soldiers.

He was both surprised and displeased that Robert was not amongst them. He had placed Alyssa in his brother's care with the expectation that she would not be allowed out of his sight.

But, having searched the face of every man who had acted as her guard, Dillon knew that Robert had remained at Westcott.

Michael entered the hall.

Dillon resolved to ask him news of Robert and strode toward the table to join him.

His questions surrounding his discovery of Alyssa's dishonesty would have to wait until she was rested.

Then Dillon would demand his answers.

As well as her trust.

CHAPTER FOURTEEN

Alyssa assumed at first that she dreamed. Dillon's mouth closed over the sensitive tip of her breast, tasting and teasing, tempting her to respond. His large, rough hands spread fire along her body.

Moaning, she tunneled her fingers through his thick, dark hair and urged him closer.

Instead, he abandoned her breast and kissed his way up her neck. "Forgive me, love," he whispered. "I could wait no longer."

A smile stretched her lips. Opening her eyes to the dim light of a curtained bed, she wrapped her arms around him and stroked his broad, muscled back. "How long have I slept?"

He captured her lips in a long, deep kiss, plundering and exciting her to a fevered pitch.

"Since you arrived yesterday shortly after the noon hour. 'Tis morning now."

So long?

She practically purred when he nipped the sensitive skin beneath her ear, then laved it with his tongue, his hand finding her breast at the same moment.

"After holding you in my arms all night," he continued, his warm breath tickling her ear and sparking a shudder of pleasure, "and stroking your soft skin…" The rough hand at her breast slipped to her side, followed the curve of her waist, over her hip and down her thigh. "After hour upon hour spent with your sweet, luscious body pressed to mine…" When she raised her knees in response, he settled himself more firmly against her, teasing her with his arousal. "I find my patience has come to an end."

She arched into him, eager for more.

Dillon groaned. "I burn for you, Alyssa. I tried to wait, wanted you to rest. But I am so greedy for you. I have to have you."

His hands shook when they renewed their rough-tender exploration of her body, seeking all of the places that would bring her pleasure. "I have never known such need as this," he admitted, voice husky as he lowered his mouth to feast on her breast once more.

Her gift told her he truly did feel remorseful, as if awakening her to such ecstasy was somehow selfish of him. But he would hear no protests or condemnations from Alyssa. Her body felt rejuvenated, responding eagerly to the touch of his hands and lips. As it should. She guessed she had slept almost twenty hours. Could not even remember entering the castle or sending word to Robert of their safe… arrival.

She groaned. "Robert." She had not sent him the missive. She had sworn she would as soon as she arrived, knowing how he worried about his brother. But she had fallen asleep before she could. Now 'twould take a day longer to reach him.

Dillon's body went still. For several seconds he seemed not to breathe. Then, flattening his hands on the bed to either side of her, he slowly raised his upper body until his arms were straight, his elbows locked, and he could glower down at her.

Alyssa's eyes widened with shock when they met his and she saw the desperate need to do violence in them. Rage unlike anything she had ever felt before abruptly screamed through him, forcing its way into her at every point they touched and scorching a path to her heart. Mingled with it was such incredible anguish that she could barely suppress it enough to seek its cause.

Dillon thought she had been imagining 'twas Robert making love with her.

Appalled, she gaped up at him as he swiftly lifted himself off of her and backed away to the far side of the bed, dragging most of the blankets with him. Cool air flowed over her like tranquil river waves, soothing her fevered skin, but doing little to assuage her rising ire.

"I imagined naught of the sort!" she exclaimed. Sitting up, Alyssa yanked a blanket away from him and dragged it up to cover her breasts. "How dare you accuse me of such!"

"I do not recall accusing you of aught," he snapped.

"I know not whence came this erroneous belief of yours that your brother is more proficient with women than you are, but 'tis beginning to twist your thoughts," she nigh shouted. "The fact that he has bedded more women than your entire army does not in any way suggest that you cannot make women scream with just as much pleasure as he can. *More* so, were I to judge by my own response to you."

He blinked in surprise, then frowned, clinging to his anger. "You called his name."

"I did not call Robert's name because I was imagining 'twas him making love with me." She could not halt a slight grimace at the thought of anyone's hands other than Dillon's touching her so intimately. "I did so because I only then recalled my promise to him."

"Which was?" he asked neutrally.

"I vowed I would send him word of your welfare and news of what has transpired here at Pinehurst. He was so worried about you, Dillon. We both were. He would not let me come to you until I revealed the vision I had had of Camden's perfidy.

'Twas a struggle to make him understand my urgency even then. And when he did, he felt it, too." Alyssa bit her lip, guilt consuming her. "I should have sent word that you were safe as soon as I arrived. But I was so weary… I can barely remember you helping me down from my horse."

Dillon's jaw slowly unclenched. "I sent Robert word of your safe arrival and of Camden's defeat yesterday whilst you rested."

She relaxed, relieved that Robert would soon hear that his beloved brother was well and would not be made to wait because of her negligence. "Thank you."

He nodded curtly. "Now explain to me how precisely you discerned my *accusation*, since I never voiced it."

Though Dillon appeared much calmer now, Alyssa hesitated. Almost afraid to tell him. Afraid he would think her freakish or, at the very least, be angry that she had not confessed it sooner and consider it a violation of his trust.

"Alyssa?"

Sighing, she relented. "There is something I have not told you, Dillon."

He stared at her expectantly.

"I am different," she began.

His expression lightened as his lips twitched. "Think you I have not noticed this ere now?"

Dropping her gaze, Alyssa plucked at the bed linens. "Nay, I… When the other *gifted ones* came to heal my wounds and restore my life, it… changed me. I am different now." She risked a glance up at him.

He sobered. "In what ways?"

"Well, there are the visions. When I saw Camden's army beneath the keep, 'twas as if I were there, Dillon, walking amongst them, stepping over their feet. One of them seemed to look right at me. And I could feel the dampness of the cave, smell their foul stench. For a moment I stood right behind Camden, listening to him boast as he outlined his strategy. As soon as I realized what he intended, I sought to warn you."

"You did. I saw you as clearly then as I see you now. Standing over there by the hearth and commanding me to awaken and call my men to arms. I thought you had disobeyed me and followed me to Pinehurst against my wishes."

Alyssa stared at him in astonishment. "You saw me that clearly?"

"Aye. I knew not what to think when I set Gideon to guard you only to turn around and find you had vanished."

She swallowed. She had known some part of her message had reached him, but this… "I have had other visions on the journey here. I saw you with your men. Twice. And watching for me from the wall walk."

"I saw you as well, more faintly than before. None around me did. But I could hear your voice, whispering that you were coming."

Distracted for the moment, she pondered the significance of that, the contradiction in the visions and possible causes of it. "Do you suppose 'twas because I was weary? The reason the first was clear and the others less so?"

"I know naught of these things, Alyssa."

She frowned. "Nor do I, but I fear I must learn. And quickly."

"These visions did not begin until your healing?"

"Nay. The dream I had of Camden stroking the cats… *that* is how the future normally visits me. Dreams that lack the clarity present in these more recent visions."

"What else?" There was an air of anticipation about him as he awaited further revelation.

"I also…" She faltered.

"Alyssa?"

"I seem to have acquired the ability to…" Swallowing, she said the last in a rush that emerged barely coherent. "Read others' thoughts."

Dillon's eyes locked with hers, forbidding her to look away.

"Could you read my thoughts ere your healing?"

"Nay," she answered in a small voice.

"Not at all?"

"Occasionally, if I concentrated very hard and you *consciously* sent your thoughts to me as you did when you admitted you wanted a... a wife, I was able to form a general understanding of them. But I could never read them as clearly as I do now."

He nodded. "And after your healing, when you realized you could?"

"Your emotions affect me much more strongly now, Dillon, overwhelming me at times. I assumed at first 'twas *them* I read and that the rest was my imagination. I did not want to believe 'twas aught more than that."

"Is it only *my* thoughts?"

"Nay. 'Tis anyone I touch. But you are the easiest for me to read. Most likely because I ... care for you more than anyone else."

The tension seemed to melt from his body. "Why did you not tell me? Why keep the changes hidden?"

She shrugged one shoulder. "These new gifts frighten me. I do not understand why I have acquired them."

"The *gifted one* who spoke to me—the tall fellow who called himself Seth—said healings affect you differently than they do me. I thought at the time that he referred to your fever. Mayhap *this* is what he truly meant. Mayhap when the other *gifted ones* healed you, you absorbed not just their healing energy, but some portion of their gifts."

"But I cannot control them." Her voice rose as her agitation increased and she poured out her fears. "Whenever I try, I find only pain. I was in my chamber when the vision of Camden struck me. I lost consciousness, Dillon. It took Robert over two hours to awaken me. My body was hot to the touch. He said I had been quivering and muttering something unintelligible. I have no memory of that. And this morning, moments ago, when you became so enraged and I tried to read your thoughts, I felt as though I were being seared inside by the flames of a torch. How can I accept these *gifts* when I cannot check them? How can *you?*"

And there lay the heart of her concern—Dillon's reaction. His acceptance, or rejection, of the transformation taking place within her.

Would he still love her now that he knew?

Would he spurn her?

He reached a hand out to touch her face, but frowned and withdrew it at the last moment.

Her vision blurred as tears filled her eyes.

She had her answer.

"Do not weep, Alyssa," he whispered, yet came no closer.

Swiping at the tear that slipped down one cheek, she shook her head and bit back a sob. "*This* is the true reason I would not tell you."

"What is?"

"I feared you would not want me. That you would spurn me. And you have. You cannot even bear to touch me."

His dark brows slammed together. "Alyssa, you just told me that the last time I touched you it caused you pain. I do not do so now because I do not wish to harm you. But that does not mean it is not killing me to keep from wrapping my arms around you and squeezing you so tight our heartbeats become one."

Sniffing, she stared up at him and drew in a fractured, hiccupping breath. "It is?"

"Aye!" He said it so forcefully she could not doubt his sincerity.

Joy leapt in her breast. Smiling, she threw back the covers and started to launch herself at him.

"Wait!" Dillon threw up his hands to ward her off.

Disgruntled, she frowned and sat back on her heels. "What?"

"I do not want to hurt you!"

"You will not." To prove it, she reached out, took one of his hands in her own, and brought it to her cheek. "See? No pain." Turning her head, eyes still clinging to his, she pressed a kiss to his palm, nibbled her way up his index finger, then drew it into her mouth and caressed it with her tongue. "Only pleasure."

Growling, he dove at her and drove her back against the pillows. Alyssa squealed in surprise. His lips found hers amidst the curtain of her hair and proceeded to kiss her breathless.

Rising above her, he grinned down at her. "We shall ponder your new gifts later. Right now I am more interested in exploring this pleasure you mentioned."

She laughed and murmured teasingly, "Then I shall let your thoughts be my guide." Leaning up to bite his chin, she smoothed her hands over the muscles of his shoulders and back. "Whatever you desire, whether you speak it or nay."

She got no further before heated images flooded her mind and inflamed her body. Burying her hands in his hair, she pulled him down for a devouring kiss, then pushed him onto his back and straddled him, restraining him with a hand on his chest.

* * *

Dillon's mouth dropped open. Verily he had not taken her seriously. The images had just popped into his head in response to his arousal and the press of her body against his. Her hands on his skin, her sultry voice washing over him, and those lips made him burn.

So when she lowered her mouth to his chest and began a slow descent down his body, doing exactly what he had unconsciously asked her to, he groaned both in shock and in ecstasy and buried his fingers in her tousled hair.

Her small hands curled around his arousal as she lowered her mouth and tasted him, first with a long, slow lick.

Lighting sizzled through his veins.

Casting him a look that was both shy and brazen at the

same time, she swirled her tongue around the sensitive tip, closed her lips around him, and drew him in deep.

"Alyssa…"

She read his need, his desires, his every thought easily, her mouth enacting every fantasy until his body was as taut as a bowstring and he teetered on the brink.

Growling, he drew her up and flipped her beneath him. Parting her legs, he settled himself between them and rubbed his throbbing shaft against her moist center.

She was ready for him.

Dillon plunged inside her, delighting in her moans of ecstasy as she wrapped her arms around him, her small hands sliding down his back to grip his backside and urge him on. She was so tight. And as needy as he. Dillon held naught back, muscles bunching as he drove himself into her whilst she arched up to meet his every thrust, the pleasuring building and building until they found their release together.

Panting, Dillon stared down at her, so very much in love with her.

He brushed a gentle kiss to her lips, then rolled them to their sides.

"Alyssa," he whispered, then said naught more.

Seeming to understand, she snuggled closer and rested her head against his chest.

* * *

"Here, love."

Having finished braiding her hair, Alyssa looked over her shoulder. Dillon stood nigh the door, fully dressed, with her black robe dangling from his hands.

Warmth unfurled inside her as she approached him and stood patiently whilst he carefully enshrouded her in darkness. "I wish, sometimes, that you could read *my* mind and heart," she told him, smiling as he clasped her hands and brought her fingers to his lips for a series of kisses.

"If I could, what would I see?"

"How much it gladdens me to hear you call me that, to have you touch me and look at me so tenderly."

Guiding her hands to his waist, he cupped her cheeks with his own. Callused from years of wielding weapons, they slid in rough contrast over her smooth skin. "If you see me as clearly as you say you do," he whispered, "then you know that I love you."

I love you, Alyssa.

Her throat tightened. She had waited so long to hear those words fall from his lips. How she wished she were free to act upon them. That they both were.

Unable to speak, she lifted her lips to his for a slow and sensuous kiss full of the love she bore him.

"And I *have* looked into your mind and heart," he murmured, pulling back to gaze down into her eyes. "You led me there yourself only yesterday."

I love you, Dillon. I wanted to tell you ere you left Westcott, but did not think I had the right.

Alyssa froze, her heart thumping so loudly she could hear naught else. Naught save her own voice replayed in Dillon's mind, confessing her love.

I love you, Dillon.

She shook her head, as if she could deny the truth of the words she had spoken.

"Let me hear them again," he beseeched her. "Give me the words I wish for the most. Now, when you are no longer walking in your sleep."

A kind of panic seized her. "I… I…"

His thumb swept across her lower lip in a brief caress. "Never mind," he murmured, not quite able to hide his disappointment. "I am a patient man when it suits me. I shall wait until the thought of speaking them does not strike such fear in you."

"I am not afraid, Dillon," she denied. "'Tis only that what you are asking, what you want between us, is—"

"'Tis *not* impossible."

* * *

D illon dipped his head and captured her lips. Filled with a desperate need to brand her and imbue her with the determination he felt, he slid his arms around her and hauled her small, slender form up against his. Anger and frustration over her refusal to believe they could have a future together pummeled him until she leaned into him and wrapped her arms around him, coaxing him back toward gentleness.

He softened the kiss, his lips now teasing instead of inciting. Releasing her, he grasped the sides of her cowl and raised one dark eyebrow. "Have you so little faith in my brother and the seeds of doubt he sows?"

Alyssa stared up at him, humor entering her deep brown eyes. "You know about that?"

He smiled. "Michael mentioned it last night when I spoke to him." Kissing her one last time, Dillon forced himself to draw the hood up to hide her face and hair, then led her from the chamber.

He settled a hand possessively on her lower back as they turned toward the stairs. Though not as narrow as those at Westcott, the steep steps similarly followed the inner curve of the donjon and boasted a high stone wall that kept the two of them hidden from view of the great hall.

"He would have me believe that half the village has accused the other half of sorcery. And that all are too busy nurturing their fear and loathing of each other to sustain their customary fear of you." Leave it to Robert to find a way to turn the people's fears against them.

"Faugh!" she whispered, slipping into her aged wisewoman voice.

Dillon laughed.

"You laugh now. But, when you return to Westcott, there is no telling what chaos will reign."

He shrugged. "Methinks 'tis a clever ploy." And he would

welcome the chaos if 'twould ultimately aid their cause.

"You would."

They started down the stairway side by side. "Why did Robert not accompany you on your journey here? I was most displeased when I saw that he had not."

"I felt very strongly that he would be needed at Westcott."

"With Camden dead, I know of no imminent threat."

"Nor do I. Yet the feeling persists."

Considering her new gifts, Dillon hoped 'twas just a feeling and not a premonition.

"Was it you, Dillon?" she asked, voice hesitant. "Were you the one who took Camden's life?"

He glanced down at her, wishing he could see her face. "Nay. When they realized their ruse had failed, that my men were not asleep and were rapidly decreasing their numbers, those still able to fell back the way they had come. We followed them into the tunnel."

"Oh, Dillon."

"Since you were there yourself, in a manner of speaking, you know the conditions for fighting were less than adequate. 'Twas narrow, inhibiting movement. And dark, more so after they extinguished all but two torches. Faces were largely indiscernible. Did my men not assiduously keep their armor shined and polished, I fear we would have had a much more difficult time distinguishing friend from foe. 'Twas not until we had dispatched them all that light was brought in and we were able to search the corpses for Camden."

"And he was there?"

"What was left of him. He had taken a mace to the face, amongst other grisly things. His hair and eye color identified him more than aught else." Since he was touching her, she no doubt felt how much he regretted not being the one to strike the death blow. Did she think less of him for it?

Her cowl swung from side to side as she shook her head. "Nay. He tried to kill you. And, mayhap, tried to kill Robert as well in the attack that left Robert limping to Westcott's gates."

Dillon had considered as much.

"You sent the body to Westmoreland?"

"Aye. I thought Lord Everard would want the boy buried beside his mother." Dillon dreaded the response he would receive. If he received one at all.

When they reached the bottom of the stairs just outside the great hall, Alyssa paused and turned toward him, enough to face him, but not enough to shake his hand from her back. "He will place no blame with you, Dillon," she said, knowing his thoughts. "Camden incurred the king's wrath with his avarice and arrogance, injured your brother, mortally wounded you, and would have slaughtered your men where they slept had you not stopped him."

"And nigh caused your death as well."

"You should feel no regret. Lord Everard knows the truth about his son."

Dillon sighed. "He is the closest thing I have had to a father in recent years. I would not wish to lose that."

"You will not."

He tried to take comfort in her certainty.

"Ere you begin your duties, I would appreciate it if you would take me to your men. I have waited overlong to see to them."

"Simon took care of them after your arrival yesterday. They are all rested and have been sent to aid in the construction in the village." 'Twould take every able body to make the repairs before the first snowfall.

"Not the men who accompanied me," she clarified. "Those who fought beside you in battle. 'Tis time I saw to their wounds."

Dillon abruptly moved away, severing all contact. "'Tis not necessary."

Her cowl tilted. "None were injured?"

Shrugging, he glanced back up the stairs. "Their wounds

are paltry at best. You need not concern yourself." 'Twas the first time he could recall lying to her. But he could not bear the thought of her harming herself to heal them.

"I have seen the wounds you consider *paltry*," she scoffed. "'Twould not take much for them to lead to either death or loss of limb. Particularly with your men's penchant for treating them with a dirty piece of cloth tied tightly about them."

He would wash the cursed wounds himself if 'twould prevent her from using her gifts to heal them. "'Tis just a scratch here and there. Naught life-threatening."

Alyssa crossed her arms over her chest and said naught.

Dillon fought the urge to squirm beneath her unseen regard.

When she reached out to touch him, he backed away. He did *not* want her to know his thoughts.

"All right, Dillon. What do you hide from me? Why do you seek to keep me from your men?"

"You worry for naught, I tell you," he stalled. He would have to discuss this with her sooner or later, he would just prefer to do so later.

She straightened, lowering her arms to her sides. "Do they hate me so much now that they no longer wish me to heal them?" she asked in a small voice, her whisper forgotten for the moment.

Regret filled him. "Nay. I would not have you believe so, for 'tis not true. *I* am the reason." He extended his hand toward her with resignation.

Hesitantly, she took it. Her shoulders relaxed. "Dillon," she said indulgently, covering their clasped hands with her free hand and stroking his, "the pain is fleeting."

"Any pain is unacceptable."

"Unacceptable to you, but familiar to me. I am accustomed to it. I have lived with it all my life and know how to control it." When he would have interrupted, she squeezed his hand. "Nay. What you saw was uncommon. 'Twas a unique situation,

Dillon. You were minutes from death. 'Tis not the same when I heal less severe wounds."

"I saw the scars," he reminded her in a low voice, still furious with himself for having caused them.

Sighing, she dropped his hand and threw hers up in the air. "What would you have me say? 'Twas my own selfishness that resulted in those, Dillon. As endearing as the few scars you bear are," she said, referring he assumed to the faint scar at his chin, the one that divided his eyebrow, and those that decorated his hands, "I did not wish to see you further marked, so I pushed myself and my gift further than I normally would. You are perfect as you are. Can you blame me for wanting to keep you so?"

That admission, belted out in as close to a normal voice as she had ever dared use in a place where they might be overheard, brought him to a stuttering halt.

She thought him perfect?

Dillon frowned and grumbled, stunned to feel a warm flush creeping up his neck. "Nevertheless…"

"I *will* heal your men, Dillon," she declared, implacable. "Whether it be now or as soon as your back is turned I shall leave up to you. I would remind you, however, that putting it off and allowing the wounds to fester will only result in more *pain* when I eventually get my hands on them."

He swore.

She smiled. "I knew you would see it my way."

"Contrary, disrespectful—"

"But utterly loyal," she quipped, folding her hands placidly in front of her. "Now. Shall we go?"

"Very well," he barked. Scowling, he continued forward, marched through the castle doors, and headed for the tower in which the men were temporarily garrisoned. "But we shall do it *my* way."

"As you wish, my lord," she said, a smile in her voice.

* * *

280 | DIANNE DUVALL

Two figures stepped from the shadows nigh the great hall's entrance, unnoticed by the quarreling duo. For several long minutes, they stared after the couple, then looked at each other.

"I know not what to make of that," Simon said, his face wiped blank by surprise and confusion.

"Nor do I," Michael responded, equally baffled.

"What do you suppose all that about the pain was?"

"I know not. It almost sounded as if healing us harmed her in some manner."

Simon grimaced. "I like not the sound of that."

"Nor do I." Michael frowned. Recalling the many times she had healed him over the years, easing his suffering during his many attacks, he hated to think that such had caused the elderly wisewoman pain.

"Her voice seemed changed as well."

"Aye. 'Twas odd."

"So unlike her. Almost…" Simon trailed off, seeming flustered.

"What?"

"Well, 'twas sweeter on the ears than the raspy whisper we are normally subjected to."

Michael silently agreed.

"And Lord Dillon. Did you notice aught amiss with him?" Simon ventured.

Michael nodded slowly. There had been no formal distance between Lord Dillon and the healer, though there always had been in the past. In fact, Lord Dillon had had his hand on her back when they had entered, settled there in an almost absent gesture of… affection? And the way she had taken his hand… "'Twas much the same with Robert at Westcott, now I think on it."

Eyebrows shooting skyward, Simon spun toward him. "Robert? But he has ever been leery of her."

"Not any more, or so 'twould seem. They have been thick

as thieves since she healed Lord Dillon." Michael glanced around, then leaned in to whisper, "I thought for a moment, ere we left, that Robert was going to embrace her."

Simon's mouth fell open. "Did he?"

"Nay. But she touched his arm and he covered her hand with his own, holding it in place so she could not release him."

"Did she strike him down?"

"Nay. They seemed quite fond of each other," he said with a shake of his head. "And Robert has made it his campaign to improve the people's attitude toward her. You would not believe what has transpired there since you left. Your wife has even befriended her."

"Ann Marie?"

"Aye. Ann Marie seems to have found quite a bit of favor with Lord Dillon, too."

Simon's expression darkened. "Just what are you implying, Michael?"

Michael raised his hands in a gesture of peace. "Not what you believe I am. I suspect he is only grateful because she aided the healer in caring for his wounds."

"Did she?"

"Aye, but only for a few days."

His feathers slowly unruffling, Simon relaxed. "All right, then."

Michael cast him a worried frown. "Although, as your friend, I should warn you…"

Simon's hackles rose again. "What?"

"'Tis just that I overheard some of the men talking and… I do not agree with them in the least, but…" He cleared his throat uncomfortably. Simon was known for having a rather fiery temper. "They seem to believe that Dillon has… taken Ann Marie as his leman."

The roar of fury Simon emitted was nigh as fearsome as Dillon's. Michael's eyes widened upon hearing it, then swiftly squeezed shut when Simon's fist connected with his nose.

Michael staggered back a step, then moaned and cupped his throbbing nose with his hands. "'Tis not true," he growled as pain careened through his head and blood poured over his upper lip.

"I know!" Simon shouted.

"Then why did you strike me, you horse's arse?"

"Because I am angry and you are here," he gritted, then sighed and visibly fought to leash his fury. "Forgive me." Stepping into the entrance to the great hall, he motioned to someone out of Michael's line of sight.

A servant girl approached.

"Have you a cloth?" Simon asked her. "My friend here has suffered an accident."

Accident, my arse, Michael mentally grumbled. Mayhap he should not have told Simon.

The servant hastened to hand Simon a cloth she pulled from a pocket in her skirts.

As Simon offered the cloth to Michael, his face full of apology, the girl hurried away.

Michael dabbed at the nose that felt twice its normal size. Pain continued to radiate through his head from it, making it feel as though someone kept hitting him in the face with his shield. The damned thing bled profusely, too. Tilting his head back, he studied Simon carefully. "Dillon would not betray you in such a way."

Simon nodded. "He would not betray me at all. My anger is directed at the men who spoke ill of my wife, not Lord Dillon."

Michael nodded, relieved. A few minutes later, he lowered the cloth. "How does it look?"

Simon grimaced. "I fear the ladies will not think you so pretty now."

Warm liquid again slipped down over Michael's lips. Swearing, he once more raised the cloth to his now-unsightly nose.

CHAPTER FIFTEEN

When Dillon had informed Alyssa that she would undertake the healing of his men *his* way, she had had no idea what he intended.

The first floor of the tower to which he led her was divided into two chambers. She knew not what purpose they had previously served, but they were now being utilized as sleeping quarters for Dillon's soldiers. Each sported neat rows of pallets, a couple of long benches and his men's gear, which was haphazardly strewn about.

Dillon evacuated one chamber and led Alyssa over to a bench, settling her upon it. Whilst the servants retrieved her bag of medicines and the other items she would need to cleanse and bandage the wounds, he ordered any and all wounded men to line up outside the large oaken door.

When all was ready, she waited curiously to see what he would do.

One by one, under her fascinated, amused, and intermittently irritated gaze, he allowed the men to enter. Dillon firmly closed the door behind each new patient, shuttering the curious gazes of those who would follow. He then blindfolded the *victim,* led the already uneasy man to the bench in front of Alyssa, and directed him to seat himself.

At Dillon's silent command, Alyssa then removed her cowl and bared whatever part of her body she intended to heal on the wounded man. She had not understood the reason for this until Dillon had touched her and silently informed her that he planned to watch her carefully for any signs of pain, to be certain the wounds did not open upon her own skin, and to ensure she did not push herself too far, as she had with him.

None of that happened, of course. She healed the wounds partly with her hands and partly with herbs as she normally did. 'Twas less of a strain that way. Dillon stopped her only twice, immune to her glares of reproof, all over a little grimace she had been unable to suppress.

She knew not whether she wanted to hug him for his concern or strangle him for his heavy-handedness.

When the last man had been healed and hurried to take his leave (the blindfolding and Dillon's bizarre behavior had certainly not eased the people's fear of her), Alyssa was surprised to see Michael step into the doorway. Bowing sheepishly, he held a crimson stained cloth to his nose, which bled rather plentifully.

"What the hell happened to you?" Dillon demanded.

Her ears straining to catch the words, Alyssa thought Michael muttered something about striking the messenger.

"What?" Dillon asked impatiently. Verily, his mood had deteriorated with every man she had healed.

Rolling her eyes, Alyssa whispered, "Come here, Sir Michael. Let me look at it."

"'Tis not as bad as it appears I ab sure, Healer." He slowly approached. "I just caddot seeb to stop the bleedeeg and wanted to ask you what I should do."

Dillon raised one eyebrow. "Aside from staying out of the path of other men's fists?"

Poor Michael. His face went nigh as scarlet as the blood

that coated his hand at that sarcastic aside from his lord.

Alyssa bit her lip to keep from laughing. "Sit down and lower the cloth." As gently as she could, she ran her fingers over the swollen bump, finding two places his nose had broken. Her eyes widened. *Simon* of all people had hit him. "Oh dear." She spoke involuntarily, shocked by the idea that leapt from his mind to hers.

Both men snapped to attention. Dillon yanked her arm away as Michael watched her carefully, noting his lord's actions.

"What is it?" 'Twas Dillon who growled that question, worried that she had experienced some pain.

Refining her whisper, she shook her head. "'Tis broken in two places. I must heal it with my hands."

Michael instantly looked as if he wished he had not come. His eyes widened when Dillon retrieved the blindfold and moved to stand behind him.

"You must not, my lord," she protested. "'Twill cover the breaks and interfere." Only Alyssa saw his responding glower as she waited with some measure of trepidation for his response.

Would he refuse to let her use her gift? Would she be forced to oppose him in front of Michael? To disobey him?

Because she would, if it came to that. She would not allow Dillon to forbid her the use of her healing ability.

"Michael," he snapped.

"Aye, my lord."

"Close your eyes."

The man did so, unquestioning.

"Should you open them ere I bid you do so," Dillon warned, "I shall blind you as punishment."

Michael paled slightly. "Aye, my lord."

Grunting his satisfaction, Dillon nodded for Alyssa to remove her cowl.

Pursing her lips, she tossed it back and told him with one disgruntled look, *'Tis only a broken nose, Dillon!*

One dark brow rose as his eyes seemed to say, *You shall do as I say or you shall not heal at all.*

Another sigh escaped her. Freeing her hand from her robe, Alyssa placed it on Michael's nose, closed her eyes, and concentrated on mending the breaks. Heat raced through her body, down to her arm, then to his nose. Soon her own began to ache. Bone shifted position beneath her fingertips, weaving itself back together. Something warm began to tickle her upper lip.

"Cease!"

Startled by Dillon's abrupt command, she jumped and released Michael, whose eyes remained steadfastly screwed shut. Her gaze flew to Dillon.

Jaw clenched, he leaned forward around Michael and drew his finger across the skin beneath her nose. It came away wet with her blood. "No more," he ordered in a tone that brooked no argument.

Alerted to his distress by his touch, she nodded and raised her cowl.

Dillon moved to stand beside her. "You may open your eyes, Michael."

Complying, Michael raised a hand to his nose and explored it experimentally. It was straight once more, no longer bleeding. The throbbing and much of the swelling had vanished as well. "My thanks, Healer."

She nodded.

"Return to the village and aid in the repairs," Dillon bid him curtly.

"Aye, my lord." Standing, Michael bowed respectfully. He froze for a moment as he started to turn away. Alyssa saw his gaze go to Dillon's fingers, still painted with her blood, then fly to her.

In the next instant, he was gone.

Dillon kicked the door shut, then returned to her side and lowered her cowl. Picking up one of the clean cloths she had set aside to use as a bandage, he grasped her chin and tenderly dabbed her nose with it, wiping away the blood. "I like this not, Alyssa," he told her.

"I know." Her body had already begun to heal itself. The bleeding ceased even as he watched. "'Twould not have affected me at all," she assured him with a smile, "were I not weary from healing so many other *paltry* wounds before it."

Dillon dropped the cloth with a groan and pulled her to him, locking his arms around her as he rested his cheek upon her hair.

* * *

When Dillon and Alyssa emerged from the castle, they found Michael deep in conversation with a knight whose back was to them.

"Does no one around here follow orders?" Dillon snapped, startling them out of their huddle.

Michael's companion turned.

"Simon," Alyssa whispered.

His eyes flew to her cowl.

As did Dillon's.

"Aye, Wise One?" Simon asked.

"I would speak with you in private." She wanted to thank Simon for trusting in Dillon's honor rather than in the foul rumors Michael had exposed.

And to suggest that mayhap 'twould be best if he kept a tighter rein on his temper in the future. Either that or unleash it upon the *source* of his anger rather than whomever happened to be standing in front of him at the time.

Dillon eyed his second-in-command with suspicion.

The large man swallowed nervously. "Have I done aught to displease you, Wise One?"

"Nay." But she did not want to mention the rumors in front of Dillon. "There is a matter I would discuss with you. If—"

She felt a tug on her sleeve. Frustrated at being interrupted,

Alyssa stopped mid-sentence and turned to Dillon. "Aye?"

He glanced down at her. "You wish my aid in this?"

She frowned up at him. "Nay, I—"

Again her sleeve was pulled.

Alyssa drew in a quick breath and eyed the space between them. 'Twas not him. Dillon had not touched her. He had not moved at all.

Confused, she looked to her left, to her right, behind her. All inhabitants of the bailey were hard at work and paid her little attention.

"Wise One?"

Dillon's voice drew her attention back to the men. Simon and Michael regarded her cautiously. Dillon watched her with some disquiet, most likely cursing his inability to view her features.

She felt yet another tug, this time on the hem of her robe. Glancing down, she stifled a gasp. Written in the dirt just in front of her, as though drawn by a finger, was the word *orchard*.

Her head jerked toward the neglected, thickly overgrown orchard that peeked around the corner of the donjon. "You men have work to attend to," she whispered, surreptitiously swiping a toe through the dirt. "We shall speak of this later."

Dillon caught her arm when she would have left. "All is well, Seer?"

"Aye. I have neglected my duties, my lord. 'Tis time I discovered what medicinal plants Pinehurst has to offer until some of my cache from Westcott can be retrieved."

Accepting her explanation with some reluctance, he let her go.

Ignoring her audience's inquisitive gaze, Alyssa headed straight for the trees. By the time she reached the corner of the donjon, she practically skipped in her haste.

The tall grasses at the edge of the orchard parted as she approached, inviting her within.

She smiled now, knowing who had summoned her, and

began to run. Through weeds. Past errant saplings. Into the shadows. Out of sight of the bailey. Cursing branches that ripped the cowl from her head and sought to detain her from her quest.

Ducking beneath a low-hanging branch, she caught a glimpse of a man up ahead and stumbled to a surprised halt. Her eyes widened.

This was not whom she had expected to find waiting for her.

As she stepped nearer, she saw that he was a boy, not a man as she had at first believed. Not much taller than herself. His clothing was filthy and tattered, the hat that hid his eyes beyond redemption.

Legs braced apart, arms folded across his chest, he stared at her insolently, saying naught.

"Forgive me. I… I thought you were…" Squinting at his features, she discerned a hint of familiarity. "*Meg?*"

Bright, feminine laughter filled the orchard as her visitor doffed the hat, allowing shoulder-length raven curls to tumble forth. "At your service, cousin."

Laughing, Alyssa hurried forward to embrace her. "Why are you garbed like a boy?"

She shrugged. "People leave me be when I travel so clothed."

Alyssa wrinkled her nose and took a step back. "Mayhap 'tis your aroma and not the clothing that keeps them at bay."

Meghan laughed. "Well, when one spends one's time searching musty caves littered with animal droppings, one can hardly emerge smelling of flowers."

"Musty caves?"

"I shall explain in a moment. First, how fare you, Alyssa? We have all been so worried about you."

She smiled. "I am well, as you can see."

"Geoffrey wanted to return to Westcott to see how you fared, but feared Lord Humphrey would mark his absence."

Alyssa frowned. "Another battle?"

"Aye."

There seemed to be no end to them on Broughston lands. And, since Lord Humphrey lacked the large, disciplined army Dillon maintained, the peasants were often called upon to fight.

"I would have come sooner myself," Meg said, "but Grandfather cannot travel, and 'twas difficult to talk him into letting me come alone."

"You should *not* have come alone. You should have waited for Geoffrey." 'Twas not safe for any woman to walk the roads unescorted. 'Twas one of the reasons Alyssa so rarely visited her family.

"Faugh! I need no man to protect me. I have my gift. If any man threatens me with a weapon, I can rid him of it and fling it back at him with a thought."

'Twas the truth. Meg had been born with the ability to move objects with her mind. But Alyssa now knew from experience that killing a man—even a villain like Gavin—was neither easily done nor easily forgotten. "Well, I am glad you are here."

Meg looked her over carefully. "'Tis happy I am to see you so well. Verily, I know not how you survived."

"You saved me. You and the others. Thank you, Meg. I am in your debt."

"You are as a sister to me. There is naught I would not do for you."

"And there is naught I would not do for you," Alyssa responded, meaning every word.

"You must promise me you will never be so foolish again," Meg entreated. "You cannot sacrifice yourself for him, Alyssa."

"I fear I cannot make that promise."

Meg took her hand and gave it a squeeze. "You love him still?"

"More every day."

With a sad smile, her cousin drew Alyssa over to the stump of a tree that had been felled by lightning. "He is an earl."

Alyssa sighed. "I am aware."

"He can never be yours," Meg reminded her gently. "He must wed a woman of noble birth."

"I know." The slim hope Robert had raised in her crumbled. He and Dillon seemed to be the only ones who thought the circumstances of her birth and her station at Westcott meant naught. For a moment, Alyssa had begun to believe them and hope that she and Dillon could have a life together. Meg did her a kindness now, ensuring she saw the truth of the matter. "Tell me of your cave explorations," Alyssa requested, wanting to change the subject. "What do you seek in them?"

"Not what, but whom."

The two attempted to make themselves comfortable on the lumpy wooden natural bench, then gave up and sat on the ground.

"I seek the *gifted ones* who helped us heal you," Meg said at last.

Alyssa frowned. "Dillon said there were seven of you."

"Aye, but only six of us were *gifted ones*. The one called Seth allowed Matthew to accompany us so he would not worry." The tale she told next was a fantastical one of Seth coming to Meghan's door and taking her—in the blink of an eye— from her home to Broughston lands to find Geoffrey, then to Alyssa's mother, then to Westcott.

"You said there was another with Seth?"

"Aye. His name was Roland, but he spoke very little. He said only that Seth is the eldest and most powerful amongst us."

"Did you not say Seth appeared young?"

"Aye. No older than Lord Dillon. 'Tis a mystery, is it not?"

Alyssa nodded. "In truth, I knew not there were any others out there. I thought our family the only ones born with unusual gifts."

"As did I." Meg shook her head. "I know not who Seth is, but I sensed such immense power in him, Alyssa. 'Twas he who told us you would not perish if we healed you and—since your grandmother lacked the strength to do so alone—showed us how to help you."

"Dillon said as much, but I know not how you did it. Only Grandmother has the healing gift."

"Roland was a healer, too. I think Seth was as well, but he did not participate. He just told us the healers could draw strength from the rest of us and… 'twas exactly what happened when we healed you."

Alyssa shook her head. "'Twas not all that happened." She explained the changes that were taking place within her. Her visions. Her ability to read thoughts.

Meg stared, her gaze fascinated. "You've acquired new gifts?"

"Aye. And have little control over them."

"I have never heard of such."

"Nor have I." They sat in silence for several long moments, wooed by the birds singing in the tree limbs above them. "Who *is* this Seth?" Alyssa asked. "How does he know so much more than the rest of us?"

"I know not. But he is more powerful than all of us combined. And tall," she marveled. "Seth was so tall that he even dwarfed Lord Dillon."

Alyssa could not imagine it. Dillon was the tallest man she had ever met.

"I intend to find him," Meg said again as a determined gleam entered her brown eyes.

Alyssa did not attempt to dissuade her cousin, knowing such would prove fruitless.

Long moments of quiet passed.

"Why a cave?" Alyssa asked curiously.

"I asked your mother to seek him in a vision and she saw him in a cave with a shadowy figure. So I searched every one I came upon on my way here."

"'Tis not much of a guide."

"I know, but how long can a giant go unnoticed?"

"Hmm."

Meg gave Alyssa a speculative look. "So, what does your handsome warrior earl think of you now that he has seen you unshielded by your robes?"

Alyssa forced a smile. "He thinks himself in love with me."

Meg bit her lip and again took Alyssa's hand. "Oh dear."

* * *

"You are quiet, my lord."

Dillon pried his eyes away from Alyssa's hands and glanced at her face.

She had not looked up when she had spoken. Her attention seemed riveted to the dried herbs she currently ground into powder, yet another treatment she prepared for the neglected people of Pinehurst.

A month had passed since her cousin Meghan had visited. A strange young woman, that one.

During that time, much had been accomplished.

Dillon spent every day from sunrise to sunset laboring alongside his men, shoring up the keep's defenses, making repairs, tearing down structures that were unsound and replacing them with new ones. In the evening, he retired with Alyssa to the lord's chamber, which also served as the solar and had rapidly become their haven away from duty and prying eyes.

The people at Pinehurst, like all those weighted by superstitions, were wary of the healer and feared her peculiar gifts. Yet they seemed to lack any real hostility toward her, mayhap because they had quickly come to understand the value Dillon placed on her and did not wish to displease their new lord in any way. He was, after all, turning out to be much more generous than his predecessor, though Simon told him they found his presence formidable and his reputation downright frightening.

Their manner toward Alyssa was more one of caution than hate. She had visited many of them in their crumbling huts, asking after their health, which more oft than not had suffered under Camden's brutal rule. Though all feared having her heal them with her hands—something only permitted in Dillon's presence, behind closed doors, whilst blindfolded—they treated her with respect and always thanked her for her troubles.

Each night, as Dillon sharpened his weapons or mended any number of items that required care at Pinehurst, Alyssa worked diligently at the table he had ordered installed in the solar, filing away the herbs she had collected and mixing her miraculous cures. Sometimes they toiled in companionable silence. Other times they laughed and talked and teased. They even sang on occasion.

This night differed, however. The hush that gradually settled upon their shoulders was heavy with words unspoken.

Seated at one end of the table, Dillon found himself watching her as was his wont. Her lovely profile. The graceful curve of her throat. The full breasts nigh hidden beneath the material of her robe. The thick braid that dangled down her back and danced with every movement. The motions of her dainty fingers.

And, as he watched, his own hands grew slack, forgetting the task he had assigned them.

"You are quiet," she repeated now.

"Aye."

"Does aught trouble you?"

"Aye," he confirmed.

An expectant pause ensued as she waited for him to speak his mind.

"I fear you have been less than honest with me, Alyssa."

Her head snapped up, her lips parting slightly in surprise. "What?"

"You have not been honest with me."

Her brown eyes widened in astonishment. "You accuse me of lying?"

"Mine own eyes have confirmed it."

She frowned at him with dawning aggravation. "I have never lied to you, Dillon. If your eyes tell you otherwise, then 'tis *they* who have been untrue."

He shook his head. "You are keeping something from me. I would know why."

A strange expression flitted across her face as she fell still. Releasing the mortar and pestle, she turned to face him, one arm resting on the table, the other at her side.

"Do you deny it?" he persisted when she said naught.

"What is it you believe I have kept from you?" she asked carefully.

"'Tis obvious to any who have eyes and care to see," he retorted, his gaze dropping to his target.

The hand at her side twitched, as though she had instinctively begun to raise it, then thought better of it.

"Dillon," she began.

He looked up. Her expression had softened, her eyes pleading for understanding. But he did not let it move him. "Why did you not tell me you had acquired other powers during your healing?" he asked, hurt that she had not.

Her brows drew together. "Powers?"

"Powers. Gifts. You know of what I speak."

"I *did* tell you of my new gifts. The first morning I awoke in this chamber. Do you not remember?"

"I remember well. But you failed to disclose the whole of it."

Alyssa folded her arms across her chest. "I told you of my ability to read thoughts. I told you of the visions. What more could there be?"

"Your ability to move objects without touching them."

She opened her mouth to respond, then shut it again.

"What?"

"Why did you not tell me you can move objects with your mind?"

Dillon knew not what response he had anticipated, but the laughter that abruptly escaped her caught him unawares.

"I have been with you for seven years, yet your rare jests continue to surprise me." Eyes sparkling, teeth flashing in a wide smile, she drifted closer until she stood between his knees.

Dillon struggled to hold onto his anger as she leaned her body into his and slid her hands up his chest and around his neck. She was so small and he so large that even seated he was taller than her.

"Move things with my mind," she murmured merrily, her lips lifting to meet his, making his heart race. "I love it when you tease me, Dillon."

His arms closed around her of their own accord as her mouth settled upon his and stole his breath. The intimacy they shared amazed him more every day, extending so much further than the lovemaking they lost themselves in when darkness fell and the rest of the keep slumbered. A look. A touch. A melding of lips. They were both so hungry for affection.

Dillon had always been secure in the love of his brother. How often had they hugged or draped an arm around one another's shoulders, slapped each other companionably on the back, or rumpled each other's hair in jest? He had thought little of it at the time, mayhap taking it too much for granted. But Alyssa…

She had been so isolated for most of her life. Feared. Hated. Ostracized. Utterly untouched. Even he had avoided physical contact with her, touching her rarely when not employing her gifts, ensuring that a respectful distance remained between them at all times, never considering how much she might need an occasional brush of his hand.

However now that their relationship had changed and

deepened and evolved, Dillon could not keep his hands off of her.

Whenever they were alone, he felt compelled to touch her hair, tunneling his fingers through it if she left it loose or smoothing his hand over it when it was not, tucking wayward strands back into place. The silky texture of her cheek always seemed to beckon, demanding a brief caress. Her shoulder fit so perfectly beneath his large palm. 'Twas only natural that it would itch to go there. And even more natural for his fingers to glide down her arm to link with hers.

The small of her back, the curve of her hip, the stubborn thrust of her chin, her tiny feet, that special place behind her ear that called out for a nuzzle, the little crinkle that formed between her brows when she was concentrating or angered all drew him like a magnet, their pull irresistible.

'Twas new to him, this adoring yet nonsexual compulsion to touch her and display his affection. And the more he gave in to it, the more comfortable Alyssa seemed to grow with his love, surprising him with similar gestures of her own.

Like this kiss that awakened within his body desires he dare not give in to until this matter was settled.

But 'twas so very tempting.

Gathering his strength, Dillon regretfully drew back and set her away from him, severing all contact.

Face flushed, lips rosy and slightly swollen, she looked up at him in confusion. Blissful, beautiful, sinfully arousing confusion.

"I assure you I am in earnest, Alyssa," he said, his voice a tad unsteady, and waited for his words to register.

When they did, she took a step back, that beloved little crinkle forming between her brows again. "You did not jest?"

"Nay."

Her head swiveled slowly from side to side. "Dillon, whatever would lead you to believe such a thing? I move objects the same way you do. With my hands, not with my mind."

Rising, he began to pace.

Why did she continue to deny it? How could she persist in speaking falsely after giving him vivid proof to the contrary? "If you did not wish me to know of your new talent, why then did you display it in my presence?" he asked. "Did you think it would escape my notice?"

She threw up her hands. "*What* new talent? The only skills I have displayed are—"

"I saw you move them!" he snapped, frustration rising. How could she still not trust him?

Shocked by his outburst, she stood mutely before him.

"I saw you move them," he said again, more controlled.

For several long minutes, she stared at him as though he were some inscrutable puzzle she could not fathom how to solve. When at last she spoke, her tone reminded him of that which Thomas often used to soothe skittish horses. "What did I move, Dillon?"

He gestured toward her work table. "Whilst you were preparing your potions and salves and such. Thrice as I watched, you reached for a pouch that was beyond your grasp and it slid across the table into your waiting hand."

Her brow furrowed. "I do not understand."

"You moved them, Alyssa. Without so much as a touch of your little finger."

"I must have jostled the table and—"

"You did not."

She chewed her lower lip. "Mayhap the table is unsteady and—"

"You know 'tis not. You placed it there yourself and would have noticed such a flaw long ere now." To confirm his words, he pressed on one corner of the table, which did not move. "'Twas *you*, Alyssa. The pouches moved at your command."

"But such is not possible, Dillon."

"Why do you deny it when just moments ago I witnessed

it?"

Alyssa gripped her hands together in front of her and eyed the table as though she feared the jars upon it would leap up and fling themselves at her.

Dillon frowned. Could it be that she had not known?

It seemed unlikely, yet her surprise and unease appeared to be genuine.

"Could you not have imagined it?" she suggested hopefully, face falling when he shook his head. "I do not understand," she said again.

Regretting his burst of temper, Dillon moved forward and wrapped his arms around her. "Did you truly not know, sweetling?"

"Nay." She sounded a bit dazed. As well she should be, he supposed. Dillon thought that, of all the gifts she had demonstrated, this one was the most daunting.

Well, nay. That was not precisely true. Her newfound ability to appear before him in visions and project that lovely translucent image of herself wherever he may be was more unsettling, though not unwelcome. He treasured every glimpse he was given of her.

Even so, seeing objects move at her command, silent or otherwise, had made his breath stop.

"I should not have shouted," he told her gruffly, unused to offering apologies.

She tightened her hold about his waist. "Had I thought what you thought, *I* would have shouted."

Sighing, Dillon pressed a kiss to the top of her head and leaned back so he could look down at her. "I thought you kept it from me apurpose as you did the others because you feared I would spurn you if I knew the truth." When she smiled up at him, he smoothed his hand over her hair, once more compelled to caress. "It angered me to think you had so little faith in me."

"Nay. I was wrong in that. I know that now. And had I

known that those were not the only gifts I had acquired, I would have told you. I *do* have faith in you, Dillon. Whatever the future may bring, never doubt that."

Bending his head, he brushed his lips across hers in a gentle kiss. "My temper is atrocious," he muttered.

"Your temper is endearing," she retorted.

Dillon stared down at her in horror. "*Endearing?*" Men throughout the continent quailed at the mere sight of his scowl and this little bit of a woman claimed his temper was *endearing?*

Her lips twitched.

His eyes narrowed.

"Only when directed at me and driven by love," she conceded, kissing his chin.

He snorted, reveling in her attentions. "You are making me soft, I vow."

"'Twas not what you told me last night," she teased, her smile turning provocative.

His body instantly rose to the bait. "Do not think you can succeed in distracting me from my purpose, wench. You have yet to admit to possessing your new gift."

Her lips pursed in a pout. "'Tis difficult to acknowledge a gift I have never utilized. Knowingly," she added at his pointed look.

"Then do so now."

"Now?"

"Aye. Demonstrate your new gift for me so that you may be convinced it can be done."

"Oh, I know it can be done," she muttered. "I have seen Meg do as much many times."

"Not whilst she was here."

"Aye, she did. 'Twas how I knew she awaited me in the orchard."

"Hmm." He had noticed naught unusual.

Taking her by the shoulders, Dillon turned her so that she

faced the table upon which her jars and pots and packets of herbs and medicines were neatly arranged. "Now, choose an object and attempt to summon it to you."

She stared up at him, face full of doubt. "Did I speak any words to make the pouches move?"

"Nay. You merely reached your hand out and they slid toward you."

Nodding, Alyssa drew in a deep breath and dramatically flung her hand out toward the table.

Naught happened.

"Try again."

Lips tightening, grumbling beneath her breath, she repeated the gesture.

A small pot with a loose stopper rattled violently, then sped forward, left the table, and hit Dillon squarely in the chest, spilling a foul-smelling, gooey concoction across the front of his tunic.

"Oh!" Alyssa's dismayed cry accompanied the sound of the pot shattering as it hit the floor at Dillon's feet, spattering his hose and boots with the rest of its contents.

Grimacing over the noxious fumes engulfing him, he saw her pretty umber eyes widen, her mouth fall open. His first instinct was to bellow a protest, his second to laugh. She looked so horrified, though, that he feared neither would be appropriate and sought a more diplomatic response.

"Ah… not bad for a first attempt. I am certain that with practice your aim will become more true, love. No need to worry."

Her eyes fell away. She began to nibble her lower lip.

He frowned. "What is it?" His eyes began to water from the stench.

Did her lip tremble?

She met his gaze hesitantly. "You will not be angry?"

There it was again! Suspicion rose. *Was* that a tremble? Or was it a twitch?

His burning eyes widened. "*You did this apurpose!*"

"I did not believe I could do it!" she stressed hastily. "I just thought… Well, you were being so *lordly* about it all, refusing to be distracted when I was trying so charmingly to seduce you and-and-and…" She sighed. "Aye, I did it apurpose."

A moment of silence passed. Absolute *reeking* silence.

Dillon burst into laughter. Brushing her hands aside, he yanked her into his arms and squeezed her close, smearing his tunic against her.

"Dillon!" She squirmed and tried to break his hold. Wonderful, musical laughter rained upon him when she could not, pleasuring both his ears and his heart. "Ugh! Cease!"

"'Twas *your* fit of temper," he reminded her joyfully. "If I have to smell like this for… how long?"

She controlled her amusement long enough to say, "Two or three days."

"Two or three days!"

She laughed harder. "Aye!"

"Then you will, too!"

They wrestled and laughed and tickled and growled and teased until, breathless, they collapsed onto the monstrous bed. Smiles still adorning their faces, they lay on their sides, eyes locked, unspeaking as their pulses returned to normal.

"My temper is atrocious," she murmured.

"Your temper is adorable," he returned, reaching up to brush his hand over her hair.

"I have been so waspish of late. Will you forgive me?"

"There is naught to forgive, love. I have yet to find a single thing about you that does not delight me."

Alyssa sighed and burrowed her face into his chest, then coughed and hastily drew back, blinking furiously.

Dillon laughed. "Forgot so quickly, did you?"

"Aye," she croaked, then coughed again.

Sitting up, he glanced down at the rank stain that darkened his clothing and grimaced. "What is the purpose of this foul substance? Is it truly medicine? Or did you conjure it up just for me?"

She sat up beside him with a smile and wiped at her shiny face and watering eyes. "'Tis good for clearing the head and chest."

"I can vouch for that," he muttered as his nose began to run.

"I admit I have been tempted to burden those who have been less than kind to me with its use. Lead them to believe 'tis a necessary part of the healing process for whatever ailment they have brought to my attention."

He grinned down at her. "'Twould be just punishment, do you ask me."

Chuckling, she pushed herself to her feet. "You know I could not."

"I know." Reaching out, Dillon drew the fingers of one hand down her pale cheek. "Since I was so boorish as to rebuff your earlier attempts at seduction, what say you I make it up to you with a shared bath?"

Turning her face into his hand, she buried her lips in his palm. "Will it be like last night's?"

His blood warmed just thinking about it. "Aye," he promised, then grinned, "only with a bit more scrubbing to rid us of this salve of yours."

Laughing, Alyssa stole a quick kiss, then raised her cowl. "I shall see to it immediately."

CHAPTER SIXTEEN

The room was unfamiliar to Alyssa. A peasant's hut by the looks of it. Clean, but one of more modest means than that in which she had been raised.

The dirt floor, worn smooth, had been neatly swept and bore no rushes. The hearth contained a stack of wood and kindling that remained unlit. The small dwelling boasted only one window through which she could see sunlight shining outside. Black draperies hung to either side of it.

A man sat before the window with his back to her, staring out at something she could not see. Beside him, on a small table carved from a tree trunk, rested a single burning candle.

Slowly, she walked in a half circle until she could see his face. 'Twas Matthew, her stepfather, garbed in clothing that was far finer than those she was accustomed to seeing him wear.

"Father?"

He heard her not. Just kept staring through the window.

Wishing to get a glimpse of whatever held his interest, she moved closer and peeked outside.

'Twas a boy. Very young, not long out of swaddling. Cloaked in innocence and little else. He dug in the dirt, giggling, making a mess of himself, and enjoying every minute.

A smile crossed her lips as she looked again at her father who, having been blind these many years (old wounds such as his were often beyond her or her grandmother's ability to heal), now miraculously could see.

The candle flame danced wildly, drawing her gaze. As she watched, the candle began to burn rapidly, the wax slithering down its sides like a snake to pool at its base, then slip over the edge. The shadow her father cast on the dirt floor deepened, lengthened, blending into the darkness already there until one was indiscernible from the other.

"Father?"

Beneath her uneasy gaze, the dwindling flame flickered, then went out. Ghostly tendrils of darkness escaped the wick, reaching toward the ceiling with charcoal arms that disappeared into nothingness.

* * *

"No." Alyssa slowly came awake and stared up through the Stygian blackness.

Dillon's arm tightened around her waist. "Alyssa? What is it?"

"I dreamed of my father," she whispered.

He must have heard her rising distress, for he pressed a quick kiss to her throat, then raised himself onto one elbow. "Do you need parchment and ink?"

"Not this time."

Easing back against the pillows, he drew her into his embrace.

Alyssa wrapped her arms around him, so thankful he was there with her, and squeezed as close as she could get. A sniffle escaped her as tears burned her eyes.

"Tell me," he murmured, pressing his lips to her ear.

"He could see, Dillon. And he was dressed in such finery, but… the candle… and the shadow… and the draperies." Her breath hitched. "I fear it means he is dying."

"Shh." His hold on her tightened. "Please do not weep, love."

Alyssa knew it upset him. She could feel it. His concern. His search for the right thing to do, the right thing to say to calm her, to ease her burden. The way her sorrow became his own.

Oh, how she loved him. How she needed him. Needed this. The strength he offered her. The comfort. The love that had become so necessary to her in such a short time.

"I must go to him. I must see if I can heal him. I am stronger than my grandmother now. If whatever illness has befallen him is beyond her ability to heal, mayhap we can do as Seth instructed and combine our strength to save him."

He nodded. "We shall depart on the morrow."

Relief mingled with the worry flooding her. "Thank you."

"I would do aught for you, sweetling."

She smiled. And she could face aught with Dillon at her side.

Then duty reasserted itself. For a moment, she struggled against it, then reluctantly surrendered. "Dillon, you should not leave Pinehurst now." Although she craved his company, she could not in good conscience tear him away from these people whose very lives depended upon him.

"Simon shall remain and oversee the keep whilst I accompany you."

"Simon is a capable leader," she acknowledged, "but Pinehurst will need more than that in the coming weeks. Winter fast approaches and there is much left to be done. The people are only now beginning to doubt the terrible tales Camden poisoned their minds and your name with. If you stay, you will have both their loyalty and their love by first snowfall. They need you here, Dillon."

"But *you* need me with you," he contended. "Are you trying to talk me out of accompanying you?"

She frowned. "I do not wish to, but as your advisor—"

"I *will* accompany you."

"All right," she answered, glad he would be by her side even though she knew she should continue to counsel him otherwise. "Thank you, Dillon."

"Rest now. A difficult journey awaits us."

Alyssa closed her eyes and listened as his breathing slowly deepened into sleep.

The dream would not cease haunting her, however, and kept her awake until just before sunrise.

* * *

The fates conspired against him, Dillon vowed. He arose early in the morning, intent on accompanying Alyssa to her father's sickbed. Kissing her awake, he bid her rise and make ready for their journey, then sought out Hamon the stable master. In short order, he chose a handful of men to accompany them, ordered Hamon to prepare their mounts, then went in search of Simon.

A loud disturbance in the stables drew his notice shortly thereafter. That lunatic horse that had carried Alyssa to Pinehurst had apparently taken an instant disliking to Hamon, who failed to mention this to Dillon because he feared displeasing his new lord. *Damn Camden and his sorry lies!*

And damn Dillon's fierce reputation as well. It had proven to be more of a hindrance of late than an ally. Though the people seemed pleased with his treatment of them thus far, they appeared to expect him to lose his head at any moment and begin torturing individuals at random.

Well, the blasted horse went mad when Hamon attempted to saddle him and, after missing several times, finally managed to kick the poor man in the head, knocking him senseless, but thankfully not killing him.

Let loose of his stall, the horse ran amuck through the already weakened stables, bucking and rearing, kicking and causing monumental damage, terrifying the other horses, and injuring half a dozen stable lads ere Dillon made it to the scene and ordered the idiots to stand back.

As he tried to soothe the frenzied beast with serene words, the crowd parted and Alyssa approached with slow, deliberate steps. His heart in his throat, Dillon watched—spellbound—

as she strode toward the snorting animal, whispering words that did not carry. Eyes rolling, the horse reared one last time and backed away a step or two, uncertain. Then, to Dillon's and the crowd's utter astonishment, it docilely ducked its head and moved forward to nudge her hidden hand with its nose. Seconds later she led it, meek as a lamb, outside the stables.

The damage had been done, though. Years of neglect, coupled with the heavy rains of the past few days and the new holes and broken beams provided by Alyssa's manic destrier (it was most certainly hers now), left the structure ready to collapse.

They barely managed to hasten the last horse out before it did.

One more undertaking that could not be delayed.

Nevertheless, Dillon remained determined not to let Alyssa leave alone. 'Twould not be fair to her. She needed him.

At least, 'twas what he told himself. More accurately, he *needed* her to need him. Such would prove that she did indeed love him, despite her continued reluctance to speak of it when lucid. His desire for voluntary verbal confirmation of her feelings grew stronger every day, making him restless and impatient.

Alyssa healed those injured by her stallion, then accompanied Dillon to speak with Simon.

Dillon rapidly fed Simon orders for the construction of a new, larger, stronger stable.

"Comparable to Westcott's," Simon murmured.

Dillon nodded. "I wish to install a much larger garrison here and of necessity the stables must be able to…" He trailed off as a rumbling sound arose, swiftly gaining in volume. "What now?" he growled, looking up.

Alyssa, who stood at his elbow, ready to offer counsel, glanced up with interest.

Before their astonished eyes, a large portion of the western curtain wall abruptly collapsed in a jumble of mud, stone, and debris.

All activity in the bailey ceased.

Simon spoke uneasily into the leaden silence that followed. "Mayhap tunneling under it weakened it despite the care we took."

Beyond furious, Dillon let loose a loud, long stream of expletives.

Surprised, Simon glanced from him to Alyssa, then apologized to her on Dillon's behalf.

"Ready your horse, Simon," Dillon ordered, knowing what Alyssa thought without her having to say a word.

Simon looked at him in confusion. "My lord?"

"Do as I say. I shall remain at Pinehurst whilst you accompany the healer in my stead."

Alyssa nodded. "'Twould be wise," she whispered.

"Take double the originally intended number of men."

"Aye, my lord." Simon sketched Alyssa a quick bow and left to follow his lord's orders.

"You said I should not go and now it seems I shall not go." Turning to stalk away in anger, Dillon felt her hand on his arm and stopped.

"Dillon," she began. Now that none were nigh, Alyssa spoke in her normal voice. "What would you have me do? Tell you to forget all of this? Beg you to accompany me?"

"Aye! If you truly wanted my company, you would."

"'Tis not how it works. You know that. You are the earl—"

"My title has naught to do with this."

"It has *everything* to do with this!"

His lip curled as he turned to face her. "You use my title as an excuse to avoid discussing our future!"

"Nay, I use it to remind you that we *have* no future. You may delude yourself into believing our positions mean naught, but eventually reality and your king will convince you otherwise." Taking a deep breath, she released it slowly. "Dillon, please, you must understand. I did not relinquish my role as your advisor when I became your lover."

Hearing the regret in her voice, he wished, as always, that he could see her face.

Glancing around, she reached up and eased her cowl back just enough for him to glimpse her features whilst keeping them hidden from the view of others.

Her misery mirrored his own.

"As your advisor, I cannot support your leaving Pinehurst and the people here who need the stability and protection of their new lord in order to sit by your leman's side and hold her hand whilst she nurses her ailing father." When he would have protested, she shook her head. "As your lover, I desire naught more. But I cannot let that influence me. You belong here."

Dillon cursed his inability to touch her then, to draw her close and slip his arms around her.

"Do not be angry with me," she whispered. "You know 'tis how it must be."

"I am not angry with you," he assured her. *Circumstances* infuriated him, not her. Because, as always, she was right. 'Twas not a good time for him to leave Pinehurst, no matter how strong his desire to do so. The damned place was falling down around him. The people wandered about like lost children seeking the guidance of a parent. And, with Camden dead, he had little reason to fear for Alyssa's safety.

As for the other, 'twas merely frustration that had made him lash out at her. He knew she was not ready to admit they belonged together, regardless of the impediments they faced. "In truth, I simply dread being parted from you again so soon."

She nodded. "As do I. But I shall take with me your love to hold close in the coming days. And I shall visit you in visions so that we might not be long apart."

The urge too strong to resist, he slid his hand inside her cowl and cupped her face, brushing his thumb across one silky cheek. "Nay. 'Twill tire you too much to do so and well you know it. You will need your strength to aid your father.

I would not have you drain your energy in visions simply to pacify me. 'Twould not be fair to either of you."

Reluctantly, she agreed. "Then I shall return to you with all due haste, my lord."

"I shall be waiting."

She turned her face into his hand. "Until then…"

"Good journey, love."

Her gaze roaming his face, Alyssa pulled her hood forward once more and left to retrieve her things. Soon after, she joined Simon and the others assigned to protect her.

The thunder of hooves accompanied their departure as mud splattered in their wake.

Left behind in the crowded bailey, Dillon had never felt so alone.

* * *

The first day of travel proved to be pleasant. Though recent rains had left the road muddy and difficult to negotiate in places, the sun shone brightly all day. A brisk breeze pinkened their cheeks and noses whilst it kept the men cool in their armor and thickly padded gambesons.

Lamentably, the same could not be said for the days that followed. The rain returned the following morning, a steady downpour that lasted all day and continued into the next. Despite Simon and Michael's entreaties, Alyssa refused to seek shelter until the storm passed, insisting on plodding forward however slowly.

In addition to Simon and Michael, twelve knights rode in their party. None offered a word of complaint. The men merely tucked their chins to their chests and pulled their sodden cloaks closer about them in an effort to block out the worst of the weather.

Simon insisted that Alyssa wrap his cloak about her, leaving him exposed. Michael had offered his first. And there had been a tense moment when she had refused it. She had feared the poor weather would make his lungs protest and had not wanted to aggravate his condition further by removing his only source of protection and warmth. Unfortunately, explaining her reasons had only darkened his mood further.

He had spoken nary a word since.

Exhaustion began to take its toll on Alyssa and 'twas only their third day of travel, which admittedly was much less taxing than her last expedition. Sleep had eluded her the previous night. Worry over her father had plagued her, compounded by disquiet over the argument she and Dillon had engaged in when last she had seen him. 'Twas only the first of many arguments, she suspected, because her father was not her only cause for concern.

Her belly roiled with nausea with every step her destrier took. What would have merely tired her before, now left her barely able to hold up her head. The scents around her seemed magnified, a constant aggravation that made the nausea worse. And her breasts were tender and heavy, confirming what she had already guessed weeks ago.

She carried Dillon's child.

And feared he would do something rash when she told him.

He would not wish her to leave Westcott, would want her to remain so the two of them could raise their child together. But how could she stay and maintain her guise as she ripened with his babe? How could she keep their child safe if Dillon insisted she abandon the elderly wisewoman guise that had protected her with rumors of immortality?

Alyssa's mother had been set aflame as a girl by those who feared Alyssa's grandmother's gifts. Alyssa would not risk the same happening to her own son or daughter.

One of the men behind her sneezed, startling a few birds from the surrounding trees. Each of the burly knights had been chosen from her previous escort and no doubt thought her deranged as well as wicked. Alyssa hoped Robert would not be too disappointed when they arrived at Westcott and he discovered that she had single-handedly sabotaged his noble efforts to transform the men into her friends by making them all ill.

The downpour dwindled to a drizzle, though she saw no break in the leaden clouds. Glancing around her, Alyssa realized they were roughly halfway to Westcott. A discussion with Simon and Michael was thus in order.

Nudging her mount, she pressed forward through the protective barrier of Sir Rolfe and Sir Alain and eased her massive destrier between Simon's and Michael's.

Simon regarded her with some surprise whilst Michael continued to brood.

"'Tis time we discussed our destination," she rasped in her elderly wisewoman voice.

"Are we not escorting you to Westcott?" Simon inquired with a frown.

"Nay, our destination lies elsewhere. Lord Dillon did not feel the need to explain when he thought he would accompany me himself. Alas, when our plans changed, there was not time ere we left." Keeping her gaze on the road ahead of them, she wondered how she might convey her needs without revealing too much. "I find myself in quite a quandary as result. And I fear I must ask a boon of each of you ere we go any farther."

"We shall aid you in any way we can, Wise One," Michael assured her, his interest piqued.

"Aye, Healer," Simon seconded. "You need only ask."

'Twas just the reaction she had hoped for. "There is one who requires my aid," she began. "One who is very dear to me and whose safety would be threatened were his location to become known." As well as his relation to her.

The men exchanged a quick glance.

"Aside from Lord Dillon and Sir Robert, along with Harry and Ann Marie," she added, refusing to leave out her two friends, "there are none at Westcott whom I trust more than I do the two of you."

They stared at her so long she began to fear her cowl had slipped.

"You honor us, Wise One," Michael said gravely.

"Aye. 'Tis a great honor," Simon agreed.

Alyssa smiled. She had been right to place her trust in them. "We shall reach a point on the morrow at which time your men will halt and travel with us no farther. Only the two of you may accompany me on the rest of the journey. And you must pose no questions when we reach the location I seek."

Twin frowns greeted her words.

"Lord Dillon entrusted us with your safety, Wise One," Simon said with some concern. "I fear 'twould not be—"

"I shall be safer there than I am here," she assured them.

They remained silent, doubtful.

"No villains or cutthroats tread where we shall venture," she informed them wryly.

Simon swallowed. "Does *any* mortal tread there?"

A startled laugh escaped her before she could cut it off.

Their jaws dropped in astonishment.

"Forgive me," she beseeched them, struggling to contain her amusement. "'Tis only—"

That bizarre buzzing abruptly took up residence in her ears as painful pinpricks of unease raced through her body. Pulling hard on the reins, she stayed her horse and motioned for the others to follow suit.

"Wise One?" Michael questioned.

She held her arm out to quell him.

His hand went to the hilt of his sword, as did Simon's and the other knights'.

The air was still, heavy with the constant threat of storms. No birds twittered. No rain fell. Only the soft patter of moisture falling from drooping leaves broke the silence.

The buzzing increased. The scenery around her blurred, shifted.

She stood within the forest, looking out on her party from a distance.

Around her, seemingly a part of the sopping foliage, men armed with swords and longbows cloaked themselves in shadows.

Many men. Awaiting a signal.

"Wise One." Michael's voice wrenched her back. "Are you ill?"

"Nay," she responded, head swimming.

"Then what—?"

"Ambush," she warned shortly.

"Where?" Simon demanded, his sharp eyes studying the forest around them.

"The trees up ahead. On both sides of the road where it bends. Men, heavily armed, outnumbering us four to one."

"To arms!" he called.

As soon as the men drew their weapons and raised their shields, swiftly closing ranks to surround Alyssa, arrows showered down upon them.

Simon yanked his shield above Alyssa for her protection and grunted when an arrow embedded itself in his shoulder.

"Worry not about me!" she shouted. "Save yourself!"

Fear, fury, and pure rabid energy raged through her as men poured from the forest and sped toward them, roaring battle cries. It filled her ears and scoured her flesh, made her head ache, her veins burn, as she struggled to control the skittish beast beneath her. The horse could sense it, mayhap could even feel it—the scorching, searing power that screamed inside her and demanded an immediate outlet.

When another flurry of arrows flew their way, Alyssa thrust a hand toward the sky without thought. Lightning crackled above them. Thunder rumbled through the air. As though blown by a powerful gust of wind, the arrows reversed their course and targeted the archers who had let them fly.

Dillon's knights gaped and hastily crossed themselves, now more fearful of *her* than of their attackers.

"Fight, damn you!" she roared. "Fight!"

The villains set upon them in the next instant.

Still in the center of their protective circle, Alyssa retrieved two daggers from beneath her robe and prepared to throw them should any of her defenders need her aid.

Swords clashed. Warhorses reared, kicked, trampled those fallen. Grunts and cries of pain abounded. Curses flew from blood-stained lips. Armor flowed crimson.

Sour sweat and the metallic scent of blood assaulted her as Alyssa spun this way and that within the fray. More men joined the melee, slowly luring her protectors away. She had lost count of how many there were, but knew not how so few knights could stand against them.

A bearded man covered in mud and filth broke through the ranks and attempted to drag her from the back of her horse. Alyssa lashed out at him with her dagger, slicing him from forehead to chin, then drew her knee back and kicked him as hard as she could. He stumbled backward, howling as he grasped his bloodied face and went down. The powerful destrier beneath her took care of the rest.

Another followed, then another. Alyssa soon found herself fighting alongside Dillon's men. When her third adversary went down, she glanced over at Simon and Michael to see how they fared. Both fought with valor and skill, sending one after another to his death. Yet, as she watched, a second opponent came up behind Michael and prepared to strike him, unseen.

Alyssa swiftly threw a dagger, impaling the man in the back, the blade tearing a path to his heart.

Michael dispatched his enemy and spun around at the second man's cry. His eyes flew from the crumpling form to Alyssa, then widened. His mouth opened. Words emerged, but were drowned out by the chaos that surrounded them.

A warning?

Breath catching, she raised her remaining dagger high and drove it down and backward with all her might. Her weapon met with flesh and sank deep seconds before pain exploded in her head.

She never saw her assailant.

The world tilted, darkened. All strength left her limbs.

Alyssa tumbled from the saddle, the ground rising up to pummel her. Her horse's hooves danced only inches from her face. The sounds of battle grew muffled, muted, soon silencing altogether as she wrestled against the blackness that rose up to claim her.

* * *

Whispers filled her ears. Adamant. Arguing.

"We must remove her cowl." Simon. 'Twas Simon who spoke so emphatically.

"Nay. As long as I have drawn breath, the wisewoman has kept her face hidden from all. I will not betray her now by revealing it whilst she lies so vulnerable."

"We agreed, Michael," Simon said. "We agreed that did she not awaken after a full day, we would remove her cowl and see what must be done."

"Naught can be done, I tell you. I reached beneath her hood myself and felt the lump on the back of her head. The bleeding has stopped. With no herbs to apply to it, there is naught more we can do."

"But she is injured," Simon persisted.

"None knows that better than I," Michael hissed. "'Twas *my* fault, Simon. *Mine.* She was guarding *my* back when the bastard struck her down, instead of looking to her own. Had I been more vigilant—"

"You are not responsible," she interrupted, her feeble voice unfeigned for once. Pain radiated through her head and down the back of her neck. Nausea twisted her stomach into roiling knots until she had to fight to keep from retching.

"Wise One?"

She lay on a cold stone floor, the material of her robe protecting her cheek from the abrasive surface. Her damp, chilly clothing raised gooseflesh on her arms and legs, inspiring an occasional shiver.

"Where are we?" Bracing her hands beneath her chest, Alyssa pushed herself up to sit with her back against the intersection of two slimy walls. She appeared to be scrunched up in a dark, dank corner. All else around her remained hidden by her two protectors' bulky bodies as they crouched on their haunches and hovered over her.

"Westmoreland's dungeon," Michael responded, one hand extended in case she should need his support.

"Westmoreland?" she parroted, disbelieving. "That cannot be." Lord Everard loved Dillon like a son. More than his *own* son, it often seemed. She could not conceive of his attacking Dillon's men to avenge Camden's death.

"'Tis true, Wise One," Simon confirmed, his smudged face grim.

"How came we to be here?" she asked slowly.

Simon glanced at Michael.

Michael looked at Alyssa. "After you fell…"

"Wait," she interrupted. "'Twill be quicker if you show me."

Confusion creased his brow as she reached out and curled her blood- and dirt-encrusted fingers around his wrist.

Images flooded her mind. Of herself, a pool of black material inundated with mud, her loyal destrier standing guard over her and keeping her from being trampled by the many knights and horses that surrounded her. Of the opponents who kept Michael from reaching her side and steadily conquered and disarmed the others, killing seven, inflicting wound upon wound on the rest. Of Michael and Simon surrendering their weapons because they feared for her safety should they continue to fight to the death and leave her alone and defenseless.

The dead men left behind.

The unconscious and dying carelessly tossed over the backs of horses.

Those men who remained conscious, but broken, being

bound by long ropes attached to their enemies' saddles and forced to walk or be dragged all the way to Westmoreland.

And Michael nigh losing his life when he stumbled to her side and, refusing to release her, insisted upon carrying Alyssa instead of handing her over to the men who itched to punish the *Cursed Witch*.

She swallowed. That kind of loyalty went beyond Dillon's orders.

How had she come to possess such staunch defenders as these?

Sliding her hand down, she took Michael's hand and gave it a squeeze.

Startled, he looked down at their joined hands, then back up at her, his desire to see beyond the shadows of her cowl almost tempting her into removing it.

But she did not. Instead she thanked him, knowing she was at least partially responsible for the difficulty he was having breathing.

Aye, she could hear his breath, wheezing in his chest, despite his attempts to appear and speak normally.

"Thank you, Sir Michael." Reaching out, she found Simon's hand as well. "And you, as well, Sir Simon. You saved my life, most likely at the expense of your own. I shall remain in your debt for as long as we live."

Simon shifted. "I fear that may not be for very long, Wise One. I know not what Westmoreland has in store for us, but think 'twill not be to release us."

"Nay," Michael agreed. "We suspect he has gone mad."

She nodded. "Lord Everard loves Dillon like a son. I know not what else would have driven him to do this."

She felt a little jolt go through both men and realized she had spoken Dillon's name familiarly, forgetting his title. Withdrawing her hands, she tried to peer over their shoulders. "Where are the rest of the men? I know Sir Rolfe and six others were slain, but what of the rest?"

Simon frowned. "How…?"

"Michael showed me. Where are they?"

Michael stared down at his arm where she had touched him as though it were some foreign object just come into his possession.

"Where are the men?" she repeated when neither knight responded.

Mute, they sat back on their heels and parted like a pair of double doors swinging open. Beyond them, on the other side of their prison, she could see the rest of her guard slumped in a jumble of arms and legs amongst the filth that littered the floor. They had been stripped of their mail and hauberks, leaving them clothed in only their hose, braies, and linen shirts. The mud and blood that liberally coated all of them had dried to a dark crust that cracked a little more with each jagged breath or fitful movement.

Four of the five were unconscious. The fifth stared at her, forehead beaded with moisture, gritting his teeth against the pain.

They would die if she did not heal them. All five of them. And without her medicines, under these squalid conditions, she would have to heal them as completely as she could in order to avoid losing them later to fever from infection. Simply stopping the bleeding would not suffice.

Could she do it? Had she strength enough not only to help them, but to help them *without* harming the babe she carried?

Her grandmother had continued to use her gift when she was with child. Alyssa could only hope 'twould be safe for her to do so as well. For she could not let the men who had fought so hard to save her life lose theirs if she could save them.

"Let me see your shoulder, Simon."

"My shoulder?" he asked, surprised.

"Aye. I shall heal the two of you first, then take care of the rest. Quickly, now. Remove your shirt."

He hesitated. "My shoulder is fine, Healer."

The unexpected falsehood rendered her speechless for a moment. "You would *lie* to me?"

Swallowing, he looked to Michael for assistance.

Michael's wheezing worsened. "'Tis not a lie…, Wise One."

"You, too?" she retorted, undone. "Think you I did not see Simon take that arrow for me?"

"'Twas, uh, poorly aimed," Simon stuttered. "It barely penetrated my hauberk. 'Tis but a paltry scratch and requires not your aid, Healer."

Scowling, she latched onto their wrists again to learn what drove their protests.

Michael had guessed that healing hurt her and had told Simon. Now both sought to spare her.

Rolling her eyes beneath her hood, Alyssa tossed their arms away from her with an indelicate snort. "You are both as bad as Dillon," she muttered, unthinking. "Now remove your shirt, Simon, or I shall snap my fingers and make it doff itself." An empty yet quite effective threat.

Fearful of another show of her mystical powers, he peeled the garment off without another complaint.

"You men and your *paltry* wounds," she complained beneath her breath as she wiped one hand on her robe to clean it as best she could, then placed it above the jagged hole he revealed.

The feverish heat that had already bloomed in his skin where she touched him drained away as she closed the festering wound.

"'Tis your turn, Michael," she said when finished, her shoulder throbbing minutely.

"You need not… squander your gift on me, Healer… There are others who need you more."

"But your difficulty breathing—"

"Is not grave."

"And your leg?"

"'Tis naught."

"I shall have to curb this new tendency of yours to spout falsehoods," she murmured, healing the wound in question despite his protests. The worry and guilt her statement spawned flowed into her alongside the pain that settled in her thigh. Once the jagged tear was securely sealed, she gave him a reassuring pat. "I jest, Michael. Do not fret. I understand that you seek only to protect me."

A ruddy flush crept up his cheeks, inspiring a grin as she used her gift to ease his breathing, then rose and crossed to the other men.

Kneeling before the one who had been staring at her as he stoically bore the torment of his ghastly wounds, she took his bloody arm—torn open from wrist to elbow—gently in her hands. "'Twill only take a moment, Sir Philip. Then your pain will be no more than a memory."

"My thanks, Healer," he managed to grind out.

One by one she healed them, taking away their pain, reducing their fever, restoring consciousness. Their wounds were deep and numerous, requiring more strength than Alyssa had believed she possessed. More even than Dillon's had required. She could only assume that the gifts she had gained through her own healing had indeed heightened her power. For, when the last raging laceration had been mended, she yet lived.

A moan escaped her.

Aye, she lived. But such agony assailed her that it took all of her concentration to control it.

Most of her body either ached, burned, or screamed with pain. Even her belly cramped and continued to churn horribly, making her fear for the babe. Chills racked her with annoying constancy, a result of the blood pouring from wounds that had opened on her limbs, torso, and face as her strength was depleted and she lost the ability to heal herself. Though no injury afflicted her lungs, her breathing grew as ragged as Michael's had been, echoing loudly in the oppressive silence.

The knights all watched her black-enshrouded form uneasily, hearing her struggle and wondering what it meant.

Simon and Michael knew. Their faces paled with downright fear as they listened to her fight for breath, saw her robe's violent quaking, and feared she would expire in the next instant.

Michael knelt beside her where she crouched, unable to rise. "What can we do, Wise One?" he whispered with such compassion.

She shook her head. "Help me to the corner… away from the others." He moved in front of her, clasped her elbows, and drew her to her feet. "I must… ressst." Collapsing against him, she let darkness surround her and blessedly steal the pain.

CHAPTER SEVENTEEN

Dillon sighed as he watched shadows cast by the dying flames from the hearth dance upon the ceiling.

Sleep eluded him. He could not seem to quiet his thoughts.

He missed Alyssa. Her smile. Her laugh. Her touch. Even her sharp tongue.

He liked not that they had quarreled ere she had left. Again and again since her departure, he had cursed himself for allowing frustration to get the better of him. She had worried for her father's health. And Dillon had whined like a pup over not being able to accompany her and had raged over her refusal to relinquish her role of advisor for just one moment and have faith in him. Have faith in his ability to secure a future for them.

Sighing, Dillon rubbed tired eyes.

He must find a way to secure a future for them.

Thunder rumbled outside, heralding more rain.

'Twould help if he could deny her arguments, but Alyssa spoke the truth. Noblemen did not wed peasants. Ever. In all of his life, he had heard nary a rumor of such taking place. Some noblemen took peasants as lemans, but even that was frowned upon if it lasted too long, because the nobility believed those of lower birth beneath them.

He snorted.

Noblemen married noblewomen. To unite families. To end hostilities. To acquire a wealthy dowry. To secure a title. To gain power. Land.

Not for love. Love had naught to do with marriage amongst the nobility.

He recalled hearing once of a young noblewoman—barely more than a girl—who had run away with a peasant she loved. Her parents had put a swift end to it, separating the lovers and forcing the girl to submit to an arranged marriage.

Dillon himself had been destined for a marriage that had been arranged for him at the age of seven. But illness had taken the girl's life ere she had seen twelve years. Dillon had not known her. Had not spoken with her. Had not loved her or longed for her as he did Alyssa.

He closed his eyes.

There *must* be a way for them to be together as more than lord and leman.

The crackling of the fire faded, as did the rumbling of thunder and patter of rain.

The bedding rustled.

Opening his eyes, Dillon turned his head and smiled. Pleasure rushed through him as Alyssa settled herself beside him.

He rolled onto his side to face her, spirit lightening. "You are here."

She wore only her shift. Her lovely midnight hair, unconfined, pooled on the bedding beneath and around her.

She reached for his hand and curled her fingers around it.

"I would have thought you halfway to Westcott by now," he murmured and frowned as the chill of her flesh seeped into his palm.

"I miss you," she told him.

"And I you."

Withdrawing her fingers from his, she curled a small hand around the nape of his neck and drew him to her for a kiss.

Dillon knew not why she had returned or if she would leave again on the morrow and did not care. He was too happy to have her with him.

Breaking the sweet contact, he leaned back to smile down at her.

His smile died ere it could finish forming. His fingers tightened around hers.

A deep gash now sliced open her forehead as though she had been lashed by a whip. "Alyssa?"

As he watched in horror, blood trailed down and striped her forehead. A second cut opened her cheek from the base of her ear to the corner of her eye. A third grazed her neck.

Fear struck. Pulse racing, Dillon lurched up to better see her.

The waves of her glossy hair flattened, the strands dampening and becoming caked with mud.

What was happening? How was this happening?

"Alyssa?"

Her pale skin darkened with purple and brown bruises in too many places to count. Crimson stains formed on her white shift as more wounds opened on her slender body.

He leaned over her. Touched a hand to her face.

She rolled to her back, her dark eyes full of pain. A single tear slipped from the corner of one eye and forged a path down her temple. "I love you, Dillon."

His heart clenched. How he had longed to hear those words cross her lips.

Smudges of dirt streaked her skin.

"Tell me what is happening," he implored. "Tell me what to do!"

She opened her mouth, tried to speak once more, but no sound emerged. Her eyelids fluttered closed.

"Alyssa!"

Dillon jerked awake.

Heart pounding, he bolted upright and turned to find the bed empty, the covers beside him cold and undisturbed. A quick survey of the chamber confirmed he was alone.

Relief rushed through him.

A dream. It had just been a dream.

Not a vision. Those came to him whilst he was awake.

But a dream.

Lying back, he sought to calm his racing pulse.

He drew in a deep breath, let it out slowly, the sound of her pained voice speaking her love for him ringing in his ears.

Just a dream.

Closing his eyes, he slid one hand over the bedding beside him. Though it bore no warmth and lacked her scent, Dillon found the image of her lying there, sorely wounded, a difficult one to banish.

* * *

Whilst Simon paced back and forth in the gloomy cell, Michael sat in the corner beside the healer.

Curled up in a ball, she shivered as she slept.

"We must warm her," he murmured.

"With what?" Simon asked. They had no blankets. Had nothing but their hose, braies, and cold, damp shirts.

"Should I… should I hold her? Warm her with my body?"

"'Twould not be proper," Simon muttered.

"Think you that matters down here?"

Another shudder racked the healer's form, drawing a moan from her.

"She is an old woman," Michael said, his brow furrowed. "Weakened as she has been by healing us, she may not survive the cold and damp. Would Lord Dillon not want us to do aught we can to help her?"

Recalling the conversation he and Michael had witnessed— the one in which the healer and Lord Dillon had seemed so close—he nodded. "Do it."

Michael carefully eased the wisewoman over onto his lap and wrapped his arms around her.

Though she moaned again, she did not rouse.

It worried Simon. And not just because he feared Lord Dillon's wrath if they failed to prevent her from perishing. Every man here owed her his life. He did not wish to see her

328 | DIANNE DUVALL

lose her own.

After several minutes of being spared lying on the cold stone floor, the wisewoman's shivers finally eased.

"I do not understand," Philip said, confused. "You say this is because she healed us? That, when she heals others, she is harmed herself?"

"Aye," Simon responded shortly.

The other men had been shocked by the healer's collapse and were slow to grasp the truth.

"You must be mistaken," Lambert murmured, his craggy face creased with doubt.

Two others agreed.

"Simon?" Michael questioned in subdued tones so as not to wake the wisewoman.

"Aye?"

"From what wounds did the healer suffer when we were forced down here?"

"A blow to the head."

"Naught more?"

"Nay."

Michael shifted his focus to the brawny skeptic. "And where were you injured, Lambert?"

"My right arm, just beneath the shoulder. Damn nigh lost it entirely."

Michael nodded. "Ere you discount our words, I suggest you pay close attention to this. I shall only demonstrate it once."

As the others watched him, Michael ran one hand gently down over the healer's right shoulder. When he reached the top of her arm, she whimpered involuntarily and shrank away from his touch, curling into a tighter knot and burrowing into his chest as though to escape the pain.

His hand came away wet with blood.

Simon swallowed miserably, given this proof, whilst the others all crossed themselves.

Noise sounded outside the cell, followed by the rumble of voices and clank of the bolt sliding back. Light flooded in as the door swung open, alleviating the gloom that had previously been broken only by a small, fizzling wall torch.

A large, stout figure stepped into the doorway, sword in hand. A second joined him, a whip in one hand, a sword in the other.

"We come for the witch," the first announced.

* * *

Alyssa regained consciousness when someone yanked her up and forced her, stumbling, through the open doorway.

Fighting and bellowed protests erupted behind her, subdued but not silenced by the crack of one gaoler's whip and the bite of the blade he brandished.

Dazed, she relinquished her hold on dreams of Dillon and listened with dread as the door closed with a loud clank. Rough hands latched onto each of her arms and jerked her forward. Though Alyssa thought the bleeding had stopped, most of the wounds she had incurred still afflicted her, making walking sheer torture.

Either oblivious or uncaring, her jailers propelled her onward, dragging her when she stumbled, until she finally dug in her heels and snarled through clenched teeth, "Do you not remove your hands from me this instant I shall lay a curse upon your heads that will place every member of your families, including yourselves, in the grave ere All Saints' Day."

Terrified, the men released her.

Alyssa straightened her shoulders, ignoring the pull of dried, crusted wounds, and tilted her chin up. "Now, take me to your lord. I would share a few words with him."

They would have taken her there anyway, of course. Their orders had been pounding through each of their not-very-bright minds whilst they held her. Now they led her more slowly down a dark passageway, up two flights of stairs, and into the great hall of Castle Westmoreland.

What happened here? she wondered, her unsettled stomach sinking as she surveyed the damage.

What had formerly been an impressive, neat, and orderly keep now lay in shambles. The soiled rushes beneath her feet reeked of decaying food and animal excrement. A thick layer of dust, soot, and grime covered nigh every surface, including the whitewashed walls, which now appeared gray. Insects and rodents scurried to and fro. The servants all huddled in corners whilst unwashed, uncouth soldiers far beneath the Earl of Westmoreland's usual stock lolled about the hall, drinking heavily and shouting coarse jests to one another, occasionally latching onto a servant woman and groping her against her will.

"The prisoner, milord," one of the guards announced.

Her newfound ability to read minds identified him as Gareth. The other guard's name, she now knew, was Walter. Both relinquished their possession of her with much relief.

Following Gareth's direction, Alyssa glared in furious disbelief. "You!"

From his position in the large, elaborately carved throne that rested in the center of the raised dais, Camden smiled down at her and offered her a mocking bow of his head. "At your service, Witch."

"I would not *have* a fool such as yourself in my service," she retorted, pleased to see crimson color flood his face when a few of his mercenaries unwisely snickered. How did Camden still live? Dillon and his men had been certain they had slain him, so certain they had sent the body back to Westmoreland. Who had they felled?

"Silence!"

And where was Westmoreland? Were any of his men even present?

A quick glance about showed her a few of them stationed uncomfortably around the hall, well away from Camden's refuse.

"Fool am I?" Camden inquired, rising. Auburn-haired and of average height, he had garbed himself in his father's finery. The rumpled fabric hung loosely on his more slender build, lending him the appearance of a child playing dress-up. Though *he* no doubt thought himself quite dashing. "If I am such a fool, how have I managed to foil Lord Dillon's plot to confiscate my father's holdings?"

"Is that what you have told the earl? What you have told his men?" she questioned, keeping her elderly whisper calm. "What other lies have you poured into their ears?"

Westmoreland's men cast each other edgy glances.

Camden scowled. "No lies. Only the truth. The truth of Westcott's treachery!"

"'Tis your father and his men who have been betrayed if they believed your falsehoods. Where *is* your father, *boy?*"

"'Tis naught of your concern." Ignoring her slur, Camden descended the steps and approached her with deliberate, arrogant steps. His handsome face lit with evil relish. "At last, I have managed to steal Lord Dillon's most prized possession," he purred. "His healer. His seer. His sorceress."

She stood immobile as he walked in a slow circle around her.

"For years now, I have wondered what horrid features you hide beneath that cowl." Stopping in front of her, he smirked. "Methinks 'tis time we have a look."

Alyssa gripped his wrist when he reached toward her, staying his hand. "I would not, were I you," she warned him. "'Twill only cause you grief. This I vow."

Shaking off her hand, he swiftly yanked back her cowl.

Gasps filled the hall. In a flurry of movement, men and women hurried to cross themselves and ward off the evil eye. Camden himself did naught. He merely stared, mesmerized.

Gradually, an evil smile blossomed. "Well, well, well. Mayhap when I listed your many titles, I overlooked the most important. His *leman*, I do not doubt."

Alyssa's heart began to pound.

"No response?" he asked glibly.

"Such lunacy deserves no response," she bit out, no longer camouflaging her voice.

He took a step closer to her, his foul stench nigh making her gag. Leaning in, he said for her ears only, "How think you Dillon will react when I take you as my whore? When I use you until I have had my fill, then give you to my men? When I shackle him and make him watch? Hmm? What think you, Sorceress?"

Tension and fear flowed through her, yet she refused to let it show. "You could not."

"Are you so certain?"

Still smiling, he rested one hand firmly on her injured shoulder. As soon as they touched, his thoughts inundated her. Every sordid deed he had performed. Every obscene act he schemed to commit. His plans. His desires. His heinous dreams of making Dillon pay in the most monstrous of ways for always being the better man in his father's eyes. For always being first with the king and the rest of the nobility despite their fear of him.

His loathing for Dillon was a bitter, twisted thing that would not cease governing him even were he to successfully remove Dillon's head and place it upon a pike for all to see.

Thunder crashed outside, the roar of some fantastical beast. Power surged through Alyssa as rage consumed her, burning, crackling, then racing toward Camden's hand. Even those in the farthest corners saw the spark of energy that leapt from her to him.

Howling in pain, Camden stumbled backward, tripped, and landed hard on his backside amidst the stinking rushes. For long moments he could not speak. He could only sit there, his body twitching, breath whooshing in and out through clenched teeth like the air in a blacksmith's bellows.

"You w-will p-p-pay for that, W-W-Witch!" he finally

managed to growl.

Careful to maintain her calm facade, Alyssa deliberately raised her cowl. "I did warn you."

"T-T-Take her!"

A terror-stricken Gareth and Walter guided her back down to the dungeon.

Simon and the others were all pacing anxiously when the door opened and she strode into the cell.

"You are well, Wise One?" Michael asked.

"Well enough to raze this keep in an instant should they continue to try my patience," she hissed for the benefit of their audience. Unfortunately, Dillon's men appeared to take her at her word, and she despaired that they would never cease crossing themselves in her presence.

As soon as the guards closed and bolted the door behind her, she staggered and grabbed Michael's arm for support.

"You are *not* well!" Simon exclaimed. "What did Westmoreland do to you?"

She waved off their concern and painstakingly settled herself in the corner that had so quickly become her own, feeling as old as these men still believed her. "'Tis not Westmoreland behind this, but Camden."

"Camden!"

"But he is dead!"

"I saw the corpse myself!"

"Nay," she broke in. "The corpse you saw was Camden's cousin, slain by his own hand to deceive you all. Camden is above in the great hall, as are all of his remaining band of hired swords and then some."

"And Westmoreland?" Simon asked.

She sighed, saddened by all that she had *seen*. "He lies abed in the lord's chamber, nigh death."

"What ails him?"

"Poison. A servant loyal to Camden has been feeding it to him since just before the siege of Pinehurst began so his illness would come upon him gradually and his death go unquestioned."

All lapsed into pensive silence.

"What next, Wise One?" Michael posed, seeking her counsel.

Alyssa leaned her head back against the wall and closed gritty eyes. "You must watch over me for a time. I have a task I must perform."

Neither Michael nor Simon understood her meaning, but faithfully settled themselves on either side of her to wait.

* * *

Westcott was quiet, peaceful. No threat had arisen since Robert had received word that Camden had been slain. Yet he continued to maintain a watchful vigil, posting double the usual number of guards and letting no stranger through the gates.

Most of the keep slumbered now.

Having just returned from walking the walls to ensure that every guard remained at his post, Robert entertained himself in Alyssa's chamber. His conscience tweaked him a bit for being there in her absence, but largely went ignored. He leaned over the cages in the corner, intending to toy with her serpents.

"Robert."

"Sorceress!" Startled, he spun around and regarded the wisewoman guiltily. "I mean Alyssa. I knew not you had returned."

"I have not."

His brow creased with confusion, then smoothed out in shock when he realized she was no more than a ghostly image. "You—"

"I have been captured, Robert," she informed him, "and am being held at Westmoreland."

She doffed her cowl.

And Robert felt rage engulf him.

Bruises and abrasions aplenty painted her delicate features.

A long, nasty gash began at the end of her right eyebrow and traveled diagonally across her forehead into the hair above her left temple. The trails of dried blood beneath it resembled the rusted bars of an iron cage. Another began an inch below her left ear and parted her cheek to end a hair's breadth from the inner corner of her left eye. Yet another peeked out from the neckline of her tattered robes.

"Sir Simon, Sir Michael, and a handful of others are here with me, but we shall not live long if Camden has his way."

"Camden! I thought Dillon slew Camden!"

She shook her head. "The body Dillon found was that of Camden's cousin, killed by Camden's own hand because he bears a resemblance to him and Camden wished to deceive us into believing him dead. He has seized Westmoreland and holds us in its dungeons. You must get word to Dillon. I could not reach him, drained as I am. The distance is too great."

Robert nodded. "As swiftly as I can."

"And Robert…"

"Aye?"

"Say naught to Dillon of my wounds. 'Twill infuriate him and make him careless."

He silently agreed. "Will you be all right until we reach you?" Even as the words passed his lips, she faded from his sight.

Shaken, Robert dashed from her chamber, through the great hall, and out into the bailey. He must gather men, shore up the castle's defenses, and fly like the wind to his brother's side.

* * *

All was black when Alyssa awoke. The puny wall torch the dungeon boasted must have extinguished itself whilst she slept.

Throat aching, she swallowed hard. Fever flayed her from the inside out. Just as she had feared for the brave men who shared this cell, infection had found a home in all but the most minor of her wounds. Though her belly had ceased cramping, she worried for the health of her babe. Feared the toll this would take. Though her grandmother had continued to heal others whilst she had carried Alyssa's mother, Alyssa doubted she had taxed herself to this extent.

Shifting position, Alyssa noticed for the first time that Michael had at some point transferred her to his lap. His determination to do all that he could to make her more comfortable warmed her, but she was unaccustomed to having any man save Dillon—and Robert the time he had comforted her as she had wept—hold her.

When she gathered her flagging strength and prepared to pull away, Michael's arms tightened.

"Remain where you are, Wise One," he ordered gently. "You will benefit from my warmth."

"I am burning," she protested hoarsely.

"What?" Simon's voice, full of worry, sounded close beside them. "Has fever taken hold?"

Michael freed one hand and slipped it beneath her cowl to feel her forehead. She gasped and jerked back, bumping his chin, when his rough palm met the tender flesh there. Startled by the feel of the ugly, blood-encrusted gash, he swore beneath his breath and softly begged her forgiveness.

"Michael?" Simon questioned louder. "What is amiss?"

"Naught," Alyssa blurted, tears threatening as throbbing pain assaulted her. Rising, she staggered away a step or two. "Naught. Just leave me be."

"She burns with fever," Michael told him.

"I know not what we can do for that," Simon admitted.

"There is more," Michael added bleakly. "Her forehead is—"

"Do not speak of me as though I were not here," she snapped irritably. "I shall be fine until Dillon comes to our rescue."

Silence.

"Was… was that the sorceress speaking?" Sir Philip asked in a low voice.

She had forgotten to use her elderly rasp.

"Lord Dillon knows not we are here, Healer," Simon reminded her after a moment.

She shook her head, swaying when it inspired a momentary dizziness. "Robert races to inform Dillon of our capture even as we speak."

"How can that be?" Michael posed. "Robert knows not what has happened."

Mutters on the other side of the door spared her from having to concoct an answer.

The bolt slid back with a clank. Seconds later, the door creaked open to admit a slender, solitary figure. Alyssa could see naught of the man but his silhouette, blinded as she was by the sudden light of the torches Gareth and Walter held.

Turning away, the man said, "'Tis too dark in here. Give me those torches."

Simon and Michael moved to stand on either side of Alyssa.

Scowling, Gareth grudgingly thrust two torches into the man's waiting hands.

"My thanks, Gareth. 'Twill be all for now."

The gaoler closed the door with a grunt.

Holding the torches high, the mystery man turned to face his hostile audience.

A priest.

Even in her growing delirium, Alyssa felt fear grab her by the arms and shake her. Of all the men at Westmoreland, this one posed the greatest threat to her. One word from him and she would suffer the same fate her mother had nigh met as a child. Burned at the stake. A torturous death if ever there was one.

"I am Father Markham. Mayhap you gentlemen would be good enough to see to these for me," he suggested with a tentative smile.

Simon made a motion with one hand.

Sir Lambert stepped forward and retrieved the torches, placing them in the rusted wall sconces.

That taken care of, the priest turned all of his attention upon Alyssa.

He was young. About Robert's age, she guessed. Thin. Half a head taller than herself, with light brown tonsured hair and… *kind* hazel eyes? Nay. That she could not believe.

When Michael and Simon tried to move in front of her, Alyssa stayed them by gripping their arms. She would have to brazen this out on her own as she had so often in the past.

"Come to administer the last rites, Father, ere you burn this witch at the stake?" she asked caustically.

"I mean you no harm, Wisewoman." His smile died as he listened to her ragged breathing and saw her sway where she stood. "Do you require the last rites?" he queried.

"Nay. Not yet." She jolted her two protectors with that, alarming them, though she had not intended to. In all honesty, she began to fear she might not survive this ordeal. It may take Dillon too long to reach her.

Simon nodded toward the priest and demanded belligerently, "If you mean her no harm, why have you come?"

Father Markham seemed to ponder that. "In part, to escape the wagging tongues of my flock."

Alyssa's lips turned up in a cynical smile. She could well imagine the frantic chattering to which he had been subjected since their arrival.

"And, too, I seek the truth. If I may…?" He reached toward Alyssa's cowl and immediately found his wrists manacled by strong, muscled fists.

"Nay," Alyssa told them, staying their angry protests. "Let him see the sorceress whose blood his *pious* congregation wishes to spill."

Her willingness to let this man look upon her unveiled

when no other had ever done so—as far as they knew—
stunned them into immobility.

"Wise One?" Michael asked uncertainly.

Abandoning her hold on them, she stood as tall as her
compact height would allow her, her hands fisting at her sides
when her wounds tightened painfully. "Do as I say. Release
him."

They obeyed with clear reluctance, but continued to crowd
her on either side, ready to attack should the need arise.

Alyssa sighed. "Michael, Simon, please join the others
behind me." Neither moved. "Should he attempt to harm me,
he shall experience the same punishment Camden did."

"Then Camden *did* harm you!" Simon blurted, his face
darkening.

The priest's lips twitched. "I was not there, mind you, but
from what I have heard, he had not the chance." His eyes
remained fixed on Alyssa's dark hood. "Know you that he
took to his bed after you left the hall and has not risen since?
Nor can he speak without stuttering."

"'Tis less than he deserves for his wickedness. Michael.
Simon."

The moment stretched.

Just as Alyssa opened her mouth to issue a sterner order,
they slowly backed away, giving her the feigned privacy she
desired.

"Proceed, Father."

The man peeled back the dark material of her cowl and
stared, stunned.

No doubt the men behind her did the same. Although they
could not see her face, her hair—a glossy black instead of the
anticipated white or silver—was unmistakable.

"Then all was *not* a lie," Markham murmured. Taking her
chin in his hand, he tilted her face up to better view it *and* the
cuts, bruises, and swollen flesh that marred it. "Who did this
to you, child?" he asked with such concern that her eyes began

to burn.

"'Twas my own doing."

He looked from her to the men behind her, then back again. "Is it true that you healed these men with your hands?"

"Aye." Determined to show no weakness, she jerked her chin out of his grasp.

"How?" He dropped his hand to his side.

"The same way I have always done."

"You will not share your methods with me?"

"I see no reason to."

He nodded, as if he understood her reluctance to trust. "Have you ever looked upon the face of evil, child?"

"I have felt its influence many times in the men and women around me. As for its face... I would not care to see a face more evil than Camden's."

"Nor would I," he concurred with a grimace, surprising her. "You have made no unholy pacts, then, in exchange for your gifts?"

"I have not."

"They say your appearance is a result of sorcery."

"You have already guessed 'tis not."

His narrow shoulders rose and fell in a shrug. "I felt compelled to ask on behalf of the people. Westmoreland has been home to me but two years now, Wisewoman. As you know, you are the subject of a great deal of speculation. But, unlike those who spread the rumors, I kept both my ears and my mind open as I listened." He paused. "You are not the same healer who resided at Westmoreland ere she transferred her loyalty to Westcott, are you?"

"Nay, that woman was my grandmother." Muttering sounded behind her. "I succeeded her the day Lord Dillon took Brimshire." Still dizzy with fever, she gave Father Markham a moment to assimilate her words. "This is not the only truth you seek."

"Is it not?"

"You wish to know of Westmoreland, how he fares."

He stared at her with wonder. "How did you know that?"

"The moment you touched me your thoughts became mine, as did all that resides in your heart."

"You are a seer as well?"

She inclined her head slightly.

"Then you know I speak not falsely when I say I mean you no harm."

She frowned. "'Tis true your thoughts indicate as much. Yet I find it difficult to believe, knowing the actions of your predecessors toward my mother and grandmother. Will you not seek to use my gifts to line your pockets?"

"Nay, child." He gave her a warm, reassuring smile. "Such gifts as yours are given for a reason, and I am quite certain 'tis not to beget profit."

Alyssa did not return his smile. Verily, his attitude baffled her. "Westmoreland lies nigh death," she informed him. "His son has been slowly poisoning him and using his delirium to usurp control of this keep. Dillon never swayed from his loyalty to the earl. 'Tis all a lie Camden formulated after enraging the king and losing his own estates."

Father Markham's lips tightened. "I feared as much."

She eyed him thoughtfully. 'Twas *she* who touched *his* face then with one small, filthy hand, startling him. "You are loyal to Westmoreland."

"Aye."

"Loyal enough to deceive his son?"

He considered the question carefully. "Camden long ago surrendered himself to wickedness. Aye. If I must, to save the lives of the good people here at Westmoreland as well as your own, I will deceive him."

He spoke the truth.

Withdrawing her hand, she clasped it with the other in front of her. "Lord Dillon and his men will arrive two or three days' hence."

"Wise One!" Simon protested.

"I assume that you are allowed to come and go as you please, Father," she continued.

"Aye. Camden and his men pay me little attention."

"Then seek you Lord Dillon outside the gates. I know not his designs, but ask that you aid him in any way you can."

"Know you *where* outside the gates?"

"Nay."

"Fear not. I shall find him, one way or another."

"I have good reason not to trust men of the cloth, Father. I pray the fever plaguing me has not clouded my judgment."

"It has not," he vowed. "Is there aught I can do for *you*, child, to ease your suffering?"

His sympathy, unfamiliar as it was, made her uncomfortable. "We have none of us had aught to eat or drink since we were captured. Some water and mayhap some bread would be much appreciated. Think you the guards would allow it?"

He tapped his lips thoughtfully with one forefinger. "Gareth and Walter will not. But 'tis almost time for Jordan and Hugh to relieve them so the former can drink themselves into their nightly stupor. Hugh is very concerned about his soul and would likely go along with my wishes. And Jordan, being a simple-minded fellow, follows his heart more often than his orders. I should have no difficulties there."

"Would they free us if you asked?"

"That I cannot do," he said regretfully. "Camden would slay them and their families as soon as he learned they were responsible."

"What of you? Will you not be made to suffer?"

Again he sent her a smile. "The church is my protection."

"I have one last request, Father."

"Aye?"

Leaning forward, she whispered in his ear.

He studied her a moment. "As you wish."

A few thumps on the door roused Walter and Gareth

and allowed him his freedom. They would have insisted on retrieving the torches, but—upon glimpsing Alyssa's face and narrowing eyes—they opted not to enter and let them be.

Silence settled around her, stiflingly thick, once the door closed. Abandoning her show of strength, she let her shoulders slump and wondered what reaction she should expect from the men behind her.

"So," she commented hoarsely, "all is finally revealed." Turning to face them, she let them have a good long look.

Every eye went wide. Every mouth dropped open. And, aye, a few hastily crossed themselves, though they had all just heard the priest accept that her youth was not a result of sorcery.

"I suppose you will all fear and revile me more than ever now," she grumbled, weary of the pain, in truth feeling a little bit sorry for herself. Shuffling over to her corner, she leaned back into it and slid down to the floor, unable to suppress a grimace as the gash in her thigh protested. "I would remind you of your oaths to Lord Dillon. Should I come to harm at any of your hands, he will slay you the instant he arrives."

"Then we are as good as dead!" Sir John, the youngest amongst the knights, declared.

Frowning, she affixed her blurry gaze on him. "You would slay me, then?"

"Nay, but 'tis my wound that adorns your forehead!"

Sure enough, a pink mark divided his forehead in the same pattern that the blood encrusted fissure divided hers.

"The mark on your cheek is mine," declared Sir Vincent.

"And that on your neck is mine," Sir Philip added.

All leapt in then, claiming responsibility for her pitiful condition, all apparently believing 'twould mean their deaths.

Closing her eyes, she shook her head. "There is only one Dillon will blame for my wounds. And it may not even matter then."

CHAPTER EIGHTEEN

Dillon rode hard for Westcott, the chilly afternoon breeze stinging his cheeks. He had awakened in his bed at Pinehurst, drenched in a cold sweat and trembling in reaction to having more dreams of Alyssa. Dreams that had been so real, so vivid, so disturbing that he had been unable to shake the feeling that something dreadful had happened to her. Half an hour later, he had departed with as many knights as could be spared, the gates locked tight behind them, not even certain where to begin his search for her.

Where would she be? At Westcott? At her stepfather's side? Somewhere between here and there?

What could have happened? Had her stepfather died? Had Alyssa's grief and distress simply become his own?

Was she safe and he merely overreacting to what could be unpleasant dreams brought on by his longing for her and his regret over their having argued ere she had left?

Or had some new foe arisen, yet another thirsting for Dillon's wealth and power? One who had intercepted her and defeated her guard ere she could reach her family?

When he rounded a bend in the sodden road and

encountered Robert and a substantial number of his men racing toward him, the last glimmer of hope Dillon had been nurturing sputtered and died.

The two brothers pulled up short a few feet apart, horses lathered, and stared at each other.

For several seconds, Dillon could not bring himself to ask the question as he took in Robert's grim countenance. "Who?"

"Camden."

Camden! Shock swept through him. *Impossible.*

"She and your men are being held in Westmoreland's dungeon."

He swore. Robert's voice held not an ounce of doubt.

If Camden lived, then whose body had Dillon sent to Westmoreland? He had been sure that it had been Camden, as had Simon and the others. Yet the bastard had fooled them all and, because of Dillon's error, now held Alyssa in his clutches.

Apprehension rising, Dillon nodded curtly and tore off in the direction of Westmoreland, everyone else thundering after him.

Should Camden guess that Alyssa was Dillon's lover, there would be no end to the cruelty he would inflict upon her, with or without his father's consent. The brutal dreams that had driven Dillon to take to the road this morning would become a reality and Alyssa…

He swallowed hard.

He could not lose her.

"How did you know?" Robert asked, gaining his side.

For one instant, Dillon could not conceal his inner fear as the nightmares that had plagued his sleep hammered through his mind. Images of Alyssa's broken, bloodied body—of her lovely brown eyes staring up at him, sightless, as she drew her last breath—arose again and tightened his chest before he regained control and wiped all emotion from his face. "Not now."

"She said Camden has seized Westmoreland, but said

naught of Lord Everard. Think you he could be part of this?"

Dillon's fury deepened. "If he is, he will meet the same violent end as his son."

* * *

Like the others, Michael gazed at the small form curled in a shivering ball on the pallet across the dank cell from them. Father Markham had been right about the other guards. Jordan and Hugh were as agreeable as Walter and Gareth were *dis*agreeable. Both Jordan and Hugh were Westmoreland's men, unlike the latter two, and seemed such nice fellows that Michael suspected they had been bullied into guarding the dungeon at night so the others could indulge in drinking and wenching. Camden was certainly irresponsible enough to allow it.

If he even knew.

Jordan had proven to be quite useful. Simple-minded he may be, but his heart was as big as a siege tower. Having never lain eyes on them before, Jordan had been shocked to discover there was a woman in the prisoners' midst. Shocked and *appalled* when he got a good look at her face.

No fear at all did he exhibit, leaving Michael to wonder if mayhap the man did not understand that she was a sorceress. Instead, furious on her behalf, he had suspected the other prisoners of abusing her and had threatened to pummel them one and all until the priest had managed to convey some moderate understanding of the true source of her injuries.

Which was when Hugh had termed her a saint.

Hugh took the priest's desire to protect her as a sign that the wisewoman was a messenger from God or some such and all but fell to his knees, praying to her. He seemed willing to do aught she asked of him.

Aught but help them escape, that was.

'Twas Jordan who had provided her with the pallet she slept upon and the blankets that now covered her. And 'twas Jordan who had hauled in clean cloths and bucket after bucket of water, then set about patiently cleansing her wounds.

Michael had been dismayed to see how many and how gruesome they were.

Jordan had even brought in some crushed calendula petals to apply to them as he said his mum often did to *his* cuts and scrapes.

The wisewoman would allow no other nigh her. Not even Michael or Simon. Only Jordan would she permit to change her bandages. And 'twas Jordan who fed her and coaxed her to drink. He even kept a chamber pot in the dungeon's only other cell and helped her limp in there so she would not have to relieve herself in front of the men.

Michael and the others were always tempted to make their escape then. But they had all been weakened by blood loss before their wounds had been healed and feared they would not get far without weapons. Should they try and fail, they did not doubt the healer would pay the price.

So they waited, speculating upon the numbers they might encounter in the hall and hoping they could convince Jordan to aid them in their escape as his attachment to the healer grew.

What pained Michael the most was that the wisewoman feared them now. In her delirium, she believed he, Simon, and the others meant to harm her and no amount of reasoning would convince her otherwise.

She also thought Jordan was Lord Dillon.

Michael supposed he could see why. Jordan did have a bit of the look of him. He certainly was as tall and broad as Lord Dillon with somewhat similar features and hair about the same dark shade, but lacking the gray at the temples.

A familiar clunk echoed off the slimy walls, warning them of another visitor. Jordan poked his head in, glancing at the others ere he sought out the wisewoman.

Opening her eyes, she looked listlessly toward him, then smiled, her battered face lighting up. "Dillon. What took you so long?"

Confusion wrinkled Jordan's brow as he stepped into the cell and closed the door, his weapons left outside beyond the prisoners' grasp. In one large, scarred hand he carried a tankard of steaming, fragrant liquid. "'Tis Jordan, Mistress. And I come as quick as I could," he said, crouching down beside her and taking the hand she offered him with such affection. "I cannot come during the day on account of Walter and Gareth. They have little liking for you, I fear."

An understatement if Michael had ever heard one. Had it been up to those two, she would be dead. They *all* would be.

Her smile turned melancholy. "You know I am accustomed to scorn, Dillon. It matters not to me as long as you are here."

A quick look at the others confirmed that they felt as remorseful as Michael did over disdaining her in the past. But their expressions also held a certain fascination.

They would have to be blind not to see the love the wisewoman felt for Lord Dillon during these moments when she thought 'twas him leaning over her. It shone through her pain like the brightest of candles, illuminating the goodness within her for all to see and shaming them, every one.

At her urging, Jordan sat down beside her, his back to the wall, and stretched out his long, muscled legs. As soon as he did, she inched over and rested her head in his lap. One slender arm, swathed in white dressing, came up to drape across his thighs. Her badly abraded hand settled on his hip.

"'Tis so cold, Dillon. Make me warm again."

Face flushing a bright red, Jordan sent Michael and the others an uncomfortable look. He may be simple, but he knew 'twas not proper for her to touch him with such familiarity.

Michael would have protested, but she took such comfort in Jordan's presence, believing him the one she loved. After she had saved his life, Michael could not bring himself to deny her whatever peace she might find in what he feared would be her last hours.

Simon must have felt the same way, for he, too, issued no protest.

Jordan awkwardly patted the healer's uninjured shoulder as he searched his overtaxed mind for something to say. "I told my mum I was ailing so she would make some broth." He held it up for her inspection. "I will have to confess the lie to Father Markham, but 'twas worth it if 'twill make you well."

"I have no appetite," she admitted.

"'Tis tasty," he persuaded. "And 'twill warm you. You *must* drink it. I always feel right as rain the day after I quaff it."

"'Twill please you for me to do so?"

"Aye."

Her gentle smile returned. "All right, Dillon."

Jordan was right. If naught else, the warmth of the broth stilled her shivers and soon lulled her to sleep. It took some maneuvering for him to ease out from under her and settle her back on the pallet, the blankets drawn up to her bruised chin.

Even in sleep she did not wish to relinquish her hold on him.

Nodding to the others and vowing to bring additional food soon, he knocked lightly on the door and waited for Hugh to open it.

"Do not be sad, Dillon," the wisewoman murmured suddenly. "I do not regret it."

The door swung open as Jordan looked over at her with both concern and bewilderment. "Regret what, Mistress?"

"Giving my life to save yours. I have loved you for years, you know."

Frowning, not understanding, he ducked out of the cell, closed the door behind him, and slid the bolt home.

"I just could not tell you," she added.

Michael stared at her as sleep claimed her once more, silencing her disturbing words.

"I feel a sudden need to confess to Father Markham myself," Simon muttered gruffly.

"As do I," Sir Philip added.

One by one they agreed, acknowledging the wrong they had dealt her, and vowed—should she live—to make amends.

* * *

Steeped in darkness, Dillon and Robert heard the man's approach long before he reached them. He made no effort at all to muffle his footsteps. Verily, he seemed to be stumbling about in the night with no singular destination in mind.

Dillon waited impatiently to see what errand he was about and whether or not he would take pains to avoid them.

He did not. He walked right into Dillon's chest.

"Oh! I beg your pardon!" After regaining his footing, he glanced up… and paled.

"Release one cry for help and they will find your head two leagues from your body," Dillon warned him.

His swallow audible, the stranger nodded, too frightened to utter a reply.

Fisting a hand in the man's tunic, Dillon led him back through the forest to the place where the rest of his party waited and thrust him into a diluted ray of moonlight.

Robert stepped up to Dillon's side. "A priest!" he spat, his face twisting with disgust.

'Twas true. It had been too dark for Dillon to notice much of the stranger's appearance. Now, after giving him a swift once-over, he shoved the useless man at his brother. "Get rid of him."

"W-Wait!" the priest cried with something akin to panic. He must think they meant to kill him.

Dillon had no such intention, of course. He simply did not think a religious man would be the best choice to aid them in their search for a purported sorceress.

Robert grabbed the priest's arm and began to drag him away.

But the man dug in his heels, craning his neck to see Dillon. "I-I-If you are the Earl of Westcott, I have come to help you," he stuttered.

Frowning, Dillon gave the man another look. "Robert."

"Aye?"

"Let us hear what he has to say. And quietly, if you value your life. I would rather not alert the countryside to our presence."

Sublime relief melted the man's features. "Thank you, my lord. Thank you." Once free of Robert's hold, he gathered his tattered composure. "I take it that you are Lord Dillon, Earl of Westcott?"

Dillon saw no reason to deny it, since he planned to allow the man no opportunity to use it against him. "Aye."

"I have a message for you from the one you seek."

Robert snorted. "How know we this? You could have come at Camden's bidding."

Eyeing Robert nervously, the priest sidled away from him.

Dillon folded his arms across his chest. "My brother asks a valid question. What proof have you that your words are not false?"

"Sh-She knew you would not trust one such as I and did bid me give you her name as proof of my good will."

Dillon's heart skipped a beat. Stepping closer to the man, Robert with him, he asked carefully, "What name did she offer?"

The priest swallowed again, his wide eyes flitting between the two large warriors. "Alyssa."

Air whooshed out of Dillon's lungs. "She lives then."

The man nodded several times. "Aye, but not for much longer, I fear."

"Dillon!"

His growl of fury drowned out his brother's startled hiss as Dillon lifted the man up in the air and shook him violently. "What did you do to her? Burn her? Attempt to drown her? All because you think she is some vile *witch?*"

Robert pried at his hands. "Dillon, stop! Release him! I do

352 | DIANNE DUVALL

not think 'twas him!"

The red haze of fury that coated his vision peeling back, he looked over at his brother and set the priest down with a jarring thud. "What know you, brother?" he queried, advancing on him menacingly as Robert held up his hands in a placating gesture and backed away. "What have you kept from me?"

"Now, Dillon, she bade me not to tell you. I could not gainsay her wishes."

"What has happened to her?" he demanded, stomach knotting.

Robert halted, a ring of Dillon's inquisitive men blockading him, and answered in a low voice. "Judging by what I saw of her and by the guilt that crossed her face when she did ask me not to tell you, she has been healing your men again."

"Some or all?"

"*All* of them would be my guess. She did not look well, Dillon."

Which was why she had not visited him in any more visions. Dillon had expected her to and had wondered why she had not, why she had visited Robert instead.

She must have been too weak.

The fists at his sides clenched until his knuckles shown white. "Was she as bad as she was after she healed me?"

"Not when I saw her, nay. But enough time has passed that she may be now."

"She is quite ill, my lord, taken with a high fever," the priest confirmed, having silently rejoined them. "Two men I trust are watching over her and making her as comfortable as possible, but I fear she may be beyond our help."

"She is *not* beyond help," Dillon snapped.

Why did she keep doing this? Why did she continue to sacrifice herself this way, pushing herself further than she knew she should? How could she forfeit her life so easily? Did she value herself so little? Did she think *he* valued her so little? Did she not know how desperately he needed her?

Or did she merely trust him to always be there to pull her back from the darkness?

"Priest."

The man mustered a tentative smile. "F-Father Markham. Aye?"

Dillon endeavored to tear his mind away from thoughts of Alyssa moldering away in the bowels of a dungeon. "How think you you may be of service to us?"

"I have been considering that and believe I have the answer. I happen to possess knowledge of a secret passageway, my lord, that begins in the chapel and ends some distance beyond the postern gate. Hidden by tangles of brush, 'twas meant to be a route to freedom for any who sought sanctuary in the chapel in the event of Westmoreland being taken. I thought you might use it to gain entry and catch Camden unawares."

Another secret passageway. "Camden knows naught of this?"

"Nay. Westmoreland once confided in me that he had decided against informing Camden when he saw the path his son had chosen. Now that Father Piers is gone, Westmoreland and I are the only two who know."

"Robert, what think you?"

"I trust him not," he answered without hesitation.

"Alyssa trusted him enough to give him her name."

"Mayhap she did not do so willingly. Mayhap he beat it out of her."

"I did not!" Father Markham huffed indignantly. "I did not even ask it of her. Did not think to. She whispered it in my ear ere I left to obtain food and water for them. And bandages. The poor girl's face was marked in so many places…"

Gasps sounded all around. He trailed off, clearly puzzled, and studied the shocked faces of Dillon's men.

An uneasy hush settled upon them.

"You saw her face?" Dillon asked, voice dangerously soft. Mayhap the man before him *was* responsible for Alyssa's injuries.

"Aye," Father Markham confirmed. "Two of the knights with her attempted to stop me, but—"

Dillon's hand closed around his throat. "You forced her? You touched her?"

"Her cowl," he choked out, face mottling. "Only her cowl *after* she gave me leave to do so."

Scowling, Dillon freed him. Why would Alyssa consent to such after guarding her identity so tenaciously all these years? And why reveal herself to *this* man, whom she must fear above all others at Westmoreland?

Did Dillon dare trust him? Believe that Alyssa had placed her faith in Father Markham, intending for *him* to do the same?

What choice had he really? Camden would kill Alyssa at the first signs of a siege. And Dillon lacked the manpower to do so now even if he thought Camden would not. The drawbridge was raised, the portcullis lowered and the walls guarded so vigilantly that he had no hope of sneaking over them.

"You will lead us to this passage," he commanded.

The priest nodded. "Aye, my lord. As you wish."

"Robert, a word." Dillon led his brother away from the others.

"You trust him?" Robert asked, his worry evident.

"I have no choice. I must reach Alyssa as soon as possible and see to her wounds. But you shall not be with me, brother. I have another, more important task for you."

* * *

Alyssa came awake with a start, heart pounding, senses tingling.

Dillon.

Her mind firmly focused on him, she bolted upright.

Pain zigzagged through her, so fierce she cried out and brought a hand to her sundering head.

Across the room, Michael rose to his knees with alarm, but came no closer. "Wise One?"

"He is here," she gasped, feeling blindly for the wall with her other hand. Upon finding it, she braced herself and shakily tried to rise.

"You should not," he cautioned.

She was so weak. Her muscles burned. Every limb ached. "He is here," Alyssa repeated firmly. "Help me, Michael. Please."

Leaping to his feet, he rushed to her side and helped her stand.

Alyssa was so weak she had to lean against him. Her forehead brushed his neck, so cool against her warm brow, though she was surprised to note that her fever seemed to have abated somewhat.

"You should rest, Wise One."

She shook her head and straightened, clinging to him for support. "He is here. We must act quickly."

"Who is here?" Simon inserted as he and the others rose.

"Lord Dillon."

The men shared a look.

"Nay, Healer—"

"He is here!" she insisted urgently. "Above. Fighting Camden and his mercenaries and Westmoreland's men." She waved toward the door. "Simon, who stands guard?"

"I believe 'tis still Hugh and Jordan."

Alyssa frowned. She recalled Hugh, but could not match Jordan's name with a face. "Can you and the others disarm them?"

"Aye."

"Then call them in and do so. Take their weapons and join Dillon and his men above. There should be sufficient dead already to arm the rest of you."

The men glanced at each other uneasily.

"Why do you hesitate? Do as I say!" she shouted. A fit of harsh, guttural coughing racked her.

At last, Simon obeyed. Striding to the door, he pounded on

it until it opened. "'Tis the wisewoman! She is failing! Come quickly!"

The door flew wide and two men rushed inside, faces distressed, forgetting the weapons they carried, which Simon and the others swiftly confiscated.

Alyssa froze. Hugh she recognized, but the other… She thought at first 'twas Dillon until she got a closer look at his face. *Oh. Aye. The simple man who gave me a blanket.*

It took him longer than Hugh to understand the ruse. But, when he did, Jordan exhibited alarm, not anger. "You cannot!" he exclaimed. "They will kill you! And the woman here after you."

"The wisewoman believes our lord is above. We must join him and fight."

"Alyssaaaaa!"

Jolted, the men all looked toward the ceiling, where that dragon's roar seemed to have originated.

Alyssa's heart leaped. "Dillon," she whispered thankfully. Her knees buckled as pain ripped through her abdomen.

"Wise One!" Michael caught her and, as gently as possible, lowered her to her pallet.

"Alyssaaaaa!"

Moisture sprang to her brow. Her jaw clenched. "Go!" she ordered, breath coming in gasps as she called upon the last shreds of her gift to try to save her babe. *"Go!"*

Kneeling beside her, Michael looked up at the men hovering around them in a semicircle. "You heard her. Take the weapons and go. I will stay and watch over her."

"Alyssaaa!"

All eyes flew to the door. The voice was closer now. Close enough for them to recognize it as Dillon's.

"Lord Dillon!" Simon called. "In here!"

"Alyssa!"

She peered toward the entrance, barely glimpsing it through the raggedly clad legs that fenced in her pallet.

Seconds later, Dillon filled the doorway, chest heaving, eyes wild, his helm gone.

His sword dripped blood. His surcoat and armor were stained crimson with it, his face smeared and spattered with it.

Not one drop of it appeared to be his own.

Sighing with both relief and despair, Alyssa let her eyelids close and hugged his presence to her.

* * *

Breathing hard, Dillon focused on the men clustered in one corner of the squalid, stinking cell. *His* men. All but two, who were unarmed and posed no threat.

They parted as he watched, exposing a crumpled black figure with long sullied tresses and a bruised and battered face.

His heart stopped. Was he too late?

The sword slipped from his fingers, clattering to the floor as he hurried forward and skidded to his knees beside her.

"Alyssa?" Dillon hastily removed his mailed mitts. His hands shook as he slipped them beneath her and gently lifted her into his arms. "Alyssa?" Cradling her against his chest, he smoothed her hair back in a familiar, tender gesture, careful not to touch the gash that bisected her forehead.

Her eyelids fluttered open. "I knew you would come."

Crushing her to him, Dillon buried his face in her neck and fought the tears that, despite his wishes, began to fall. He had nigh been driven mad with fear for her as he had followed the priest through the webbed and dusty tunnel. Markham's belief that she would not live long had torn through his skull.

Would he reach her in time?

Would Camden or one of his cohorts race for the dungeon and dispatch her as soon as the battle began?

Dillon had never fought so hard or so savagely in his life as when they had breached the great hall. And for the first time ever, he had left his men to finish the battle whilst he searched for Alyssa, praying he would find her alive.

And she was. But she was so frail and weak and feverish.

Had he cut his way through Camden and his men only to watch her die in his arms?

Do not leave me, Alyssa. Please, do not leave me, he begged silently, terrified of losing her.

"I will not," she promised, her arms finding their way around him and squeezing him as tightly as her sapped strength would allow.

He nodded, unable to force a response past his tight throat.

"But, Dillon…"

When she said naught more, he drew back, fearing she had lost consciousness.

She had not. Alyssa stared up at him with such anguish in her tear-filled eyes that he felt dread sour his stomach.

"What is it?" he prompted.

"You will be so angry," she whispered. "You will scorn me."

"I shall *never* scorn you, love. Why would you think such a foolish thing?"

Her chest hitched as a sob tumbled forth from between her cracked lips. "Because I fear our babe will not survive."

Everything within him froze. "Our babe?"

"Please forgive me, Dillon." Crying in earnest now, she clutched his surcoat and hauberk with desperate hands that were covered with scrapes and scabs. "I have tried so hard to keep him strong. But I am so weary… and weakened from the fever… I do not think I can continue."

A son. Alyssa carried his son.

Stunned, he rested a large hand on her sunken stomach.

And she believed that only the tattered remnants of her gifts kept the babe alive.

"I had to heal them," she sobbed. "I know you are angry, but I *had* to. I c-could not let them die. They f-fought so hard to p-protect me, Dillon. I *had* to help them."

"I know love," he soothed, shifting his hand from her stomach to beneath her knees. "I am not angry."

"B-But the babe…"

Rising with her in his arms, Dillon left the cell, his dumbfounded men following after him. "'Twill be all right," he promised.

Michael and Simon slipped past them and, wielding Jordan and Hugh's swords, hurried forward to guard their front. Dillon lost sight of them as they raced up the stairs at the end of the passageway. The sound of steel meeting steel ensued, and a body tumbled down to land at Dillon's feet.

Alyssa moaned, one hand going to her belly.

Dillon stepped over the body and swiftly scaled the stairs, jarring her as little as possible. "'Twill be all right," he said again, and knew not if he meant to convince her or himself. "I have already sent Robert for your family. They will be here anon, to restore both your health and that of our babe." *Our babe*, he thought with equal amounts of awe and fear.

She nodded and tried to slow her hiccupping breath. "I love you, Dillon."

Joy and pain surged through him. How he had longed to hear those words cross her lips.

"Forgive me for n-not saying it ere now. I have been so foolish. I have loved you for so long. And, w-when we were taken, I feared I would not have the chance to tell you."

He clutched her tighter. "Shhh. Worry not, sweetling. We are together now. 'Tis all that matters."

The great hall was a mass of carnage when they entered, littered with bodies and body parts, the air filled with groans and tainted with the odors of death.

If possible, Alyssa paled even more as she took in her surroundings. "Where is Camden?"

He nodded toward the dais. "Over there."

Following his gaze, she shuddered. "Where is the rest of him?"

He nodded in the opposite direction. "Over there."

"You are certain this time 'tis him?" she asked, but no

condemnation accompanied the words. Only a deep desire to see the threat ended.

He ground his teeth. "I am certain." And almost wished the knave were still alive so he could run him through and take his head again.

Sprinting up another set of stairs, Dillon burst into the lord's chamber. Sickness hovered heavily in the room. The only occupant, hardly recognizable to them both, rested in the huge bed, barely forming a wrinkle in its surface.

Emaciated and gasping for breath, Westmoreland neither moved nor opened his eyes.

Dillon turned to leave, swallowing his sorrow at seeing his friend on the cusp of death.

Alyssa threw out one hand and clutched the door. "Wait."

He paused, looking down at her.

She stared at the bed as though seeing a specter. "Dillon... the dream..."

Dream? "What dream?"

"The dream that drew me from Pinehurst."

It seemed as though years had passed since then. But, after a moment, Dillon recalled she had dreamed that her father was ill and... dying. His gaze flew to Westmoreland, then returned to Alyssa, who looked flabbergasted.

"Dillon, I...I think Westmoreland is my father."

CHAPTER NINTEEN

"You are fidgeting again."

Ignoring Dillon, Alyssa turned to look over her shoulder at the long procession of soldiers on horseback that followed them. "Do you suppose Lord Everard is all right?" She could not locate Westmoreland amongst the other men. "Mayhap 'tis too soon for him to make such a trip. 'Twill tire him."

"'Tis but a short trip."

"We should have postponed it another fortnight."

Dillon sighed. "I have already allowed you to postpone it twice, sweetling. Did you have your way, we would not leave Westmoreland until the snows thawed."

She frowned at him. "But he has not yet recovered all of his strength."

"He is strong enough."

"And 'tis so cold."

"'Twill only grow colder do we wait," he responded patiently.

"Spring is not so very far away. We could have waited until then."

He grinned. "You will be too round to sit a horse by then, love." Reaching out, he gave her still-flat stomach a gentle pat.

Heat suffusing her cheeks, she batted his hand away.

"Can you not call him Father?" he broached softly.

She bit her lip. "'Twould make me feel disloyal to the one who raised me."

"Matthew knows he will always be the father of your heart. The one who helped you take your first steps and learn your first words. The one who helped you grow into the wondrous woman I fell in love with. I do not think 'twould trouble him if you called the man who sired you Father, as well."

Whilst Dillon had liberated Alyssa from the dungeon, Robert had raced to retrieve her family.

As fate would have it, her mother had seen in a vision that Alyssa would need them and had already sent for Geoffrey and Meghan. Together with Matthew and Alyssa's grandmother, they had set out to aid her not long after she had been captured. So Robert had, thankfully, encountered them all on the road to Westcott and had returned with them posthaste.

Dillon and Matthew had instantly liked each other, much to Alyssa's relief. And, though she doubted the two men would ever be friends, there seemed to be no animosity on Matthew's part toward Westmoreland, who Beatrice finally admitted had sired Alyssa. Matthew alone seemed unsurprised by the revelation, leading Alyssa to believe that her mother had confided in him long ago.

It had hurt, learning that her mother had lied to her all these years, vowing she knew not the name of Alyssa's father. Declaring him lowborn in all of her tales.

Fear had driven Beatrice. Fear that, were the truth known, Westmoreland's wife might harm Alyssa. Or mayhap harm Beatrice herself. After all, Beatrice had aided Westmoreland in siring a son on his wife when she wished not to conceive. And had demanded he give her a child of her own as payment, though Westmoreland knew naught but that she had wished to share her body with him for a night.

When Camden's dissolute nature had become obvious, Beatrice had been more determined than ever to keep her secret, fearing that Westmoreland might return and take Alyssa from her if he learned he had sired a daughter. Or that Camden might kill Alyssa to ensure that his inheritance went undivided.

In the weeks that had passed since Dillon slew Camden and Westmoreland learned he had sired a daughter, Westmoreland *had* expressed a desire to declare Alyssa his heir. So her mother's fears might not have been in vain.

"Lord Everard cannot truly name me his heir, can he?" she asked, uncomfortable with the notion.

Dillon grunted. "Now that Camden and his cousin are both dead, Westmoreland has no other living relatives."

Alyssa refused to think about Camden having been her half brother and once more turned her thoughts to Matthew. "It makes me feel as though I am abandoning Father in order to gain wealth and property."

"You are not abandoning him at all," Dillon assured her. "Nor does he think you are. Matthew will always be welcome in our home, Alyssa. And you may visit him in the home of your birth anytime you wish… once our son is born."

"The babe is fine, Dillon," she promised, noting the concern that darkened his brow. "Healthy and strong."

Turning his head, he met her gaze. "If he is healthy and strong, why do you have such difficulty keeping food in your belly?"

She grimaced. Everything she put in her stomach seemed to come right back up again. "Such is normal for a woman who is breeding. 'Tis the mark of a healthy babe, my grandmother says, and 'twill soon pass."

"Well, I like it not," he grumbled, reaching out to capture her hand in his own.

She laughed. "Nor do I. If you did not insist on remaining

by my side at all times, you would not be subjected to such unpleasantness."

His face softened. "Twice now I have nigh lost you. Can you blame me for wanting to keep you always within my sight?"

Her heart swelled. "Nay."

A cold breeze rose up around them. The barren branches of trees crackled and clacked as they swayed and collided with one another.

Worried that Westmoreland might take a chill, she looked over her shoulder again.

"He is fine, Alyssa. Cease your fretting."

She tossed Dillon a petulant frown. "We should have waited."

"You are only using his supposed frailty as an excuse to postpone the inevitable."

"Faugh!"

"You will have to face the people of Westcott sooner or later, love. The longer you put it off, the more difficult 'twill be."

She snorted, attempting to hide the nervousness that plagued her and had made her nausea worse that morn. "I have faced your people many a time."

"*Our* people. And not like this, you have not."

Glancing down, she plucked at the luxurious cloak lined with fur that kept her warm. Beneath it, she wore a long, pale green tunic softer than anything she had ever owned topped by a surcoat carved from yards of beautiful velvet in a lovely emerald green.

The clothing of a true noblewoman.

Dillon had insisted she leave her hair loose this morn, free from any restriction save the jeweled circlet he had placed atop her head himself. Two new daggers reposed at her waist, replacing those she had lost whilst fighting Camden's soldiers. New boots fashioned from the most supple leather graced her feet. A trunk full of clothing as grand or more grand than that which she now wore lumbered along somewhere behind her. Even her undergarments were of the highest quality. Dillon had seen to it all, choosing it whilst she had remained abed, recovering from both her injuries and her second healing.

Alyssa was unaccustomed to such grandeur. "I feel a complete fraud," she grumbled.

"You are beautiful. A countess in every way. I am proud to call you wife."

"I fear your people will not agree," she countered.

"*Our* people have been made well aware of who my bride is and will welcome you with open arms." Glancing away from her, he muttered, "Or risk losing their heads."

Amusement rose up inside her despite her concern. He was so protective of her. And so very stubborn. Dillon had decided he would make his people love her, and still seemed to think he could actually accomplish such an impossible feat.

Alyssa smiled, letting her gaze trace his handsome profile. She could scarcely believe he was her husband, wed to her at Westmoreland in a ceremony conducted by Father Markham at Dillon's own insistence. And with the king's blessing.

Alyssa had been staggered by their good fortune and had feared Dillon had beggared his estates, buying King Richard's approval. However, when asked how he had accomplished such a miraculous feat, Dillon had simply said he possessed knowledge of their lionhearted ruler that King Richard wished to remain private. He would not tell her *what* and managed to keep his mind frustratingly blank whenever she tried to riffle through his thoughts in search of the answer. Alyssa could glean only that it had something to do with King Philip of France.

When Dillon had vowed to forever maintain his silence as long as the king voiced no objections to their union, King Richard had accepted the wealth of gold that had accompanied Dillon's missive and had offered them both hearty congratulations.

Alyssa shook her head in amazement. Dillon had known she feared wedding him without the king's blessing and had dared to blackmail the fierce monarch in order to procure it. As little time as King Richard spent in England, he needed Dillon's loyalty and sword arm too much to simply slay Dillon to ensure his silence. "Have I told you today that I love you?"

His lips tilted up in a warm smile that she thought would always make her insides melt. "Aye. A dozen times or more. But 'tis not enough."

She laughed, then gasped when he suddenly leaned over, grasped her about the waist, and lifted her to sit sideways across his lap. Barely settled, she clung to him helplessly whilst he dipped his head and captured her lips in a long, passionate kiss.

"Dillon, your men," she protested breathlessly when he finally drew back. She peeked over his shoulder, then groaned at their amused grins, sly glances, and knowing nudges.

Not at all concerned, Dillon hugged her close. "My men are well accustomed by now to seeing me accost my wife. 'Tis no secret that I love you dearly and cannot keep my hands off of you."

She grinned, wrapping her arms around him and nestling her head to his chest. 'Twas true. The man had no shame, no sense of propriety. If he wanted to kiss her, he kissed her. Wherever they might be. Whomever they might be entertaining. If he wanted to slip his arms around her and cuddle her close, he did that, too. And he had no qualms whatsoever about scooping her up in his arms at the most unexpected moment and carrying her up to their chamber to make wild passionate love to her, leaving his intentions no secret to those who witnessed their retreat.

"I shall soon have to pound some sense of propriety into that handsome head of yours," she lied. Alyssa adored his spontaneity. 'Twas a playful, boyish side of him she had not seen often enough.

"I admit my actions this time were not purely motivated by pleasure," he confessed.

She sat up straighter, arching her brows. "Oh?"

He sent her a sheepish grin. "Westcott lies ahead and I feared you might bolt."

Head snapping forward, she swallowed hard as her stomach turned over. "I am going to be sick."

"Nay, you are not," he retorted instantly.

"I am, Dillon. I am going to be sick. You must stop."

"Alyssa, look at me."

Worries tumbling through her head, she did so.

"All will be well," he promised. "Will you not trust me in this?"

She sighed. How could she say *nay* when he looked at her with such tender concern, as if there were naught he would not do to ensure her happiness. "Aye," she whispered, feeling no better.

Alyssa did not delude herself into believing that the rest of the nobility would accept her as Dillon's wife and would not scorn Dillon for marrying beneath him. Only half of the blood that coursed through her veins, after all, was noble. Nay, the noblemen and women may be coldly polite when in the king's presence, but they would never welcome her, never accept her as one of their own, and would no doubt issue barbs and cutting remarks every chance they could get. Fortunately, Alyssa would have only sporadic contact with them and Dillon did not care what they thought of him. Mayhap because his fearsome reputation would keep them at bay.

Here at Westcott, however…

She would see these people every day, was expected to lead them at her husband's side, and held little hope that they would welcome her presence in their lives with more eagerness than they had the evil sorceress they had long imagined her to be.

Dillon gave her a reassuring squeeze.

When they cantered across the drawbridge, through the

massive gate house and into the outer bailey, they found it deserted. Disheartened, Alyssa wondered if the people had been so upset by their lord's choice of brides that they had refused to greet them upon their return.

When they passed through the barbican into the inner bailey, however, she gaped at the sight that met her eyes. "Are they *all* here?" she asked, staring about them in wonder.

"By the looks of it, I would say so."

The people of Westcott packed the bailey. So many that they left only a narrow path open from the gates to the steps of the keep, where Robert, Father Markham, Ann Marie, and Simon waited with smiles of greeting. Off to the side a bit stood Michael and the rest of her former cellmates, all grinning from ear to ear.

When Alyssa's eyes alighted upon another figure, she frowned. Hugh, the jailer from Westmoreland who had been so concerned for his soul, bowed and scraped as though they were royalty. Whatever was he about?

Dillon slowed his destrier to a plodding walk, giving the people time to adjust to her appearance. Alyssa could not tell whether they were pleased or displeased. None uttered a single sound. Even the children remained quiet, gazing up at her with silent awe. Then...

"Where is the sorceress?" someone mumbled in a loud aside.

"Right there, you dolt," another muttered.

Alyssa searched for the speakers, but could not find them in the sea of faces to her right. Nor could she identify either of the voices, pitched low as they were. But both belonged to men.

"Where?"

"He holds her in his arms. Are you blind?"

"Well how was I supposed to know? She does not wear her robes."

"She is the only woman in the party, you fool!"

Dillon coughed to cover the laughter she felt shake his shoulders and jostle her back.

Alyssa felt her own lips twitch and bit back a nervous giggle.

An older man to her left cursed. This one she could see quite clearly.

"What?" his weathered wife demanded. "Stop crumplin' yer face up like that or you will have the countess thinkin' you do not like her."

"'Tis not that," he denied. "I was just rememberin' all of the bawdy jests I told in 'er hearin', thinkin' 'er a crusty old wench like you." He winced when his wife's hand abruptly made contact with the back of his head. "And now to find out she's so young and innocent and a saint an' all…" He shook his head. "I fear I have cleared myself a wide path to Hell, Edith."

His wife snorted. "You cleared that path long afore we came to Westcott."

Dillon chuckled again.

Alyssa's amusement waned. "Dillon," she broached, "of what does he speak? A saint? Who told him that?"

"I suspect Hugh has been spreading tales."

A groan escaped her. "I thought Father Markham cleared up that misconception ere they left."

"Evidently not."

"Well, I cannot let these people believe I am a saint."

"Better a saint than a sinner—oomph! Watch the elbow, wife."

"Sister!" Robert's boisterous welcome distracted Alyssa from the sharp retort that had formed on her lips. "I trust you had a pleasant journey."

Smiling, she let him help her down from Dillon's horse. "Aye, Robert. Quite pleasant."

"You are well?"

"Aye."

"Nay," Dillon negated, dismounting beside her. "Every morsel I coax her to eat comes back up and finds a home in whatever container or bush is nearest at hand." He hastily caught Alyssa's elbow ere she could drive it back into his ribs again.

"Husband, 'tis not appropriate to discuss such things in front of others." Flushing hotly, she assured Robert, "'Tis naught. I am well, truly."

He looked confused for a moment until understanding dawned. "Ahhh. 'Tis my future nephew who disturbs you so."

Gasps sounded around them.

Father Markham beamed at her over Robert's shoulder, already a party to their secret, whilst Ann Marie blurted ecstatic congratulations.

Amidst the ensuing chatter, Dillon took her hand in his much larger one and led her to the top of the steps. Alyssa's stomach fluttered nervously as he turned them both to face his people. And she worried for a moment that she might be sick right there in front of all.

A hush fell over the crowd that had been alive with discourse as news of her pregnancy passed from person to person like a breeze through trees.

Her heart pounded with both dread and anticipation, thudding against her ribs.

Would they mock her? Would they loathe her? Would they accept her, grudgingly or nay?

Commanding her attention, Dillon raised her hand to his lips and winked at her to ease her fears. "People of Westcott," he called, his deep voice loud and majestic. "I present to you my wife, my advisor, my heart. Mother of my heir. Wisewoman and healer of all. Lady Alyssa, Countess of Westcott!"

Cheers exploded through the bailey.

Alyssa started violently.

Laughing, Dillon yanked her into his arms and captured her lips in a lengthy kiss, goading the cheers to a deafening roar.

Dizzy with surprise and relief, Alyssa stared up at him in amazement. "Did you truly threaten to behead them if they did not accept me?"

"Nay."

"Then how did you accomplish it?"

Dillon assumed a smug expression. "Think you I lied when I said 'twas not impossible?"

Grinning, she raised her arms and linked them around his neck. "Nay. But I believe *I* have been right all along."

"About them?"

"About you," she corrected as she tunneled her fingers through his soft, thick hair. "I knew there was a hint of sorcery coursing through your blood."

Much to the delight of those present, he leaned down to nibble her ear. "How else could I claim a sorceress of my own?"

Another melding of lips followed, poignant and sweet. For long moments, they gazed at each other, oblivious to all save themselves, looking forward to the future they would share at Westcott, a future both had once thought impossible. The children they would raise. The utter, marvelous chaos that would embrace them were any born with her special gifts.

"I love you, Dillon."

"I love you, Alyssa," he responded warmly.

Smiling shyly, her arm around his waist and his looped around her shoulders to keep her firmly anchored to his side, Alyssa turned to face his people.

Nay, *their* people.

The cheers rose to a roar, stealing her breath, bringing tears to her eyes.

At last, she thought, glancing up at the man at her side.

He glanced down, his hand tightening on her shoulder. *At last.*

ABOUT THE AUTHOR

Dianne Duvall is the *New York Times* and *USA Today* Bestselling Author of the *Immortal Guardians* paranormal romance series and *The Gifted Ones* historical romance series. Her debut novel, **Darkness Dawns**, was nominated for the RT Reviewers' Choice Award for Best Vampire Romance by *RT Book Reviews*, for Best Paranormal Romance—Vampire by The Romance Reviews, and for Best Book of 2011 by Long and Short Reviews. **Darkness Rises** was also nominated for the RT Reviewers' Choice Award for Best Vampire Romance. Dianne's novels are routinely deemed Top Picks by *RT Book Reviews*, The Romance Reviews, and/or Night Owl Reviews. Reviewers have called Dianne's books "utterly addictive" (*RT Book Reviews*), "fast-paced and humorous" (*Publishers Weekly*), "extraordinary" (Long and Short Reviews), and "wonderfully imaginative" (The Romance Reviews).

Dianne loves all things creative. When she isn't writing, Dianne is active in the independent film industry and has even appeared on-screen, crawling out of a moonlit grave and wielding a machete like some of the vampires she so loves to create in her books.

Connect with her online:

Website — www.dianneduvall.com
Blog — dianneduvall.blogspot.com
Facebook — www.facebook.com/DianneDuvallAuthor
Twitter — twitter.com/DianneDuvall
Pinterest — www.pinterest.com/dianneduvall
tsū — https://www.tsu.co/DianneDuvall
Goodreads — www.goodreads.com/Dianne_Duvall
Google Plus — plus.google.com/106122556514705041683
YouTube — www.youtube.com/channel/UCVcJ9xnm_i2ZKV7jM8dqAgA?feature=mhee

Made in United States
North Haven, CT
19 December 2024

63080918R00224